The Sublime Transformation of Vera Wright

The Sublime Transformation of Vera Wright

*A novel by
Rea Nolan Martin*

Copyright © 2012, Rea Nolan Martin, Wiawaka Press New York

All rights reserved. No part of this book may be reproduced, stored, or transmitted by any means—whether auditory, graphic, mechanical, or electronic—without written permission of both publisher and author, except in the case of brief excerpts used in critical articles and reviews. Unauthorized reproduction of any part of this work is illegal and is punishable by law.

This is a work of fiction and, as such, it is a product of the author's creative imagination. All names of characters appearing in these pages are fictitious except for those of public figures. Any similarities of characters to real persons, whether living or dead, excepting public figures, is coincidental. Any resemblance of incidents portrayed in this book to actual events, other than public events, is likewise coincidental.

ISBN 978-0-557-07495-2

Library of Congress Control Number 2009936127

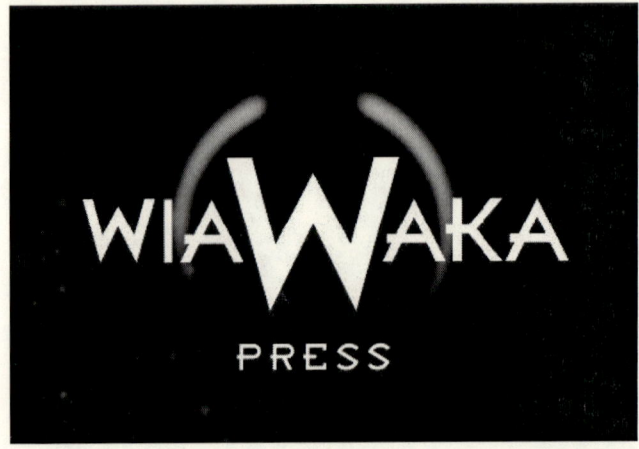

About The Author

Rea Nolan Martin lives with her family on the shores of the Hudson River where, in the mesmerizing rise and fall of tides, she finds infinite inspiration. She has published short stories and poetry. This is her first novel.

This book is dedicated to her personal miracles: Charley and Zach.

— Mystic Tea

"There comes a moment when the children who have been playing at burglars hush suddenly: was that a real footstep in the hall? There comes a moment when people who have been dabbling in religion suddenly draw back. Supposing we really found Him? We never meant it to come to that! Worse still, supposing He had found us?"

-- C. S. Lewis from Miracles

Chapter One

The clouds hang like ghostly druids over the small town of Canaan, New Jersey, and the sky, what can be seen of it, is cinder gray. It's as dismal a Labor Day weekend as Vera Wright can remember in all of her sixty-three years. Like walking in a fog, she thinks, as she scrambles through the church parking lot behind her husband, Monk. Not just a "fog" fog, but the kind of fog that steamrolls over your entire life obscuring all the guideposts you once took for granted. Oh for heaven's sake, she thinks, what in the world am I doing, borrowing trouble like that? But still, it's all very...ominous, really. *"Om-i-nous,"* she repeats to herself. Great word.

Monk reaches back impatiently to grab her hand, so tiny in his huge paw, and practically lifts her up the stone steps into the handsome Romanesque-style Church of St. Jude the Apostle. Late as usual, thanks to Monk, they arrive at the end of the opening hymn.

"In the beauty of the lilies Christ was born across the sea," wails the choir from the raised platform behind the impressive marble altar.

Vera smiles vaguely to her neighbors and acquaintances as she follows Monk into a nearly empty pew at the front of the church, singing, *"With a glory in his bosom that du da du da du dee..."* Such a patriotic tune, she thinks, and a little strident for church, perhaps. But oh well, it is a national holiday, after all. She pats her hair in the back to see if her trendy little flip survived the drizzle. Wouldn't do for a beautician to be seen with straggly hair. Not with potential clients present, anyway. And really, isn't everyone a potential client? Why, even a priest needs a haircut now and then.

"As he died to make men holy, let us live to make men free..."

As she arranges her daisy print clutch purse and buttercup yellow trench coat from Marshalls on the seat behind her, she wonders if perhaps the choir chose this sort of marching-band-half-time-tune on purpose in order to attract young people back to the church. God knows, attendance has been sparse this summer, due no doubt to the many priest scandals that sent the unfaithful packing. Oh, Vera understands their confusion; she has her own. But after a lifelong investment in the Roman Catholic Church, she is not about to start shopping for a new religion now, and neither, as far as she knows, is Monk.

"While God is marching on!"

Not that their faith is so powerful, no, she wouldn't say that. But just the inertia of it all. At her age is she really going to start waving her arms and singing out the odd 'Amen,' or 'Hallelujah' in the middle of a simple and obvious remark? Is she going to suddenly clap her hands and dance a jig on her way to Communion? Not likely. It isn't in her nature to do that. Quiet and deep reverence for the Lord was impressed upon her as a parochial school child. Not that all Protestant churches encourage spontaneous outbursts, she realizes, but she would have to learn which churches did and which did not. And that would be a lot of work. And besides, Catholicism suits her. She knows pretty much what her spiritual obligations are, fulfills them, and gets on with her busy life.

"A reading from the book of Wisdom," announces the lector.

And anyway, thinks Vera, isn't St. Jude's the lucky parish having recently engaged Father Max Alter as their new pastor—Father Max with his exuberant energy and persuasive oratorical skills? Why, he is so articulate, he could practically run for Congress. If priests were allowed to run for Congress, and why not, she thinks, why aren't they? It seems priests aren't allowed to do anything, even date. Never mind marry. Vera never saw the sense in that. Why, if Monk had been able to marry, he might have become a priest. Not that he's too priestly these days, far from it. But early on he'd entertained the idea of becoming a priest in much the same way kids fantasize about becoming President of the United States or Spider Man. To please his devoutly religious parents, however, Monk had kept the fantasy going right up until the day he met Vera.

Before long, the congregation stands for the Gospel, and Vera takes this opportunity to sneak a discreet peek behind her, shocked all over again by the low attendance. Even the latecomers have filed in by now, and the pews are nearly empty. Oh well, it's Labor Day, after all, she thinks. Probably a lot of parishioners are still vacationing at the Jersey shore. She counts the attendees to herself, and goodness, there must be less than a hundred in a church that could easily fit ten times that number. Well...whatever.

She picks a speck of lint from her sunburst sweater set and adjusts the belt of her white cotton skirt. Last day for white, she thinks. Vera wouldn't be caught dead in white after Labor Day, no matter what the fashion gurus say. What do they know, anyway? They're the same geniuses that sell cutoff Capri's to people with short fat veiny legs. Not that Vera's legs are short; they're not. Vera can easily handle the Capri fad, unlike many of her stout friends. But she draws the line at white after Labor Day. That's an immutable law. She loves the word *immutable*, which she used just recently in the Sunday crosswords. It has such a ring to it. "Im-mu-ta-ble," she pronounces under her breath.

"What's that?" says Monk.

"Nothing," she says, shaking her head. As if a wrestling coach would understand the beauty of the word *immutable*.

All at once Father Max's voice booms from the microphone. "'No one lights a lamp and then hides it under a basket,'" he says.

The force of his baritone reminds Vera that she should pay attention. This is one more thing she likes about Father Max. He takes command; snaps her out of her incessant daydreaming. She checks her watch. Goodness, she has missed almost half the Mass. Where is her head!

Father Max continues, "Jesus went on to say, 'Instead, the lamp is put on a stand to give light to all who enter the room. Your eye is a lamp for your body. A pure eye lets sunshine into your soul. But an evil eye shuts out the light and plunges you into darkness. Make sure that the light you think you have is not really darkness. If you are filled with light, with no dark corners, then your whole life will be radiant, as though a floodlight is shining on you.'" Father Max closes the book ceremoniously. "The Gospel of the Lord," he says.

"Praise to you, Lord Jesus Christ," responds Vera with the rest of the congregation. She sits down and wiggles back into her seat expectantly, settling in for Father Max's homily.

He takes a moment to study the congregation. He is so intense, Vera thinks he might be counting attendance, as she did, and is concerned that the low numbers might offend him. He is such a handsome man, she thinks. Why, he could have been anything—a model or a CEO.

"Look around you," says Father Max. "Look around you, because today I see something very special in this church of ours." He pauses. "Does anyone else?"

Vera looks around. Apparently not.

"Does anyone else here notice that everyone in this church today is...dying?"

Vera's hand flies to her chest as she gasps.

"Each and every one of you has a terminal condition," he says. He shakes his head sadly. "It's called the human condition."

There are sighs of relief and smiles as they all look around with knowing glances. Phew. He really tricked them this time.

Father Max wags his finger. "Are you relieved?" he says. "Don't be. If ever there was a reason to crank up your spiritual life, it's that. The human condition. We're not built to last in the physical sense."

He takes his microphone off the pulpit and walks to the center of the altar. "I've known people with terminal cancer who defied the odds by a decade. I knew a healthy person, the spouse of a terminal patient, who walked out the door for groceries and was killed by a passing car." He steps down from the altar and points to the front row. "Do you all feel sorry for John Lorenzo over here?" Pause. "Well, do you?"

No one responds, although everyone certainly does feel sorry for John, who sits bent-over in his wheel chair week after week, his head hanging lower to the ground every Sunday.

"As most of you know, John's got an advanced case of Parkinson's Disease." He pats John's shoulder gently. "But don't feel sorry for John. He's had notice. Gotten his exit package, so to speak. He made his peace with the Lord a long time ago, didn't you, John?"

John tries to crane his bent neck upward, but doesn't get far. Instead he lifts his right hand and says, "Amen."

"Feel sorry for yourself," says Father Max to the crowd. "Because you might die a lot sooner than John does, and maybe you haven't made peace with the Lord. Maybe your eyes are still filled with darkness. Maybe your light is dim. Are you waiting for a terminal diagnosis to get to know your Lord and Savior? Because I've just given you one. My advice is to get down on your knees today and ask the Lord to send his Spirit into your life now. To let the light in. Not in the theoretical sense. Not in the once-a-weekend-on-Sunday sense. Not out of a sense of duty. Rather, do it out of love and a yearning for redemption. Because only then can you reach your full spiritual potential. Ask him to consume your heart with his light. Can you do that?" He gazes meaningfully at the congregation. "How many of you are afraid to do that? To turn yourselves over completely?"

A few people raise their hands, not Vera or Monk. People like Pauline McIsaac and Mary Ellen Palmeri who are constantly turning themselves over to the Lord as far as Vera can see. Why, they practically live at the church. If those two haven't turned themselves over, there's no hope for the rest of them.

"The act of turning oneself over to God is a constant job," says Father Max. "There's no end to the surrender. You dive under one wave, and there's another one right behind. Sometimes you don't have time to dive at all, and you get mixed up in the whitewash, swallowing water and scraping the bottom until you don't know where you are. But once you've done it..." he raises his arm, "...surrendered completely. Well, then you have nothing to fear. Not injury, sickness or death. For those in the light, death has already been conquered."

Vera sighs. As far as she knows, she has not turned herself over to anything but her beauty clients. And Monk, of course. And their daughter, Mia, although not so much anymore. Not since Mia has seen fit to exclude them from...well, everything. It might be a relief to let someone else do all the worrying for a change, Vera thinks. To float on a cushion in space while someone else sweats the details. She wonders what it would be like to worship God that way. To become holy, even. To be filled with light.

Father Max returns to the pulpit and replaces the microphone. "Statistics tell me that in a group this size, only half of you are really listening, and only one of you will attempt to act on my advice. But if even one of you does what I suggested—lets the Lord shine light on your darkness—well, then that one courageous person will have made my entire priesthood worthwhile." He bows. "God bless you all."

The rest of Mass flies by on a series of hymns, antiphons and a chorus of automatic responses, but for some reason Vera's mind is stuck on the words of Father Max. Afterwards, back in Monk's filthy Suburban truck, complete with the team's unfinished lunches and skanky wrestling uniforms from yesterday's meet, Vera tells Monk she thinks Father Max may have a point. "Because we don't know when we're going to die," she says earnestly. "We really don't. And I don't feel okay with that, do you?"

Monk pops a Chiclet from a piece of foil and throws it into his mouth. "Yeah, I'm okay with it."

"I don't believe you," says Vera. "If you found out this afternoon that you had a good case of some barnyard flu, I don't think you'd be fine with that, Monk Wright." She clicks her seat belt in place. "If you're being honest."

He backs out of the parking space, snapping his gum. "Just saying, if you ask me, Max's sermon seemed a little on the hysterical side."

"*Father* Max," corrects Vera. "You should be more respectful of his station."

"Yeah, well, he's too young to be my father. He should be calling *me* Father."

Vera sighs. "It's what he represents," she says wearily. "You know very well..."

Monk chuckles. "Gotcha," he says winking.

"Honestly," she pouts. "The things you waste time on..." She shakes her head. "Anyway, we are going to die, Monk. That's a guarantee. There's nothing hysterical about that. Our parents are dead. One day you just disappear from the face of the earth." She snaps her fingers. "And that's that."

"I'd rather focus on living if you don't mind."

"But aren't you afraid of dying?"

"Nope."

"Well, he also mentioned our spiritual potential. What about that? Maybe God wanted me to be more than a beautician." She raises her chin. "I got good grades. I could have been...well, something else, don't you think?"

He grins. "A hot little stewardess."

"I was thinking more of a teacher, Monk, or a manager at a large company."

"What kind of company?"

She shrugs. "A magazine publisher. Maybe even *The New York Times*. Just saying—I haven't really reached my potential." She flips down the visor mirror to check her lipstick. "I hate getting old."

"You ain't old, Babe." He leans over and pats her knee with his huge hand.

"Aren't. Aren't old."

"You'll never be old to me, Vera," he says. "I mean that."

She blushes, though she is used to his compliments. "But, Monk," she says, "just yesterday I found myself loaded with a full tank of envy over Marjorie Whitestone, of all people."

"Good God," he says. "She has nothing on you."

"Well, it turns out she does," says Vera primly. "It turns out she has a firm chin. No wattle whatsoever. Can you imagine being jealous of an unattractive fifty-five-year-old woman just because her chin doesn't sag? That's when I realized...as if for the first time...that I am almost a decade older than Marjorie. I am...old." She sighs. "And my chin sags."

He stops short at a red light and they both swing forward. "Your chin does not sag," he says. "You look more beautiful now than you did the day I married you."

She swats the air. Love is definitely blind when it comes to Monk. No reason to emphasize her flaws, she supposes, but honestly, sometimes she wonders if he even looks at her. Even sees her at all. Yes, okay...she does have a nice well-proportioned body "for her age." She stays youthful and up-to-date with her hair and makeup, because after all, she is a beautician. She has no obvious facial flaws, it's true—no Dumbo ear lobes like Edith Sorrento or droopy hound dog eyes like her best friend, Louise Lambert, as much as she loves Louise. And it wasn't too long ago that Vera was able to catch the eye of many a wayward male, but lately that attention has slowed down to a few passing glances from half-dead invalids. She folds her hands on her lap and looks out the window. Count your blessings, Vera Wright, she tells herself. You're a lucky woman.

Over the course of the day the dark clouds peel off like an old scab, revealing a brilliant cornflower blue sky. Vera is reminded of the words of Father Max: "Shine light on your darkness." At some point after she has folded the laundry, ironed Monk's shirts, and prepared the marinade for their short rib barbeque, it hits her gently, a flash of whimsy, nothing more. Why not? After all, who wouldn't like to be a better person? And right there in the middle of the kitchen on the black and white star-patterned linoleum floor, she drops to her knees and says, "Lord, please enter my heart."

She blesses herself then rises quickly, feeling a little...funny. But that's ridiculous, she thinks. What's the big deal? The Lord is already in my life. Why, I was baptized and confirmed! I receive Communion every Sunday! Well, anyway, there. I've done it. I've made Father Max's priesthood worthwhile. Good for me.

She walks to the gilded mirror in the front hall and stares. Her sienna brown hair in a perfect flip, her deep navy eyes still bright, though the lids are definitely caving in to gravity—not as bad as Louise's, but still. She sighs. Maybe God entering her life in a different and more meaningful way can help her to see herself as Monk sees her. As God does. Not old, but eternal. Not that she intends to stop taking care of herself. No way. That's who she is. She's in the beauty business, for heaven's sake. She reapplies her Pink Sand lipstick, pinches her cheeks, and shakes her finger at the mirror. "I'll get the better of you," she says to her image, and scoots back to the kitchen to prepare Monk's favorite lima bean salad.

Chapter Two

For over a month now, Vera has been attending daily Mass. Part of her commitment to holiness, perhaps—court the Lord as the Lord courts her. And anyway, she's wondered for a long time what it is besides false piety that these die-hards get out of so much church. Probably nothing but each other's company, but oh well. Not that Vera plans to do it forever. But with Louise by her side, it's an agreeable way to start the day—minus the religious know-it-alls who shriek out the hymns as if singing at knifepoint. Oh, to be that oblivious of your shortcomings. What bliss!

On this particular Wednesday morning, a burst of crisp October air blows through the open windows of St. Jude's, re-circulating the intoxicating aroma of myrrh. Vera finds this air invigorating, inspiring even. She inhales slowly, deeply, with her eyes closed. As she exhales, she opens her eyes in time to see light cutting like a sword through the crimson robes of Jesus himself on the stained glass window ten pews in front of her. The light slices the room in half— half the congregation redeemed, half stained with the blood of salvation—or maybe the other way around.

"Why look at that," Vera whispers to Louise.

"What?" asks Louise in her usual shrill church whisper. She rises beside Vera for the reading of the Gospel. Rosemary Pastorello and Doris O'Rourke turn their heads to register disapproval of the chatter. "Look at what?" repeats Louise.

"Oh nothing," Vera says, though the spectacle is as obvious as an asteroid. Sometimes Louise is just too self-involved. But on the other hand, so is everyone else here at St. Jude's. Every day at Mass: stand and sit; sit and kneel. Like robots! How this phenomenon of light isn't creating hysteria in the pews, Vera can't imagine. It's as if the Lord himself were making a statement as definitive as the division of goats and sheep on the last day.

Vera holds up her arm discreetly to the crimson filter and wonders which side of paradise she has been called upon to occupy. She stands dead center. She could crane her neck for redemption; arch her back for damnation. Possibly Father Max would mention the light in his homily. Well, he practically has to, she thinks. There's no way for him to ignore this miracle.

Father Max bows and prays silently, then raises his youthful head of curly black hair and proclaims wide-eyed and joyously, "A reading from the Gospel according to Matthew."

"Glory be to you, oh Lord," mumbles Vera along with the other fifty or so faithful weekday congregants.

As Father Max reads the Gospel, the crimson light deepens to blood red, enlarges in scope, and illuminates a thousand motes of dust like diamonds. Vera has to force herself to tune back in.

"'...and the disciples saw this and were astounded,'" Father Max reads. "'The disciples asked, 'How did the fig tree dry up so quickly?' And Jesus answered, 'I assure you that if you believe and do not doubt, you will be able to do what I have done to this fig tree. And not only this, but you will even be able to say to this hill, 'Get up and throw yourself in the sea,' and it will.'"

Father Max surveys the congregation, until finally he makes eye contact with Vera. "If you believe this, word for word with all of your heart, Vera Wright, then from this day forward, you will receive whatever you ask for in prayer and more than you ever bargained for."

Vera's eyes twirl like pinwheels. *What!* she thinks. Me? Why me? By now she sees that the crimson robe of the Lord has bled over the entire congregation, with the exception of her, who alone is encapsulated in a spotlight of pure transparent gold. She stares at Louise, who is listening politely to the remainder of the Gospel as if Vera's name had never been mentioned. How can she be so blasé!

"The Gospel of the Lord," says Father Max.

"Praise to you, oh Lord, Jesus Christ," repeats Vera with the others, although the words tumble out of Vera's mouth like pebbles.

"Louise," she whispers. "Why did he say that?"

"Say what?" screeches Louise, and automatically the others turn around.

Vera shrugs. "Didn't you hear him say my name?"

Louise pats Vera on the knee. "Let's discuss this afterwards," she says. "We're annoying the cherubim."

Normally this comment would crack Vera up, but not today.

"What does Jesus mean by this statement?" asks Father Max. "I'll tell you what he means." He looks directly at Vera and points his finger emphatically. "He means that these wonders and more will be performed in his name by you, Vera Wright. Your gifts will be given in abundance with the grace of God, and for the good of all nations. And because you have consciously invited him into your heart, these gifts will thrive even in the seeming desert of your life."

Vera's mouth drops open and it feels as if her brain is leaking through her nose. Father Max continues, but Vera can no longer hear him.

"I have to go," she says to Louise.

"What?"

"I have to go." Vera slides out of the pew, pulling the corners of her favorite lavender tweed jacket together with shaking hands. "Oh my purse," she says, reaching back. She hurries out to the blinding light of the autumn sun which follows her like a searchlight into her modest VW sedan and holds her captive until she arrives safely home at #7 Destiny Drive.

Chapter Three

Louise Lambert peers expectantly into the decorative hand mirror at her freshly coiffed head. "My goodness, Vera Wright, you've done it again," she trills. "You have totally transformed me!" She winks at Vera. "It's enough for me to forgive you for that little lapse at church yesterday. What in the world got into you?"

"Oh, that," says Vera dismissively. After an entire day of pacing, she'd decided that she'd imagined it—made it up from start to finish. Why, it was absurd, the things she was seeing and hearing. And after all, no one else had noticed a damn thing. "A hot flash I suppose," she says to Louise. "Although I thought I was over that. Maybe it was that pile of B vitamins I've started taking to improve my stamina."

Louise nods. "Hypervitaminosis," she says. "I heard about that on Dr. Oz." She scrunches her face. "But I mean you never really told me what exactly happened. What was it that you saw?"

"Oh nothing," says Vera. "The light. Just the way the light colored the room. It was just, I don't know...profound."

"I'll tell you what's profound," says Louise. "This sassy new haircut of mine." She swings her head. "It's not too young for me, is it?"

"Absolutely not," says Vera. "Who says we have to look like a museum piece the minute we turn sixty?"

Louise giggles. "Sixty? I'll take that as a compliment. And wait till Stanley sees me tonight. Katie bar the door!"

She raises her hands and wiggles them hokey-pokey style with a wild look in her eyes.

Vera chuckles. She knows as well as Louise does that Stanley Lambert is not the least bit capable of monkey business. Ten years Louise's senior, Stanley is eighty-one years old and, God help him, spends three-quarters of his time drooling in a wheel chair with the TV on all the livelong day. This leaves Louise to tend to his necessities, minus three hours a day that the aides come in to help. And here's poor Louise, vacuum-packed with enough energy and life to entertain four active husbands her own age. Life isn't fair, but that's not news to either of them.

Louise taps an envelope against the bureau top and out slides a $100 bill which she hands to Vera.

"Oh no," Vera insists. They go through this drill every time. "The facial is on me, Louise. Just a little extra to take the sting out of your day. After all, you could be going to a luxurious spa somewhere. I appreciate the business, believe me."

Louise strikes the usual pose, hands on hips, eyes to the ceiling. "Oh for heaven's sake," she says, "there isn't a place I could go to in Canaan that would charge me under $250 for everything you just did." She holds up her fingers one by one. "Facial. Color. Cut. Set. Style! Why, I'm almost as lovely as you now." She places the $100 bill on Vera's desk and walks out grinning at her victory.

Once Louise is gone, Vera plops down on the velveteen tufted settee in the salon that Monk built with his own hands over thirty years ago. It's a simple salon, but complete with all the essentials: open sink, two recliners, two chairs with hair dryer attachments, a hot light, Victorian oval mirrors, and plenty of storage space for color and perms. Not that it couldn't use some updating. But over the years it had allowed Vera to work from home and spend more time with their daughter, Mia, when she was young. And even though Vera still brings in some good extra cash from her dozen or so loyal customers, Monk's salary as a high school Phys Ed teacher has been the primary income for the 39 years of their marriage. They make do.

At the age of 63, Vera is luckier than most of her clients whose doddering mates are already equipped with the odd aftermarket parts—valves, pins, prosthetic knees and hips, not to mention the kidney Howard Gleason's doctors harvested from his own son. Thank heaven, Vera is still blessed with a rollicking husband her own age who is more youthful and vibrant than she is. Not that he doesn't work at it. Monk won't go two days without running his treadmill to Kingdom Come and lifting his weights right along with the wrestling team he coaches after school. And where is he right now, but somewhere in Delaware with a bus full of wild teenagers on their way back from a full week cooped up at the Model U.N. Make no mistake about it, Vera knows, the wildest one on that bus is Monk Wright.

And that reminds her that the dear man will be home in less than two hours and she has a dinner to shop for. She peers in the mirror, fussing with an auburn-pearl curl here and a streak of autumn berry there. She hopes he likes her new colors, nothing too drastic, really, just enough to make him wonder. After all, Vera has to keep up with the times, doesn't she? If people spot her around town looking the slightest bit disheveled or out-of-date, she could lose even the most loyal clients. Not to mention the occasional teenager whose parents agree to a streak or two of daffodil yellow, wild ochre or cinnabar red, provided it's temporary and Vera does the coloring. "All coloring is temporary," she says on the kids' behalf. "Hair grows!" She thinks the colors are fun, and certainly good for business.

As for her own cosmetic adjustments, she likes to keep Monk guessing. A little healthy doubt is good for a marriage, and their marriage, Vera knows, is as good as it gets. It still makes her blush the way that big bald lug teases her, and oh, why not say it—lusts after—the oversized breasts she is constantly threatening to surgically lift and reduce. She shakes her head at the ridiculousness of a man who has been looking at her nearly every day through such a huge floating chunk of life insisting that she alter not a single atom of her sagging, aging body. Where does that kind of love come from? Well, it's almost too dear to imagine.

Not that they haven't marinated in an occasional sulk, they have. Or even worked up to a shouting match or two over something so absurd she can hardly remember the reason. Well, there was the time he'd left the moon roof open on his own car during the blizzard and made every attempt to blame her. Vera shakes her head, remembering. How could she possibly have done it — she'd been sick in bed with the flu and hadn't driven the car in ten days! Even worse was the time he turned a deaf ear to her when she was trying to discipline Mia after she'd been crowned the Official Queen of the Underground Beer Chugging Team at Canaan High. Oh yes, Vera remembers how hilarious Monk thought that little caper was at the time. "It's what kids do in high school!" he'd remarked with a mouthful of mashed potatoes mixed with peas. Well it certainly wasn't what Vera had done. Or Monk either. Anyway, she knows he doesn't think it's so funny now, what with all Mia's problems.

Vera leans her petite body closer to the mirror and studies her eyes for makeup flaws — clumped mascara, uneven liner — then stretches her full lips and carefully applies tawny frost lipstick. She is always advising her clients that bland, colorless lips on a mature woman advertise old age. "If you do nothing else — apply and reapply your lipstick!" she counsels. "People will be drawn to your lips and not to your wrinkles!"

She is loaded with useful tips and secrets she has collected from famous aestheticians she has seen in seminars or on TV. Her business and her clients are important to her. Not that the beauty business was her first choice as a career, but even part-time college had proved an impractical luxury, especially after her parents died in the car crash. And then of course, there'd been Mia a little earlier than planned. But before all that, college was certainly an option. Vera graduated in the top ten percent of her high school class, and was the number one best English student ever, according to Sister Perpetua.

Even now, unlike most people she knows, Vera isn't the least bit averse to lifelong learning. Her library is filled with self-improvement books by Wayne Dyer, Deepak Chopra, and more recently, Dr. Phil. She never opens one of them before placing a collegiate dictionary on the table right beside her, and each new word is readily incorporated into her everyday language. "Stanley's behavior is simply *nefarious*," she would say to Louise, as if Louise—(even with all her money!)—would know what to do with the word nefarious. Or, "My goodness, Louise, your hair color is ubiquitous. We must do something to make it more unique." Louise's lack of comprehension is not Vera's concern. Vera knows if she doesn't use the word, she'll lose it. And using the exact right word to her is like finding the perfect new color for a client's hair. She isn't one to be satisfied with the gist of a message. To Vera, words are like a giant pile of free jewels. If you know what you're doing, you can select an exquisite diamond. Or you can just stick your hand in the pile without looking and come up with a cheap piece of glass. Up to you.

She grabs her coat and purse and gives one last approving glance around the wedgewood-blue living room, flinching slightly at the overstuffed rocker they inherited from Monk's mother, Gert. For maybe the millionth time, Vera thinks: what an ugly godawful piece of worthless trash, and then lets her thought go to the winds, as Deepak Chopra is always suggesting in his books. This chair is her only concession to Monk's ongoing list of preposterous interior design proclamations. "Let's put a pot belly stove in the living room!" is another. Or... "If we cover the dining room walls with mirrors the room will look bigger." Classic unthinkable decorating comments from meddling men. All men do it, Vera knows. She knows everything that happens in people's lives, because for some reason she has never fully reckoned, no one inspires more confidence than a beautician. Vera could easily hang out an additional shingle for therapeutic gossip and make twice as much.

She exits their cozy old Colonial into a brilliantly lit autumn afternoon. Burnt sienna, caramel, butterscotch and carmine red leaves are spread like mosaic tiles over the terrace. Such a lovely home, she thinks as she strolls down the cobblestone path. Her home is a stubborn tribute to the past when houses were homes and not idols of pagan worship. The neighborhood has changed considerably, however, from sensible hardworking families to affluent upstarts in the business of demolishing perfectly livable homes to be replaced with architectural monstrosities.

Of course Monk has made friends with all of the new neighbors, but Vera has not and never will. She simply cannot reconcile the neighbors' wasteful and reckless values with the values that have taken her so adequately through her own conservative life. Anyway, she thinks, what kind of out-of-control bombastic ego does it take to construct such a monument to one's wallet? And now, of course, with the economy crumbling, they'll be lucky if their precious mansions aren't seized from them in the night! Surreptitiously converted into military hospitals and federal prisons! And then what will become of the neighborhood?

Next door, Jessica Carmichael waves to Vera, "Hello, Mrs. Wright!" she calls out gaily as she unloads Neiman Marcus shopping bags from her Escalade. Vera nods politely, though she has no intention of getting involved in a conversation with one of those excessive SUV personalities, even if she does live next door. Get a job, she thinks. Do something useful. Knock down half your home and plant a few trees so we can all breathe again, for God's sake.

Vera moves along down the path thinking that the time is fast approaching when she and Monk should be moving into the country where people and values are real. The Poconos maybe, or the Adirondacks. Just someplace where people plant their own gardens and mow their own lawns. Where the town mascot is not a golden calf. Of course they would never see their daughter, Mia, if they made such a radical move. Not that they see her now. Mia Wright, the grand reincarnation of Cleopatra! Adorning herself with the gold coins of her husband Frederick's grand inheritance in between hair extensions and self-tanning. But Mia's narcissistic lifestyle is another concern entirely. Half the time Vera would like to wring her daughter's neck, but she has no time to think about Mia now.

In the Stop & Shop, Vera passes the courtesy desk and smiles at the manager, squat and sturdy old Bridget Stack, whose five unappealing children Monk taught all those years ago.

"Nice to see you, Bridget!" she says.

Bridget waves.

"I recommend the corn today," says Bridget. "Very tasty, and probably the last good batch we'll have for some time."

"Thank you," says Vera, and then under her breath, "Where's your lipstick, Bridget? Is it fun looking twice your age?"

She navigates her cart to the produce aisle to inspect the corn. It does look fresh, and after all Monk has been known to devour three or four ears from a good batch. She selects an ear and peels the husk. Not that she doesn't trust Bridget, but the Stop & Shop makes it a policy not to discourage husking, so she might as well take advantage of the privilege. But what is this? Her head throbs, not to mention her heart, as the naked cob reveals not kernels, but some kind of horrific picture she can hardly unscramble. Where is it coming from, this vision of...Monk?

God help her, it is Monk, stacked up against the fern green wall of his study on Destiny Drive as if tossed carelessly from the ripped seam of an overstuffed tornado. His sallow flesh is piled apologetically around his midriff—a giant 6'3" beanie baby—not a bone or muscle in evidence. His eyes are rolled back in his head.

She gasps and drops the corn.

"Everything all right, Ma'am?" asks the sweeper.

"Sure, yes, of course," she says. She refuses to flee, as she had from St. Jude's, or to submit the slightest credence to this freakish occurrence. But is she losing her mind? Is this how that sort of thing happens, like a car engine that putt-putt-putts and then just stops cold in the middle of a highway? No, she thinks, it's nothing. Nothing at all. A brilliant cinematic scene projected ever so matter-of-factly onto a dimpled ear of white shoepeg corn. And who needs corn, anyway? Why it's practically November! Now that she has talked herself out of the hallucinogenic corn, she moves down the aisle in favor of the green beans. Nothing to husk; no tragic vision to expose.

She scoops a handful of beans into her plastic bag, and as she returns to the pile for another scoop, she sees it again: Monk splayed against the wall of his study, mouth ajar. How had she not noticed the slackened jaw before? Even more horrible than the first vision! She moves mechanically to the last wicker basket in the produce corner, the neglected brussel sprouts. Not a favorite of hers certainly, but a favorite of Monk's, so why not? He would be delighted at her thoughtfulness. But there it is again. Vision with a capital V now, brighter and more demonic than before, pulsating before her, and...she glances around... before anyone else? But seemingly no one else is being victimized by poor Monk's demise.

Vera moves frantically through the store now, running from the persistent grip of the Vision. On through the fresh fruit, beneath the Macintosh apples and the last batch of late summer berries... Monk. Behind the Roquefort dressing and the catsup and the scrod...Monk. Next to the last box of microwave popcorn, a flash of fern green wall, a speck of reflective flesh from poor Monk's shiny bald dead head. She practically whiplashes her neck turning away, her hands over her eyes, but she is not fast enough. She takes quick tiny steps to the pasta aisle, where he lurks behind the fettuccini, and to the bakery, where his royal blue and gold Canaan wrestling team sweatshirt announces itself behind the Italian loaves.

Vera exits the store with a bag full of who-knows-what, a mishmash of cans and boxes and bags of frozen prepared foods, foods she has never brought home before. She can't imagine what kind of concoction this will make for dinner, or where she will purchase the presence of mind to concoct it.

Safely in her VW sedan, she studies her hands, which are shaking spastically, and wills them to stop. "Stop it," she tells them in her strictest staccato alto. "Stop. It. Stopitstopitstopit." And slowly, they stop, though the vibration is then transferred to the rest of her body, which shivers. Monk is on a bus, she reassures herself. A bus with sixty teenagers and a driver. He is nowhere near Canaan. He is certainly not propped up in the northeast corner of his home office, inanimate, for the love of God. Okay just say it: *dead.*

And oh, she thinks—how Monk would cackle at the sheer absurdity of this situation. Ha ha ha! She can see him now, doubled-over at the sudden and involuntary ordination of his wife into the world of the ridiculous and the sublime. The supernatural! No way. Unless, could it be? Was it possible that this sort of thing happened regularly to women over sixty? Not to Louise, maybe, but who knows? Would Louise tell Vera if it had? Might she have instead buried it in the crawl space of her subconscious never to be unearthed in social circles?

Maybe the odd supernatural experience is one of those unspeakable syndromes that women never discuss, even with their beauticians, such as their own snoring, discreet plastic surgery, and other vagaries of age. The sort of scary and unmentionable topic that women stopped discussing at some critical point in history after, say, the witch hunts at Salem.

Vera carefully turns the key in the ignition and grounds herself by focusing on the practicalities of her dashboard. Her gas tank is three-quarters full, and no, she does not have her seat belt fastened. Let's see if she can do it. Yes, with some effort, she can and does: click. Reassured, she pulls out of her spot carefully, concentrating. Piece of cake. She is at least fractionally functional. She can steer the car.

Once confidently on the road, she thinks that she might be onto something important. Women share all kinds of rites of passage, and bizarre visions are possibly the vein of femininity that draws them together, the ancients and the moderns alike. From Sarah and Rebecca all the way to Vera's second-cousin-once-removed on her father's side who regularly beat the odds at the track. Not that her own mother would have bothered to share such an essential fact with Vera or with anyone. Regina Lord had not shared the most basic things—menstruation, garter belts or the shocking realities of the male anatomy. And as an only child, Vera was on her own. She had researched these things herself, then confirmed them with the experts—her girlfriends, Monica and Nora O'Reilly.

Monica and Nora came from a disheveled and passionate Irish household where no indignity of the body or mind was held sacred. "Nora's on the rag!" one of her brothers would proclaim in the middle of dinner. And this, then, would precipitate a decathlon jog out of the house and up the block with Nora running wildly after whomever until she tired of the chase.

The older O'Reilly boys, Sean and Kevin, quoted Donne and Hopkins as easily as they quoted Mick Jagger or Huckleberry Hound. They were wildly attractive with slate-black hair and flame-blue eyes, and played the piano and guitar—rakish and utterly unaccountable troubadours. They were the only two people in all the history of humanity that Vera would have married in prison, not that they'd ever been sent there, but there were more than a few opportunities. Luckily they'd treated Vera like a sister and never once asked her on a date. So marriage to them had not been an option.

And then there was Monk—literally given that nickname because of his early intention to become a priest. The exact opposite of the O'Reilly's! Vera smiles as she remembers spotting Monk across the dance floor in tenth grade. It was almost in slow motion, Monk striding with his long gait—could it be toward her? "You're the most beautiful bloom in this room," he said. She blushed feverishly. He continued, "What does that make you then—a rose? Nope, a gardenia. An exotic tropical flower." Vera turned every shade of red, thinking this must be some kind of football team dare, a prank at her expense. But no, he'd meant it. He dated her eagerly and loyally, finally dropping all pretense of priesthood in favor of marriage about the time her parents were killed in the crash.

As Vera drives back up her driveway, she is relieved to see that Monk's car is not there. He's not even home, never mind dead in the corner of the second floor office. How asinine! She lugs the grocery bags from the car and into the kitchen wondering what to do now that she has no possible way of making dinner from these ingredients. Or does she? Three bags of frozen vegetables in cream sauce, a can of white beans, a jar of tomato sauce, a bunch of green onions and a bag of noodles shaped like...she inspects more closely...some sort of cartoon character named Sponge Bob. Oh, for heaven's sake! Monk will think she checked her brain out with the groceries.

She pulls out her stew pot and throws everything inside but the pasta and adjusts the flame to low. She'll blame the recipe on a misprint; he'll never know. She places the lid on the pot and decides to walk upstairs to the scene of the crime just to put her mind at ease. Her heartbeat rises radically as she climbs the stairs. Her breath shortens. "La la la," she sings to distract herself. "La la la."

She forces herself to look at the study from the hallway where she can clearly see that the treadmill is inactive. There is no noise in the room, no sign of occupation. She takes one step and then another, her hand at her chest, then turns to face the hidden corner next to the desk where the vision had taken place. Nothing. She exhales slowly, deliberately, and has to sit down on the edge of the desk chair to catch her breath. Monk is definitely not splayed in the corner, never had been. She wonders how he would ever have fit there in the first place, considering the position of the file cabinet.

"So silly," she whispers aloud as she turns back. Then, almost at the carved oak banister in the center hall, the Vision returns. "Aaaaaaa," she screams, running across the hall to their bedroom with her hand at her throat, from there to the bathroom, to the guest room, and every room in the house. Monk is everywhere and yet...*nowhere*. Just to be sure, she runs downstairs to check the salon. Nothing. The phone rings and she answers overenthusiastically, "Hello?!"

"Your frog prince returns!" says Monk.

Like a prayer she sighs, "Mooonk. Thank God it's you!"

"Why? What's up?"

"Oh, nothing," she says. "I just...really missed you this time."

He calls out to the students, "She misses me!" And they all cheer and clap. "I'll be home in ten minutes," he says. "Maybe I'll take you to dinner."

Vera thinks about the slop she's got cooking on the stovetop and says, "Well isn't that a nice idea?"

"Good," he says, "that's solved. I'll just need a half hour to run the treadmill, a quick shower, and then we go."

"Oh no!" she says. "I...I'm absolutely starved. Let's just relax and go to dinner."

"Starved? I don't believe I've ever heard you use that word—what with your pint-sized appetite, but okay. Fine. We'll make it an early bird special and save some money."

"Thanks!" she says with forced enthusiasm, and hangs up. She runs to the kitchen to turn off the stove and back to the salon to touch-up her lipstick and hair. Thank God he's skipping the treadmill, but still...she can't keep him off it forever. As she stares into the mirror pulling this curl down and that one over, lifting her hair at the crown for fullness, she gets an idea and jogs up to the office. On her hands and knees, she pulls the treadmill plug and tucks the cord under the platform. This will do for now. The way Monk over-thinks everything mechanical, the plug would be the last thing he'd suspect.

Fifteen minutes later she hears, "Hey baby!" and rushes to the door in time to see him drop his duffel bag on the floor and his boom box on the table. He places his hand on his chest and says, "Whew! Am I glad to be home."

"We'd better have that checked out," says Vera.

"What? Get what checked out?" He enfolds her in his huge body and kisses the top of her head.

"Oh, just, you know, your heart. You were tapping your chest just then, and I thought...well, when was the last time you saw a cardiologist anyway?"

He holds her at arm-length, frowning and says, "Never?"

"Well, then, at your age, it's about time you did. And me, too. It's time I saw one, too."

"You can go if you want," he says, shaking his head. "But as for me, I'm more fit than half the kids I coach. You should see me bench press with them. Nobody can believe it." He strikes a pose. "I the man!" He leans over and presses a button on the boom box and it belts out some scratchy Chubby Checker song at a deafening volume. At this, he launches into his cage dance routine, mashing his feet against the floor. "Hey? What am I doing?" he says tauntingly.

"For heaven's sake, Monk."

"Come on!" he says, moving faster.

"Fine. Mashed potatoes."

"That's my girl!" Then he jumps on his toes, bringing his knees high.

"The pony," she shouts out quickly so he'll stop.

"That's right!" he says grinning. He grabs her by the hand and starts twisting, though Vera just stands there.

"Let's doooo the twist," he sings along, shaking his finger in the air. "Come on, baby, let's dooo the twist!"

"Oh for God's sake, Monk." She does a wimpy little twist and pulls away.

Laughing heartily, he flips the switch off and jogs up the stairs, still singing, "Let's twist again, like we did last summer..."

Hands on her hips, Vera shakes her head. "Honestly," she says. "Honest to God."

At the restaurant, she gradually calms down, even relaxes enough to sip her favorite—a strawberry wine cooler—while Monk enjoys his Dewar's.

"Here's to us, babe," he says, grinning broadly. "You and me and the best life I've ever had!"

She giggles. This is so like him—this reckless animation. And who in the wide world, she thinks, could ever be as happy and grateful for such a simple life as this dear man? She feels warmth spread through her heart, and realizes suddenly that there's no way anything will happen to him. Why it's all her, she's certain. She's the one who should be making the trip to the ER, not Monk! After all did he have the vision? Well not one, but a dozen. A dozen visions in three days! People have been committed for less.

"So the kids were great," says Monk. "And Marcus Shotke did the funniest..."

Vera can't hold onto his story no matter how hard she tries. His words slip like change between the cracks of her worthless and obsessive thoughts. Maybe she's experiencing what they used to call flashbacks way back when. Flashbacks from what though? she thinks. It's not as if she has a history with drugs. But come to think of it, there was that one hash cigarette she reluctantly smoked behind the beauty school with Crystal Lipinksi in 1967. Oh my goodness she'd never forget the way Crystal had made her laugh that day—mimicking all the cheap customers who'd taken advantage of the school's free beauty services. Laughed so hard she was literally seduced into following Crystal anywhere—which turned out to be right into the deep pine woods to smoke a cigarette rolled in a plump and vulgar manner that Crystal assured Vera would calm them both down. Well, why not? Vera thought. Why the hell not?

But afterwards, it was worse. Her laughter turned to near hysteria as she could not put a period on the end of a laughing jag. It just went on and on until her stomach convulsed with laughter and she begged for merciful sobriety. She didn't dare go back into the school. God only knows what she would have done to her customers! So she sent Crystal back in to make excuses for her and drove straight home—if you could call the way she drove home that day straight. She would never forget the way the red traffic lights bled into the streets and the monkey birds— their mangled feathers and disturbing overbites. Oh God, she could barely stand to think about it even now. She'd been so relieved to see her parents' car gone. Thank God they weren't home to see what had become of their earnest daughter.

But all that youthful indiscretion and hilarity had washed right off when she'd answered the phone bearing news of her parents' accident. And wasn't it she, Vera, who should have died in a crash that day? Wasn't it Vera who had driven home stoned as a post and not her parents who, with all their marbles in place, had watched in certain horror as a brand new Dodge Dart unhitched from its position on the car trailer and flew promptly into their windshield?

She is startled out of her reverie when Monk takes her hands across the table. "Hey, what's happened to you?" he asks brightly. "You eating out?"

"Oh, heavens no," she says. "I'm right here with you, Monk. Right where I want to be." She sips her drink. "How was your day, dear?"

Chapter Four

In her salon, Vera sips coffee and nibbles a cranberry nougat biscotti. She has twenty minutes before her next client, and oh, why not—she decides to take the plunge and call Mia. No sense thinking it through too deeply or she may never do it. Tap tap tap. She cannot control her fingers as she awaits her daughter's voice.

"Yes?"

"Mia?" says Vera eagerly. "Is that you, dear?"

"Well it's not Frederick, Mother, so it must be me."

"It must be I," corrects Vera.

"Oh, for God's sake, does every conversation have to begin with a grammar quiz?"

Vera shifts her weight. "It's just that, well, in your position, Mia...and after all we did to send you to Wellesley...it would seem appropriate to hear you speak the King's English."

There is a moment of silence, and then Vera thinks she hears Mia lighting one of those godawful cigarettes. "Don't you agree, dear?" Of course she knows Mia won't agree.

There is a long inhale, and then, "Oh what do you really know about the King's English, Mother? Isn't that a little pretentious? I mean, when did the king teach you grammar anyway—at beauty school?"

Vera raises her chin. "No point in sarcasm now, dear, is there?"

"What's up? I've got a million things to do today."

"Just thought I'd make a little appointment with you, that's all. A little appointment to go shopping or do something girly. Something fun."

"Not today, I'm busy. And tonight we're dining at Jardinique with Frederick's parents."

"Oh my," says Vera dreamily. "Ritzy."

"Ritzy for you, Mother. Not for them. For them it's the equivalent of a hot dog and fries at the corner cart."

"Well then why bother?"

"What's that supposed to mean?"

"I just mean, why bother to dress up for the corner hot dog vendor, that's all? If that's all it means to them."

"I can't have these conversations, Mother. Seriously. What the Tophet family dresses-up for is just about the most insignificant... I can't even believe it! It's ridiculous! Ridiculous even to mention it. I don't get you." Mia takes another audible drag.

"Well perhaps Sunday then?" Vera says through gritted teeth. "How would that be? You and Frederick can come here for dinner."

"Won't work. I'm hosting a meeting for the Central Park Women's Club on Sunday."

Vera raises her eyebrows. "Really? That's wonderful, dear. You'll be helping out all kinds of charities then, won't you? Good for you. We should always give more than we get."

"No charities, Mother. It's a designer trunk show."

"Well how fun! Would I be allowed to attend?"

"Not unless you want to spend a thousand dollars on a sequined thong."

Vera gasps. "You wouldn't do that, Mia, would you? Not in this economy! Why people are homeless!"

"People will always be homeless, Mother. Look, I know it's not your thing—not Marshalls or Kohl's. Not exactly a bargain. But it's my thing, okay? I'm young and beautiful and I enjoy parading around in sequined thongs. And Frederick likes it too."

Vera swallows hard. "I bet he does."

After a long pause, Mia says, "These conversations are really tedious, don't you think? How about I get back to you in the next week or so?"

"That's what you said last week, Mia, and you never called."

"I tried; I did, but look... I just don't have a life that revolves around..."

"Around what, dear? Around your mother?"

Mia's voice gets thinner and thinner as her words race each other to the finish line, toppling over and under each other until they are all one giant familiar word that Vera has heard a thousand times: "Youdon'teventrytounderstand-youneverdidokaygoodbye."

Vera slams down the phone. Where does she get the nerve, that one? she thinks. Marshalls or Kohl's? What's wrong with saving a little money? And how demeaning is that, anyway? Not good enough? Too simple for the elegant Tophet aristocrats? Too out-of-date for the Central Park Women's Club? Too cheap for their hotsy totsy designer trunk show? Vera has a good mind to get in her car on Sunday, drive straight to that trunk show and purchase one of those thongs just to show her daughter who's with the times and who's not. Sequined thongs. Huh! Maybe she'd make her own at senior craft night.

Vera bites a big chunk of her biscotti and chugs the remaining coffee. She is trying not to be pissed, but that conversation has not helped her escalating nervous condition, that's for sure. Not that she would ever trouble Mia with her visions of Monk, not at all, or even Father Max's bizarre indiscretion in church. But sooner or later she would have to tell somebody, wouldn't she? It wasn't the sort of experience one could swallow and digest without regurgitation. At some point, she would need advice.

The shop bell rings and Louise breezes through the door. "Hello Vera! It's me. Or should I say, 'It is I'?"

"You should say 'it's me', Louise, because otherwise I wouldn't know who it was."

"Ha! You think I don't know good grammar?"

Vera shakes out the plastic smock and ties it around Louise's neck. "What do you think Monk would say if I showed up in a sequined thong?"

"A what?" Louise lays her handbag on the counter and relaxes into the chair.

"A thong," says Vera. She cranks the chair back and turns the hose on Louise's hair. "You know, one of those rubber bands that passes for underwear these days."

Louise screams over the rushing water, "I think he'd have a heart attack!"

"A what!" Vera turns the spigot off. "What in the world would make you say a thing like that?"

"For God's sake, Vera, it was just a joke."

"Oh. Of course," Vera says. She tries to control the tremble in her hands as she shampoos Louise's hair, rinses it, and wraps it in a towel. She hums some ridiculous upbeat circus melody to keep her mind from replaying the vision. Later on, Vera pulls a hunk of Louise's hair with the round brush and rolls it as she applies the dryer to the shank.

"Ouch!" says Louise, wiggling. "That dryer's hot."

"Sorry," mumbles Vera and adjusts the heat.

"And anyway, are you listening to me?" Louise says.

"Oh, sorry," says Vera. "I got a little distracted."

"As I was saying," snaps Louise, "Stanley looks right up at me from that pathetic wheelchair and says...he says, 'Helga, I almost married you, but my mother wouldn't allow it. I'm sorry, Helga. It wasn't my fault. We were only 19-years-old. I couldn't go against my mother's wishes at that age. But you're the only one I've ever loved, the only one. Come over here right now and let me give you a smacker.'"

Vera flicks off the dryer. "Excuse me, Louise, but who's Helga?"

"Well exactly!" says Louise. "Who the hell is the little slut? Fifty-one years of marriage, and never once has Stanley ever so much as hinted at another liaison in his youth."

Vera considers this. "There was the war," she says.

"Oh please, as if there was anyone in Korea named Helga!"

"Huh," says Vera. She starts the blow dryer again and raises her voice above it. "Well what did you say to him after that?"

"I'll tell you what I said!" Louise raises her fist. "I said, 'Stanley Lambert, my name is NOT Helga. Whoever the hell she is. The little tart. And furthermore, you'd best not ever mention her name in my house again!'" She clenches her fists. "I tell you, Vera, I wanted to wheel that man out to the patio and shove the chair right down the terrace and into the pond. You want a smacker, butthead? I'll give you a smacker!"

Vera can't help it; she starts to giggle. This gets Louise going, too, and they treat themselves to a first class laughing fit. Louise is bent over on her chair, and Vera steadies herself against the counter with her head flung back.

"I can't believe I just said that," says Louise, still chuckling as she dabs the tears from her eyes. "I mean the man is totally losing it, Vera, out to lunch at a diner on Pluto, for God's sake. And here I am pampering myself and getting hysterical with you."

Vera breathes deeply. "I'm sorry, Louise, but if we don't laugh we'll shoot ourselves, won't we?"

"Well not you, exactly, Vera, let's be accurate. What with your manly man. Believe me, Monk Wright knows exactly who you are any day of the week. He hasn't lost a single tool from his belt."

Vera resumes humming as she blows out Louise's bangs. How will she ever keep from revealing her secret?

"Well, has he?" insists Louise.

Vera shrugs.

"What the hell is wrong with you, anyway?" shrieks Louise. "What exactly are you hiding from your so-called best friend?"

Vera rocks her head back and forth, considering. Oh, what was the use in pretending? She drops her shoulders and looks at Louise in the mirror. "All is not perfect in paradise."

Louise whips around in the chair. "What? Don't even tell me that man is stepping out on you. You and Monk are the last real hope for the future of matrimony. I'll kill him before I kill Stanley!"

"Oh no, it isn't that." Vera shuts off the dryer and sinks into the adjacent chair. "As far as I know, Monk is as pure as the day I met him. But lately, I've been...I mean, I myself...have been on the verge of..."

Louise gasps. "No! Don't say it. And for God's sake don't do it! The minute you leave that man, the women of Canaan are all over him, young and old. You'll never get him back."

"Oh goodness no, not that. It's just that I think something might be wrong with me...not Monk. Me. I've been having...well this is a little embarrassing, but..."

"Vera, just say it."

Vera rubs her palms against her apron. "Okay, then, remember that day in church?"

"Well, yes, sort of. It's not as if you ever told me the whole story."

Vera swallows. "I have to tell somebody, Louise. I can't stand it anymore." She nods her head up and down, back and forth. "I've been having well...unpleasant...I don't know what to call them so I'll just say it." She stammers for a second. "Visions."

Louise takes a Q-tip from the counter and twirls it in her ear. "Excuse me, Vera, the shampoo in my ear... I thought you said 'visions'."

"I did say visions," says Vera. "Visions is exactly what I said. And don't think it's easy for me to say. It isn't."

"I see."

"I know it sounds weird."

"It is weird."

"Nevertheless, last week I had a vision—nothing else to call it—of Monk, well...dead."

"A vision of Monk?"

"Right in the corn at Stop & Shop. While I was husking."

"Dead in the Corn?"

"Not actually *in* the corn, Louise. *Reflected* in the corn. He was in his office, collapsed on the floor near the filing cabinet."

"And you're sure he was dead?"

"Completely dead. It was awful. Horrible. I still have nightmares."

"Have you told him?"

At this Vera stands and takes the curling iron to the crown of Louise's hair. "No, I haven't told him. What would I say? 'Monk dear, prepare to be dead in the near future.' He'd never believe it, that's for sure. I don't even believe it myself. Aside from the horror of the vision, whatever would I do without Monk?" She picks out random pieces of hair to augment Louise's hairline and disguise her unusually high forehead.

"That's wild," says Louise.

Vera lifts a can of hairspray. "Close your eyes," she warns, and sprays liberally.

Louise makes a show of choking on the spray as she always does, then checks her face in the mirror and leans over for her purse. "In my opinion, Vera, you've just had a teensy little breakdown, that's all. Nothing to worry about. She pulls out a card from her wallet. "Just in case, though, this is the name of Stanley's cardiologist. If you ask me, he's a little too good at what he does. Stanley should have been dead ten years ago."

Sniggering, Vera takes the card and reads it, "T. Charles Guthrow, M.D."

"And don't give it another thought," says Louise. "The visions, I mean. We all have them; we just never discuss them."

"We do?" says Vera. She fans her face. "You have no idea what a relief that is."

"Well sure," says Louise. She roots through her wallet for money then glances up at Vera. "Why, just the other day I saw a woodchuck vacuuming under the bed in the guest room."

Vera stares at Louise agape, and after a minute, Louise bursts out laughing.

"Very funny," says Vera. "Ha ha ha."

"Just kidding," says Louise. "But seriously, I have had the odd...premonition."

Vera pulls out the broom and sweeps Louise's hair into a tidy pile.

"After all, I dreamt that Stanley was kissing another woman, and right on the heels of that dream comes the story of Helga the Harlot. Women have intuition about things. Sensitivities, that's all. Don't indulge them."

Vera nods. Finally something makes sense to her. "That's exactly what Deepak Chopra would say—don't give it any energy. Just let it go."

"That's probably where you got your crazy vision from anyway," says Louise as she presses a handful of bills into Vera's palm. "Too much of that Eastern woo woo will give you ideas."

"I'm just trying to improve myself, Louise."

"Yes, well it's one thing to try and improve yourself, and another thing entirely to turn yourself over to every radical foreigner with a gimmick."

"What about Dr. Phil? He's not a foreigner."

"Still..."

Vera pulls out a twenty from the pile of bills and tucks it back into Louise's pocket.

"Well, see you at church in the morning, dearie!" sings Louise. She opens the door, pulls the twenty out of her pocket and tosses it into the air behind her, leaving the door ajar.

Vera hollers, "Thanks, Helga!" As she closes the door, she mutters, "Oh and by the way, your hair is thinning."

Cleaning up for Karen Zostra, her next appointment, Vera allows herself a good chuckle. Intuition, she thinks. Intuition on overdrive! That doesn't really make her feel any better about Monk's health, though. She takes a few minutes and calls the cardiologist for an appointment, but his office is closed.

Vera chats her way through Karen's conventional cut and blow-dry, as well as Melissa Wubbold's usual touch-up and style. She concentrates hard as she dyes Melissa's eyebrows the perfect shade of chestnut and then waxes them to an exquisite arched form.

Melissa is probably Vera's most sophisticated client—tall with aristocratic carriage so rare in these days of common inelegance. Even so, Vera had the urge earlier to utterly reinvent Melissa, change everything about her hair and makeup. It was a wild impulse that she'd forced herself to suppress. Dye her chestnut hair raven black perhaps. Chop it into something gothic. Something out of one of those vampire shows.

But Melissa wasn't the only afternoon temptation. Before Melissa, Vera had had the urge to convince all of her afternoon clients, conservative and liberal alike, to do something wild and free, something utterly unconventional with their hair and makeup. Brand new creations by Vera Wright! But she'd suppressed those urges, which has sadly only served to turn her into a veritable Vera Scissorhands, prepared to cut the hair of any unsuspecting deliveryman or hapless solicitor. She doesn't know what's gotten into her.

Melissa lifts the hand mirror and admires herself. "Oh Vera, what would I do without you? You're the best aesthetician in Canaan."

Vera blushes. "Oh no, I'm not, but thank you very much. When I went to school there was no such thing as an aesthetician. Only beauticians, and oh, I suppose, makeup artists."

Melissa primps in the mirror. "Well there you go, Vera. I know an artist when I see one."

Melissa pays then blows Vera a kiss from the doorway. "Goodbye, dear," she says. "See you next week."

Vera waves from the doorway then plops down on one of the styling chairs. In a minute she leans into the counter with her head in her arms. What a day, she thinks nervously. If only she could shake the image of ...well she would, dammit, that's all. She damn well would. No aberrant vision would do her in. She remembers from many of the self-help books she's read that there is power in reciting affirmations. She begins with the obvious, "I am fully sane," she says, and repeats this several times. "I am in full possession of my right mind..." "I am an intelligent human being...blah blah blah..." She cannot even keep the affirmations straight. She tries again, "I am fully insane... I mean sane! I am fully sane."

In a few minutes the low monotone of Vera's mantra is shattered by a booming base vibrato that resounds through the floor, walls, and into the atmosphere as if being transmitted through water. "Verrrrrraaaaaaaaa," it says.

Vera pops her head up like toast. "Who?" she says. "Where? Where are you?" Every muscle in her body taut and ready for battle, she rises slowly, grabs a hot curling iron, and carefully inspects every corner of the salon, closets included, poking the curling iron in and out. Satisfied that the disembodied monster is not hiding in the salon, she then races through the rest of the house opening closets and cabinets and poking her hot wand under the beds. Nothing. No one, and no other voices.

"I'm hearing things," she says aloud. She walks fearfully back into the salon, flattening herself against one of the walls and walking sideways in anticipation of her predator.

"Verrrrraaaaaa," she hears again. "Don't be afraid. I have come to teach you."

She freezes against the paneled wall of the supply room. "Who...who are you?"

She listens hard, though hears nothing but a tiny voice inside her own head, which tells her to go to her desk. She follows this powerful impulse, though she is not sure why. Still brandishing the curling iron in her left hand, she marches robotically to the desk. She picks up a pen and a pad of paper printed with the words "Memo from the desk of Vera Wright," and all at once drops the curling iron beside her. She writes and writes and becomes lost in her writing.

She is lost in time and space and even in the very core of her identity, and twenty minutes later, she emerges from her writing, remembering nothing of what she's written, or if it was even she at all who had done the writing. The only thing she knows for sure is that someone has certainly written something, because ten memo sheets are filled to the brim with tiny cramped letters of the alphabet that appear to be grouped into words.

Sweat pours down her face. She rises stiffly and walks to the prep room for a glass of water. She drinks the water. Motivated more by curiosity than courage, she returns slowly to the desk to see what is written on the memo pad. As she flips through the pages, she can see that it certainly is her handwriting, though not her neatest penmanship. And luckily, at first glance, she can see that at least there are no pictures of Monk lying dead in a corner from a heart attack. Not that Vera had ever been gifted at illustration, but still, not even a single stick figure is in evidence.

She puts her glasses on and reads aloud: *"Vera Wright, I am the guide who will usher you through this period of spiritual growth, as you have been chosen by the Lord to prepare the world for his will."*

Vera wants to pass out, but forces herself to remain alert. If she passes out, she's afraid she'll never regain consciousness. Instead of Vera discovering Monk in the study, it will be he who finds her dead in the salon. A sick game of Clue imposed upon them by a sadistic poltergeist. This experience feels like the end of something to Vera. The end of her life, perhaps. Or maybe the beginning of something horrific, as if she'd just inadvertently lifted a concealed emergency exit and leapt out of her mind. She wonders how much more time she has before striking pavement. She has a feeling not much. She spreads her fingers over her eyes and peeks through them to the pad of paper: *"Do not be afraid,"* it reads.

"Do not be afraid!" she screams. Even in her condition she knows this is the most preposterous statement of all. "Do not be afraid? Who do you think I am, the Virgin Mary!?" Well, she is certainly not the Virgin Mary, which may be the only thing she still knows for sure. Though it could be argued that she is indeed more innocent than most. After all, she did have only one man in her entire life, but still. She lowers her eyes and reads: *"You will be told what to do when the time comes. For now you must listen within yourself for the instructions you will need to carry out this transformation."*

Vera slams her hands against the paper, covering the words. Glancing around to make sure nobody has observed her, she then opens the desk drawer and stuffs the memo pad as far back as she can reach. Is God crazy? She cannot possibly carry out his will for mankind. Though she is certainly curious and smart enough—she did get accepted into Montclair State, after all—she nevertheless was not able to actually attend the school. She is basically a simple and self-educated spirit. And even if she weren't—how utterly ridiculous, let's face it! She is many things: the dedicated wife of Monk Wright; a whimsical beautician—a colorist really, okay—an artist even, whose job is to help people improve their appearances. Why, just yesterday she streaked the front of young Jolene Neiner's hair chartreuse green! Somebody please tell her which chapter and verse of the Bible says that Noah streaked somebody's hair an unnatural color and then braided it in a hundred tiny cornrows. Or Daniel. Or Moses.

And notice they were all men, she thinks. In all of history there has been no room for women in this most exclusive of clubs. What would you call it? *The Propheteers!* And she wasn't about to be the first to sign-up, either. Leave the insides up to God, is her new motto. First thing in the morning she will throw these useless notes into an envelope and send them to the Vatican. Maybe the Pope is up to the task of sorting out the future of mankind. Isn't that what he gets paid for?

She walks to the mirror and picks up her sheers. Studying her all too innocent and saintly visage, she pulls at the front of her hair and chops it into spikes. "Ha!" she says. "You want a prophet; I'll give you a prophet!"

A few minutes later Monk opens the door and strides eagerly toward her, then stops cold when he sees her hair. "What the?"

Vera lays down the sheers then tumbles into his arms. "Oh Monk," she says happily. "Thank God you're home. I've missed you. I don't want you to go to work anymore. I want you to retire."

Monk pushes her back an arm's length. "You trip over a weed whacker?"

She pulls at this hair and that as if measuring uniformity. "You'll see when I'm finished, it'll look great," she says too eagerly. "Very modern. I have to stay modern, Monk. Youthful." *Sane, she thinks. I have to stay sane.*

In the morning Vera dresses mechanically for 8:30 Mass. She is very suspicious of God, and is not sure she wants to show up for any more special attention. But even as a recent daily Mass attendee, she would already be missed by many. Which would attract even more attention. She isn't up to the phone calls: "What happened to you, Vera?" "We were sick with worry!" Ha! Vera knows how even the holy rollers enjoy spreading a juicy rumor. She rummages through her closet and rejects anything conservative or saintly. Instead, she chooses her most stylish outfit—a form-fitting raspberry knit pantsuit with a lovely poppy vine embroidered asymmetrically on the left arm and leg. This should do the trick nicely, she thinks—the perfect antidote to the gravitational pull of uninvited spiritual activity.

Or was it mental breakdown?

Whatever it was, Vera will fight it today by concentrating on her exterior, her *packaging*. By ramping up her stylish persona as much as possible, which is easier now considering her new spiked hairdo. Very modern and youthful looking, she thinks, though slightly unbalanced since she had to ask Monk to finish the back of her head while she supervised the job via a handheld mirror. Thankfully a little gel disguised his inexperience. The important thing is—she's practically unrecognizable even to herself, and so maybe then also unrecognizable to her spirit stalker.

No doubt whoever is heckling her from the beyond thinks he's going to turn her into a nun, or worse—a half-starved locust-eating sandal-shod saint in a sheepskin loincloth. But Vera is sure this will never happen. Not to her. If Vera's picture is going to end up on a holy card, it's going to be with freshly painted auburn highlights, waxed eyebrows tinted to match, and a stylish scarf concealing the loosening flesh on her neck. As she's applying her deep nude lipstick, she thinks for the hundredth time, oh for heaven's sake, Vera, as if God would pick a part-time beautician. She pinches her cheeks and plumps her lips. But even so, why not Delores Lablanca down the street with the brand new 25,000 square foot designer home? Delores has enough money to stage the Apocalypse. Why not her? Or even Monk—why not him? He's the one who'd wanted to be a priest in the first place! Vera had never once entertained any such fantasy.

She walks outside into the crisp wind which is blowing the leaves into dozens of tiny gold and scarlet tornadoes on the lawn. As she pulls her jacket closer, her eyes are drawn upward beyond the shedding trees to the popcorn clouds floating against a brilliant field of powder blue sky. These joyful colors are a cruel backdrop for her anxiety and suffering, so she will not allow the suffering. Instead, she will savor the blessed ordinariness of this day.

In her car, one block away from St. Jude's, however, white-hot angst starts to flow almost imperceptibly through her veins and arteries, rising gradually in force until finally the chambers of her heart are flooded with a gully-wash of anger. How *dare* a so-called representative of God intimidate her like this! she thinks. She can't help her outrage. Her angst rages against her obstinate optimism, growing and growing until it is larger than Vera's radical makeover. Larger than her asymmetrical pantsuit. Larger than her entire wardrobe. It bubbles up from her pelvis through the nerves of her intestines, abdomen, lungs and throat, and finally, out her vocal chords. Much to her own amazement, she is sitting in her car in the parking lot of St. Jude's Church screaming at God at the top of her lungs as if she were married to him.

"How dare you!" she bellows. "How dare you unsettle my life in this manner, just when Monk and I are preparing for our twilight years. I am sixty-three-years-old, if you haven't noticed. That is not exactly young! Joan of Arc was a girl, and to my recollection, none of your model saints was on the verge of retirement!" She exhales deeply to regain control. "Why not pick on somebody your own size! Somebody omnipresent and immortal! Somebody without a family to care for! Somebody not crippled with the handicap of original sin!"

She cannot believe her own courage. The gall of it is intoxicating, and just as she is starting to believe in the gist of her own argument, there is a knock on the car window. Vera is startled out of her mind and shrieks involuntarily, causing seventy-year-old Margaret Vitella to return the shriek reflexively. This volley goes a few rounds before Vera is finally composed enough to roll down the window. "Oh, Margaret, I'm so sorry," she says. "Forgive me. You scared me."

Margaret throws her hand up to her massive bosom. "Whatever is the problem, dear! You were...screaming at someone. Is everything alright?"

Vera searches the car wildly for an excuse and says, "Um. Well, you see, I've been listening to this audio tape on screaming. Primal screaming? It's very good for you. You should try it. Very therapeutic." She forces herself into a ripple of what she fears is hideously false laughter, but eventually Margaret catches the ripple and giggles herself.

Before long Margaret's contagious giggle evolves into little uncontrollable tee hee's followed by huge raspy inhalations that really do make Vera laugh. She is quite happy to be taking this tiny break from total psychosis. Or is hysterical laughter just part of the same script? It occurred to her last night that it might be happening because she's alone too much. She is beginning to fear her entire solitary life, pining for Monk or Louise, or even her daughter, Mia, good Lord, to fill in all the empty gaps of solitude that she used to treasure.

They walk companionably up the brick walk, Margaret's hand on Vera's shaking forearm. "What's happened to your hair, dear?" asks Margaret. Margaret's hair is snow-white and curled in an old-fashioned bubble cut. Vera's hairdo has no hope of making sense to Margaret.

Vera reaches up to touch the stiff peaks of her new spiked hairdo. "Oh," she says shyly. "It was time for a change, that's all."

"That's good, dear," says Margaret. "It's not falling out then?"

"No!" says Vera. "Absolutely not!" Is that what people will think? She brushes the remark aside. God knows she has more to worry about than her hair at the moment. She walks Margaret into the vestibule and they part ways—Margaret taking her usual left turn to sit with the *Martha Society*, the church housekeeping volunteers—and Vera to the right to sit with Louise.

All of these distractions aside, today Vera plans to listen attentively to Father Max's homily so that no misconceptions are drawn. If she hears her name come out of his mouth, she will address him promptly after Mass. No more of this pretending. If Father Max is in on this little supernatural conspiracy—if he is perhaps even the source of it—he should be man and priest enough to confront Vera directly.

The vestments and altar cloth are purple today, or more accurately, a vibrant cabernet. They are lovely and trimmed with a richly detailed gold-threaded edging that is most striking, both on Father Max's tall imposing figure and on the altar itself. It's easy for Vera to get lost in these ornate details, because these constitute much of the reason she enjoys attending daily Mass. For her, Mass is both a tribute to the Lord and a privileged tour through a living museum. The pageantry and the deep resonant music, the luminous windows and the friezes of Christ's passion—all of this has captivated Vera since she was a child, but even more so today, this day of renewal. It is a tribute to millennia of spiritual richness, forgiveness and healing purchased with the blood of martyrs. So dramatic, she thinks. My goodness, who could resist! Today Vera plans to take advantage of this abundant inheritance by receiving Communion and requesting that she be fully healed of her troubles.

In spite of Vera's determination to pay close attention to every word spoken, she is drifting in and out of her own thoughts only to find herself well past the readings and at the brink of Father Max's homily. She clasps her hands and raises her chin. She will hear every word he speaks from now on. She forces herself to listen.

"Do you think you are weak?" he asks gently. Then more forcefully, "Do you think you are too weak to help the Lord in his earthly mission? His mission to save souls?"

Vera is thunderstruck, as this was the exact premise of her earlier argument with God. Well, of course I'm too weak, she thinks, practically mouthing the words. I'm a pathetic and uneducated middle-aged human on the verge of a mental breakdown.

"I have news for you," he continues, surveying his audience. He pounds his fist on the podium and waits for its echo to resound. "God does NOT choose the strong!"

Is it Vera's imagination or is Father Max looking directly at her again?

"God chooses the weak and makes them strong." His finger points around the room. "You and you and you and you..."

At least she's not alone this time. At least he's including a few others in his little club.

"When you hear the call, you must do something about it. No excuses. DID YOU HEAR ME, VERA WRIGHT? NO EXCUSES!" His face is flushed and he is leaning forward. "You might not be much. You certainly aren't perfect. But you are all God has. And he needs *you*." Bolts of lightning project from the fingers of Father Max's hands. Light descends from the altar.

It is all Vera can do not to pass out.

Chapter Five

Other than the special effects, Vera barely remembers the rest of Mass. For example, she remembers the Communion wafer gliding magically through the air from Father Max's hands straight down the aisle and into her mouth before she could even bless herself or say Amen. She remembers Louise asking her why she wasn't receiving Communion at the altar, and telling Louise that she had already received Communion in the pew. Then there was Louise's confusion to be dealt with, followed by her outright exasperation, not to mention the little dig about Vera's new hairdo. Vera does not remember anything else about the Mass, though. She does not remember Father Max's blur of a homily, the sign of peace, the Lord's Prayer or the recessional hymn. She could not say who was sitting in front of her, behind her, or directly to the right of her. She could barely say her own name.

But somehow, who knows how, she survived to the end, ditched Louise, and now finds herself sitting in the unappealing, nearly colorless living room of the rectory. It is a haphazard mess—seemingly decorated by a drive-by designer, or perhaps a Salvation Army delivery man. She straightens a corner of a paint-by-number original of the *The Last Supper* in the hall, and sits on a wooden settee where she awaits Father Max's counsel. Or explanation, really. Did he use her name in his homily or didn't he? Did he send the Communion Host down the aisle to Vera like some two-bit telekinetic psychic? Or did he not.

Her eyes shift sharply to the left as something suddenly occurs to her. Isn't it Halloween today? And aren't churches haunted on Halloween? It makes sense that they would be. Or at least could be. Maybe not all churches—not cathedrals, certainly, or basilicas. But ordinary churches containing ordinary distracted people. After all, goblins did not like God. Did they? Goblins were the opposite of God. Or... she raises her index finger. Perhaps this little display of magic was simply a clever trick mastered by Father Max in the seminary. After all, who knows what seminarians did with their spare time?

Vera knows she has to be careful here. She does not want to expose herself completely. Not yet. A teensy weensy bit of her understands that it might not be Father Max at all, but she, Vera, who is somehow making these things happen. If they're really happening at all.

She hears footsteps in the hall. "Is that you, Mrs. Wright?"

She turns and is caught off guard by his outfit—faded jeans and a loud Hawaiian shirt in shades of lipstick red, fuchsia, and a near blinding electric banana. "Oh, well, yes," he says. "I see now that it is you, but I was thrown-off by the new hairdo. Very... sharp."

Thrown-off, thinks Vera. I don't think so. You knew exactly who I was when you sailed that Communion Host down to me, Father Max. She examines him more closely. Had he worn those clothes under the vestments this morning? Was that possible? Why, he looks like a kid on spring break! Much too young to be providing spiritual counsel, and yet... just the right age for a good prank.

He reaches out to shake her hand. "What can I do for you today?" he asks.

She withdraws her hand—*(is he holding a buzzer?)*—and then, after inspecting, extends it again.

"Hello, Father," she says, a bit awkwardly now that she is confronted with his more casual, and dare she think it—unpredictable and extremely unpriestly persona. "I um, just..."

"Would you like a cup of coffee?" he asks brightly.

"Sure," she says. "That would be nice."

"Follow me, then, Mrs. Wright."

"Oh please call me Vera," she says. After all, she thinks, didn't you just call me Vera from the altar! "Mrs. Wright is so formal." She can't believe she's saying this to a what...thirty-five-year-old? Forty at most.

"Vera it is," he says, and pours her a mug of coffee from the carafe. "You can call me Max." He smiles. "Just kidding. A little joke."

A little joke!

They settle into his office—Vera into the threadbare tartan-plaid couch facing his desk, and he into the swiveling oak chair behind it. He pushes a bowl of candy corn in front of her, and she selects one, less out of hunger than a sense of obligation. "Mmmm," she says.

"They're my favorites," he says, and pops one into his mouth. "Here, have another."

While sipping coffee and chewing her candy corn, Vera admires the religious notions—a Lucite block with a ghostly image of the Crucifixion, an antique carving of St. Jude, and a bottle of holy water marked *Lourdes*. Well, he certainly has the right affects, she thinks. Nothing suspicious or worldly— no Waterford decanters filled with whiskey, for example, and no atomizers of Calvin Klein cologne ready to be spritzed. At least nothing obvious. Of course, who knows what's in the drawers.

She crosses and uncrosses her legs, and then says, "I'm um, wondering if you've noticed anything unusual about your homilies lately." She reaches over and jingles the sacristy keys on his desk to appear almost disinterested in the answer.

He regards her quizzically as he slides his arms down the ink blotter and rests his chin on his fists. "What do you mean, Vera?"

"Well...I mean, do they seem a little personal to you?"

"Personal? In what way?"

She glimpses the ceiling. "I'll just come out and say it then, Father. Save us some time. We're both busy people." She doesn't know where her boldness is coming from. "It seems to me that you've been talking directly to me from the pulpit. Using my name, if you will. I feel as if you are insinuating that the Lord intends to take me, Vera Wright, the weakling...and make me strong. It sounds as if you are trying to give me a direct message that you could just as easily give me in private as humiliate me in front of the entire congregation, that's all." She stretches her fingers in front of her and inspects her nails. "That's all I'm saying."

Father Max's chocolate brown eyes narrow as he sizes Vera up. He retreats back into his chair and says in a near whisper, "You got the call." Then he grins broadly. "By God, Vera, not only did you get the call, but you heard it!"

She uncrosses her legs again and sits upright. "I, um...I heard something alright."

"God bless us and save us," says Father Max, his arms raised high. "Has anything else happened, Vera? Anything unusual?"

"No," she says. "Just that. Just hearing the call is all." She does not want to risk credibility by revealing the visions yet.

"I see."

"But, well this...this 'call'...it's made me a little anxious," she says. "A little freaked out, you could say. A little berserk, in fact." She plays with her wedding band. "For instance, I don't know what to do to stop it. How to stop the call."

He shakes his head vehemently. "Oh you can't stop it, Vera. When God reaches down to bless a soul and inspire the gifts of the Holy Spirit, that process can't be stopped. That's a divine pact between you and he."

"You and him," she mutters while clearing her throat.

"Excuse me?"

"Oh, nothing," she says. "Go on." Shouldn't a priest know how to speak proper English? she thinks.

Father Max reaches over and takes Vera's hands. "We have free will, Vera. The Lord will only penetrate the spirit that has asked for these gifts in one way or another. He will not force himself on anyone. So there is something within *you* that has sought the Lord in a special way." He releases his hands and raises them openly to the ceiling. "And glory be to God, you well might have gotten your answer."

She blows air out of her cheeks and shrugs as if to appear casual. "And so, um...what next?" She drops her head, mumbling, "Winged demons in the attic?"

"Excuse me?" he says.

She shakes her head. "Nothing."

Father Max swings his chair around to face the side window, and strikes a contemplative pose. "Next is discernment, Vera. Do you understand discernment?"

"Maybe." She wrings her hands. "I mean, I'm not sure what I'm really dealing with here. It doesn't come with a manual. And some of it seems, well, supernatural."

He shrugs. "Well, that's because it is supernatural. The Holy Spirit is a real and present supernatural force."

"But how do I know? How do I know what's from the Holy Spirit and what's not? After all, it is Halloween."

He laughs out loud. "You won't find goblins in the church, Vera. At least not St. Jude's! Ha ha ha."

She blinks.

"Discernment only comes with prayer and fasting," he continues. " 'Pray unceasingly,' saith the Lord."

"Unceasingly?" This strikes Vera as excessive, considering she has a husband to care for and a business to run. Not to mention an overall life.

He nods emphatically. "Unceasingly. And eat lightly so that your body is clear and not distracted by the digestive process. Listen carefully to your heart." He cocks his head. "Tell me, Vera. What does your heart say?"

She does not have to think about this long. "My heart says: 'Vera, for no apparent reason, your whole life has changed mid-air, so get out of this mess as soon as you can. In fact, run.'"

"I see. That's because you're afraid. But if this call truly does come from the Lord, Vera, there is no reason to fear. With enough prayer, you will know what to do. The Lord promises peace to those who do his will and peace he will provide."

Vera nods tentatively. He seems so sure of himself, she thinks. Maybe he does know what he's talking about, in spite of the shirt. She almost shares her visions with him, but then decides against it. "Exactly what should I pray?"

He makes his hands into a little tent and taps his fingers. "Pray the rosary. Start with that. Do you have a special affinity for the Virgin Mother?"

"Not really."

He reaches into his drawer and retrieves a tiny teal blue velvet pouch, pulls the drawstring and laces a beautiful silver rosary through his fingers. "These came from Garabandal," he says. "In Spain. The Virgin appeared there many times. Maybe it will help if you use a special rosary, blessed just for you. The Blessed Mother is our most powerful intercessor."

He blesses the beads, and for the first time Vera feels a flicker of hope. He knows what she's going through. He has not suggested psychiatric care. He's heard of this..."call." He's given it a name, and blessed a rosary just for her. She smiles spontaneously. "I'll do it," she says. "I'll pray unceasingly."

"To see what the Lord is calling you to, exactly," he says, then winks. "He may want you to join the Martha's. We could use a few more housekeepers, you know."

Vera is shocked by this presumption. "Oh no," she says. "That would be a terrible disappointment. I don't think God would go through all these shenanigans just to get another

Martha. Why, those Martha's are..." She restrains herself. "Well, not the Martha's themselves, but the job...is not for me."

"Well, maybe a Mary then?"

Vera considers this—Mary who? Mary Magdalene? Didn't she start out as a prostitute? And here Vera had never bedded a single soul until her own husband came along, and even then, not until their honeymoon. "No," she says, "not Mary either."

He smiles uncertainly. "Remain open to the will of the Lord," he cautions. "Do not get in his way. He will tell you exactly what he's got in mind. But you must have the ears to hear."

Vera dangles the rosary for a moment, admiring the perfect tiny beads—the size of early peas—then drops them into the velvet purse. "I'll let you know," she says, though she has no intention of letting him know much. The Martha's, she thinks. Ha! What a gossiping bunch of dust bunnies! Not to mention that the youngest one is a good ten years older than she is.

As she's leaving, he hands her a pocket-sized prayer book and bids her goodbye.

Vera sinks into the cushion of her car seat and drops her forehead forward onto the steering wheel, inadvertently blowing the horn. She rockets up. Good Lord, will she ever be calm again? As she settles back down, she repeats the mantra, 'Pray unceasingly'. If it sends the spooks away, she'll do it. She'll do anything to send the spooks away. She blesses herself with the cross and begins the rosary aloud with the Apostle's Creed. "I believe in God..."

All that day, Vera prays unceasingly. She prays in the shower, at church, in the car, and while pushing the vacuum back and forth over the new Berber carpet in the basement. This is easy now, she thinks between prayers. This is my day off. But what about tomorrow when Lori Andersen brings in her three shrieking kids for haircuts—what then? How do I pray the rosary while listening to all the petty grievances of the day, not to mention waxing Edith Sorrento's unsightly moustache?

She tries not to leap ahead of herself, though. "Stay in the moment," Wayne Dyer always says, not to mention Deepak. And Vera is trying her level best. She prays while preparing the sausage lasagna for dinner, continues to pray through dinner, wondering when and if Monk will catch on, and how she'll deal with it. She can't finger the beads and butter her bread at the same time, so she tries to count in her head.

"How about a little more pasta," he says, smacking his lips.

Vera nods absently. She has only one more *Glory Be* to go before the end of the Glorious Mysteries, her thirtieth rosary of the day. She would like to finish.

"Vera, did you hear me?" asks Monk.

"...world without end, Amen," says Vera. By the time she realizes she is praying aloud, it is too late.

"Huh?" he says. "What?"

"Oh." Vera pokes at her salad. "Just thinking about Father Max's homily today, that's all. About the end of the world. Revelations, you know. 'No one knows the time or place...' and all that." She stands. "I'll be happy to get you some more lasagna, Monk. And maybe some salad?" She turns and races up the steps to the stovetop before he can quiz her any further.

"You're thinking about church an awful lot lately," he says. "Aren't you? Or something. You're thinking about something." He pivots his weight in Vera's direction. "Is it really church, Vera? Or something else?"

She watches her hand holding the knife as it slices easily through the lasagna. "Church," she says. "Just the way the readings are hitting me lately, that's all."

"Huh," he grunts. Monk does his Sunday duty, but ever since he dropped the idea of joining the priesthood, he hasn't been one for extracurricular church talk.

She tries to look attentive as he reports on the day's wrestling events at Canaan High. All she really remembers is that one of the boys injured himself on the weights after school. She does not remember the boy's name or the exact nature of his injury.

After dinner, Vera prays as she washes dishes and prays as she scoops candy into little bags decorated with witches and ghosts. What an odd custom Halloween is anyway, she thinks between Hail Mary's. Who in the world thought it up? She barely remembers going door-to-door when she was a child, and wonders if the custom started later than that. And what was the point of it, really? To scare away the goblins, or to entertain them?

Through all her preparations and mental meanderings, Vera continues to pray. She prays as she answers the doorbell and prays as she distributes the candy to the little tricksters. She prays as she listens to the soft rustle of the nearly denuded treetops and the squealing of the packs of children in the streets. Later on, she prays herself to sleep.

The next day, Vera awakens with the Joyful Mysteries on her mind and the first prayer, *The Apostle's Creed*, right there on her lips. "I believe in God..." She prays and prays all morning, saying who knows how many decades in the string of ten Hail Mary's. Or meditating on how many of the twenty mysteries of the rosary as she washes and moisturizes Edith Sorrento's over-processed hair. Why, washing Edith's hair is like washing a broom, Vera thinks between prayers. Well, that's Edith for you. She never listens to advice. *Glory be the Father, to the Son, and to the Holy Spirit...*

"Darn!" she says as she drops her brush. *As it was in the beginning, is now...*

"And she had to have a C-section," says Edith.

Hail Mary full of grace...

"And even then, the baby's head was so malformed you'd think it was made of Silly Putty."

Blessed art thou amongst women, blessed is the fruit of thy womb...

"And then not two days later it popped into shape. A normal human head! It was an outright miracle."

After treating Edith's hair with intensive conditioners, Vera highlights sections of it with golden-sunlight dye and wraps each section with squares of foil that Edith hands her one at a time. Every time Edith hands her another piece of foil, Vera mutters a Hail Mary to herself. Sometimes she loses count and has to count the pieces of foil on Edith's head to know exactly where she is in the decade. Working with her hands is a huge distraction since she can't finger the rosary beads while she's working. Not to mention Edith's incessant chatter.

Vera removes the foils, washes Edith's hair and begins the blow-dry.

"And not two weeks after that scare," says Edith, "the cousin of the father-in-law's half brother went and got himself a fatal concussion trying to dodge underneath the garage door because he was too damn lazy to look for his remote. Isn't that always the way? So now, I don't know if there's going to be a wedding or not. If I've got my facts straight, that jackass was supposed to be an usher. So at the very least, the funeral will delay things. And not only that, but guess what? You'll never guess."

World without end, Amen.

"Vera, have you been listening to me?"

Vera switches off the dryer. "Well, of course, Edith."

"It's just that your lips are moving when I'm talking and you seem to be humming something."

"Not at all," says Vera. "I'm all ears, really."

It was all Vera could do to get through the day. Five styles, six colorings—two of them double process, one facial, and one trial makeup for a wedding portrait. When they are all gone, she unwraps her apron, cleans up the salon, and bursts into tears.

"I can't take it anymore," she sobs, falling to her knees on the cold floor. She raises her arms and opens her hands. "Do you hear me, whoever you are? I can't take it anymore! I'm a beautician, not a cloistered nun! I can't pray unceasingly. I can't mutter prayers all day long and still pay attention to my customers' hair and makeup, not to mention the occasional manicure. Why I don't even know what I did to them today! I can't remember anything!"

She sobs and sobs, surrendering utterly to her frustration, and it feels so good. Screw it, she thinks, and then shouts, "Just screw it! Screw it! Screw it! Screw it!" She realizes what she's saying and then arches her back and beats her chest. "Ha ha ha ha ha!" she shrieks. "That's the funniest thing I ever heard. Screw! It!"

And then, in the middle of her cathartic tantrum, like the fin of Jaws on a perfect summer day, comes the deep and penetrating underwater voice. "Pray," it says. "Pray unceasingly."

Vera grabs a round brush from the counter and hurls it in the direction of the voice. "You pray. How about that? YOU pray unceasingly." She hurls a comb after it and a few dozen pink perm rods followed by an entire carton of hair straightener. "And see just how you like it. See how you damn well like praying until you lose all your customers and your tongue falls out."

Eventually she picks herself up and moves to the desk, where she grabs the memo pad and, barely registering the activity, begins to write. She writes and writes and writes, remembering only bits and pieces. *I am with you,* she remembers writing, but only that. *I am always with you.* But when she inspects the notes, she can find no real alphabet anywhere on the papers, only sticks and circles. Has she reverted to pre-school, for heaven's sake? She stuffs the papers into the back of the desk drawer and flees the salon.

She wants to take a shower, but barely has enough time to make Monk a halfway decent meal, so she foregoes the shower. Instead, she defrosts ground beef in the microwave and throws it in a bowl along with an egg, a cup of onions, some breadcrumbs, and a few dashes of hot sauce, why not? The hotter the better—take her mind off the lunacy of the day by numbing her tongue with red hot pepper sauce. She tosses in a few more drops, and kneads the mixture through her fingers, getting lost in the process. Just meat squeezing through fingers—so visceral, she thinks, remembering clearly having used that word recently in a New York Times crossword puzzle. A wonderful word: *visceral.* Physical and earthy, like the meat. Nothing the least bit supernatural about it—just meat. Meat and breadcrumbs and fingers.

And just as these thoughts descend upon Vera, so does an unearthly light, so real she can see its golden tones like tiny sparklers surround her. Unearthly, yet tangible. She can see the light; she can feel its warmth like the noonday sun on a beach in August. And before she knows what's happened, she is splayed out on her floor in a state of divine ecstasy. The sparklers, the light—her heart filling with light and love. She is a bottomless pit, an empty chalice that fills and fills, and while it is filling, pins her firmly to the floor.

She is euphorically unaware of her physical surroundings—just the warm and sparkling light from the ceiling that won't stop pouring in. The next thing she knows, she is in Canaan Valley Hospital Center on a roller bed in the ER, her hands still sticky with raw meat and egg.

Chapter Six

Monk paces outside her partially draped cubicle, then stops and stares wide-eyed at Vera. He turns and screams, "She's awake! Somebody come in here and help! Doesn't anyone hear me?" He whips open the rest of the drape. "She's awake I said!"

Vera eases up onto her elbows, and Monk turns at the noise.

"No, no," he says frantically. "Lie down. You're in no condition...you might have had..."

Vera shakes her head. "I feel fine," she says. She pauses to assess her condition. Why, her spirit is inflated like an inner tube, and she is so happy it hurts! How can this be? She has never been this happy in her life—not on her wedding day. Not even on the day Mia was born. She says, "Monk! The Lord has blessed me!"

"Indeed he has," says Monk. "I thought you were a goner." He catches himself mid-cry. "Honest to God, baby, I thought it was curtains for you."

"Get me out of here," she says.

"What! You can't leave! You had tests. They have to get the results. He scratches his neck. They don't know what you have." His face is stricken. "You could have a concussion, or a heart blockage...or...or a stroke! There are more tests coming. You can't leave, Vera. For God's sake, you gave me the scare of my life!"

A doctor strides in and says, "Ah, Mrs. Wright." He studies her. "Well, don't you look improved!"

"She's conscious, at least," says Monk eagerly. "And she can talk..."

"I feel great," she says, smiling. "In fact, I feel ebullient."

"Ebullient," repeats the doctor. "Well, that's not a word my ER patients use too frequently. Or any patient for that matter. At least your vocabulary hasn't suffered."

"She does the crosswords," says Monk proudly. "No college either. Just born smart."

"You may feel ebullient, Mrs. Wright, but can you tell me what day of the week it is?"

"Why, yes, it's Tuesday, November 1st. She narrows her eyes, searching, and then says, "All Saints Day! Now isn't that interesting?"

Monk squeezes her hand. "What?" he says. "Why?"

"I received the spirit on All Saints Day."

"Received the spirit?" asks the doctor.

Vera stares at his nametag. "Dr. Guthrow?" she says in disbelief.

"That's right," he says.

"Why, you're the cardiologist that was recommended to me by my best friend, Louise Lambert. You're Stanley's cardiologist!"

He draws up a seat beside her. "Had you been having symptoms prior to this episode, then?"

"Me?!" she says. "Oh no, not me! My husband."

Monk frowns. "Vera, I told you, I'm healthier than a twenty-one-year-old decathlete. I haven't had any symptoms whatsoever. Not even indigestion."

"Maybe not," says Vera, "but it seems to me that any sixty-five-year-old male ought to be checked out by a cardiologist at least once in his life, wouldn't you say, Dr. Guthrow?"

"Of course I would, Mrs. Wright, but at the moment, you're my primary concern."

"Well, yes, but I'm worried about my husband," she says. "And that could impair my own health, could it not?" She puts on a little pout for affect, but secretly she is thrilled, because she is certain that the coincidental appearance of Dr. Guthrow is a sure sign that Monk will be healed by the Lord.

"Fine," says the doctor. He hands his card to Monk. "Give my office a call," he says. "You really should at least have a stress test." Then he jots down some notes on his clipboard. "So far the tests reveal no indication of a heart attack," he says to Vera, "but considering the lack of consciousness, I'd like to keep you overnight anyway."

"Oh my no!" says Vera, pulling herself up against the pillows. "I'm fine. I'm better than fine. I could run a 10K right now."

Dr. Guthrow chuckles. "Not so fast." He puts his hand in front of her eyes. "How many fingers?"

"Three."

"Okay, well I'm going to have the neurologist stop by and check you out, and it will be up to her. She'll probably want an MRI of the brain before you go. So be prepared to stay awhile."

After Dr. Guthrow leaves, Vera sighs. "I'm sorry about the meatloaf, Monk."

He pets her head. "What do I need with a meatloaf?" He wipes a tear from his cheek. "What the hell is a meatloaf without a wife?"

Hours later, Vera is discharged and wheeled to the front lobby where Monk picks her up and carries her to the car. "Oh! Silly! You!" she says, the words bouncing out of her mouth like balls of compressed rubber. "I told you—I've never felt better in my entire life."

He closes her door, then walks to the driver's side and slides in beside her. "You're very brave," he says. "I have to admit, I never thought you'd be this calm in such an emergency."

"But it really wasn't an emergency for me, dear, now was it?" she says joyfully.

As he pulls out of the driveway, tears bound down his cheeks and his shoulders shake. "My God, girl, have you no sensitivity? I thought I'd lost you."

"Oh, Monk!"

"I almost called Mia. Almost risked talking to that butthead Frederick." He pinches his fingers. "I was this close."

"Oh, not Mia," says Vera. "Mia would not be the one to call." She shakes her head. "I'm not sure at all how Mia would react." If she would even come, thinks Vera.

"You don't understand," he says. "I thought it was the end of you."

As they enter the house Vera cannot explain the quality of the euphoria that grips her. In spite of Monk's insistence that she go straight to bed, she leaps from the covers the minute he leaves the room. She cannot wait to land on her knees. "Father," she says. "You have lit a tongue of fire within me."

"Yes," says the voice, and this time, she is not in the least bit scared. "Now you must go forth and ask forgiveness of all those upon whom you have trespassed."

"...upon whom you have trespassed," Vera repeats. *Upon whom...* Her eyes light up—she can hardly believe it! The King's English! Why, this is the very sign of discernment for which she'd prayed. Who else would speak the King's English but the Lord himself? She would get herself a new dictionary and have it blessed. Who knew how many new words she would learn now that she had the Lord for a teacher? Certainly no evil spirit would bother using good grammar. An evil spirit would dangle participles all over the place. An evil spirit would say, "Go find every sucker you trespassed upon and kick 'em where it hurts."

She repeats the holy words aloud, "...u*pon whom.*" At least she knows for sure that it isn't Louise, or even Father Max. Neither one of them would ever get it right. "*...Upon* *whom you have trespassed."* And God knows Monk isn't in on this little conspiracy. Just Vera and the Lord and the exact right grammar to get her attention.

"Pray," says the voice. "Pray for your enemies and for your friends, and for the brokenness of the world."

"Oh, absolutely!" says Vera in an enthusiastic whisper, hoping Monk can't hear. There is no task too large. Nothing the Lord couldn't ask of her now. "There is so much I want to pray for," she says. "My family—Mia and Monk—and the whole world! How will I ever have the time to do all the praying I want to do?"

"Just bring me two fishes," he says.

"Two fishes?" she asks.

"Two fishes," he says. "And five loaves of bread."

She cocks her head. "What kind of bread?"

"Two fishes and five loaves of bread, and I will multiply your efforts a thousandfold."

"A thousandfold?"

"Together we will feed the world."

The *world? S*he stands and twirls. "But I barely make a passable meatloaf!" Where is the energy coming from? "This is amazing," she says. "I am amazed. I am absolutely and positively...in LOVE! I can do anything and everything. Nothing is impossible."

She hears the steady clunk of Monk's steps on the stairs and dives back under the covers. "Keep a journal," says the voice. "So the world will know."

I will keep a journal, she thinks. Several journals. A library of journals! She can hardly wait to start writing.

Monk steps into the room, gingerly carrying a tray with a bowl of something or other, along with a bud vase containing a single plum-colored chrysanthemum. "Minestrone soup," he says. "And some saltines. If you finish this, I'll make you some fish sticks." He sets the tray on her lap. "And I brought you some pickles." He picks one up and crunches into it.

She laughs. "I'm so hungry I could eat the flower."

"That's a good sign," he says. He watches her for a moment then strokes her cheek. "I don't tell you this enough, but I love you, Vera Wright." He kisses the top of her head. "I knew I loved you, but I didn't know how much. I just didn't realize how much."

She nods tearfully.

"But now I do."

She grabs his hand and kisses it. "I'm very lucky," she says.

"Not as lucky as me."

"As I," she says.

"What's that?"

"Not as lucky as I am, Monk. I'm the luckiest person in the world."

The next day, Thursday, Vera buys a leather journal that she keeps her eye on all day long, in between clients, just laying there on the desktop waiting to be filled. As the day progresses, she knows just what she will write.

November 3rd — *Let it be known that the Lord has asked me to keep a journal, and I have agreed. I received the Holy Spirit on Tuesday, November 1st at 6:15 PM while making hot peppered meatloaf on my kitchen counter. The best I can explain is that the Lord lifted the lid off the top of my head, poured forth the spirit of love and joy from his own heart into mine and replaced the lid. All of this in the space of a minute and a half while squeezing the meatloaf through my fingers, tenderizing the meat and blending the egg and breadcrumbs with the meat and spices. An old family recipe, minus the hot sauce. We were never to eat the meatloaf, however, because the Lord's work pinned me to the kitchen floor. I was such a weakling that I landed in the hospital—Monk misinterpreting my ecstatic state for a coma. I was helpless to change this course of events, though it was and remains extremely confusing— why me?—I still think, but then the Lord answers, 'Why not you, Vera?"*

Ever since then, it's as if a part of me is busy running around in the spirit world at the exact same time I am attending to the duties of my physical life. I don't know who or where I am half the time. I am hoping this condition will soon change as I grow into my new and improved spirit. Otherwise, I am doomed to a sanitarium.

The very next day, November 2nd—All Soul's Day—after Mass, I drove all the way to Junior Sanborn's trailer near Kingston, New York. I was moved to tell him that I was the one who had sent him the fake invitation to Julia Gannon's pre-prom party in 1960, even though I'd known darn well that Junior didn't have a prayer in hell of going to the prom with anyone. Julia, of course, turned him away, as I must have known she would. It may have been the only truly mean thing I ever did, and I can't even remember why I did it. Probably some dare I had no business taking. At any rate, my conscience could no longer bear it. Thank God Junior was gracious enough to forgive me and invite me in for a catfish sandwich, which, sadly, I could not accept. Instead I drove two hours back home to Canaan to confess the deed to Monk, who was even more shocked than Junior had been, not so much that I'd deceived Junior, but that I'd driven all the way up to Kingston to confess it after all these years.

Humility, Vera is thy name.

Chapter Seven

The total and absolute power of the Holy Spirit notwithstanding, Vera's transformation does not take place all at once. She is at times joyful, if not *on-fire*, with enough energy to circle the earth twice. Then all at once the joy wears off the edges—just when she really needs it. She has a hard time holding onto the joy, for instance, when Katrina Baughman pitches one of her regular twitching fits during an eyebrow tint, causing the foam to drop onto her puny lashes and from there...well. Let's just say one of these days that woman is going to blind herself with ebony hair dye, and as a full-fledged attorney-at-law, she will not be suing herself. Vera silently blesses Katrina, as the Lord has instructed, but the effect of it is not as automatic as she would like. She still fantasizes about ejecting Katrina from the chair.

Part of this might be because, over these last few weeks of holy inspiration, Vera has not gotten much sleep. In fact, she is downright exhausted. God talks to her at the most inconvenient times: just as she is falling asleep, or in the middle of the night when she gets up to go to the bathroom. "Vera...Vera," he says, like a little kid just waiting for her to wake up. Not to mention early in the morning before she's even had a chance to brush her teeth. A few times Vera even found the salon door unlocked in the morning, her desk drawer ajar, and she took this to mean that she'd had another writing session with the Lord in the middle of the night. These writings are the most mysterious of all. She does not know what they say, because, though very small parts of them are legible and in English, the great majority is written in little hacked-up twigs of an alphabet—sticks and circles with spaces here and there. But she keeps these writings, nonetheless, stuffed in the back of her drawer, because she feels that the Lord must have his reasons, even if she does not understand his methods. After all, it is his bidding, not hers that has brought about this holy calling. "You are here because the Lord has brought you here," says Father Max.

Thankfully, however, when the Lord speaks to Vera outright, he does so in plain English, although even then she is not always sure what he is talking about. Sometimes it's the simplest reminder, such as, "Vera, the philodendron needs watering," or, "Vera, you left the curling iron on." And other times the language and concepts are so big and slippery, Vera cannot slide her mind or even her extensive vocabulary into them without landing upside down and backwards.

One of these times the Lord was trying to teach her about two things he calls imprint ether and kinetic ether. She told him she knew about ether all right—that foul smelling gas the doctor had administered right before her tonsillectomy at the age of four. This was not the same kind of ether, according to the Lord, but another kind that we all use every day, whether we know it or not, to form ideas that either inspire the world or haunt it. This is serious business, he says. Just when we're idly half-entertaining some seemingly innocent naughty thought in the privacy of our own brains, that same thought is busy taking form in some part of the universe—or many universes, as the Lord points out—the infinite parallel universes that comprise the unconscious world.

The Lord recently directed Vera to an article about these universes in the Tuesday New York Times science section. She loves the fact that the Lord reads the New York Times.

Read it—why, he probably inspires the reporters who write it! And not only the articles, but what about the crossword puzzles? Anyway, according to the article, certain physicists have already concluded that we reside not in a universe at all, but a multiverse. The Lord says that's the reason for war right there—nasty idle thoughts formed unconsciously with kinetic ether in other parts of the multiverse. Well, of course, the Lord went into a lot more detail, but all the detail in the world didn't completely clear it up for Vera.

Because what did that mean exactly, in practical terms? When Vera is trying to say a prayer while rolling Louise's perm and Louise won't stop yakking and Vera imagines herself stapling Louise's tongue to the roof of her mouth, does this mean that somewhere in the multiverse Vera is actually stapling Louise's tongue? And if so, wouldn't that be a useless way to run the world? Is the Lord in charge, or isn't he? And if he is, then how can he allow unconscious human beings to perform vicious invisible acts in the middle of Canaan, New Jersey? People cannot be arrested for using invisible ether to commit invisible crimes, whether it's tongue stapling or murder. There's no law against it. Where's the evidence? So what's the point? Well anyway, this is not for Vera to question, she supposes. She is only the court stenographer, not the judge and jury.

But all in all, Vera thinks the Holy Spirit is doing a good job turning her into a better person. She tries to be more aware of her thoughts and how spiteful and nasty they can be if she isn't monitoring them every single second. For instance, if she catches herself thinking, "Why can't Monk pick up his own damn underwear," instead she will force herself to say aloud, "Monk is an excellent provider and a loving husband," thus turning a negative thought into a positive statement. This small act of faith may change the world for the morning, if not eternity, saith the Lord.

And Monk is amused by her "perkiness", as he calls it, and her uncharacteristic willingness to forgive almost anyone's transgressions, not to mention her heroic efforts in the kitchen. For dinner, Vera slaves joyfully over a three-course prime rib feast, beginning with shrimp cocktail and ending with homemade cream puffs. This pleases Monk so much, that Vera intends to become more organized so she can cook this way every night. And if not at night, then possibly a simmering slow-cooked crock pot banquet that she can throw together in the morning before her clients arrive. Of course, first, she would have to dig her crock pot out of the appliance graveyard in the basement.

And perhaps, to multiply her efforts, the Lord himself would consider contributing some loaves and fishes. Asiago cheese loaves and halibut would be nice. Not to mention a glass or two of ordinary spring water transformed into merlot, why not? After all, an outright miracle would certainly go a long way to converting Monk, which would also support Vera mightily in her own pursuit of faith. And wouldn't that serve the Lord's purpose, too? What goes around comes around, saith the Lord. Or at the very least, saith Vera. She claps her hands. Oh, how she intends to enjoy her new life in the spirit and its access to unlimited new dimensions of giving and receiving. *Your faith will move mountains.* Vera intends to take the Lord up on that.

As they begin the prime rib dinner, Vera says, "A lovely new home is going up behind the Morgenstern's." She sips her wine cooler. "The house has an indoor swimming pool and its own post office, I heard."

"That so?" says Monk.

"Oh, yes," she says. "It's huge, of course, and imposing. Worth quite a lot, I'm sure. Isn't it nice to be surrounded by such wonderful expressions of architectural innovation?"

Monk dips a jumbo shrimp into his cocktail sauce. "Vera?"

"Yes?" she says brightly.

"Are you on drugs?"

"Ha ha ha!"

He squeezes lemon onto his shrimp. "Well just explain to me then why former *hideous monstrosities with the carbon footprint of a herd of tyrannosaurus* have suddenly been reconstituted into *wonderful expressions of architectural innovation*? Why the change of heart?"

"Oh, well, I just feel that it would serve me better to be more...positive, that's all." She pats her lips with her napkin. "There's nothing we can do about them anyway."

"Okay then." He nods his head repeatedly, trying to absorb this. "That's great, Vera. Maybe you'll be a little chattier with our neighbors then? Or is that pushing it too far?"

"Oh no," she says. "Not far enough, really. I'd actually like to invite them over. What do you think?"

He grins broadly and bounces his fist staccato-style on the table. "I don't know what's come over you, my dear, but it suits you. I always knew you were sweet at the core. I just never knew how to get through the grizzle."

"And another thing, Monk... I'd like to...well, it's just that now the Lord has given me the energy to...deal with our daughter." She swallows. "I'd like to clear this mess up by Thanksgiving. I'd like us to celebrate Thanksgiving with our daughter."

Monk's eyes turn suddenly sad. "You think you can clean out a viper's nest in three weeks?" He shakes his head. "Nah. She leads her own life. We don't have the authority to 'deal' with her, I'm afraid."

Vera places her fork carefully on the side of her plate. "A little unconditional love can change the world."

"Maybe the world, but not Mia. Don't forget we tried that."

"Yes, but...two fishes and five loaves of bread blessed by the Lord will manifest a thousandfold."

He frowns. "You think the Lord wasn't with us a year ago, Vera, when Mia landed upside down in a convertible on the median and cracked her skull? Or a month ago when she ranted at you at the top of her lungs right in the middle of downtown Canaan? I mean, you've been through some kind of experience, I will grant you that. The proof is in the pudding here, and I do see a change. Is that the Lord, though?" He shrugs. "I don't know. And if it is, why would he do anything different now than he's been doing all along, which is basically pacing on the sidelines, the same as you and me. Don't forget how many prayers we've been saying for Mia for what now...four years? And let me remind you that she and her alcoholism—because that's what it is, Vera, alcoholism, not to mention vanity—were some of the reasons you started to go to daily Mass in the first place."

"Well then, she's done me a favor, hasn't she?"

Monk raises his eyes. "She's the one who needs the favor, Vera, not you. And I don't see her getting one."

"Are you saying she's hopeless? That there's nothing the Lord can do?"

"To be honest with you..." He sighs. "Sometimes I feel like the Lord's just left us down here to rot. I don't know, maybe it's just me." He throws his napkin on the table as he stands up. "I need another beer. You want more wine and soda?"

"No dear," she says quietly. She does not want to convince him with words, but with actions and physical proof. "I'm going to surprise Mia one of these days," she says. "Just drop in and see how she is."

He glares at her. "I'd be careful if I were you."

"A mother should be able to drop in on her only daughter— her only child, actually. Don't you think a mother has that right, Monk?"

"I do. But just prepare yourself, is all I'm saying. I mean, Jackass could be home—or should I say—God Almighty in his three piece custom-tailored suit." He pops the tab on the Miller Lite and chugs it on his way to the table. "We don't even know what he does all day," says Monk as he slips back into his chair. "What the hell does he do, anyway?"

"You know very well what he does," says Vera. "He invests. The family has a lot of money, and according to Mia, he... he invests it for them."

"That's not a job," says Monk. "That's gambling." He bites his lower lip. "I tell you what, bring your cell phone and call me if the Jackass is home."

"Let's call him Frederick."

"You used to like calling him Jackass! In fact, I believe you were the one who named him that. Not to mention the little cheerleading act that spelled it out." He waves a hand in the air and jumps into a V stance. "Give me a J. Give me an A!"

She blushes. "Yes, well. That wasn't very kind of me either, was it?"

"Kind? No. But bulls-eye accurate, yes. After all, Frederick is a Christian name." He frowns quizzically. "Isn't it? There must be a Saint Fred somewhere." He sips some beer. "Anyway, a jackass like him shouldn't be allowed to use a Christian name."

Vera forces herself not to correct Monk's grammar. Instead she says, "Let's stop blaming Mia's weaknesses on Frederick."

Monk pushes his plate away. "I've lost my appetite."

Vera pushes it back. "Oh, Monk, I never intended to spoil your dinner. Look at it this way—I'm back on the case, that's all. I have the strength and the commitment to help our daughter now. You should feel good about that."

"You're gonna get screwed again."

"That's impossible."

He sighs. "Okay. But don't forget your cell phone. You never know what's going on over there. And carry it on you—right in your pocket or snapped to your belt." He points his finger at her. "Do not leave it in the car. And remember to press 5. That's my automatic number."

"I always forget that," says Vera.

"Well, remember it," says Monk. "I want you to be prepared for anything."

Vera tires herself out forcing sprightly conversation through the rest of dinner to cheer up Monk. She does not want him sabotaging her efforts to corral Mia back into the fold. She wants him to disappear into the scenery for a while so she can let the Lord work through her — use any kind of ether in his palette to snap Mia out of her lazy selfish life.

Monk sulks a bit, picking at the rest of the dinner, but improves by dessert when he polishes off three cream puffs. "Okay, then," he says. "I'm off to the gym."

"To the gym?" she says.

He picks up his plate and brings it to the sink. "Yeah, I can't get that damn treadmill to work. I've called the shop. They'll be here on Saturday to check it out."

"You think it's a good idea to work out strenuously after consuming a 5,000 calorie meal?"

"No better time."

As she's clearing the table, she says, "Maybe you shouldn't work out until you've had that stress test."

"Will you stop harping on that?"

She winces.

"I'm seeing the doctor next week," he says more gently. "You know that. You also know I'm in great condition." He winks at her and wiggles his butt. "Remember last night?"

"It's just that..."

He turns on the oldie station and starts to mash his feet. "What am I doing, Vera?"

She rolls her eyes. "Mashed potatoes."

"That's a girl...now what?"

"Oh, Monk."

"Vera!"

"Okay, the pony."

He finishes his cage dance and twists out the door. Vera watches from the kitchen window as he pulls out of the driveway in his old rust trap. Oh Monk, she thinks. Don't ever leave me. Please don't ever leave me. Slowly, she draws the rubber gloves over her hands, submerges them in the soapy water, and begins another rosary.

That night, the Lord speaks to Vera in a new way. It seems like a dream, but it's no ordinary dream. An extremely extreme dream is what it is—something like Vera imagines it would feel like to be dropped on the peak of Kilimanjaro from a helicopter with gale force winds at her back and nothing to slow her down. And it involves her parents.

In the dream, it feels as if she is walking the earth with her physical body, and yet, she knows she is not. Her senses are on heightened alert—the dewy grass beneath her feet is slippery and cool. The Heaven Scent powder on her mother's neck is sweet and nostalgic. She inhales the pungent smoke of her father's pipe tobacco while she is still in route—still in the helicopter, you could say, before she even knows she will be seeing him. And also it feels as if Vera can change the dream if she wants to, though it is too riveting to change. She would never change it, in fact. It's been too long since she's seen her parents. She is not a witness to this dream, but an active participant in it, complete with a snowy white eyelet gown and ginger-highlighted hair laying in long ringlets down her back. She is a child, and yet not a child. She thinks like an adult.

First she feels her strong new super-sized spirit ditch her material body and wander through a carnival freak show of every dead person she's ever known. There is Uncle Bartholomew, Aunt Kitty, Nora Ferguson, Louis Tanty and Ronald Lynch—all of them reaching out to her behind red velvet ropes as if she is a celebrity. One good thing she notices is that she is attached by a silver life rope to her naval and feels confident that she can find her way back, hand-over-hand, if need be. Though she has no idea how long this rope is or how far she has already gone.

Eventually, she meets up with her parents, whom she has not seen in a good long while—forty-three years to be exact. Her mother is glowing; her spirit shimmers like an opal. She is dense with light, while at the same time slightly translucent. She is dressed in a skirt made of layers of white organdy and a pearl white sweater that looks as if it had been spun from a cloud. Her hair surrounds her youthful, lovely face like a silver halo of tight curls. Her eyes are the color of jade with a glint of emerald. She looks even prettier than Vera remembered. She is every bit like her own version of the Good Fairy, and Vera wonders if she has landed in Oz.

Her mother extends her hands and touches Vera's. Her hands are warm and Vera relishes the heat. The last time she touched her mother she was cold as stone. But not now. Now Vera can tuck that memory away, because now her mother is alive. "My mother is alive!" she exults. "Oh, Mom, is it really you?"

"It is," says her mother dreamily.

Well, it is Vera's mother, and yet not Vera's mother in a lot of ways. For instance, this is definitely not the same woman who dumped laundry all over Vera's bedroom floor in one of those all too frequent housewife tantrums about clean versus dirty clothes. Vera had her fair share of these tantrums herself when Mia was young. And this dignified woman does not the least bit resemble the mother Vera spotted late one night at a neighborhood get-together in their living room shooting peas through a straw to knock down the plastic figurine set-up on Mr. Walter's butt as a target. The woman floating in front of Vera now is not a party animal. She is an exalted being who has risen above the weight of the earth's pettiness.

"We're happy here," says her mother. She waves her right arm elegantly outward, as if she is a model on the Price Is Right pointing out the Amana self-defrosting refrigerator behind door number two. "Have you ever seen anything so lovely?" she asks.

And right then Vera can see why they are happy. They are still living in the heavenly version of Canaan—the same brownstone colonial in which Vera grew up. The stone shimmers with a wash of pinks and maroons; the slate roof sparkles with crystals of silver and gold. A white angora cat she has never seen before curls into a wicker chair on the porch. Everything in her parents' heaven is lit from within. No central source of light is apparent, and Vera has never seen anything like it. It is not blindingly bright. More like New Jersey on a pleasantly overcast morning in November. As Vera notices this, she also realizes that she and her mother are brighter than their surroundings.

"Come," says her mother, "let's visit your father." She brushes Vera's shoulder to guide her indoors.

Her father is sitting in a corner of the dining room in his old red leather chair—the one now stored in Vera's basement. Curls of aromatic smoke rise from the pipe on the table beside him. He raises his eyes slowly from the newspaper, keeping his finger about one inch from the top on the left to mark his place. As he looks up, the paper relaxes in his lap. Vera notices that his spirit is not as bright as her mother's, and wonders why this is so. In fact, if she is honest, he is as dim as a ten-watt bulb, his edges blurred in places by the similar tone of his surroundings. Like a half-drawn picture, it is hard to know where he begins and ends. The pine-paneled dining room is the same as she'd remembered—diamond-paned windows, the long oak table, and the expansive stone fireplace— inviting, but dark as dusk.

Vera is suddenly overcome with excitement. "Daddy!" she calls out. She can barely contain herself, but wants to give him a chance to welcome her. After all, this is his heaven, not hers. Not yet.

"Who is it?" he says, and places one hand like a visor to protect his eyes from the glare. It is clear that he cannot see too well.

"It's Vera, dear," says her mother.

Her father nods and says, "Ah, Vera, honey, finish your homework," then snaps his paperback open and says, "Hey, Regina, get me a beer, will you?"

Vera is devastated and, like a child, yanks the back of her mother's sweater for attention. "What's wrong with him, Mom?" she pleads.

Her mother sighs, then turns and guides Vera out the door where the light is brighter and more agreeable to Vera. They stroll for a while in the garden, which is filled with the velvet iris and satin pink peonies that her mother has always loved. "They bloom all year," she says smiling. "Can you imagine living in a place where the spring flowers never stop blooming?"

From the garden, they can hear her father repeating, "Hey, Regina, get me a beer, will you?" He uses the same intonation again and again, like a robot.

As Vera's mother rises to get the beer, Vera says, "Let him get his own beer."

Her mother smiles. "He can't, dear. He doesn't have sufficient awareness or form to leave his chair."

Vera is chilled by this answer. What does it mean, exactly? If he's in heaven, why can't he leave his chair? And why is there a chair in the first place? Why isn't he lounging on a cloud, for instance? She waits for her mother on a wrought iron garden bench near a koi pond that Vera doesn't remember. The steady whoosh of the small waterfall nearly puts Vera in a trance.

Her mother returns and says, "Your father wants everything to remain exactly the same—the house, the yard. Me. He has frozen these images in his mind, and remains in the past. The only alteration I've made to the property is this pond because he isn't able to enjoy the yard anyway. It's too bright out here." She leans forward and spreads her fingers under the water, tickling the fin of a shimmering silver fish as it passes by. "I figure by the time he's able to move by himself, he will also be able to appreciate the change. Other than that..." She drifts off, and Vera doesn't probe.

In a few moments, her mother turns to Vera meaningfully. "Other than that, your father refuses to believe we're dead." She shakes her head ruefully. "He just can't accept that we left you behind."

Vera peers into her mother's jade eyes and says, "What! He doesn't know he's dead?"

"That's right, dear. He has no idea. It's a real hindrance."

"How can he not know he's dead? I mean, how can anyone not know he's...dead?"

"The mind goes on," says her mother. "And the mind goes on deceiving."

"But why don't you tell him?" She stands up abruptly. "I'll do it," she says. "I'm going to march right in there and tell him he's dead."

Her mother pulls Vera down gently by the arm. "It's no use, dear. I've told him a thousand times already."

"But maybe if I...?"

Her mother shakes her head side to side in long, slow, fluid movements.

Vera cannot believe this one bit. This is not at all what she thought. Or to her knowledge, what anybody thought. Or what she'd ever read anywhere or been taught out loud. Why, this existence of her father's defies every catechism lesson in the book. "Mom," she says, "the nuns taught us that when we die we would be greeted by the Lord and whisked off to heaven." She shakes her head emphatically. "Nobody ever mentioned the possibility that we could die without knowing it and be paralyzed in a recliner for eternity." She points to the garden. "I mean, it's lovely out here, but..."

Her mother nods. "But they do discuss purgatory I believe."

Vera is shocked. "So this is..." She can't believe this either. "I'm in...you're in...purgatory?"

Her mother tips her head thoughtfully. "It's an in between place, let's say. A place for people who are stuck in fixed belief systems that no longer apply. There are still lessons to be learned here."

"So heaven is heaven?" says Vera hopefully. "Heaven isn't...this, right? Right, Mom? Heaven isn't purgatory?"

"There are many levels to heaven, dear. '*Many rooms in my Father's mansion,*' as you have heard from Father Max's pulpit. Infinitely as many rooms as the mind can create."

Vera's eyes light up. "You know Father Max?"

"Ah yes, well, you are the one thing missing from our lives, Vera. Naturally I'm interested in your progress." She smiles admiringly and pulls one of the ringlets of Vera's hair. "Your spirit is very bright, dear. The Lord has big plans for you if you can manage to stay on the path. And if you can, you will have many choices when you arrive here."

"Choices?" she says. "I thought all that went away when you died. I mean, I thought we automatically surrounded the Lord like a choir of angels to sing his praise."

"Sing his praise, certainly," says her mother. "But we can only ascend according to the density of our light. If our light is not equal to the light in our environment, we would get... burned. And that would... well, let's just say that would not be heaven. The Lord in his mercy appoints us to a realm compatible with our resources."

Vera wrings her hands. "You and Dad don't have the same light," she says. "Why isn't he bright like you or me?"

"Like you or I," says her mother, winking.

Vera blushes. Her mother shifts her light toward Vera. This is the first time Vera realizes how bright her mother really is. Or maybe the light is coming from her—from Vera. It's hard to tell; their energy mixes.

"Vera," her mother says patiently, "it is important to awaken on earth. To do whatever it takes to awaken down there. Your father can awaken; it's not impossible. But it's much more difficult here, and it takes a great deal of energy and many prayers from his loved ones on earth. He can't do it on his own because he did not want any part of it on earth."

"He prayed," protests Vera. "And he attended Mass!"

Her mother cocks her head sympathetically. "Indeed, but he did that for you, dear. So you wouldn't get thrown out of Sunday school. Showing up at church every day is no guarantee that your heart will be emptied enough to receive the Lord. Your father went to church because he was told to, but did he ever really believe any of it?" She sighs. "Apparently not. His consciousness is low, and his heart remains closed and suspicious. He did not *believe* in it then, so he has no access to it now. His life is hazy and muddled, like a forgettable dream."

"He believed in me," says Vera, sniffling. "He took good care of me."

"That he did. And that attachment also keeps him here."

Vera purses her lips. "What about you, Mom? What keeps you here?"

"I could leave," she says wistfully. "If I wanted to, I could ascend. My light is dense enough to move several levels closer to the core realm. Closer to the Lord." She regards Vera lovingly. "But your father would not be able to accompany me. And I'm willing to wait."

"He's a good man," says Vera. "Anyone can see that. God should be able to see that."

"You can help him," says her mother. And then, as her image dissolves, she says, "Pray for him, Vera. Pray unceasingly."

And before she knows it, Vera is blasted like a rocket back into her rickety aging body and by the time she awakens, she is already sitting upright like a stake has been driven down her spine. She is sweating and trembling and desperately thirsty. She is an all-around wreck. Lying beside her, Monk snores like a rhinoceros. She nudges his shoulder until he turns over, and then slips out of bed for a glass of water. Though she reaches for the details of her dream, they are gone by the time she crawls back in bed.

***

"Wake up!" shouts Father Max too close to the microphone as he paces back and forth on the altar during his homily. "Wake up, or by God..." He stops and points accusingly at the congregation. "God will be happy to do it for you."

Vera hopes Father Max is talking in general and not directly to her again. She thinks it's about time somebody else got a wake-up call, like Louise. Louise has been a real crank lately. Or Dorothy Michaels from the rosary society, the way she wails out the Joyful Mysteries like a screech owl, holding every one of the parishioners a personal prisoner while she hangs out the "Aaaaaammmeeeeen" like the last flag in a parade. Does she think this relaxes people? Makes them any holier? Because it does not. It makes Vera want to use skeins of kinetic ether to commit etheric murder. Even saints have some consideration for other people's time, do they not? Not that Dorothy Michaels is a saint. Vera catches the thread of this dark thought and halts it in its tracks. "God bless Dorothy Michaels," she says a little too loudly.

"What's that?" whispers Louise.

Father Max is still talking, so Vera bug-eyes Louise to be quiet.

"Did you just say something about Dorothy Michaels?" Louise says in a slightly lower pitch.

Vera simply stares forward as a good example of what you should be doing in the middle of a priest's homily when you're sitting in the second row and the priest is looking directly at you.

The static from Father Max's microphone bristles in the air. "Do you think the Lord came down to this tiny, nearly inconsequential planet merely to make you and me more comfortable?" He inhales audibly, gathering oxygen and steam. "Because he did not!" says Father Max. "He did not make a round-trip journey from paradise to buy you or me a silver blue Porsche Boxster or a restaurant quality stainless steel outdoor grill."

The way he described these items, Vera can't help but wonder if he'd actually priced them out. She imagines him tooling down Sheridan Avenue in an onyx black convertible sports car with the top down, his cardinal red vestments waving behind him in the breeze.

He throws his head back and booms, "The Lord made this arduous and tormenting journey to comfort the AFFLICTED." More quietly, he adds, "And to afflict...the comfortable."

Vera's head bobs up and down in agreement. She knows all about affliction. She knows the truth when she hears it. "Amen," she whispers.

"But it will be well worth your while to serve the Lord," he continues, "because if you pray the rosary and attend daily Mass, in the end you will be gifted with a body so glorious...so luminous...as to blind the mortal eye. And this is our reward...our *uniform* so to speak. In taking on this gift, we will be appropriately outfitted to eternally survive the presence of the Lord God Almighty. To experience him in full and glorified relationship."

Before she knows what she is doing, Vera raises her index finger and blurts, "Well, not exactly..."

Father Max surveys the congregants for signs of dissension. "Does someone want to share?"

Louise elbows Vera and Vera elbows Louise back.

"Vera?" asks Father Max. "Did you want to add something to the homily?"

Vera pulls tightly on the string cords of her sandwashed ultrasuede vest. "Yes, well. No," she says. "No."

"I think you do," he insists.

She clears her throat. "Well, okay then, maybe...yes." She rubs her hands together. "Okay, well, it's just that I think there's no guarantee of receiving the glorified body you want just because you attend daily Mass, that's all. Or because you pray the rosary. I mean, I wouldn't want to give anybody that impression, because it isn't automatic." She bites her bottom lip. "It won't happen to everyone."

A tidal wave of murmurs crashes over the congregation. *Who does she think she is?* But Father Max recovers nicely. "I think Vera has a point there, people, don't you?"

No, not yet they don't. At least no one is willing to speak up.

"I mean we can't very well walk out of this church every day and run our Buick Skylarks into schools full of kindergartners and expect to be outfitted by the Lord for the heavenly banquet, now can we?"

There is a smattering of giggles.

"But I think most of us can expect a fine and luminous wardrobe when it's time for our spiritual journey. Barring acts of outright evil."

"Our spiritual journey is now," blurts Vera. "We can't wait. It's now." She is not sure where she is getting this information, but wishes she would shut up.

At this, Father Max bows, returns to the altar and begins the Offertory. Somehow Vera forces herself to stay for the completion of Mass, hoping and praying that the Host will sail down to her pew to spare her the embarrassment of receiving Communion directly from Father Max. Why did she have to say that? Why? And vaguely she remembers a dream involving her parents, though she cannot recall a single helpful detail.

After Mass, Louise struts over to Vera in the parking lot with her hands planted firmly on her hips. "What exactly has come over you, Vera Wright?" She wags her index finger. "You're getting to be very outspoken, you know. Bold. Nearly irreverent."

Vera takes long strides ahead of Louise to outpace her, but Louise takes short little butt-wiggling high-heeled steps to catch up. "You didn't used to be so outspoken," says Louise. "Not like that, anyway. You used to make me laugh. You don't make me laugh anymore, Vera. I don't know what's happening to you. You've changed."

Vera pauses at her car door. "Do you think I'm crazy, Louise? Because if you do, you should just say so."

"Maybe I do." She blinks. "Maybe I don't."

Vera beeps her remote to unlock the car. "Ah, yes, well, I've got a lot on my mind. You can blame it on that."

"Like what exactly?"

"Mia for one."

"Oh, yes, well, Mia."

"I'm going over there later," Vera says. "To her place."

"I'll say a prayer, then," says Louise.

Vera nods. "You do that, Louise. You say a prayer. A really big fat one with whipped cream and cherries on top." She opens the car door and tosses her purse across the passenger seat.

Louise frowns. "What's that supposed to mean?"

"It means that a lot of people say they're going to pray when they have no intention of praying. It's like saying 'How are you?' when you don't really care."

Vera dips into the seat, and just as she's about to slam the door, Louise whips her hand inside to flick Vera's shoulder. The door catches on Louise's wrist and bounces back.

"Aaaaaaa!" screeches Louise, grabbing her hand. "Mary, Queen of Angels, spare me the pain! Aaaaaaaa!"

Vera swings the door open and jumps out. She has already had it with this day. "Let me see," she says, and goes for Louise's hand.

Louise yanks her hand back protectively. "Aaaaaaaa!" she shrieks. "I have to go to the hospital. Aaaaaaaaa!"

"Well, let me see it at least!" exclaims Vera, but Louise is too busy jumping around in little circles shrieking.

Vera is getting disgusted. She did not even close the car door that fast or that hard. Louise's hand couldn't possibly be broken or even sprained—a little bruised, maybe. And anyway, isn't Louise the biggest damn baby in the nursery? Why, Vera remembers once in the salon she'd wailed like this when a bobby pin was removed. "Ouch! Ouch! It's sticking! You're hurting my head! Ouch!" And what in the hell was she doing sticking her hand into the car in the first place? Who sticks her hand in someone's car when the car door is in the process of being closed? Good God in heaven, exactly what kind of satanic adventure was this spectacle turning into?

"Aaaaaaaa!" screams Louise. "Aaaaaaaa!"

"Okay, okay," says Vera. "Get in my car and I'll drive you to the hospital." She pushes Louise from behind. "Come on. Let's go. I have to get to the city."

Louise turns her head, her lower jaw dropped in an odd and exaggerated manner. "This is how you apologize?" she says. "Are you kidding me?" She jerks away from Vera. "I'm not going with you," she says. "Stanley would take better care of me than this. A ferret would take better care of me!"

Vera's whole body shudders with frustration. "Oh for God's sake, Louise," she snaps, "get off your cross; we need the wood."

"Uhhh!" gasps Louise angrily, squinting. "Why, you...!"

From the corner of her eye, Vera sees an approaching flock of feathered hats and plaid mohair suits from the 1960s. Apparently Louise's screams had created chaos inside the church during the recitation of the rosary, and now the rosary society, not to mention the Martha's, are scooting full speed across the parking lot to investigate.

"What's going on!" demands Margaret Vitella at the head of the flock, her hands wagging in the air. "Call 911! Somebody call 911!"

"No reason to call 911," says Vera calmly. "It's just a bruise."

Louise gives Vera the evil eye and screams, "Aaaaaaaaa! Aaaaaaaa!"

Margaret comes to a full breathless stop in front of Louise's limp, outstretched hand, and gasps, her hand to her broad chest. "Oh, my dear, dear girl," she says, then turns and barks orders to the other Martha's, "Hasn't anyone called 911 yet? Call 911 now!"

A rustle of purses soon produces several cell phones, each of the callers competing to be the official rescue call.

Margaret places her hands consolingly on Louise's shoulders. "Dear dear," coos Margaret. "Come sit over here on the bench and we'll wait for the ambulance." Out of breath herself, she has to lean on Louise's shoulders as they walk. "I used to volunteer at the hospital," she reassures Louise. "I worked in the snack shop, but believe me, we were all trained to know exactly how to manage emergencies." She turns around and barks into the crowd, "Somebody get ice!"

Louise turns and glances smugly at Vera.

Vera rattles her keys. "I've got to go," she says.

"Well then go," says Louise.

"Mia, remember?"

Louise raises her chin and struts off with Margaret and the other ladies.

Oh, the hell with it, Vera thinks as she jumps back in the car. It's a bruised muscle, nothing more. Let Louise get pampered to death with fuss, just the way she likes it. This kind of behavior is probably what made Stanley sick in the first place. Let her be chauffeured to the hospital in a damn ambulance attended by four surgeons, for God's sake. Sirens wailing. The whole catastrophe. In less than an hour she'll be released with a bag of ice and some Tylenol. How embarrassing. And she'll be lucky if she can shake off the Martha's by dinner. The Martha's love a willing victim. Not to mention the hamburger casseroles they'll be feeding Louise for a month.

Vera zooms out of the parking lot, hoping not to run over any small children from the adjacent grammar school. Once on the road, she drowns out her thoughts by whistling, "I'm a Yankee Doodle Dandy" as she passes the school, the rectory, Rocco's Diner, Anthony's Hair and Nails, The Little

Flower Shoppe, and stops short at the first traffic light. Whistle whistle whistle. Not a thought in her empty head. "Real live nephew of my Uncle Sam. Da da dum. Born on the fourth of July. Da da da..."

Ten minutes later, when she makes a left onto Destiny drive, she has run out of lyrics and says, casually at first, "Okay, then, Lord, exactly what was that all about? Can you give me a hint?"

Then, as she pulls into her driveway and stops the car, she punches the dashboard hard with each word. "What. Are. You. Doing. To. Me. Down. Here. Lord!" She opens her mouth wide and screams, "That is, besides prodding me awake at night; confusing me with cryptic little teachings; preaching my name from a pulpit; and landing me in the hospital with a pretend 'coma'?" Her voice gets shriller and her breath fogs up the windows. "And let's not forget the little incident with the CORN!! Is this my reward for praying unceasingly? Am I going to lose my best friend next? Is that the finale to this little soap opera? Or do you have even more nefarious deeds planned!"

As she shuts the motor off, she shrinks in her seat and cries, tears streaming down her face, absolutely ruining her ultrasuede vest. It is all just too much. She might as well walk the plank blindfold toward fifty killer whales with unhinged jaws. Vera is not in the mood for any of this. She starts her engine back up.

She is in the mood to tell off Mia.

Chapter Eight

Vera is feeling better, because all the way down Route 4 and over the George Washington Bridge, the Lord and all of his messengers are giving her the silent treatment. No chatter. Total shut down. Vera thinks her screaming fit has shut them up, at least for now, and this makes her happy. Overjoyed, in fact. Finally, she has figured out how to exert some control over this black hole of another world that is sucking her in like space junk. Well, they can just find themselves another martyr, she thinks, because Vera Wright has been burning at the stake long enough.

She inhales deeply, down to the belly, feeling a brief sense of composure and stability. When she yells at them, they leave her alone, just like Monk does. And hopefully, Louise. And maybe even Mia, if Vera is lucky. Let them all put on long faces and pout in the corner. Just as long as they leave her alone, she does not care about the repercussions. She will darn well keep screaming, too. It is her version of the thumb in the bursting dyke, and she will not take it out until she is good and ready. Possibly never.

And then, out of nowhere, "Take a right," says the Lord. "Take a left."

Before Vera knows what's happening, she has taken a right and a left, and is somewhere she has never been before.

"Under the overpass," says the Lord. "Right at the light."

Vera's wheels are screeching.

"Past Voo Doo Liquor, into the alley," he says.

Now Vera is surrounded by broken down buildings with shattered windows that look a lot like pictures she's seen of London during World War II. She cannot even guess where she is. Baghdad. Or Kabul.

"Take another left," says the Lord. "Now left again at the fifth light. Stay with it, Vera. Don't lose me. Stay alert."

Vera stays with it like Velcro. The voice is riveting. It's above her, below her, and reverberates in her own head louder than the penetrating bass of the radio rap in the cars around her. All she can think is, "Third light. Fourth light. Fifth light. Turn." She turns, and in obedience to the voice, screeches to a stop halfway down the block at the curb of the most horrendous gutter of a slum she has ever seen, where a woman in a black cape is staggering up the street toward her, and falls on her face just as Vera realizes who she is.

"Mia!" screams Vera, and jumps out of the car, leaving the door open behind her. "Mia!" she screams again, racing toward her daughter. Doors slam all around her, sirens wail, and the boom boom boom of the rap music underscores each of Vera's steps as her feet land hard on the pavement. She reaches the woman and turns her over. It's Mia all right. Her skin is pasty white and her eyes are glazed. She shows no sign of recognizing Vera, but is muttering something incomprehensible.

Vera tries to help her stand, but Mia pushes her away, producing a shrill frightening caw of a laugh that sends chills down Vera's spine.

"You...you're so..." Mia stutters, pointing to the air as she struggles up, and then falls again. "You're so...so out of it. So... ignorant."

Vera whips her head around toward the car, thinking: Cell Phone. Purse. Monk. But by the time she climbs up and gets her footing, she can only watch helplessly as her car is screeched into reverse by a bearded, stringy haired, pock-marked hooligan, who handily disappears around the corner in her car.

"Oh my God!" she mutters, shaking with anger, not to mention fear. She glimpses the barred windows of the washed-out buildings around her, the vacant faces of the passersby as she screams, "Help! Help!"

By now, Mia has gotten to her feet and brushed off the sidewalk scum from her black woolen pants. She straightens herself up, clears her throat, and throws her shoulders back, as if to start this tape rolling again in a more dignified manner.

"Help!" screams Vera. "Somebody help!" She is screaming reflexively, because she thinks there is probably no help to be found anywhere near here, and in fact, probably nothing but a great deal more trouble to attract on this street.

Mia staggers up behind her and says throatily, "I can get you home."

And warily, Vera picks up the unsteady rhythm of Mia's footsteps—forward three steps, back one. She takes Mia's elbow, but Mia lists hard to the right, thrusting Vera toward the curb, where she trips, nearly falling on the sewer grate. At the corner, Mia sticks two fingers in the corners of her lips and whistles for a cab, which flies two lanes over and screeches to a stop in front of them. Vera helps Mia into the cab, and just as Vera tries to get in herself, Mia slams the door and the cab takes off.

Vera stands right there on ... she looks up at the sign... Webster Avenue with her hands over her mouth and gasps. And gasps again. In her entire life, this is the only true terror she's felt since the day of her parents' death. Where oh where is the Holy Spirit now, she thinks. Then in sheer despair, she falls to her badly bruised knees and says, "Holy Spirit, where are you now?" And she is tapped on the shoulder by a uniformed cop, six feet tall and brawnier than Monk by a long shot.

"You need help, Ma'am?" says the cop in a bass so deep it scrapes the bottom of his throat.

Vera is suddenly uplifted because he looks to her like that actor from *The Green Mile* –the one with all the healing gifts. Heal me, she thinks. Heal my whole life. Her tears speak volumes for her apparently, because the cop picks her off her knees and carries her to the patrol car, where she lands like a heap of trash in the back seat, wailing and crying, and thoroughly unable to identify herself or say anything at all, besides, "God help me. Oh God, please, help me. Help my daughter." The streets of New York pass like a blur.

At the station, she manages to pull herself together long enough to call Monk and file a report, but none of this erases the brutal image of Mia from her mind. She is still shaken to the core by the unthinkable, unspeakable behavior of her own daughter. The same one she'd once cuddled and hugged and dressed in more than one starched linen sailor dress and wide-brimmed straw hat with daisies on the brim. Where is that little girl now, Vera thinks and thinks, until her brain is black and blue from thinking it, and by the time Monk arrives in a giant huff, she is doubting that it was Mia at all she had encountered on the street, but some look-alike vamp of a Harlem opium addict who didn't know Vera from Eleanor Roosevelt.

Dressed in his royal blue sweat pants and Canaan High coach jacket, Monk slides down the bench into Vera like he is stealing first base. He hugs her tenderly, then eases back and raises her chin with his index finger until she is looking straight at him. "Vera?" he says. "Baby? What the hell are you doing in the South Bronx for crying out loud? You're doing it to me again, aren't you? You're trying to scare me again."

"No," she whimpers. "I made a mistake, that's all. I made a mistake and they stole my car. And my purse." She blots her tears with her shirtsleeve. "And my cell phone."

Monk holds her at arm-length. "Who hurt you? Who stole your car?" He draws her closer. "Whoever it is, I'm gonna kill him."

An officer approaches Monk and says, "You the husband?"

Monk clears his throat. "Yes sir, that's me."

"Your wife here tells us she was driving to see your daughter and tried to help a young woman on the streets who was staggering around intoxicated."

Monk stares at Vera. "Mia?"

Vera looks down at the clasped hands in her lap and shakes her head no.

Monk turns to the officer. "Any reason to have her evaluated in a hospital?"

"No!" screams Vera. "I won't go!"

Monk squeezes her hand. "I won't make you go. I promise."

"That's up to you," says the officer, then holds out a clipboard and asks Monk to double check the stolen vehicle report. "We've got patrol cars looking for these guys," he says. "But they're fast. Your wife here was so upset it was difficult to get the information from her as quickly as we would have liked." In a minute he takes the board back from Monk. "But we'll call you when we know more."

Monk nods. "Come on, Vera," he says. "Let's get you home."

Outside the police department, he helps her into his truck, which smells like a stagnant pond. He reaches over her lap and belts her in. As he jumps in the other side, he says, "It was Mia, wasn't it?"

Vera's chin trembles. "It looked like her," she says. "But I couldn't say for sure."

She can see that he is steaming, shaking even, but trying very hard to control himself for her sake. He runs his tongue over his teeth, pondering his next step. She waits. The lump in her throat feels as hard as an unshelled walnut.

Monk starts the engine, but before he accelerates, says, "Why here, Vera? What do you know about Mia's behavior that I don't know? She lives on Central Park. Why did you drive to the Bronx to find her?"

Vera shrugs. "Intuition," she says in a whimper. "A voice in my head. 'Turn right. Turn left,' it said. And before I knew what was happening, there she was."

Monk taps his fingers on the steering wheel. "I tell you what we're going to do," he says. "We're going to pay Mia a little visit right now."

"No!"

He pulls out of the parking space and says nothing until, almost twenty minutes later they are standing in the lobby of Mia's building facing Mr. Joseph, the doorman.

"And who are you here to visit?" asks Mr. Joseph.

"Mia Tophet," says Monk steadily. "We're her parents."

The doorman's expression gives nothing away. He calls Mia's suite. "Hello, Mrs. Tophet," he says. "Your parents are here to see you." He listens attentively. "So not right now?"

Monk yanks the phone from his hands. "Listen here, young lady, exactly who do you think you are?" He taps his fingers, listening. "We'll be right up." He hands the phone back to Mr. Joseph, who listens for a second, then hangs up and says, "She's in 2022. Sign here."

After he signs in, Monk takes Vera by the hand to the elevator. Once inside, he snaps his fingers and rubs his palms against the sides of his pants. "Can you believe she was gonna blow us off?" He snorts like a bull and wiggles his head around on his neck like a bobble doll. "She has brought me to the limit, that girl."

Vera says, "We've never done this before, Monk. Never just stopped in to see her like this. Not since she's lived here."

"Not since she started treating us like the Beverly hillbillies," he adds.

As the elevator light identifies floor number 15, 16, 17, Vera says, "I'm afraid."

"Don't be. I'll take care of it." He punches his right fist into the palm of his left hand.

"How will you take care of it?" she asks.

"Don't know."

Vera's teeth chatter, and she prays to herself, *Glory be to the Father, the Son, and the Holy Spirit...*

The elevator halts and the doors open. They step into the smartly decorated black and white harlequin vestibule, and Monk rings the bell. He fidgets, shifting his weight from one leg to the other, back and forth, and then draws Vera closer to him. Five minutes later they are still waiting, and Monk rings the bell again and pounds on the door. "Mia, open the door!" he says.

The tap tap tap of Mia's heels can be heard approaching the door. The unchaining of the latch. The turning of the knob. And there, on the other side of the door is Mia, her blue-black hair turned up into an elegant chignon minus one long straight piece dangling stylishly in front of her right ear. Her hazel eyes are bright and clear, her full lips painted in poppy red. She is sheathed in a long-sleeved, body-hugging zebra-print jumpsuit wrapped at the waist with a large black patent-leather belt and diamond-studded buckle. Though she is not a tall woman, she is well-proportioned, and all in all gives the appearance of high pedigree right down to her expression which reads: bored-stiff-and-dying-fast-of-affluenza. She does not look the least bit as if she escaped a near-death experience in the South Bronx three hours ago. Beside her, Vera feels like a chipped-off chunk of lifesaver candy at the bottom of her purse.

"So what brings you two here?" says Mia evenly.

"We'd like to come in and chat for a while," says Monk.

She waves her hand inward.

Vera is shocked to see her daughter looking so Mia-like. This is unnerving. Was it Mia she'd seen on the streets or not? Lord, she prays, are you going to help me here? At least help me stop trembling.

"Hello, Mia," Vera manages, studying her daughter's eyes for guilt.

She nods. "Hello, Mother." Then she sniggers, "Nice hair."

Vera wonders what happened to just plain "Mom," but figures that word is forever buried beneath the lavish pink Venetian marble floors and antique horsehair fainting couches. "Well," says Vera, "yes, I got a new haircut. It's easier to take care of." Every word she utters feels foolish and inadequate.

Monk and Vera settle awkwardly into the embroidered loveseat.

"Isn't that a little ridiculous?" asks Mia.

Monk cocks his head quizzically. "What's that?"

"The loveseat," she says. "There are three oversized couches in this room." She shrugs. "Whatever."

"How are you feeling, Mia?" asks Monk pointedly.

"What's that supposed to mean?"

Vera shakes her head. "See what I mean, Monk? See how she is? She's defensive about everything."

Monk clenches Vera's hand while continuing to look directly at Mia. "It's supposed to mean—how are you?" he says. "It's a tradition in the human family to ask people how they are when you haven't seen them in a very long time."

Mia throws her hands up. "I'm fine. Great, thank you." She widens her eyes. "And how are you, Dad?"

"Not so good, Mia, to tell you the truth. You see, earlier this morning your mother here took a little trip into the city to pay you a visit." He crosses his legs. "Just a nice motherly visit to see how you were doing, since we never hear from you voluntarily. And while she was driving in, well..." He re-crosses his legs. "You see..."

Vera can tell he has no idea where to go with this. *Your mother happened to be driving through the South Bronx?* That would simply not do. She butts in. "I got lost," she says.

Monk nods appreciatively. "She got lost somewhere north of Manhattan. And while she was driving around trying to find her way, lo and behold..."

He clenches Vera's hand so hard he impales her with her own engagement ring.

"Lo and behold, who does she see on the street, but..." He looks directly at Mia. "Can you guess?"

Mia plops down on the red velvet chaise. "Oprah Winfrey?"

"Come on," says Monk. "Where were you at 10:00 this morning?"

Mia reaches over to a marble-top table, snaps open a silver container and pulls out a cigarette. "Excuse me?" she says. "You have to know my whereabouts at all times suddenly? As if I'm not over thirty and married?" She lights the cigarette with a gold-plated lighter and inhales deeply with her eyes closed, as if she has never enjoyed anything more. On exhale, she smiles coolly. "Where do you think I was anyway? Do you think I was walking around..." she waves her hand. "Or perhaps you think I had my chauffeur drive me... Uh! And to do what exactly? As if I would be caught dead north of Manhattan. As if my life extends beyond one square mile." She shrugs. "It doesn't. With the obvious exception of South Hampton." She taps her cigarette in the ash tray. "And Boca."

Vera reaches back and rubs the nape of her neck. It does seem unlikely that Mia would have been desperate enough to wander into the slums. After all, what in the world could she get down there that she couldn't get delivered right to her door on a platinum tray? So then who directed Vera to that neighborhood? Was it the Lord or wasn't it? And why did that woman look so much like Mia? It was all so confusing. Vera is irreparably tired.

"Then where were you?" says Monk, waving away the smoke.

Mia surveys the room. "I was at Tiffany's." She raises her index finger to interrupt the conversation then presses a button on the table. Within ten seconds, a maid appears. Mia points to the cigarette, and the maid leaves and returns with an ashtray and a can of air deodorizer, which she places on the table next to Mia.

"Thanks, Lola," says Mia in a surprisingly kind voice. Vera is happy to know her daughter is still capable of courtesy. Mia inhales, and when the maid is gone, she exhales through her nose. "Frederick doesn't like the smell," she says.

Monk says, "I don't particularly..."

Vera elbows him, and he clears his throat, then says, "So... Tiffany's."

"Honestly," says Mia. "Is that a crime? Tiffany's?"

"Of course not."

"So why the third degree?" She cocks her head.

"Because," says Monk, "what happened to your mother this morning was a crime. She stopped her car to assist a young woman who looked exactly like you."

"Well, not exactly," mutters Vera.

Monk rolls his eyes at this breach. "Did she or didn't she?" he says.

"Well, she did, but not the way Mia looks now. This woman was disheveled and... glassy-eyed." She stares at the floor. She can't look at either of them.

Mia swings her legs down from the chaise and leans forward. In an earnest voice, she says, "What happened, Mother? Did something happen? You don't look like anything happened. I mean, you're...somewhat put together."

As they try to process Mia's sudden new interest, Monk says, "They traumatized the hell out of your mother for one thing. And stole her car. Her purse is gone, along with all her money and credit cards."

"And my cell phone," adds Vera.

Mia narrows her eyes. "Did you get a good look at the thief?"

"Not really. But sort of. I don't know. The car was down the block."

"So," says Mia, "you went for a little stroll in that neighborhood? Looking for...?"

Vera musters the courage to lock eyes with her daughter. "I got lost," she says, then turns to Monk. "We're not getting anywhere here. Let's go."

Mia squashes the cigarette butt thoughtfully, and rises slowly to her feet. "Look, I'm sorry you're so traumatized, really. But...driving through the South Bronx? What did you expect?"

Vera and Monk stare at her, and Mia juts out her chin defensively. "Don't look at me," she says. "I'm hardly a suspect."

"If you say so," says Monk.

Mia shrugs. "A hundred women look like me," she says. "A thousand."

"Nobody looks like you," says Vera.

After a minute, Mia sighs. "Listen," she says, "I realize I haven't been seeing much of you two, and... I don't know. It's tough to do that when you live in the city."

"Your chauffeur can't find New Jersey?" says Monk.

Mia sucks in her cheeks. "I tell you what. How about... why don't you..." She scratches her head. "I was just thinking that maybe..." She huffs for a second then says, "Maybe it would be okay if you came here for Thanksgiving dinner."

Vera gasps, throwing her hand to her chest. Tears spill down her cheeks. "That's exactly what I've been praying for," she exclaims, then instantly realizes her mistake.

"Oh, for God's sake, Mother, as if someone actually listens to your prayers. As if prayers go somewhere."

Monk steps toward Mia threateningly, his eyes narrowed. "How dare you speak to your mother that way."

"No don't," says Vera, and pulls him back. "Let's just accept this as a new beginning."

Mia's eyes dart right and left. "I don't know about a new beginning, Mother. It sounds like such a...I don't know... such a commitment. But if you don't mind dining on quail and truffles..."

Vera raises her eyebrows with delight and says, "Well, I just love chocolate! You know that. There's nothing I'd rather eat!"

"Not chocolate, Mother. Mushrooms. Hideously expensive black diamond mushrooms that can only be found by special pigs in the wilderness of Provence."

Vera blushes. "Well, Mia, you don't have to go to that kind of trouble for us."

"It's not for you," says Mia. "Believe me. I realize your tastes are more... It's the menu Frederick and I enjoy on Thanksgiving. His family never eats turkey. Turkey is so..." she shakes her head. "The bird itself is so...I don't know. Tasteless." She holds her hand in front of her and absently inspects the five-carat Harry Winston diamond ring that Frederick gave her in exchange for her soul. She looks up suddenly, mutters, "Excuse me," and, without explanation, taps her skinny high heels on the marble floor toward the winding staircase and upward bound.

While she's gone, Monk blinks at Vera. "Quail?" he whispers, "with chocolate mushrooms sniffed by pigs?" He shakes his head. "She's bonkers. I don't want to be a guest in this asylum. Can't they come to our house? Or maybe just drive through KFC in separate cars?"

"No," says Vera. "For some reason she can't bring herself to visit Canaan. So we'll just accept the invitation on her terms and that's that."

A second later Monk whispers, "So was it Mia or wasn't it?"

"Don't know for sure," says Vera. "But whoever it was led us back to our daughter."

At that moment Mia appears on the upper landing clicking precariously on her high heels down the stairs to the landing, where she skids. "Oops," she says, grinning broadly, which is such a rare sight that it creates a ripple effect of grins on Vera and, for a second, even Monk.

Vera's heart leaps as she realizes that they haven't all grinned like this in a very long time. She is beside herself with gratitude to the Lord for all he has made manifest in her intensely exhausting day. If this is the cost of reunion, let it be! Her heart swells with joy.

November 23— *Praise the Lord! Praise the Lord! Praise him and praise him again! My cup runneth over. Why, it's as if my cup is sitting under a running faucet of his good will and generosity. I can't drink it up fast enough—it spills out of my mouth and onto the floor and all around me. It has occurred to me to get a bigger cup, but then I thought, why a cup at all? Why not a trough? Or a canyon? The Lord's love knows no bounds. It is we who bind Him.*

Here's how I know: yesterday he showed me the way back to my long lost daughter, Mia. It was no ordinary reunion, no loving hugs or weeping faces. Well, except for mine of course. My mascara and eyeliner were halfway down my face by the time I got home. But not Mia's. Mia's makeup was airbrushed-perfect start to finish, as usual, though in retrospect I was not crazy about the color of her eye shadow—a kind of cantaloupe orange, or more exactly, tangerine. And my husband, Monk, never weeps about Mia anymore. He says his tears for Mia dried up a year or so ago. "The tear bank is closed on Mia's account," he said. Now he just tries to protect me from her abuse.

So it was nothing like the reunion I'd dreamed of for years, day after day, night after night. In fact, the whole experience was downright...grim. Yes, grim is the right word. Not the actual reunion itself, which was not grim, but the manner in which the Lord chose to reunite us was dark and confusing. Like Father Max is always preaching: the Lord works in mysterious ways. I guess I had just never been desperate enough to let him show me his way before now.

I don't like to think how long Mia has been estranged from us exactly, but it can be traced in one straight line to her engagement to Frederick Spencer Tophet, IV and his arrogant family. That engagement occurred approximately three years, two months, three weeks, one day and ten minutes ago, if memory serves me. The Tophets are listed in the top ten families on the Manhattan Social Register; at least that's what they told Monk and me. We've never actually seen the book. We were also told that this distinction came about as a result of the great grandfather's maritime connections during World War I. The other factor in their social position is that the mother's family is supposedly related to Shakespeare. Her maiden name is Prigg. Mia would never have survived Canaan High with that name, I can tell you that.

This is all fine and good, though as much as I love English grammar, I have never really had a good grasp of Shakespeare, other than 'Romeo and Juliet,' the movie. Not enough schooling for that kind of language, I'm afraid. Give me a good mystery any day, and also I enjoy a nice romance now and then, not the bodice-rippers, but a good story with some juicy new words like 'acerbic' or 'insidious.' Not that those words are totally new to me, but just that I don't get many opportunities to use them based on my current relationships. Welcome to my life. So I enjoy reading about characters who can use those words without being mocked.

Anyway, after we found out that Mia was marrying Frederick, I signed right up for a course on Shakespeare at the community college. Monk will tell you, I'll do anything to improve myself— whatever the situation requires. But when I mentioned the course in front of the Tophets, well, you'd think I'd jumped right up on the table in fishnet stockings and stiletto heels and swung my bra around in circles over my head. Why, this little faux pas turned out to be a trespass so monumental as to practically get us uninvited to the wedding by our own daughter. And of course Frederick, being ten years older than Mia and wealthier than Midas, paid for the whole thing, including a honeymoon in Tahiti with grass-skirted servants at their every beck and call. Not that we ever saw any pictures.

That left Monk and me without much to offer other than a rehearsal party in our own backyard, which of course would never have worked, being such a modest-sized lot compared to our neighbors', and also, loaded with gopher holes. Even I knew enough not to suggest that. So it's not that I have anything against the Tophets; they have more to offer a beautiful and ambitious young lady than we do. More money and more culture. More influence. But other than Mia's Audrey Hepburn-esque beauty, we could never figure out what Mia possibly had to offer Frederick. Certainly not a name. Not a rung-up on the social ladder. No money, not one red cent. And Frederick is as stiff as a post no matter how funny things are. Mia could dress-up like Mister Jingles and twist balloon monkeys every morning in a fright wig and it still wouldn't make Frederick laugh. The man is so obsessively fastidious he was probably getting haircuts every three weeks in vitro.

I suspect Mia also wonders what it is she has to offer him or his family, because if she knew, she might have the confidence to be a little more generous with her own parents. God knows we don't want her money, just a little time and attention. Monk and I are just waiting and willing to fit into Mia's life anywhere she can find room. But it turns out their 6,000 square foot co-op doesn't come with an attic, which is just where you would throw a trunk of old memories and the spidery old parents who remind you of your humble past.

This is not a complaint, mind you, but an explanation of the depths from which the Lord has seen fit to return our daughter to us. Praise be to him, who will surely be present at the Thanksgiving banquet! Of course, the Lord's ways are mysterious, as I said. And even this morning I am struggling to remember exactly what happened yesterday, but believe me, it was a wild day in the Kingdom! I followed the Lord all around the mulberry bush, this way and that, over bridges and pot holes and frost heaves into the slums of the South Bronx. There, I followed his every command until finally someone unknown to me, and yet known to me in some strange and inexplicable way, appeared out of literally nowhere. Someone who looked like...well, at the time anyway, like...not Mia exactly, but Mia if she'd just spent the last thirty days in a state asylum hunting down her right mind. And then, of course, my car got stolen, along with my purse, credit cards, and cell phone, everything that connected me to the rational world. And I ended up at the station howling with grief while Officer Green Mile (you wouldn't *believe the resemblance) tried to get me to identify the perpetrator by flipping through a Sears' catalogue of drug dealers and thugs.*

Well, just as an update—they haven't found my car yet. But I'm not holding my breath, either. How could they possibly find it? I drove it straight into another dimension. It's gone! After all, what had I been doing there in the first place? Why did I jump out of a running car into a slum like that? Was I crazy? Was that really Mia? Or more likely...(what I have come to believe)...was that incident nothing more or less than a more extreme version of the Stop & Shop hallucination of Monk on the treadmill? Another little wake-up call from the Lord. "Hello, Vera? This is the Lord. Get Monk a check-up now. His heart needs healing." Followed soon thereafter by another message, "Vera, this is the Lord. Your daughter needs you. Find her before she falls apart."

I remain His servant, Vera Wright. Amen.

(Flipping through the dictionary, I like the word 'macabre' over 'grim' in the third paragraph.)

At Sunday Mass, with Monk beside her, Vera looks around discreetly for Louise, but can't spot her anywhere. She must have gone to another Mass, Vera thinks, relieved. She tries to review the whole incident with Louise in the parking lot on Friday, but gets nowhere. She can't remember what precipitated what, only that Louise claimed to have hurt her hand, oh yes, and then cried like an infant until the Martha's cuddled her. Louise certainly knows how to throw a tantrum when she wants to, Vera thinks, and this makes her rethink all the Stanley stories Louise has been selling Vera for the last ten years. "Stanley this... and Stanley that...." Notice there was never any Louise this... or Louise that... Everything was Stanley's fault. And here's poor Stanley stuck in a wheel chair with Louise running around on two healthy legs minus the unsightly varicose veins that circle her ankles like a swarm of tangled worms. Poor Louise, my butt, thinks Vera now. Poor Stanley is more like it.

"A reading from the holy Gospel according to Matthew," says Father Max.

"Glory be to you, oh Lord," repeat Vera and Monk along with everyone else.

Father Max clears his throat then peers meaningfully at his flock. "Peter came to Jesus and asked, 'Lord, if my brother keeps on sinning against me, how many times do I have to forgive him? Seven times?'

"'No, not seven times,' answered Jesus, 'but seventy times seven, because the Kingdom of heaven is like this...'"

Vera tunes out Father Max's reading for a moment, thinking it's too bad Louise isn't at this Mass, after all. Louise certainly could have learned a thing or two from the Lord's little parable on forgiveness. Not that Vera sinned against Louise, of course. Not that there was anything to forgive Vera for, God knows. Or 'for which to forgive Vera,' she corrects herself. But since Louise no doubt believes that Vera wronged her, it would be just like Louise to give Vera the silent treatment instead of forgiving her once, never mind seventy times seven times. As if Vera should have stayed in that parking lot and done what? Held Louise's hand instead of driven into Manhattan to reconcile with Mia? Ha! Treated Louise as if she'd lost the use of her entire hand? As if it had been amputated, for God's sake? Ripped off in a corn picker, for crying out loud? Shredded in a wood chipper?

Vera tunes back in to Father Max as he reads, "'And the Lord concludes, 'That is how my Father in heaven will treat every one of you unless you forgive your brother from your heart.'"

He closes the book solemnly and proceeds to go into some kind of rant that Vera doesn't really hear, because she can't get over Louise's inability to forgive. At the same time she can't get over Louise, she is ecstatic that at least she and Monk know how to forgive Mia, and for that humility the Lord has seen fit to return their daughter to them. And isn't that wonderful, she thinks happily. Isn't that just like the Lord himself in all his glory, to unload his sweet abundance on those who accept his generosity? She sighs with deep satisfaction. Living in the light of the Lord is a gift beyond the comprehension of the mortal mind, she thinks. If only she could impart that knowledge to Louise. To Mia! To everyone! But she supposes it has to come from the Lord when he is good and ready to make himself at home in the heart of his chosen ones. She can hardly be expected to shake people silly until they accept the love of God, now can she?

The next morning Vera awakens to the first powdering of snow laid out on the front terrace like a bolt of Irish lace. She claps her hands. Oh, how she's always loved November snow! But this year it's even more special. This year, the snow is a sign of gentle cleansing, not only of the atmosphere, but also of Vera's entire life. Her life has been cleansed, refreshed, and made whole again, just like her soul. "God is kind and merciful," she sings. She pages through her prayer book, reciting this prayer and that, before starting in on her first rosary of the morning as she dresses for 8:30 Mass. *I believe in God, the Father Almighty, Maker of Heaven and Earth...* Since she has a salon client directly after church, she dresses in a simple ensemble of heather twill pants and a matching turtleneck sweater. Something easy to work in, wintry and cozy. Why, the snow is making her crazy for a large mug of hot cocoa made with real milk, not water, and topped with a dollop of whipped cream. And let's not forget her famous peanut butter oatmeal chocolate chip cookies for dunking!

And this makes Vera think about how Mia used to love to dunk! Oh, and remember the time she dunked her brand new Barbie upside down into the mug, soaking the long blonde braids in the cocoa? Vera shakes her head plaintively. At the time she had wanted to spank Mia, but now? Well, now, Vera would trade all her earthly possessions just to watch 5-year-old Mia dunk that Barbie into a mug of hot cocoa one more time — her intense hazel eyes studying the effects of cocoa on doll hair. Her beautiful young face a map of human potential. Vera has a mind to stop at the toy store to buy a Barbie and mail it to Mia with an envelope of cocoa. But she won't. She knows Mia would never remember.

Give us this day, our daily bread, and forgive us our trespasses as we forgive those who trespass against us. And lead us not into temptation...

Hot chocolate and cookies is such a capital idea, that Vera intends to get a good batch going as soon as she returns from Mass. Like cartoon characters, her clients will be drawn helplessly into the salon on a tempting ribbon of aromatic steam. She wants to please everybody today. She is a pleaser. She will please the world. The Lord has filled her with the desire to please.

And she is reminded that this will be the first morning Mass with Louise since the incident three days ago. Even so, Vera is feeling generous and big-hearted and ready to forgive Louise all her trespasses, every one of them. After all, Louise has not been visited upon by the Lord. Vera has. So it's up to Vera to share her blessings with her friends. She only hopes Louise is ready to accept forgiveness, for Vera has learned from the Lord that self-forgiveness is the most difficult of all. We despise in others what we despise in ourselves. Vera will do her best to help Louise forgive herself.

She begins a *Hail Mary*.

And let's not forget Louise's beauty appointment later this morning at the salon. Louise will be her second client of the day.

Perhaps they will have hot cocoa together afterwards, or even lunch if Louise has the time. At some point Vera plans to share her good fortune about the reconciliation with Mia and the unexpected bonus of Thanksgiving in Manhattan. Louise will be thrilled for Vera. Won't she? For a second Vera is pricked with doubt. But then she thinks, well, of course Louise will be happy for her. Vera has bothered Louise with little else than her troubles with Mia for the last ten years, even before she became an almighty Tophet. Louise will be jubilant for Vera!

Vera freshens her new mulberry lipstick with some vogue new extra-shiny, long-wear lip gloss. She primps her hair, admiring the tasteful way it's growing out in little waves that are softer than the original spikes. Vera still cannot fathom what got into her the day she chopped her hair to bits. But she feels so good now as to literally erase all the scars of the last few weeks. Weeks she'd been renewing her true faith and learning to live in the light. Why, it was not the light at all, but her own darkness that had created the tension. It was as if she'd been living in a root cellar for decades and someone had finally opened the door. Opened the door and shined a bright light into her wide-open lenses. She flinches to think of it. But so far she has endured, and the light has burned through the darkness, and now Vera can see everything as it truly is. Sparkling clean, clear, and obvious as all get-out. Why, now she could practically spot a venial sin fifty stories up in the middle of Vegas.

She arrives at Mass, anxious to slip into the usual pew with Louise and eradicate any discomfort by instantly hugging her friend. Now, that's forgiveness for you, new and improved Vera-style. Not to allow even a moment of discomfort to intrude upon their relationship. Vera arrives first, however, and waits impatiently, nodding to her acquaintances as they assume their usual places. She removes her gloves and loosens the belt of her camel coat—bargain of the season at T.J. Maxx!—all the while reciting to herself, *Hail Mary Full of Grace...*

She attempts to squeeze the rest of the Sorrowful Mysteries of the rosary into the five minute space before Mass begins—an unprecedented accomplishment ever since Vera started to pray unceasingly. But one never knew—perhaps Father Max would oversleep this morning, and she would be able not only to finish those, but also get a head start on the Glorious Mysteries. Not to mention the more recently introduced Mysteries of Light. Miracles do happen!

Even now, weeks later, Vera cannot believe how much she is praying. She has learned to think and pray; to balance her checkbook and pray; to follow difficult recipes and pray. And not only that, but her prayer life is clearly paying off. In Vera's life now, prayers are worth a great deal more than money.

Father Max, resplendent in the deep purple vestments of Advent, glides onto the altar followed by a trail of Eucharistic ministers and altar servers. He bows reverently before the crucifix, then extends his arms to the congregation and says, "Grace, mercy, and peace be with you from God the Father and Christ Jesus, our Savior."

"And also with you," says Vera along with everyone else. She peers behind her, expecting to see Louise hustling up the aisle left, right, or center, but there is no Louise in any direction. Well, perhaps she has car troubles, Vera thinks, or more likely, Stanley troubles. Vera is barely listening to Father Max as he greets them joyfully, and reads to them about Abraham and Sarah and the promise of a son in spite of Sarah's old age. Instead Vera is climbing out of her skin, twitching this way and that in search of Louise, concocting all kinds of stories about Stanley's health, or whatever else might be keeping Louise from Mass, including, oh, God, help her, Stanley's passing. Vera flips the cell phone out of her coat pocket to view the recent calls and message menu. Perhaps Louise had already left her a message about Stanley's death.

Father Max winds his way through the reading about Elizabeth's pregnancy with John the Baptist, and about how Elizabeth's husband, Zachariah, was punished for his disbelief. As usual, Vera is having a hard time listening. After all, where the hell is Louise? Something dreadful must have happened to Stanley, and if not to him then possibly to, well...that was just impossible. But could it be that something...? No. If there was one thing Vera remembered clearly about last Friday, it was that Louise's hand had barely touched the car door, and the door itself had not even closed, not even a tiny bit. And this gets her thinking about Louise's reaction, which ignites the fires in Vera's belly until once again, she is stoking a bonfire of red hot anger, if not white hot rage when all at once she happens to crane her neck long enough to lock eyes with who else but Louise across the aisle. Louise is nestled smugly in the center of the Martha's, her white-plastered-hand in a sling as she offers a limp Sign of Peace to a beaming Margaret Vitella.

Next to Vera, George Tanty offers his hand, "Peace of Christ," he says.

"Uh!" blurts Vera. She does not even look at George, but instead sends the evilest evil-eye she can muster on such short notice across the room to Louise with air mail postage and extra insurance to ensure its safe arrival. How dare she! Her so-called best friend! She leans right over and collects her personal belongings. As if she's going to stay here one more minute and be the victim of Louise's abuse! She won't have any of it. No, she will not. She marches right out of St. Jude's in a blind fury, praying fervently, *Our Father who art in heaven, hallowed be thy name...*

Later, at the salon, she continues to pray—forces herself to pray the five Glorious Mysteries, as she mixes the color for Rhoda J. Preston's caramel blonde mane. She is happy to have Rhoda as her first customer, as Rhoda is quiet and will not mess up Vera's devout concentration. Praying unceasingly is no small task, God knows, and there are those who help and those who hinder. Rhoda is a helper, because she is an introverted retired laboratory technician, who still occasionally documents patient reactions for new life-saving pharmaceuticals in nearby Paramus. Rhoda's method of conversation is simple and direct, using a plethora of yes's and no's with no long drawn-out and unwelcome explanations to screw-up Vera's prayer count.

Vera applies the dye carefully to Rhoda's roots as her thoughts return to Louise. She can't help herself; she sifts through the exact sequence of events as they occurred in church this morning. When she gets to the part where she locks eyes with Louise, quite without intending to, she blurts as loud as you please, "What the hell do you think you're doing sitting over there with those old ladies? What in the Sam Hill is wrong with you," as if she is standing next to Louise in the church and not right beside Rhoda in the salon. At this Rhoda's head jerks, causing a confusing chain reaction that includes, among other things, a projectile of dye careening through the air like a Rorschach in motion and landing in what seems like a week later, right on top of Rhoda's head, not to mention all over her face.

"Oh, my goodness, my goodness. Help!" screams Rhoda. "Help, my eyes! I'm blind; I'm blind! Help! My eyes!"

Vera runs to the faucet with a towel and back again to pat the gel from Rhoda's face and eyelids, trying hard to keep calm, repeating, "It's okay, Rhoda; it's okay. I'm terribly sorry. It won't hurt you. Don't worry, Rhoda. Don't worry." At the same time Vera tries to pray without ceasing as she has been commanded, but oh my God, how many things have to go wrong before the Lord gets the picture. She can't pray unceasingly. It's impossible!

"It stings!" screeches Rhoda. "Help! Help! It stings!"

Even so, Vera somehow manages to keep calm as she blots the final drop of dye from Rhoda's eyes. But Rhoda is still screaming, so she wrenches Rhoda's head around and under the faucet hose and rinses her eyes with cold water, which...oops...turns out to be hot. At that Rhoda screeches like a jackal, and Vera merely turns the faucet handle to cold and continues to rinse and rinse. And finally, mercifully, Rhoda concedes that she is not blind. That she has the use of both eyes, though the left one has swelled to the size and color of a maraschino cherry. As she calms down, Rhoda primly smoothes the gathers of her plastic apron, her lips set firmly in a straight line. Her eyes blink madly as she adjusts her posture and expression to reflect her most professional demeanor.

From that moment forward, Rhoda does not utter another word, and this suits Vera nicely. She finishes up Rhoda's roots as if nothing at all had occurred, and as the dye sets, Vera excuses herself through the salon door to her house, runs upstairs to her bedroom and screams at the top of her lungs. "I can't do this anymore, Lord!!!!!" She looks madly about the room and picks up her favorite Lenox vase and hurls it at the window. This feels so invigorating that she lifts her beloved childhood figurine of Snow White and hurls that at the door, too, followed by Doc, Grumpy, Sleepy, Happy, Dopey, Bashful and Sneezy. She reaches for more glass and porcelain in a therapeutic frenzy and climaxes with the hand-blown cranberry glass bedside lamp.

After throwing the lamp, she splays herself out on the bed like a snow angel in full view of ...what the heck? Well, it appears to be nothing less than a full-winged messenger of the Lord miraculously suspended from the ceiling in an aura of brilliant blues. He is wearing alabaster robes and has a face so radiant that Vera cannot make out a single feature, not an eye or a nose or a mouth. Just rays of blinding blue and white light streaming out. Streaming and streaming.

"The world as you know it is nearly over," he says kindly. "Before these shocking changes, the Lord wishes you to plant your feet more squarely in the firmament of his light. Write," he says. "Write what you are moved to write, for the good of all. And pray. Pray unceasingly." At that, he dissolves into a piece of split plaster in the ceiling.

Vera rises obediently from the bed, down the stairs, and into the salon. She walks peacefully past a frantic Rhoda whose arms are flailing, who is screaming something or other about a timer having gone off fifteen minutes ago, blah blah blah. And Vera arrives at her desk, where she sits, opens the drawer, gathers her implements and begins to write and write and write whatever she is told to write. She is aware of a certain degree of chaos in the background, but she is easily able to block it out because she must. Because the angel is telling her news that, sooner or later, will matter a great deal more to Vera and to the world than the mere ruination of Rhoda J. Preston's hair.

When Vera snaps out of her writing trance, she is relieved to see that Rhoda has taken leave. As Vera recalls the incident, she is at first slightly disturbed. But in the end, she thinks, after all these years of dying the woman's hair, wouldn't you think she would know enough to rinse it when the timer buzzed? Is that so hard? After all, isn't she well into her fifth decade of life experience? Can't a person rinse her own hair by then, especially considering her beautician's obvious unavailability and communion with the Lord? Vera shakes her head as she cleans up the mess of dye and hair in the sink and on the floor. What did these people expect of her for heaven's sake?

Hours later, she returns to her bedroom with a vacuum cleaner, and though she knows she made a mess throwing a few items around, she is aghast when she steps into the room. Piles and piles of colorful broken glass and porcelain everywhere. She gets a large brown paper bag, and begins to pick up the pieces, none of it the least bit salvageable. As she is bent over the head of what she thinks is Doc because of a bit of black from the frame of his glasses, she hears a slight noise and turns to see Monk.

"Blaaaaaaaaaaaaaa!!!!!" he screams, which causes Vera to scream even louder, while Monk laughs so hard he has to hold his belly like a girdle so he doesn't herniate.

"Jesus, Mary and Joseph," she says breathlessly. "One of these days you're going to give me a heart attack that way, Monk." Scaring her, however, has always been one of his favorite past times, and she doubts he'll stop for any reason.

Monk steps into the room, still chuckling, and then it dawns on him that the room is filled with broken pieces of Vera's favorite figurines. "What happened?" he says.

Vera swallows. "I, uh..."

"Who did this?" He bends over and picks up Sleeping Beauty's shoe. "These are your keepsakes," he says. "Your childhood..."

"I got very angry," she says. "I got so angry."

Sidestepping the porcelain, he gets to her and leans down onto his knees. "What made you so angry?" he holds her face in his hands. "Was it Mia?"

Tears flow down Vera's cheeks as she realizes what she's done. "No, not Mia, I just..." There's no way she can tell him about the angel. "I had a bad day," she says. "Louise, and then...Rhoda, uh uh..."

Monk enfolds her and lets her cry. "Come on," he says after a minute, and leads her to the bed. He cleans up the pieces around her as she dissolves into a crying heap.

Chapter Nine

Vera has had it with Louise and her cheap tricks. Louise has not shown up for a single hair appointment, and also, she's still stuck like glue to the Martha's in church, not to mention the Rosary Society ladies. Well, so what? Let her. Louise has always had so much money she's probably never picked up so much as a Cheerio in her entire life. Let her scrape up the sticky juice and gum after the children's Masses. Let her clean up the rice from the weddings and pick the withered heather from the altar arrangements. Let her plunge the toilets and launder the linens. Ha! That's probably the only reason the Martha's are courting her to begin with. A new scrub woman.

Vera can hardly wait to see Louise unload the Hoover from her car trunk to vacuum the vestibule. Why, it's worth a special Saturday afternoon drive-by! She can hardly wait to see Louise, saddled with a tray of Amway cleansers, hustle her fanny into the church to clean and polish the windows and pews for Sunday Mass. Not to mention the Communion breakfasts of powdered eggs and stale bagels she'll be required to host at least twice a year in the church basement. This was the price of being protected by the Martha's. The perfect punishment for a big fat baby like Louise.

In fact, truth be told, Vera has not only had it with Louise and her new gang of sanctimonious church ladies, she has also had it with church. Who needs church every single day when she is already praying unceasingly and talking to the Lord and his holy angels in her own bedroom? She is exhausted by all these demands on her time and energy. Father Max should be bringing Communion to her. Of course, the Lord says to honor the Sabbath, and she has every intention of attending Mass on Sunday, but as for daily Mass? It has ceased to give her peace of mind. In fact, it gives her agita. She is a bundle of nerves every day wondering: Where is Louise?

Vera crosses Louise's name off her appointment book with such vengeance, she scratches a hole in the page. Well, too bad. Who cares about Louise's name on a page? Who cares about Louise? Vera can hardly wait to see what kind of ridiculous hairdo Louise comes up with when she's forced to find a new beautician. And, hmmm, whom would she pick? No doubt it would be Peg Davis at the "Hairport" around the corner. Stupid name—Hairport. It's not even near an airport, for God's sake. Oh yes, and "No appointments necessary." Well, of course not! Who in her right would make an appointment to get her hair hacked by Peg?

Vera forces a laugh that sounds hideous, even to her, and then right after that, blurts involuntarily, "God bless Louise," even before she knows what she's saying. "She is a child of God with full rights of inheritance to his heavenly kingdom, no different than mine."

Vera does not know exactly where these words came from, but she has no time to think about it, because at that exact moment, the doorbell rings. She is not expecting any clients until Melissa Wubbold at one o'clock for a perm and style. She parts the curtain slightly only to find herself peering right into the doe brown eyes of Father Max himself. He smiles sweetly.

After a moment of hesitation, she checks her carousel-coral lipstick in the mirror, and opens the door. "Good morning," she says suspiciously. Guiltily.

"Good morning, Vera!" he booms. "May I come in?"

She steps aside and waves him in. Did he come to get his hair cut, she wonders.

He removes his inappropriate puffy black ski jacket and places it on the coat rack along with his inappropriate black knit cap. His hair is sticking up from every angle in a haphazard nimbus of static electricity. He looks about nineteen years old. Don't they teach them how to dress like priests anymore, she wonders. At least he's wearing his Roman collar. But still. Other than that, he'd be at home in a pool hall.

"Well, I haven't seen you in a few days," he says pleasantly, as if he'd happened to find her salon by pure coincidence.

She peers down at her navy suede pumps. "No," she says. "I, um, well..."

"I thought you might not be feeling well," he says, "so I brought you Communion. Would you like to receive Communion, Vera?"

Her eyes widen with surprise. "Well, I guess so. Well sure, Father. That was very thoughtful of you." She cannot believe that she had just been thinking this very thought. That she should not have to go to daily Mass. That Father Max should be bringing Communion to her! How many buckets of kinetic ether does it take to produce a parish priest at your very own door with a Communion Host within minutes of thinking it? She must be pumping out ether like crazy. Next thing you know Louise will be appearing at her door completely bald and begging Vera to take her back. Vera thinks maybe she should start paying more attention to her thoughts. Lord, have mercy on the weak and powerless, she prays.

"Would you like some coffee?" Vera asks him.

"No thank you," he says. "Maybe after Communion, though." He sits on one of the waiting room chairs, and Vera settles in across from him.

"This is a very nice place you've got here, Vera," he says. "A nice little business."

"Why, thank you."

He clears his throat. "I'd like to do a reading first," he says and then flips open his book to the marker and reads the story of the infant Jesus presented at the temple and meeting up with an old man named Simeon. In the story, Simeon says more or less that the child had been chosen by God to do great things, and also that, because of the child's destiny, sorrow would pierce his mother's heart like a sword. Vera has heard that story many times, but the next part strikes her as being completely new.

"'There was a very old prophet,'" Father Max continues, "'a widow named Anna, daughter of Phanuel of the tribe of Asher. She was now eighty-four years old. She never left the Temple; day and night she worshiped God, fasting and praying. That very same hour she arrived and gave thanks to God and spoke about the child to all who were waiting for God to set Jerusalem free.'"

After Communion, Vera blesses herself and sits quietly for an appropriate amount of time, although she is so eager to ask Father Max a few questions that she is really not reflecting on the miracle of the Eucharist, praying for anyone in particular, or even thinking a single thought that is in the least bit spiritual. As soon as she thinks she can get away with it, she says, "I don't remember ever hearing about Anna before."

Father Max leans his torso forward and rests his hands on his knees. "No?"

"It's just that we don't hear very much about female prophets in this church." She glances out the window. "Not to knock the church, Father, but we don't hear much about women period."

He cocks his head. "Well, I'd have to disagree with you heartily on that one, Vera. After all, my own devotion is to the Blessed Mother. My priesthood is dedicated to her."

She nods uncertainly.

"And let's not forget the great saints; Teresa of Avila is a doctor of the church!"

"Well, what do you know," says Vera thoughtfully.

"So you see, the church honors all those who are members of its spiritual body, male and female. Each of us, male and female, is created to make manifest the love of our Creator in a particular way."

"You don't say?" She shimmies her skirt back and forth stretching it tight over her knees. "But why aren't there any female prophets?" she asks earnestly. "When I think of prophets, I think of Noah and Daniel and Moses and John the Baptist. I think of them. The women are just virgins or prostitutes. They're not prophets. Except this Anna." Vera can't believe she is saying this. "No offense," she adds.

Father Max gazes at her thoughtfully. "It's true that more men had major roles in the Bible."

"Almost all men."

"Yes, but not the real followers. The real followers of Christ stood under the cross. They were with him when the going got tough. Other than John, they were all women."

"Not that it got them anywhere," she says.

Father Max raises his index finger. "It got them to heaven," he says. "And that's all that really counts."

This never occurred to Vera before. "I suppose you're right," she says, then frowns, debating her next question. Oh what the hell. "Father Max, do you believe in prophets?"

"Well, of course. Don't you?"

"I mean, do you believe there are prophets amongst us now?" She smiles coyly, wondering even to herself how far she will go with this. Will she open the desk drawer behind him? Will she show him her pages and pages of...what? Prophecies...written in the all-mysterious stick and circle language? After all what were these pages of cryptic chicken scratch if not prophecies? Why would the Lord bother her nearly every night in the middle of the night just to draw sticks on memo pads and the back of receipts? Which reminds her, she needs to order more memo pads.

Father Max clicks his tongue, considering. "Haven't heard of any good prophets lately," he says. "Though there are a lot of apocalyptic doomsayers. But it's possible. All things are possible."

"But how would you know?" asks Vera. "I mean how would you know a modern day prophet if you heard one?" She cranes her neck forward conspiratorially. "Would the person wear robes and sandals? Eat locusts?"

Father Max chuckles. "If he came from California he might."

"*She* might," corrects Vera.

"Excuse me?"

She rocks her head back and forth playfully. "Well, it could be a she couldn't it?"

"I suppose."

"So how would we recognize her?"

Father Max opens his hands. "By her good deeds," he says. "The way we always recognize the Lord's own."

Vera nods thoughtfully as Father Max jumps to his feet. "You know what I've been wondering these last few days, Vera?"

She rises with him. "No, not really."

"I've been wondering why Louise Lambert hasn't been sitting with you."

She gasps. Why, this is none of his business.

"Not to pry," he says, "but I just wanted to make sure that I haven't lost one of my favorite weekday parishioners to a squabble."

Vera checks her watch. "I have a client arriving soon," she says.

"Oh dear, there I go opening my big mouth. I've offended you." He raises his eyes and looks directly at her. "Before you kick me out, may I just pass on a small bit of spiritual advice that my mentor once gave me?"

She inhales audibly. "Fine."

"Keep a Forgiveness Journal, Vera. I do it to this day. Anybody who's offended me, I write his name in there and wait on the Lord to help me forgive."

This might have merit.

"You see the truth is," he says, "none of us really knows how to forgive. We think we forgive, and then the very next moment we're thinking ugly thoughts again. Do you understand?"

Even though she is caught off-guard by the wisdom in this, she reminds herself firmly that this is not a confessional. She does not have to confess anything to him here. Nothing at all. Though there is something that's been bothering her, and so she responds in a sing-songy noncommittal fashion, "What if the person who offended you doesn't even bother to ask for forgiveness? What if they could care less about your forgiveness? Just saying, there's a lot of talk about forgiveness in the Bible, but you can't really forgive someone who doesn't think they've done anything the least bit wrong." She looks around the room casually. "Can you?"

"Sure you can," he says. "In the end, forgiveness is between you and the Lord."

This comes as a shock.

"'Forgive us our trespasses as we forgive those who trespass against us,'" he says. "You say it every day in the *Our Father*."

"Oh."

"Sometimes it's just about letting go and allowing other people to hold a different point of view," he says. "People fight for all kinds of petty reasons that build up to feuds."

She has had just about enough of his little innuendoes. "Louise Lambert is the petty one in this fight," she says. "She blames me for hurting her hand, and the truth is I've been so busy praying unceasingly that I had no idea her hand was anywhere near my car. And what was she doing following me so closely?" she says. "Sticking her hand in my car door? Nagging and haranguing me is my memory of it."

Father Max says, "Is that right?" He ponders this. "Well, now that you mention it, how is your prayer life going, Vera? I've been meaning to ask you that since your last visit to the rectory."

"How do you think it's going?" she says and then starts to cry. "How do you think it is—praying the rosary day in and day out while your customers jabber on about all their damn problems and you keep losing count of the *Hail Mary*'s, not to mention entire Mysteries. One day I was in the middle of praying the Sorrowfuls when I was interrupted by some hysterical client, and all of a sudden, ten minutes later, there I was praying the Joyfuls again!" She pounds her fist into her thigh. "It's difficult," she says. "But I won't stop, because the Lord is answering my prayers left and right, including returning our daughter to me and Monk."

Father Max grabs a tissue from the counter and hands it to Vera.

"Thanks," she whimpers. "And Monk and I have been invited to her apartment for Thanksgiving." Her chest heaves with the pressure of the last few weeks. "And, and...she hasn't so much as asked us over for a drink of water in three years. Uh, uh uh...and now..." She shakes her head vigorously as if to purge herself of the emotion. "This is so embarrassing."

"Not at all," he says.

"You're very kind to listen."

"That's what I'm here for." He walks over to the coffee station and motions to ask her if she wants some.

She shakes her head, no. "But you take some," she says. "It's a fresh pot. Uh uh uh..."

He pours the coffee and sits back down. "You need to move on," he says.

She blots her tears. "What do you mean?"

"You have to move on from reciting prayers to praying with your whole being."

She blinks.

"You're ready for that, Vera."

"I am?"

"Prayers are not a series of magic words that produce results," he says. "It's not a spell."

Maybe not, thinks Vera, but it sure does seem like magic some days.

"Prayer is also a manner of relating to others and to God in our ordinary every day actions," he says, then sips coffee.

She smiles. This sounds too good to be true. "But, well, how do you pray without words?"

"Read the autobiography of St. Therese of Lisieux," he says. "The book is in our parish library. Therese offered every little action of her day to the Lord. She didn't pray while she was talking to someone. And she listened carefully. Just as the Lord does. Listening carefully to the troubles or the joy of another is also prayer when it is approached that way." He grins. "Our whole lives can be one long prayer if we want them to be. If we offer ourselves to the Lord every day, that's a prayer."

"Well, that's just beautiful," cries Vera. "That really lets me off the hook with these words and words and words, even though I love words; I do! But I swear sometimes I don't even know what I'm saying anymore. Not that I don't pay attention to the words, mind you. I do. Or I did."

"But it's in your nature to listen to your clients."

"Yes," she says, realizing the simple truth of this. "That's why they like me. Because I'm a good listener. Well, I used to be."

"Then offer your listening to the Lord," he says, then places his mug on the reception desk and moves to the door.

"And no more rosary?" she asks.

"Oh, by all means, pray the rosary!" he says. "But not all day long. Not when you're at Mass, and not when you're engaged with others."

"Not at Mass?"

He picks his coat off the rack. "Certainly not. Mass is a higher form of prayer. Always give your full attention to the higher prayer."

She frowns. "I don't remember ever hearing this before," she says. "And I don't think the Rosary Society knows about this either."

"Well, we'll have to do a better job of teaching then, won't we? But for now, just open your heart, Vera. Talk to the Lord in your everyday language. Confide in him. He's your friend."

She wags her index finger. "And the forgiveness book!" she says.

"Yes, that too." As he puts on his coat and hat, he says, "Just tell the Lord your intention, and let him change your heart and the heart of the offended."

"But I am the offended!"

"In an argument, both people are usually offended."

As he walks out the door, Vera calls out, "Father Max, come by anytime for a haircut."

He waves his hand. "I just might do that, Vera." And off he goes in his inappropriate outerwear to his inappropriate fire engine red VW Beetle convertible. What kind of a priest is he anyway, thinks Vera. Next thing you know, he'll be riding past her house on a Harley without a helmet. Though come to think of it, she is highly flattered that he cared enough to pay her a visit and recommend the forgiveness book. Not to mention the fact that he realized right off the bat that Louise Lambert was the one who needed forgiving. And as far as Louise also being offended, well of course she is! Louise has invested a lifetime in being offended.

She stands there for a few minutes, watching, and then thinks, I need to buy a book, and she runs out to Barnes &

Noble for a nice leather-bound journal. She finds one that is scarlet red embossed with a big heart and a tongue of fire. It's perfect. And right then and there she scribbles in *Louise Lambert,* followed by *Frederick Michael Spencer Tophet, IV,* followed by *Margaret Vitella and the Martha's,* which sounds like a Motown band, but whatever. Oh, and one more—*Anthony Kimble.* The man who drove the truck that was carrying the new car that slipped off its hitch and killed her beloved parents all those years ago.

She pays for the book and hugs it to her chest as if to transfer all the withheld forgiveness that had been hardening her heart. I hope it works, she thinks. I hope Louise shows up tomorrow morning to get her hair fixed for Thanksgiving. She squints hard and visualizes Louise at the door of the salon tomorrow morning. She visualizes with all her might, but keeps getting pictures of Louise standing in front of her bald as a balloon. She sucks in all the imprint and kinetic ether she can, using it like crayons to create Louise out of nothing. Out of forgiveness. Louise, with all her hair.

The next morning, Vera falls out of bed onto her knees in a state of utter exhaustion and asks the Lord not to show up in her bedroom anymore when she's trying to sleep. It's not as if he doesn't have another 16 hours in the day to teach her how the world works. Of course the Lord knows that a human being requires sleep—he was one! So then she thinks that perhaps it's not just God who's bugging her at those times, but possibly an underling sneaking in his own agenda just when the Lord has retired for the night. Not her mother, she hopes! She certainly hopes her mother would not be party to the overwhelming nature of her extreme dreams.

But at this rate of sleeplessness, Vera will expire. After all, she cannot escape the fact that she has hair to style, a house to keep, and a husband to please. Not to mention a daughter and her husband with whom to reunite. And then it occurs to her. Tomorrow! Tomorrow is Thanksgiving. This thought makes her deeply and abidingly happy, and she decides to call Mia later on to see what she can bring to the feast. There must be something! A fancy tart of some kind, perhaps. Something expensive from a chic bakery that will make Mia proud in front of her in-laws. Of course the in-laws will be there, too, won't they? This has not been confirmed, but Vera will plan for the worst. She will not make anymore faux pas about learning Shakespeare. Why, come to think of it, the Tophets probably barely know Shakespeare's work themselves. Why should they? Life is not a literature exam! Just because you're related to someone famous doesn't mean you have to go around quoting him.

As she kneels by her bed, she thinks—even if Mia says, "No, don't bring anything, Mom," well, then, Vera is determined to honor that request. She will accept her daughter on her daughter's terms. That's the bottom line. Vera will be a good guest. A good guest honors and respects the wishes of her hostess.

"Lord bless my day," Vera says aloud. "Lord bless my every action and word, and make the whole day a prayer in honor of you. And also bless Monk at the cardiologist today. And if there's anything wrong with him, please find it fast. Please bless and protect Monk," she repeats with emphasis. "And Mia." As she rises, she says, "And Louise. And Frederick. And Anthony Kimble." As she says these names, she is grateful that Louise and Frederick don't stick in her throat anymore, although Anthony Kimble and his car trailer are still lodged in like a fur ball. The Lord will have to do a better job of helping her to forgive Anthony. When someone kills your parents, even if he didn't mean it, forgiveness is a lifetime job.

Vera does not go to Mass today because she wants to give Louise the opportunity to appear at the salon. If Vera goes to Mass and watches Louise with the Martha's, she's afraid it will only cast their differences in bronze. She uses her ether to keep Father Max in the rectory this morning. Even though she has no appointments today, she does not have time to entertain Father Max. She is waiting for Louise and praying with her actions for Monk and Mia. That's enough. Not to mention shopping for baked goods and artichoke hearts for Thanksgiving dinner.

As the morning advances, Vera waits patiently in her salon for Louise, whom she is now able to visualize with a full head of hair even though the hair is frizzy and poorly styled. She visualizes Louise in her quirky little lynx jacket with the big tortoise shell buttons appearing on the salon steps, her eyes lowered, her lower lip pouting with...guilt. Vera can't help it. After all, Louise is the guilty one, even though she merits forgiveness. "God bless Louise," she says aloud.

She moves about her salon prayerfully. Conscious of her thoughts and actions. Trying to make them humble and wholesome and wrapped up with a sapphire blue bow just waiting to be untied. "La dee da," she sings, as she dusts the shelves of self-improvement books. "La dee da, Wayne Dyer. La dee da, Deepak Chopra. La dee da, Bernie Siegal, Max Lucado and Anthony Robbins." Why, dusting these shelves she realizes for the first time that for her entire life she has sought to become what she is finally becoming: a holy person. A good and holy person. This thought fills her with such grace that she drops her dust cloth and reaches for the phone to call Mia.

Ring ring. Ring ring.

"Yes?" The voice is gravelly, but definitely Mia.

"Mia!" says Vera, perhaps a little too eagerly. She tones her voice down an octave. "Good morning, dear."

"Yes?"

"It's me, honey! Mom!"

"I," says Mia.

"What's that, dear?"

"I, Mother. It is I. Not, it is me."

"Well, of course, dear," says Vera, embarrassed. "It is I, then. Sorry."

"You're always correcting everyone," Mia says. "You should pay attention to your own grammar once in a while."

"Did I wake you?" asks Vera. She checks her watch. Ten o'clock.

"What?"

"Did I wake you?"

"No." After a long pause she says, "Is there something you want, Mother?"

"Um, well, just that I'm looking, well...your father and I are looking forward to tomorrow, and we wondered..."

There's a rumbling and some throat clearing, and then Mia says, "What's tomorrow?"

"Why, tomorrow is Thanksgiving."

A rustling of sheets or papers. "Oh. Right. Yes."

"And I'd like to bring something along. A fruit tart, perhaps. Or some hors d'oeuvres."

Mia sighs heavily. "Hold on a second." A door slams. Something falls. And then she says, "Sure."

"Sure?" repeats Vera. She is suddenly alive, really alive, as if someone had just shot her up with adrenalin. "Really?" she says. "That's wonderful. Which would you prefer, Mia? The tart or the hors d'oeuvres?"

"Whatever," she says. "Look, I'm in the middle of something here. I've got to go." She hangs up.

Vera considers the phone then hangs it up with a grin. Well then, she thinks happily, I shall bring them both. I shall bring... an artichoke cheese dip and a large lemon tart topped with gelled oranges and blueberries. She is ecstatic. She is beside herself. She picks up the phone and dials Monk at the high school.

"Hey," he says. "How's my girl?" He whispers to someone. "It's Vera, kids. Excuse me while I talk to my beauty queen."

Vera blushes. "Oh, Monk," she says. "I've got the best news."

"What's that, sugar?"

"I talked to Mia, and well, she was still...Mia. Still...peevish and...well anyway, she agreed to let me bring an hors d'oeuvre and dessert to dinner tomorrow afternoon."

"Vera, can you hold for a minute while I call the Nobel Prize Committee? They'll want to get that million dollar check ready."

"It's just that it's such a breakthrough, Monk. Usually she would just hang up. Or say something degrading about my culinary tastes."

Monk sighs heavily. "I'm glad you're happy, that's all. That's all that matters to me. I'll go along with all this crap just to make my girl happy."

"But Mia's your girl, too, Monk. Remember? Remember how she used to..."

"I don't have time for that. What Mia used to do and what she does now contradict the hell out of each other. I don't even know who she is anymore. She's wiped me out. Used up her daddy chits. Let's just take this one step at a time. Okay?"

"Okay, then."

"So I'll see you right after the damn doctor hooks me up with a mess of tubes and runs me to Kansas City and back. I hope he's up for the competition."

"It's for your own good."

"I'll show him! I'll outrun every one of his patients. Young and old, every patient he's ever had. I'll set a damn record."

"That's my guy."

"I gotta get out of here. I love you, sugar pie."

After he hangs up, she kisses the phone. No matter how frustrated she gets with that man...the clothes on the floor, the hair in the tub, the stubble in the sink, the snoring, the blank stares whenever she asks him if he did something she'd requested, his stubborn resentment when it comes to forgiving Mia, the disgusting way he eats corn on the cob, the way he packs his toothbrush right next to his shoes...lordy, it's a long, long list, but anyway, he loves her. It's a true thing, their love. And this fills her with warmth.

"God bless Monk Wright," she says aloud, and then repeats it at the top of her lungs. "God bless Monk Wright!"

Vera cleans and cleans and waits and waits, but she must have used up today's supply of ether, because Louise never shows up at the door with or without hair. Vera is stumped. There's no way she can go to church tomorrow and the next day just to watch Louise prattle with the Martha's, wearing her damn fake cast like a purple heart. Vera shakes her head, imagining this scene. No. No way at all. And there's no way Vera can just march over to Louise's house and ring the bell, and say what? "Hello, Louise. How are you doing? Might I come inside for a cup of tea sprinkled with a big fat honey of an apology?" Won't work.

She supposes she could find herself a new parish. There were plenty enough around—St. Elizabeth's and Holy Angels. But such a drastic action as that would only bring Father Max straight back to the salon with a long list of questions, not to mention sermons. Which she had enjoyed, it's true. But still. No, she has to stick with St. Jude's one way or the other. She pulls her forgiveness journal off the shelf and puts an asterisk next to Louise's name to emphasize the immediacy of the situation. "All things get done in the Lord's time," she remembers Father Max once saying from the pulpit. But what if that's not time enough? Dear Lord, she thinks, please move it. Wherever Louise is now, turn her around and point her in my direction.

November 25—Right in the middle of the Upper Crust Bakery, the Lord warned me about spiritual pride. I'd never heard of such a thing, but apparently I'm on the brink of it. He told me that I have been given many gifts, some I'm using, but others I don't even know about. Like what, I think. What else could he possibly pull out of his bag of tricks? Believe me, I don't want to know.

But anyway, he said these gifts were not given to me for my own use. They were given to me to save the world. What? Excuse me? I don't mind saying that this business of saving the world bothers me a lot. Not to mention that I'm a beautician. As I've said before, since when does beauty school qualify you to save the world? Anyway, I like the world the way it is, and don't see the point of saving it. And by the way, saving it from what? From whom? I wanted to ask him these things, but didn't have the nerve to start talking right out loud in the middle of the bakery. This is what I get for telling him I don't want him interrupting my sleep anymore. I get him talking to me right in the middle of a bakery transaction. Here's Ludwig the baker saying, "What's that, Mrs. Wright? Did you say a lemon tart or a custard tart? We have both." And there I am about to say, "What do you mean I have to save the world? Are you crazy? Call Superman. Here's his number."

Well, the Lord must have read my mind, because he said that throughout history he has only spoken to quiet and unknown people. I don't know about quiet, but I am certainly not famous. And also I think he should be giving these gifts to someone a little smarter. And wiser. Like Father Max, perhaps. Someone without a spouse whose life is arranged to handle spiritual intrusions complete with all kinds of people to pray for you if you get in over your head. My head is spinning from all this craziness, let me tell you. But if it gives me the inside track on Mia, I'll follow this road right off a cliff, whatever it takes.

And also I'll try to stop thinking I'm made of magic, like he said. Not that I completely understand what he's doing to me. I don't. In fact, I hardly understand it at all. And that's the truth. I mean, he's the one who informed me about ether in the first place. Does that mean I shouldn't use it to make Louise appear at the salon? And if so, then what exactly do I use it for? If I need to knit an etheric net to save the world, please tell me how big it has to be and how long it will take to create it, and I'm all yours. All his, that is. I mean, he gave Noah the exact dimensions of the ark, so is it too much trouble to let me know how big to make the net?

(Working on becoming) his humble servant—Vera Wright

Vera dumps two cups of shredded cheddar into the bowl with a half-cup of heavy cream and a jar of artichoke hearts and stirs. She hears a commotion at the door, and turns just as Monk whips open the kitchen door and pounds his chest like a gorilla.

"Me Tarzan, you Jane," he says, grinning.

Vera turns from her artichoke dip, the wooden spoon still in her hand. "What did he find?" she says. "Will you need an operation?"

Monk takes three long strides in her direction, enfolds her, and kisses the top of her head. "You're a worry wart," he says. "He found nothing. Notta. Zip."

"Nothing?" she says. "How could that be?" This does not jive with her understanding of the situation. Her understanding is that something needs fixing fast.

He dips his finger in the bowl and she smacks his hand. "That's for tomorrow," she says.

"He says my valves work great. I ran at a higher speed and incline for longer than the doc himself was able to do last week." He nods his head emphatically. "I the man."

Vera pats his cheek. "Well then, at least we know, dear."

"At least we do."

"But there aren't any more tests? And what about blood tests? Nothing else we need to wait on?"

"Nothing." He frowns. "What are you so worried about, anyway?"

She mashes the artichoke hearts. "Oh, nothing," she says as casually as she can. "Just that sometimes the doctors aren't thorough enough."

"This one was," says Monk. "Believe me."

"I believe you," she says. I don't have a choice, she thinks. And anyway, she was wrong about Louise showing up at her door, too. So maybe this is what the Lord meant by spiritual pride. Thinking you know everything about everyone else. As if the people you hallucinate about don't have wills of their own. As if their wills don't change matters altogether. She will not have pride. She does not have to be right all the time. And in this case, being right would be a very bad thing.

"Did he put you on any medication?" she asks.

"None."

"Well then, I guess you're all set."

He hugs her so hard he squeezes the breath out of her. "I'm gonna go run," he says, "now that the treadmill's fixed." He shakes his head. "I can't believe the damn cord wasn't plugged in! How embarrassing!"

"Isn't it always the obvious," she says. Lord, give me peace, she prays silently. Give me your peace of mind.

As she finishes up the dip, she whistles, hums, and then turns on the radio to her favorite oldie station. Anything to keep her mind off Monk upstairs on the treadmill. Still, she can't help herself—she sneaks over to the bottom of the hall staircase three times to listen for his heavy footsteps. She smiles as she listens to him thud thud thud to "Mustang Sally," which is blaring on the office radio. These sounds please her. They are pure Monk doing purely Monk things. Signs of Monk's glorious life. God bless Monk.

The Lord is making good on his promise to provide her with peace of mind. So all's well, except that she's still having a hell of a hard time sorting out right from wrong as far as her visions go. Not to mention her skill level at ether production. At this point she doesn't know whether or not Louise showing up at her door would be a good thing or a bad thing. Louise showing up at her door would certainly improve Vera's track record. But Louise showing up at her door would give more credence to all her visions, good and bad. Oh the hell with it, she thinks, and wraps the bowl with cellophane. It's nearly Thanksgiving, after all. On Thanksgiving, you're supposed to be grateful.

"Thank you, God, for my family, and while I'm at it, for this whole wild ride."

"Strap yourself in tightly," says the Lord. And then he leads Vera to the salon desk to download some more celestial data.

Chapter Ten

That night a human-like form obscured in a brilliant bolt of glacial blue energy introduces herself to Vera as Ranere, an angel of the Lord. She snatches Vera from her sleep and escorts her across the multiverse to a majestic mountain range in the middle of who knows where—Colorado or Nepal. It's dark, though there is the sense that it would be beautiful in daylight—a sleeping geophysical beauty on the verge of awakening. But much to Vera's shock the angel does not take her to a charming mountainside village on the outskirts of the range, but instead right through a crack in the massive stone embankment into the interior of the mountain itself. She is lucid and hyperconscious of her surroundings. This is no dream, she thinks, even though she realizes that a sizable piece of her remains in bed asleep.

Vera and Ranere travel up and down the corridors of the vast complex. There are thousands of bedrooms, tens of thousands, maybe more. And every one of them is furnished with two cots and two dressers, very much like Mia's dorm rooms at Wellesley. The light is dim, and though there are windows with velvet drapes, everything is colored in shades of pewter and steel gray. Nobody here is having a party any time soon, Vera notices. They all walk with their heads down, mechanically, and though they are able to move, they do so with little more awareness of their surroundings than Monk when he is watching TV.

These people don't talk. Not one word can be heard. Not that the air is still; it isn't. The air is dense with the rhythm and bass of machines humming, tools buzzing, and meters ticking. Click clack click clack. They work hard, like robots. Nail, hammer, slam. Nail, hammer, slam. Automatons. Some are hunkered over sewing machines. Some are varnishing woodwork or polishing brass. Others are stirring huge volumes of liquid in massive aluminum pots in the institutional kitchen. All in all, it's a busy place, though dreary and unappealing. All sweat and no reward.

Ranere takes Vera into a bedroom, which she says is all Vera's. Vera does not want the room. Why would she want to stay here? She has her own room, her own house. Her own salon. And Monk is anything but an automaton. In fact he's the opposite of an automaton. He's unwieldy and resistant and loud. He does things his own way. She wants her own room in her own house with Monk the loudmouth. But the angel convinces her that she will need a place here to lie down. "I'm not tired," she protests, and then inexplicably swoons, and the angel lays her down on the cot.

"Close your eyes," says Ranere.

Well, how can she keep them open? It's as if pounds of red-hot light are sitting on her lids. The weight and the heat are unbearable and she is scared at first, but is soon and miraculously detached from the pain.

"Trust the Lord," says the angel kindly. "We are lightening you up. Raising your vibration so you can see more, travel to more places, help more people."

Vera doesn't have the vaguest idea what Ranere is talking about, but it truly doesn't matter. She is already in the process anyway, whatever the process is, and she's helpless to stop it. She is thoroughly distracted by the warm tingling that is moving from the crown of her head slowly down her face and neck onto her shoulders, chest and belly, lower abdomen, and right on down her legs from her knees to her ankles to her feet and toes. This all takes time, she's not sure how much, and it is not entirely unpleasant. While the last bit of electric-like impulse moves through her toes, she's aware that her right hand is tightly clenched as if she's holding onto something for dear life.

When the process and sensation are completely over, she sits up slowly, opens her eyes, and behold! Her entire body is translucent—milky white mixed with a million sparkly colors like an opal. She's opalescent! Her body is the single most beautiful thing she has ever seen anywhere. More radiant than the sun or the stars or the planets. More spectacular than the most expensive jewel in Mia's safe. How can this be? she wonders. How can her body outshine the sun? Why, dressed in this magnificent designer piece, she could easily walk the spiritual red carpet on her way to the pearly gates for her eternal reward. She can see the paparazzi now—light bulbs flashing, whispering with awe into their microphones, "Well would you just look at Vera Wright gliding center aisle in a bodysuit painted directly from the palette of Original Creation Energy! You can't get more elegant than that, folks. Look for Vera to win best-dressed!" But there she goes again with her spiritual pride.

Slowly, she turns around to the side of the bed, and places her feet on the cold stone floor. It's then that she raises her right fist in curiosity and pries her tight fingers open like an oyster shell in possession of the last perfect pearl. But there is no pearl inside. Instead, there's a tiny ball the size of an acorn, hard but also rubbery. It takes her a moment to realize that the acorn is actually the compressed remains of her entire physical body. She is stunned. What? What have they done with her body? Would she ever be able to wear it again? Is she dead? She doesn't feel dead. And yet...she has no idea what death feels like. Is there any feeling at all to death?

Slowly, she stands and walks out of the room. She's able to walk; even glide. She glides into the hall, and behold once more—all has been made new inside the mountain! The corridors are lit with spectacular chandeliers and sconces. Why, it's a mansion! A castle with many unique and richly decorated rooms! Everything sparkles with Victorian abundance — the emerald green velvet of the drapes matches the deep rich emerald of the plush carpet. The heavy Biedermeier furniture has been converted into pure gold and upholstered with fine fabrics made of resplendent jewel-tone silks. Everything dingy has been made bright. Everything old has been made new. It steals her breath.

And yet, all around Vera and her vibrant, youthful, reflective and well-toned opalescent body are people who continue to work as if the mountain had not just been transformed into a crystalline empire. Vera shakes the shoulders of the seamstress, "It's been done!" she says. "Look around you! Everything is new! It's been done. Wake up!"

The seamstress tips her head upward as if in response to a breeze or a distant call, but for some reason, she can't hear Vera's voice. And neither can the cabinetmaker or the cook or the plumber or any other number of workers in the mountain.

Vera turns sideways to the angel, whose face is still too radiant for her to face directly, "What's wrong with them?" she says. "Why are they still working as if their work has purpose? As if the world has not already been resurrected?"

Ranere sighs. "That's a good question," she says. "Not just here, but everywhere. Why? Why do people sleepwalk on earth as well?"

Vera ponders this but gets nowhere. She can't wrap her mind around the meaning. What is Ranere talking about? This renewal has most certainly not been done on earth, not yet. Has it? Not since she last checked.

Ranere tries again. "Like most people, these workers operate on a lower synthesis. The lowest causal level — the component level of detail and breakdown. Until they recognize their own power, they will not be able to see the light, no matter how bright it gets. Or hear the vibration of your voice. You are lighter than they are. They are a sodden mass."

"But can't we help them?"

"You can, Vera Wright," says the angel meaningfully. "Now that you know where they are, you can help them. That's your job."

And Vera wants to help them. She does. But she doesn't know how.

That morning, Vera awakens on her left side, arms forward, knees bent. Even before she reaches full consciousness, she is staring at her outstretched arms, disappointed at the heft of her sagging body. Where did the lightness go? The opalescent glow? Even as the so-called dream fades, the weight of her body seems to be accumulating mass at a startling rate. This is downright discouraging, not to mention the crepey condition of her upper arms. She pinches a piece of flesh and drops it in disgust. And she only weighs a hundred and twenty pounds, for heaven's sake! She can't imagine how it feels to wake up at two or three hundred pounds, fighting the force of gravity from one end of the day to the next. Why, it must feel as if a giant magnet is dragging you around. Shlump. Shlump. Shlump. Being human is exhausting, she thinks. Fraught with obstacles and frustrations, not that she would want to be anything else. Not a snake, certainly. An eagle, well...maybe that.

The longer she lays awake, however, the more she makes peace with her imperfect body and this warm, wonderful bed, which she would not even be able to feel without a body. She listens to the familiar rasp of Monk's heavy breathing behind her. And this warm, wonderful husband of hers—yes, indeed, such a comfort. Spirit shmirit, she thinks. After all, being human is all she really knows. She can't let a dream change all that. Even an amazing dream. Not to mention that the idea of trading in her body and her life is downright frightening, no matter how much contact she has with the spirit world.

But this dream stays with her. It won't let go.

She pulls the blankets up to her chin and burrows into the mattress, thinking and thinking. Somewhere in the Bible doesn't it say that the earth is not our true home? Nevertheless, it's a sticky place, and darn hard to leave. Being human is so familiar that at this moment she can barely imagine what it feels like to be all spirit again. 100% what? Air? Energy? Light? Yes, that's it, light. She can barely remember the exquisite lightness of being she'd experienced last night. She squints hard. Concentrates. But, no. She knows it was amazing, but she can't bring back the feeling. Doesn't want to. She absolutely does not want to die in order to live, no matter what the Bible says.

No sooner does she produce this thought, than the Lord's voice overwhelms her. "Vera, Vera, Vera," he says, and it takes her a while to attune to the rhythm and timbre of his words. Ugh. She might as well get up now. She knows he will not let her be. In the grip of his voice, she rises and moves to the bathroom where she turns on the shower faucet. She washes her face as he talks to her. She brushes her teeth as he lectures her. She undresses as the volume rises in her head, and she steps into the shower. She must get used to this, she knows. He is never going to leave her alone. As she showers, he reminds her with some urgency about the mountain dream — that the earth has already been made new and prepared for his minions. This brings the dream back to Vera in the minutest detail — the vast village. The strange lightness of being. Her physical body compressed to the size of an acorn. The sleepwalkers. The futility of it all. But of what, exactly? She thinks hard. The futility of the people and their refusal to listen? Was it just the people in the mountain who wouldn't listen? Or was it also Vera? Vera and Monk, and Mia. Not to mention Louise.

"There is nothing keeping any of you from your birthright in my kingdom except your own refusal to open your eyes and accept my grace," saith the Lord. "Human suffering, human pettiness, even physical death, are all unnecessary. Death has already been conquered. Do you believe this, or do you not?"

Vera smiles in surprise. She is all for the abolition of suffering. She is all for the elimination of death. But how? And if this is true, why in heaven's name is the Lord telling this to her and not to Father Max? She wonders if Father Max already knows.

"Were even one percent of you to kneel down on the same day and ask to be awakened, the filth would be wiped from your eyes and from the entire earth, and you would recognize the new earth and your eternal home in that instant," saith the Lord.

"And we would all have radiant bodies?" she asks, as she scrubs her doughy knees.

"Yes," saith the Lord. "And you, Vera Wright, are the one who must tell them this."

"And this is how I save the world?" she asks.

All at once the curtain is flipped aside, and Monk's big head appears. "Blaaaaaaaaaaa!" he screams.

"Aaaaaaaaaaa!" she screams back. "Monk Wright, what are you doing! You are scaring the life out of me! Aaaaaaaaa!!!!"

He leans into the wall laughing, bends over laughing, his eyes tearing with joy. Scaring Vera in the shower is especially satisfying to him for some reason. How could she have been so distracted as to lose her guard? Why, she never even heard him enter the room!

"You tiptoed!" she screams. "You snuck in on purpose!"

He laughs so hard he belches, which makes him laugh harder. "Oh, oh, oh," he says, trying to calm himself down. He gets the hiccups, and sits down on the side of the tub. Finally, he says, "Okay, okay, enough about me. Explain what you're doing in there talking to yourself about saving the world."

She hems and haws. "You know, just...thinking about a movie I once saw."

He reaches in to tickle her, and Vera reflexively covers her breasts. This does no good at all, since it's that very act of modesty that appeals to Monk the most and always has. At this, he drops his pajama drawers and hops into the shower with her. He takes the washcloth from her and gently soaps her shoulders in big Monk circles, round and round.

"Oh, Monk," she says, swallowing water. "You're going to drown me."

"That's what I intend to do," he says in a deep John Wayne drawl. "I intend to drown you in love." He begins by lathering her back.

They are way too old and slippery to make love standing in a shower anymore, and after a while, Monk rinses her with the hand nozzle, dries her off, and leads her back to the bed, where he has his tender way with her.

Later on, as they dress for Mia's, Monk says to Vera, "A thousand dollars she isn't there."

Vera groans as she pulls on her panty hose. "Don't make me sorry I gave into you," she says.

"Just trying to prepare you, that's all. I can't picture this, Vera. Not even a corner of it. She's been so unreliable for so many years. Like the time..."

"Don't."

"I'm just saying..."

Vera picks up one of her shoes and taps it on the floor. "Don't," she says. "Don't spoil this day for me. Whatever it is, whatever it turns out to be...right now, I believe Mia will be there, and that's all that matters. It keeps me going."

He holds his hands up. "I've said what I needed to say."

She breathes deeply.

"Sorry," he says.

"That's better."

"I love you," he says.

"You big oaf," she says, and he chuckles.

She pulls her black knit top over her head. Steps into the matching pants. She can't go wrong with black, she thinks. Nothing Mia can criticize about black knit with just enough spandex to keep its shape. And she has the loveliest black crocheted tunic from Daffy's to top it all off. And a silver bracelet—so modern. She's all set. She will make Mia proud. And Mia will be there. Monk doesn't understand about ether, and she hasn't seen fit to educate him. She can't even imagine the conversation. He never enjoyed science to begin with. Not that this is physical science, but spiritual science. The science of the spirit. How it works. How it's constructed. If the Lord is teaching Vera about this, she thinks, how many others has he taught? And what about the apostles, did he teach them? When he walked on water, did he tell them how? Did he tell them why? Maybe someday she'll get up the courage to ask Father Max.

But not now. For now, the problem is not walking on water. The problem is Mia's presence at her condo on Fifth Avenue. Will she be there or won't she? Vera nods to herself. Yes, Mia will be there. She closes her eyes and concentrates on an image of her and Monk knocking on Mia's door. They wait and wait. Why isn't Mia answering? She concentrates harder and harder. Finally, the door opens and Mia answers. Vera sighs with relief. Praise the Lord! Mia answers the door.

As she applies her kohl-black liner and mascara, bits of last night's dream flash before her, and she can't help but share them. "Oh, Monk," she says, "I had the most beautiful dream last night. I didn't want it to end. I dreamed the whole world was renewed and refreshed in colors that don't even exist yet. Colors it would take months to name, if I could even find suitable names. I was in a mountain somewhere. It was a magnificent place without sorrow or pain. Although not everybody there was aware of it."

He chooses a navy blue tie with tiny orange and brown turkeys all over it. "I can't remember the last time I had a dream," he says.

"Oh, and I got a new body in the dream!" she says.

He turns indignantly. "Nothing wrong with the one you have." He wiggles his hips. "It's made this old man happy for my entire adult life. You can hardly beat that."

Vera rolls her eyes in an exaggerated fashion as she slips into her black suede pumps. She descends the stairs to retrieve the artichoke cheese dip and lemon tart from the refrigerator. As she wraps the bowls tightly, she sings, "Over the river and through the woods...da dum da dum da dum..." She puts on her black wool coat and carries the dishes to Monk's Suburban, which she hates like hell to ride in, but her VW sedan is still missing. Oh, when will they ever figure out who has it! she thinks. That is, if it isn't on the bottom of the river. Thank God Mia and Frederick don't live in a house. It would be humiliating to drive up to a grand house in Monk's old beater. And with her luck their house would probably have a circle drive and a fountain! But in Manhattan, Mia will never see the car. So who cares?

Such a petty little concern, anyway, and she refuses to let it ruin her day. "Da dum da dum da dum..." On Monday she'll give in and get a rental until the insurance company comes through with the cash for a new car. She shakes her head. She doesn't want to think about the stolen car, no way. Not today. She wants to think about this perfect late autumn day, crisp and clear—the smell of cedar smoke wafting from chimneys all around her, winter hovering nearby. Today is an historical day. Today she will dine in Mia's home.

"The horse knows the way to carry the sleigh o'er the white and drifting snow-ho!" Vera's head swings to the music. Her neighbor waves to her and she joyfully waves back. "Happy Thanksgiving, Jessica! We're visiting our daughter in Manhattan today!"

On the way back up the walk, a car screeches to a halt behind her, and as Vera turns, she sees a cruddy black Plymouth on the curb. "Hey, Ma'am, you know where I can find Vera Wright?" calls a shaggy-haired man out the window.

"Why, yes, that's me," she says. "Er...I. That is, I am she."

He jumps out of the car and runs to her with a letter. "Sign here," he says breathlessly.

"Well, what do you know?" she says. "What's this?"

"Just a letter for you," he says, handing her a pen. "Can't give it to you until you sign here."

She signs her name in her best penmanship ever, and he gives her the letter. "I thought the post office was closed today," she says.

"I'm not from the post office, Ma'am," he says, running back to his car. He drives off.

Vera opens the letter as she's walking into the house, and stops cold in the center of the hall.

"What's that?" asks Monk.

She hands it to him. "It's a summons," she says.

"Summons? What the hell?"

"From Rhoda, one of my clients." She says this deadpan. She is in shock.

Monk reads and reads, frowning and squinting at the smaller print. Finally, he pulls out his glasses and reads wide-eyed. "What the hell?" he says. "She says you permanently injured her eye!"

The air is leaking out of Vera's balloon. "Some dye dropped onto her eyes," she whimpers. "But it was her fault, Monk, I swear. I said something unexpected, and she jerked her head—like this." She jerks her head in demonstration, while tears stream down her face. "It was just...an accident...."

"Oh baby, come here," he says, and hugs her tightly. He lifts her chin with his finger. "Listen to me, babe, I'm not gonna let anyone sue you, understand?"

She nods. "Oh, Monk ..."

"It won't happen. I've known John Preston for years. Played handball with him. Taught all their kids. I won't let it happen, Vera." He mumbles something under his breath. "I won't let it."

She is so exhausted and betrayed that she cannot indulge any more energy in this summons. She will turn it over to Monk and to the Lord, and await her destiny. First she loses Louise, and now Rhoda. What next? Her salon?"

"We're going to see our daughter," says Monk.

Vera nods tearfully.

"So now you think she'll be there?" He buttons his coat. "She damn well better be."

Before they leave, Vera enters Rhoda's name in her forgiveness book, recites a brief prayer, and offers this and the rest of the day to her Lord and Savior. Whatever happens, it will be a prayer to him. Even if it's lousy, rotten and full of holes, it will be the fatted calf on her altar, and he will see it for what it is — the best she has to offer. A genuine sacrifice. She locks the door behind them and walks uncertainly to the truck.

As they ride through Canaan and onto the highway, Vera stares out the window blankly. The day has lost some of its luster, but she is trying very hard to win it back with her waning ether. She notices that ether is deeply affected by emotional outbursts of any kind, good or bad. It's not efficient to spend yourself on emotion, she thinks. And she is famous for emotion. She will have to store that information away somewhere safe. She will have to learn to watch her outbursts in order to conserve her ability to create the life she wants and deserves. The life the Lord had in mind for her even before she was born. She does not want her ether spilling recklessly out of her creating monsters she isn't even aware of. If she gives in to this disappointment, she will only create further disappointment. She must learn to treat everything neutrally. Oh my God, she thinks, fat chance.

They are in the thick of traffic on the approach to the George Washington Bridge, and Vera is still nestled deeply in thought. Monk changes everything when he booms, "Good God almighty, will you look at those clouds!" He pounds the dashboard for emphasis, which catapults Vera right out of her meditation.

"That's the second time today you scared the life out of me!" she says.

He smiles. "Then it's a damn good day!" He waits a second or two then says, "Well?"

"Well, what?"

"Well, have you ever seen anything more goddamn beautiful than those clouds?" He points to her right.

"Don't say that," she says. "Don't say 'goddamn'. It's a cuss word. And it doesn't make any sense when it's used to modify the word 'beautiful'. 'Goddamn beautiful' is an oxymoron. And it isn't pleasing to the Lord."

Monk rubs his chin. "I had no idea that the Lord disliked oxymorons, but I'll keep that in mind."

"Don't be funny, Monk. It's the 'goddamn' he doesn't like! Don't say 'goddamn'."

Monk grins. "Look to your right," he says. "Tell me that doesn't call out to you!"

Vera snaps out of her bad temper, because she cannot get over how Monk is going on and on about the clouds. It causes her to look a little more closely, and goodness gracious, she thinks, if there isn't a field of cloud poppies sitting right over the Hudson River! Why, the definition in the outline of the blossoms is extraordinary! Miraculous!

"Well?" he says. "Am I right? Am I right?"

Her mouth is still ajar. "Why, Monk," she says. "I can't believe you noticed that. Since when do you notice clouds?"

"Since they're like that," he says. "I never saw clouds like that before. Not only that, but the water is blue today. The Hudson River isn't blue! It's brown bordering on ink black. What good fortune is this? A blue river and a sky full of popcorn clouds. That's what I call a miracle. Wow!"

To tell the truth, Vera thinks, the water is not really blue—more like a deep violet with amber highlights. But Monk is slightly color blind, so why correct him? He's immune to correction anyway. And deep down, she's delighted at his new enthusiasm. She can't recall a single time he's ever pointed out a cloud formation to her, even when they dated. And then it hits her—could it be? Is it an awakening? Is Monk suddenly able to see the light all around him? Things he never noticed before? Light that others can't see? What a fortuitous day this is after all, she thinks, pleased. Perhaps the day will not be a sacrifice to the Lord, after all, but a gift to her! Why, the Lord can be such a trickster!

Chapter Eleven

At Mia's, they park in the underground garage and ride the elevator to the lobby. The lobby is all glass and onyx tile freshly decorated with several lavish museum-sized baskets of mums, marigolds, eucalyptus and assorted autumn flowers. The fragrance is pungent and the effect festive. Why, Vera's own back yard doesn't smell this earthy.

Monk whistles as he carries the Tupperware bowls, one in the palm of each hand, moving them up and down to match his stride. But Vera can't help it—she's nervous. She tries to pretend this is any other holiday, any other day, but she's unsuccessful. In fact, she's beginning to shake. Her breath is shallow, rapid. She wants this too much. Oh God in heaven, she never wants to want anything this much again.

Now her whole body is rippling, inside and out. She tries to drown her fears in a bucket of positive ether. But the bucket is leaking. She uses what little ether she has left to conjure Mia answering the lobby phone politely. "Yes, hello. Yes, of course. Oh, how delightful! Frederick, dear, guess what? My parents are here!" She imagines Mia swelling with the joy of her parents' arrival. Of entertaining her parents for the first time. On Thanksgiving, no less. Finally! Lord, have mercy on the less fortunate.

They approach the security counter. "Mia Tophet," says Monk importantly.

The guard nods and points down to the sign-in book as he lifts the phone and punches numbers on the dial pad. In a minute that seems to Vera like a month and a half, he says,

"Mrs. Tophet? Mm hmm." He turns the book around and reads Monk's scribble. "That's right," he says. "Okay, Ma'am, I'll send them up."

"Oh!" exclaims Vera with relief. "Oh! Oh!" She throws her hand to her chest and bends slightly forward. "Oh, my God!"

Monk wraps his arm around her. For once, he doesn't ask her what's wrong or what's right. For once, he knows. This tiny nonverbal communication thrills her almost as much as the fact that Mia is home and is allowing them to come up. For dinner! "This is a day the Lord has made!" she exults. And Monk squeezes her shoulders in agreement.

When she opens the door, Mia looks so elegant, she takes Vera's breath away. Her blue-black hair sweeps her shoulders in a graceful cut. She is wearing a fitted amethyst-colored pantsuit made of burnt-out velvet, with a tunic top that is slit up the sides and tied at the waist with corded velvet. The narrow feet that she'd inherited from Vera's side are sporting exquisite black pointy slides. She should have been a fashion model, Vera thinks proudly, a super model. She's that gorgeous. But Vera doesn't want to appear too eager, so she sizes down her reaction considerably.

"Hello, dear," she says as she casually pecks her daughter's cheek, as if it were no surprise at all that Mia had invited them in the first place. No surprise at all that she had actually remembered to be there to let them inside.

"Mother," says Mia, nodding. "Father."

Monk kisses her politely. Vera remembers when he used to squeeze Mia with all his might and lift her right up into the air. "That's my girl!" he'd say joyfully, right up to senior year in high school when things began to fall apart. "Oh, Daddy!" she'd laugh. "You're so silly!" Vera tries to dispel that memory, refuse it even. Go away! Don't ruin my reunion! But the memory is so beautiful it grips.

"Lola!" calls Mia.

Lola appears in a crisp black uniform, takes the Tupperware bowls from Monk, and returns for their coats. "Sir," she says, nodding to Monk. And to Vera, "Ma'am."

Mia leads Vera and Monk through the conservatory that features a magnificent black enamel grand piano, and Vera asks, "Do you ever play the piano, dear?"

"What?" says Mia as she walks into the library.

"The piano," says Monk on Vera's behalf. "Your mother asked if you ever play the piano anymore. All those lessons..."

"Um. No, not really," she says absently. "I've thought of it, but...no." She finally stops in the living room and presses a button on the wall. "Frederick," she says into the speaker. "They're here."

"Who's here?" responds Frederick in his sophisticated Gregory Peck voice. The only thing Vera ever liked about Frederick was his voice.

"My parents," says Mia.

No response from Frederick.

"For Thanksgiving," she says.

"Well, bloody hell," he says. "I forgot it was Thanksgiving."

Mia shifts her weight. "So come on down."

"Pretend we're not home," he says. "I've got a splitting headache. Tell Dickhead down in the lobby to tell them we're in Boca."

Mia leans into the wall. "You just told them yourself, genius," she says. "They're standing right next to me."

Another long pause. He clears his throat. "I'm sure they know I'm kidding," he says. "I'll be down in a bit. Entertain them for awhile, won't you?"

Vera turns to Monk whose face is so beet red, she thinks he must have popped a blood vessel. She elbows him in warning.

Mia turns around slowly and shrugs without a hint of embarrassment. "Would you like a martini?" she says.

Monk, still exhaling, checks his watch. "Well, I'll have a... um...well, it's only one o'clock, but..."

"I'll have one!" says Vera.

Monk's eyes bug out. "You'll have what?"

"A martini," she repeats resolutely. She reaches behind Monk and pinches his butt to keep him quiet. "With olives."

"Well, of course olives, Mother," says Mia, blinking.

At that point, an amused smirk creeps onto Mia's face, and to Vera, that half-smile alone is worth the risk of drinking a martini, not that she can recall exactly what kind of liquor is in a martini. She can't. Why, Vera hasn't had more than a wine cooler or two at any occasion she can think of in the last thirty years, ever since they invented wine coolers. Never mind a martini. But it sounds so sophisticated. And thank goodness she remembered about the olives. She loves olives. The olives will keep her sober.

Monk rubs his hands together expectantly. "Well then," he says. "Since I'm the designated driver here..." He poufs his lips. "How about a, uh...I don't know, gin and tonic? Light on the gin."

"Fine," says Mia, and then presses a different intercom button, ordering the drinks from central command.

They mill around the room in the meantime, Vera admiring this painting and that, Monk picking up this doodad and that, until finally, he plops into the oversized couch. A few moments of awkward silence later, he says, "I'm surprised you don't have a pooch."

Vera knows he is not the least bit surprised Mia doesn't have a 'pooch'; she never cared for animals. But at least Monk is trying, she thinks. And at least he didn't charge upstairs and strangle Frederick when he'd made that comment earlier. This makes her love Monk with surprising new force. What would she ever do without him? The big lug.

"I do have a dog," says Mia.

"Oh?" says Vera, shocked. "You never told me you had a dog, Mia! Where is the little guy?"

"It's a she."

"Well, isn't that nice!" squeals Vera. She catches herself and quickly tones down. "What nice company for you. Where is she?"

Mia claps her hands a few times and a giant long-legged white shaggy dog enters the room. It's the shaggiest dog Vera has ever seen. With the sharpest pointiest face she's ever seen. The dog charges across the room.

"Holy crap!" blurts Monk, pushing back into the couch.

Mia grabs the dog by the collar and jerks her back.

Vera stares meaningfully at Monk. "It's just a dog, dear," she says. "You've seen dogs before." She turns to Mia and forces herself to walk gingerly in the direction of the dog. "What's her name? Pretty doggie," she says sweetly. "Nice doggie."

The dog growls and Vera backs off.

"Her name is Elvira," Mia says. "She's won tons of awards. She's an afghan with more pedigree than Frederick."

"Well then," snorts Monk jovially, "maybe Frederick should have married Elvira!"

Vera grits her teeth. "That was uncalled for, dear," she says in a sing-song voice, though she knows it was totally called for.

Mia points accusingly at Monk. "This is Frederick's home, Father. Do I have to remind you of that?"

Monk is about to retort big time when Vera moves in front of him. "We do understand that, Mia," she says. "Of course we do. Don't we, Monk?"

He is really stewing. Stew, stew, stew. His mouth is moving, but no words are coming out. Hold back, thinks Vera. Hold back. She stiffens her jaw and juts her head out in a fighting stance. He stares back at her defiantly and then finally throws his hand out in defeat. "Fine," he says. "Just a little humor, that's all. Allow an old man to keep his sense of humor for God's sake."

A tall balding man enters the room. He's dressed in a gray suit and is carrying drinks on a silver tray. He extends the tray to Vera, "Mrs. Wright," he says, and hands her the martini with a cocktail napkin.

"Oh well, thank you very much," says Vera giddily. The man is very handsome, she thinks, even with the comb-over. And so solicitous.

The butler bends in front of Monk. "Sir," he says, while handing Monk a gin and tonic.

Monk accepts the drink suspiciously. "Not too much gin, I hope!" he says winking.

"No, sir," says the man.

He stops in front of Mia. "Madame?" he queries.

She shakes her head. "Nothing for me tonight, Ervin."

With a nod, he leaves.

Monk says, "Aren't you going to have a drink with us?"

"No," she says, looking across the room.

The silence is heavy, bloated with questions, and it occurs to Vera that perhaps Mia has actually quit drinking. Could this be? No wonder she'd turned over a new leaf and invited them to dinner. She'd recognized her alcohol problem and stopped drinking. Had she quit cold turkey? Attended AA? Either way, this explains a lot, and for the first time since the invitation, things are becoming apparent to Vera. Falling into place. Not such a big mystery after all—Mia's fidgety, nervous behavior. The long silences. The agitated phone calls. Vera doesn't know everything about alcoholism, but she does know that when an alcoholic stops drinking, things can get tense. Not that they aren't tense while they're drinking. Just that tension is a hallmark of an alcoholic with or without alcohol.

All at once she is bothered by a vague memory of her father drinking too much. A memory deeply buried in some dusty corner of her mind. Why now? she thinks. Had her father been an alcoholic? She can remember the beer, that's all. The constant ssssip of the air as he pulled the tab. The deep satisfied belch after the first mouthful. He could be crass, her father. And he enjoyed his beer, yes. An alcoholic? Not possible, she thinks. Her memories of her father are all good.

Vera sips her martini. "Oh my!" she says. "This is well..." She giggles. "A little...wow! Strong, I'd say! Maybe some more seltzer."

Mia rolls her eyes. "There's no seltzer in a martini, Mother."

Vera places her drink on the end table and settles into the couch. "Well then I'd better have a seat, hadn't I?" She takes another sip just for show, just enough to wet her lips, and thinks, my goodness, why not just drop two olives in a bottle of witch hazel?

Fifteen slow and tortuous minutes later, Vera has sipped half of her martini when Frederick waltzes in. He is his tall and lanky self, full of lotions, braces, tonics, and hair gel. Why, he smells like a fragrance counter, Vera thinks, and turns to head off any comment Monk might be considering. Monk's nose is high in the air, and he is sniffing audibly. Vera shoots him a fast, laser-sharp warning glance, followed by a huge fake smile directed at Frederick. He's handsome enough, Vera thinks, with the exception of his oversized chin, but all in all too smooth, too rich and homogenized for Vera's tastes. He stops at the edge of the room and stands there.

He says nothing, so Vera chirps in, "Well, well," she says. "Happy Thanksgiving to you, Frederick." She attempts to stand, but stumbles back into the couch. "Oh my," she says. "I think I'd better have a cracker, Mia, to absorb some of this liquor."

Frederick nods politely, his hands tucked safely in the pockets of his black tailored pants. His white shirt is crisp and over-starched. "How are you, Vera?" he says. "Monk?"

To his credit, Monk stands and offers his hand. After a moment of seemingly deliberate hesitation, Frederick takes it. Vera notices that Monk rubs that hand on the seat of his pants before he sits back down. She hopes nobody else noticed.

Frederick orders a scotch straight up, and in a few minutes, a tray of hors d'oeuvres arrives along with Vera's artichoke dip in a silver bowl. Vera is babbling on and on about whatever—even she has no clear idea, and then Mia says, "How's your car, Mother? Have they found it yet?"

"No, dear, they have not," says Vera. She's pleased that Mia even remembered the incident, though. And doesn't this just prove that she's emerging from the selfish me-me-me phase of alcoholism?

There's a long silence during which Vera sips a tiny bit more of her martini until lo and behold, there's nothing left in her glass but olives. She picks one up delicately and places it in her mouth. "Yum!" she says.

Mia moves to the intercom and orders Vera another drink.

"Oh no!" giggles Vera. "I couldn't. No."

"Too late," says Frederick, crossing his legs. It astonishes Vera that he's wearing no socks! With all his money and supposed taste, the man is...sockless!

"Well..." says Vera as she shifts her weight on the couch. She's at a surprising and total loss of words, not to mention the lightheadedness. And Monk is offering no relief. She looks searchingly at Mia, then Frederick, who are both seated across from her in separate gigantic chairs. "How are you two doing?" she says a little too meaningfully. "How is marriage treating you?" As soon as she says this, she regrets it. "Not that you have to tell us," she says, waving her hand in dismissal. She plops the other olive in her mouth and looks at Monk, "I mean who am I to be so personal?" She chews the olive. "It's really none of my..."

Mia leans forward and says, "Not so great, actually, Mother."

Frederick adjusts his position in the chair and rubs the back of his neck with his free hand. He looks at Mia. "As your mother said, Mia, this is none of her business."

"Is that right, Frederick?" she says. "Well, then just whose business is it? If it's not mine, and it's not Mother's, then whose is it? Father's?"

If Vera had a gun, she would shoot herself.

Frederick takes an exorbitantly long time re-crossing his legs. He stares up at the ceiling, back down again, and swishes a mouthful of scotch before swallowing.

Mia says, "Mother, I've been meaning to tell you, I'd like you to have my Mercedes."

"Huh?" says Monk.

At this moment, Lola arrives with a tray full of drinks, and this time Vera sips hers so long it could technically be considered a gulp.

Mia roots through her Ferragamo purse and produces a set of keys. She walks over to Vera, jingles the keys, and drops them in Vera's lap. "Consider it a gift," she says with no trace of a smile, then returns to her chair. "I'll transfer ownership on Monday and have Roger drop it off at your house.

"What...what do you mean, dear?" says Vera. "What do you mean you'd like to give me your...your car?"

"It's a convertible," says Mia. "Very sporty. You'll enjoy it."

Frederick clenches his jaw. "You're not giving her that car, Mia," he says.

Mia smiles brilliantly at him. "I'll give her any damn thing I please," she says. She stands and peruses the living room. "In fact...here." She lifts a glass bowl in the shape of a water lily. "Mother, I'd like you to have this bowl."

Vera looks over at Monk, then Frederick. She accepts the bowl reluctantly. It's so heavy Vera can't even hold it, and it falls onto the cushion of the couch. Mia leans over, picks it back up, and hands it to the maid with instructions to bubble wrap it and place it in a shopping bag for her mother when she leaves.

"Well!" says Vera, after taking another sip. She turns to Monk. "That certainly is a magnificent bowl. Not to mention the car."

"It's a Steuben," says Mia. "The bowl. It's a very rare collector's piece. It was a wedding gift from the Giuliani's."

Vera's eyes widen. "The Giuliani's, well. We certainly know who they are, don't we, Monk?"

Speechless, Monk rubs the top of his bald head with his palm.

"We'll have to find a nice place for it, then," Vera says to Monk, who is now staring at his loafers.

Frederick rubs the thumb of his right hand rapidly against his other fingers. Finally, he points at Mia, "That's enough," he says. "Don't take this any further."

This is clearly the wrong thing to say, because Mia takes this as a cue to stroll around the room in search of another treasure. She ends up with an ivory tusk about two feet long, illustrated with intricate ink drawings that are far too miniscule for Vera to make out from a distance. Mia has to carry the tusk with two hands.

Frederick snorts. "No," he says.

"Father," says Mia, as she hands it to him. "I'd like you to have this tusk. It comes from the estate of Ernest Hemingway."

"Wow," says Monk, so impressed he seems to have lost sight of Frederick. "I may be a jock, but I've certainly heard of him. <u>Old Man and the Sea</u>—I think I even read it. Not sure. I've certainly seen it lying around the school."

"He was a big game hunter," Mia says. "He shot the elephant himself. It was legal then...I'm told."

Monk places the tusk in his lap and studies it carefully. Vera can't tell if he's actually studying the ink drawings, or silently wondering what the hell to do next.

The butler appears in the living room with a tray holding a tiny brass bell, which he tingles three times. "Dinner is served," he says.

Mia says, "Thank you, Ervin," and tells him to wrap up the elephant tusk for her father. She looks at her parents. "Well, shall we?" she says.

Monk stands and offers his hand to Vera, who topples a bit getting up. He leans his face into hers and says chuckling, "I never thought I'd say this, but maybe you should lighten up a little on the juice?"

Vera says, "I'm fine, Monk. Not to worry about a shingle thing."

Monk wraps his arm around her waist and follows Mia, who stops in her tracks and says, "Frederick? Are you coming?"

"Not really hungry," he says. "I've been nibbling."

Mia turns to her parents, "Excuse me," she says. "Frederick and I have to discuss something, so won't you please follow Ervin into the dining room? Thanks."

"Of course, dear," says Vera, and off they go.

The dining room is spectacular; a crisp white linen cloth on what must be at least a twelve-foot table set with elegant black china plates that are painted with a single white gardenia in the center. The middle is decorated with real gardenia centerpieces, and gardenia blossoms are scattered over the surface of the table.

Vera is astonished at the trouble Mia has gone to. She wants to cry. She looks up at the butler, who towers over her, and tugs his sleeve. "Oh," she says, "it's jush so...beautiful, isn't it? Isn't it... jush beautiful? Can you believe how beautiful it is?" She crosses her hands at her chest. "I...I have never seen anything so beautiful." She dabs her eyes.

The butler doesn't respond, but holds Vera's chair for her. Monk assists her onto the chair and the butler slides her in. "Oh my," she says, gushing. She thinks she might be slurring, and takes great care to pronounce the words slowly and precisely. "Such... ser-vice!" she manages.

"Madame," he says, nodding, then crosses to the other side of the huge table to hold Monk's chair.

Monk shoos him away. "Oh for God's sake," he says. "I can sit down by myself. Do I look like a man who can't sit down by himself?"

"Very well, sir."

When he's gone, Monk juts his head out to Vera across the table and says, "Get a real job, eh? What the hell kind of a job is that for a man?"

Vera whispers, "He's...a nice man."

Monk swats the air.

Vera picks up her napkin, shakes it out, and places it on her lap, all with exaggerated gestures in order to put Monk on notice to do the same. "Put your napkin...on your lap, dear," she finally says when the charades don't work.

"Jees," he says. "No, how's that? I'll just...all this damn fuss. Let me be, Vera. I have my own manners."

"Manners are manners," she says, but it takes her a long time to say it. She is a little cross-eyed from the alcohol, so does not want to challenge Monk too much.

"Manners are invented by people," he says. "There are different manners for different people in different places for different meals. What in the name of God do you make of that? Some control freak makes some rules..."

They are interrupted by muffled voices in the other room, which grow increasingly louder.

"I will give her whatever I want to give her," says Mia. "Let me remind you that half of this is mine."

Vera plays with the heirloom silverware. "The tablecloth is Irish...lllllin-en," she says carefully. She would give anything for some food to absorb the alcohol, so when Ervin arrives with rolls, she immediately selects one from the basket and takes a huge, ungainly bite without bothering to butter it. "Mmm," she says. "Nice and...hot."

Monk is wringing his hands, and she can tell that he's miserably uncomfortable in this dining room. "Now that's great manners," he says, as if he cared less about manners. "I can only imagine what you would say if I tucked into a hot roll even before the host and hostess arrived."

Vera barely hears him. She's too busy purring as she chews. And anyway, she knows he doesn't mean it. This is what he always does when he's tense in a social situation. He takes it out on her. She goes in for another chunk of the roll. She needs this food badly. She has to sober up fast.

"Oh really?" they hear Mia say quite loudly. "Perhaps your parents would also like to know how you've squandered their little fortune..."

"That's enough," says Frederick pointedly and just loud enough to be heard.

Then a pause. A few minutes later, they enter the room with smiles pasted on their faces. "Time for dinner," says Mia, who sits at one end of the table.

Frederick takes his place at the other end, jingles the brass bell, and clears his throat. When the butler appears, Frederick says, "The Chateau Lafitte, Ervin."

Ervin nods and disappears.

"Well," says Vera. "Your father and I can't tell you...how happy...we are... to be...heeerre."

"We're happy to have you," says Mia. "Aren't we, Frederick?"

Frederick blinks.

"Aren't we?"

Vera clears her throat and says in a slow and exaggerated manner, "Where are your parents, Frederick? We thought they'd be here. We're shorry to miss them."

"They're in Switzerland," he says brusquely. "Which is where we're supposed to be." He sips his scotch. "That is if Mia were in better form."

"Oh?" says Vera, turning to Mia, then back to Frederick. "She looks good to me." She cocks her head, looking at Mia. "In fact...she's beau...tiful."

Mia gives Frederick the evil eye.

"Beautiful, yes," he says. "The most beautiful siren of them all."

"Why, Frederick," says Mia coyly, as if he'd meant it as a compliment.

Vera thinks they may have made up and can't believe she is rooting for that. Well maybe just for tonight. Tomorrow she will no doubt be using her kinetic ether to register Frederick on the next shuttle to Mars.

Vera watches Monk suffer through the consommé, staring at her in between sips as if to say, what the hell is this? Couldn't they have added something? A mushroom? A grain of rice? Vera just hopes he doesn't say anything out loud, never mind punctuate the meal with one of his long, ghastly burps.

In between cleansing sorbets they move from the consommé to the lobster aspic to the stuffed quails without fanfare and without much more conversation than Vera's simple questions and Mia's brief responses. Monk contributes a remark here and there, like, "Imagine that, lobster jello." But nothing worth remembering.

As they are about to cut into the quail meat, Frederick stands, looks at them all and says, "Excuse me, won't you?"

"Well, of course," says Vera, though Mia is looking a little stunned. But why should she? A man has to use the bathroom once in a while.

From her seat in the dining room, Vera can see Frederick in the front hall at a distance of about thirty feet. He's standing with his back to them, slipping into his black overcoat, which is being held for him by Ervin. Frederick then wraps a white scarf around his neck, buttons his coat, and walks out the door.

Vera's hands are positioned over her plate, frozen—a fork in her left, a knife in her right. Her mouth is open, but she manages to close it before turning to Mia.

Although Mia has an even better view of the hall than Vera or Monk, she is calmly cutting her meat as if nothing the least bit significant has occurred. She looks from Vera to Monk and asks blandly, "How do you like your dinner so far?"

Vera blinks. "Well...what could be better?" she says. "The best I've ever had, not that I've ever had quail before."

Monk is silent, but thanks be to God, he manages to raise his thumb in a sign of approval.

Vera thinks maybe it's all nothing. Maybe Frederick went out for another bottle of wine. He'll be back in a minute. Their ways are different from ours, she thinks. They communicate differently, that's all. She cuts a piece of meat and tastes it. It's very juicy and the gravy is quite rich and flavorful. "Mmm," she says. "Very good."

They all pick at their quail and their garnishes of fancy string beans tied with a strip of unrecognizable vegetable, no potato or starch of any kind, which Vera knows she'll hear about from Monk for months. But once the maid has cleared the table and the butler has taken coffee requests, Vera says, "Mia, dear, do you think something's happened to Frederick?"

Mia bites the inside of her cheek. With a distant look in her eyes, she stands, says, "Excuse me," and walks out of the room, slowly at first, but a minute later they hear the hurried click-clacking of her heels in the hall and up the stairs.

Monk leans in across the table and points his knife at Vera. "This is a crazy place," he says. "I told you we should have had dinner at our house."

Vera shakes her head. "They had a little scuffle, that's all. That happens to young couples."

Monk rolls his eyes. "As soon as we get home, I want you to make me a real turkey dinner. With all the trimmings. Cranberry sauce from the can, the way I like it. And stuffing from the box with that sausage you add."

"How can you talk about food?" says Vera. "You just ate plenty. Not to mention that our daughter is in some distress."

"Who says she's in distress?" says Monk. "She's as sober as a block of wood. And she's handling herself like a lady. I haven't seen her so composed in years."

Vera leans in closer. "You said it—she's a block of wood—dull and inanimate, if you haven't noticed. Not behaving one bit like our daughter." She settles back in her chair. "Not the whirling dervish we raised."

More than ten minutes later, there's the click-clacking again and some rustling in the hall, and then here comes Mia around the corner, losing her balance slightly and sliding on the marble floor. Were it not for Monk's quick reflexes, she would have fallen. Instead, she is magically caught in her father's arms. Monk looks awkward at first, but then squeezes her hungrily. The sight of it causes Vera's hand reflexively to cover her mouth, plugging the gasp that accompanies the powerful flash of memory. How Mia used to worship her father. What a daddy's girl she was. How she let Monk tease her mercilessly. Vera could almost abide Mia's rejection of her, but not Mia's rejection of Monk. They were made for each other more than any father and daughter she'd ever known. And here they are...together again. God is in his heaven.

Once Mia has her footing, she lifts her head and stares at her father as if she barely recognizes him and pushes him away.

"Mia!" he says. "Why did you do that?" He grabs her by the elbow. "Why did you push me away?"

Mia yanks her arm from his grasp, dismisses him with her hand, and returns to her seat.

To Vera this surfaces a different memory, a more recent one, and the Lord orders her loud and clear to "Go upstairs now."

She rises slowly from her chair, gets her bearings, and announces that she has to use the powder room.

"Oh for God's sake, Mother," says Mia. "The 'powder' room? Make sure you bring your powder to the powder room." Her eyes are wild and unfocused. "Powder your nose in the powder room." She picks up an invisible powder puff and pretends to powder her nose.

"What's wrong with you, for God's sake?" says Monk. "This whole civil evening, and now..."

Vera only hears his voice trailing off because she is being led up the grand staircase, through the hall to Mia's bedroom. She notices that she feels sober and wonders if it was all the food she ate or if it was the Lord himself who restored her sobriety. Martinis, she thinks. What on earth made her think she could drink martinis?

Once in Mia's room she is distracted by the luxury—the rich quilted garnet silk of the bedspread and chairs, even the walls, for heaven's sake; the princess canopied bed; the soft lighting; and everywhere the white cashmere and mink throws. Standing in the middle of this excess, she has no idea what to do next. What am I doing here? she thinks. What is my daughter doing here? She throws her hands in the air. "What now, Lord? Don't leave me here to guess!"

Since he isn't answering her, she decides to follow her instincts and open Mia's closet. She can't believe the number of designer gowns and outfits—hundreds of them, like a boutique. Millions of dollars of one-of-a-kind ensembles. Vera rifles through, amazed at the wealth of fabric, and then suddenly, she stops. What is this? She stares, incredulous, focusing and refocusing. But it's still there, unmistakable— the black cape. She walks away backwards, and shuts the door. Her stomach roils with nausea. Afraid she'll be sick, she wanders into the bathroom at the back of the master suite. As she moves toward the toilet, she leans against the wall and grabs the towel rack to hold herself up, nearly stepping on a...what? What is this? There at toe-point is a foot long tube of plastic.

And right beside it, a hypodermic needle.

Chapter Twelve

As Vera reaches the top of the staircase, she hears Monk calling, "Vera! Vera, where are you?" He sounds serious, emphatic, and for Monk, nearly hysterical. "Vera!"

"I'm here," she calls back, and waits for him to follow her voice. "Here!" she says. "At the top of the staircase."

Monk appears in the hall. "Mia left," he says wildly. "And I want to get out of here. I don't know what's wrong with her, or him, but I gotta get the hell out of here."

"I have to show you something," says Vera.

Something in her voice clearly startles Monk, because he walks upstairs without questioning her. "What?" he says. "What is it? Don't surprise me, Vera. I'm serious. This has been a damn stressful day. Just tell me what it is. What is it?"

She takes his hand and leads him down the hall and into the bedroom, where she opens the closet and pulls out the cape.

Monk stares it. "What?" he says.

"The South Bronx. The lady was wearing this cape."

He scratches his head. "They probably sell a million of those things," he says.

Vera takes his hand and leads him into the bathroom, where she points to the paraphernalia. She knows Monk will know better than she does what this is. Monk works in a high school athletic department. He's lost more than one athlete to drugs.

He walks past Vera and kneels down over the needle. "Get me a bag," he says in nearly a whisper. "Any kind of a bag. Something to put this in."

Vera roots through the bathroom cabinets and drawers, and cannot find anything, and she's not about to ring for the maid. In desperation, she walks into the bedroom, grabs a pillow, and pulls off the garnet silk case. Somehow, this seems fitting. In the bathroom, she holds it open for Monk. Protecting his hand with a bath towel, he places the needle and tourniquet carefully in the pillowcase. Then, like a madman, he opens and closes every cabinet in the room, and the next room, and the next, searching for the drugs. When it's evident he's not going to find anything, something suddenly occurs to him. "We've got to find her," he says. "We've got to get her some help."

Vera nods. She closes the case and follows Monk hurriedly down the stairs, where he is pressing buttons left and right trying to get Ervin's attention to retrieve their coats. He snaps the fingers of his left hand, waiting, while the right hand clenches the pillowcase. Finally Ervin arrives with their coats. He holds them out, and this time Monk doesn't argue, he just slips his arms into the sleeves. But when Lola tries to hand him their bubble-wrapped gifts—the lotus bowl and elephant tusk—he flicks his hand. "Some other time," he says, then grabs Vera's hand and rushes out to the hall.

In the elevator, they say nothing. It's a long ride down. Monk is practically jogging in place, he's so anxious, and Vera feels as if she is swallowing a marble. As they rush through the lobby into the parking lot and across five rows of parked cars, they see Mia about twenty feet ahead. She's leaning against a car, her eyes fixed on the ground, and taking a long drag on a cigarette. As she exhales, she tosses the butt on the cement floor and squashes it. She is apparently deep in thought. When she looks up, she sees them staring at her.

"What?" she says, planting her feet in a belligerent stance. "You're leaving? Where are you going?"

"Where are we going?" says Monk.

"Uh...yes?"

"You walked out on us," he says. "With no explanation."

She surveys the dark parking lot. "I um, well...I just..." she shrugs. "I just had to run an errand. I planned to come back. I am coming back."

"We've got to talk," he says. He and Vera move slowly closer.

Mia tenses; her eyes dart back and forth. "I invited you over here. I gave you dinner on Thanksgiving. We had a good..." she whimpers, "...time. And this is how you thank me? You...you just..." She covers her face.

Vera cannot believe her daughter is crying. It takes a moment to register, because it's like watching a hunk of scrap iron suddenly shed tears. It's like...a miracle! Moved beyond belief, Vera opens her arms and walks the final few steps toward Mia, and in response Mia takes three giant steps backwards. Vera halts.

Now Monk rushes forward. When he's close enough, he grabs Mia by the arm so she won't run away. With his other hand, he shakes the bag open. "What is this?" he says.

Mia looks away.

"I gave Mom my car," she says.

The word Mom settles achingly in Vera's heart.

"That's nice," says Monk, "but I want you to look in here and tell me what this is all about. Your mother and I want to help you, Mia. We know there's a problem, but we had no idea how bad it was. And we're sorry we haven't been around to help you with it."

Mia swallows, her neck craned upward. She will not look inside the bag.

"It's a tourniquet and a needle," he says. "What do you think of that, Mia? Isn't that something? Your mother found a tourniquet and a needle in your bathroom. She nearly stepped on it. Is this what you do with your time and your money? You shoot up?"

Tears stream down Mia's face. "How dare you pry into my personal life," she says.

"You're my daughter," he says. "I have a right."

"You..." she says, pointing, "have no right."

"I damn well do, young lady. I taught you honesty and integrity."

"Ha! That's a laugh."

At that, Monk rattles her arm hard, and Vera gasps.

Mia twists, trying to escape his grasp. "How dare you talk to me about honesty and integrity," she says.

Monk grasps more tightly. "What's that supposed to mean?"

Her eyes go wild. "It's supposed to mean Mrs. Wyste?" she sneers. "Mrs. Stella Wyste?"

Monk's mouth falls open and inadvertently, he releases Mia's arm.

"Mrs. Wyste," continues Mia as she backs away. "Did you know about Mrs. Wyste, Mom? Mrs. Stella Wyste the art teacher?"

Vera frowns, confused. "You had her freshman year? The redhead?"

"Stella Wyste the redheaded art teacher who did it with Dad in the art room."

Monk's face turns pasty white. He turns to see Vera's reaction.

"All my friends knew about it," says Mia. "Stephanie saw them together when she went to her locker during the school play. I was the laughing stock of the high school for my entire senior year." She steps back some more. "Thanks to this..." She points to Monk. "...paragon of virtue."

"It wasn't what you're thinking," pleads Monk, first to Vera, then Mia.

"You're a pig," says Mia. "I hate you."

Vera is stunned. She forces herself to say, "Mia, please let us take care of you."

Mia shakes her head, no, several times before disappearing into the darkness.

At this, Vera turns and taps hurriedly to the car where she sits in the passenger seat with her arms folded tightly against her.

Monk, shoulders sagging and head down, drags himself to the car and slips into the driver's seat. He lays his head and arms against the steering wheel. "Vera..." he says.

"Don't."

"Please. Let me explain."

"I already knew about it," she lies.

"You did?"

"Sure."

"It only happened once," he says hoarsely. "I swear, Vera. It was a mistake. Stella..."

"Don't say her name."

"But if you knew about it..."

"Just take me home."

He reaches for her and she slaps him hard in the face.

That night, Monk stays in the guest room. Even across the hall Vera can hear him sobbing in his pillow. She's never once heard Monk sob or even whimper. It feels to her like the end of the world. Like the world has tumbled down upon her, the entire universe cracking in half, birthing another whole world. A world without Monk? She can't imagine it. She forces herself to open the forgiveness book and write his name: M-O-N-K W-RI-G-H-T. How could he have done that, she wonders, dropping the pen. How could he have risked everything for that scrawny unkempt woman? That...Bohemian river rat! Poor Mia, she thinks. No wonder...no wonder, and all these years. Poor, poor Mia.

Vera tries to go to sleep, but tosses and turns so much that she considers taking a sleeping pill, and finally settles on half a tablet. She's tempted to throw some more figurines at the Lord, because she cannot believe how much she'd been looking forward to Thanksgiving, and how badly it had turned out. It was a mess; worse than she'd imagined. Her beautiful daughter is addicted to heroin. Her husband confesses to an affair. Please God, she prays, heal my daughter! She screams the thought so loudly she can almost hear it being said. Her throat hurts from forming the words so firmly, so wholly, without releasing them into the air. She raises her fist to the ceiling. Save our daughter, she telegraphs to the Lord. Save our daughter. Do anything to us, but save our daughter. And as for Monk...well, let him purge.

Eventually, Vera falls asleep long enough to visit with her mother, Regina, in the backyard of her parents' heavenly Canaan home. Her mother is diaphanous, sparkling crystalline, much brighter than Vera this time. She leads Vera by the hand to the benches beside the koi pond. Vera is not a little girl in this dream. In this dream, Vera is her age, but looks a hundred. Her mother is radiant and youthful, and compared to her, Vera looks as if she'd been pickled in vinegar and stored in a root cellar for the last decade.

"Daughter," she says gently, "you are not looking well."

Vera is unable to pull together enough energy to speak. Her mother gently strokes Vera's hand. "The Lord led you to Mia," she says.

Vera nods.

"Your child has weakened you," she says. "She is strong-willed."

It's as if there's a dense filter between Vera and her mother, as if she's being shown her mother through a screen. Vera looks directly at her mother and with great effort manages to say, "And Monk."

Regina nods. "Yes, and Monk. He has suffered for years from his deed, child."

"Good," says Vera. "Let him suffer."

"If you can find it in your heart to forgive, the Lord will heal you all."

"I forgive Mia," says Vera. The words have an underwater quality to them, as if Vera is penetrating new elements to communicate with her mother, similar to the way the Lord's voice sounds to her on earth.

"Your energy is weak," says her mother. "And you cannot stay here long, not in this state. You need healing. So listen carefully — your daughter's troubles cannot be blamed entirely on Monk. She has a strong will of her own. She is her father's daughter."

"What are you saying? That she's had affairs?"

"I'm saying that Mia will be healed of her troubles when she comes to the end of herself. Do you understand?"

Not really, but Vera can feel herself retreating — vanishing — from the scene.

"She must empty herself," her mother calls after her, "as we all must, before she can be healed."

Her mother's voice is loud, yet distant, and still embedded in Vera's mind as she awakens to a sun-drenched room at eight o'clock in the morning. Monk is nowhere to be found. Vera is relieved to find him gone; she needs time to process. She turns her mother's words over in her mind, "She must empty herself as we all must, before she can be healed." Well, Vera certainly feels empty this morning. May my emptiness be filled with love, she thinks.

Vera takes her time showering and dressing. She has no clients today, not on this long weekend. She has Rhoda's lawsuit to deal with, of course. And Monk. Yes, she has Monk to deal with, not to mention her own broken heart. They'll have to discuss the events of yesterday, and see a counselor, not just for Mia, but for themselves. There must be someone who can help. Father Max, perhaps, but no. Someone anonymous. Someone she'll never have to look in the eye at the Stop & Shop.

She dresses in an old pair of black slacks and a black sweater. Her mood is black, too, though she is trying to rise above it. After all, it was a long time ago, and Stella Wyste moved to Virginia, when was it—seven years ago or more. She tries to imagine Stella's face, but can't. She wasn't pretty, though, Vera remembers that much. Sexy, maybe. And that thought hurts. How could he? How could he have done that to her and Mia? And right in the school?

She drags herself down the stairs for a mug of coffee, and of course, Monk has brewed some, as he always does, even though he himself doesn't drink it. She pours milk into the coffee mug and stirs, sits down to the paper, which he's opened to the crosswords. A handwritten scrawl above the puzzle says, "Sorry." Vera cannot concentrate on the puzzle. She stares out the kitchen window. The sky is cerulean today. Not a soft blue, not powder blue, but cerulean blue. Powerful blue. How she loves cerulean, the color and the word. "Cerulean," she says aloud. "Cerulean blue."

Still, in spite of the magnificent sky, the day contains so many impossible problems. Putting Monk's heinous indiscretion completely aside, Vera doesn't even know where Frederick went last night or if he came home. Not that Frederick is an asset of any kind, of course. And then there was that darling butler and the maid, so Mia wouldn't have been alone anyway, that is, if she even came home. Vera presumes the help stays there, but who knows— maybe not. There's so much of her daughter's supposedly privileged life that Vera knows nothing about.

She drops a piece of oatmeal bread into the toaster and strolls into the living room sipping her coffee. The radio is on upstairs, and as she moves tentatively toward the sound—should she approach him, or wait for him to approach her—the phone rings and she answers it. "Hello?"

"Mom?"

"Mia? Oh, Mia, is that you? Honey, you've had me so worried."

"Mom..."

"Yes, Mia, I'm here."

"I...I'm sorry. I didn't mean to hurt you like that."

"It wasn't...you don't...it's okay," she says.

"I need help, Mom."

Vera's emotions implode; she can hardly talk. "We...uh...oh...oh, Mia, we'll be right there, honey. We'll be there as soon as we can get into the city. We're leaving this minute."

"No, don't," she says. "I'm coming out there. The chauffeur is driving me. I have to get out of this place before I die in this place. I don't want to die, Mom," she whimpers. "Save me."

"Don't say that, Mia. You're not going to die." She covers the speaker. "Monk?" she calls out. "It's Mia!" She catches her breath and says into the phone, "Are you sure you don't want us to come out there and get you, Mia? It's no trouble. We can be right there."

"No, just be home when I get there. Please don't go anywhere. I'll lose my nerve."

"I promise," says Vera, and hangs up.

She follows the music upstairs to Monk's office, thinking Mia is all that matters right now. *I can get past anything if it will help my daughter. We've got to help Mia. Mia wants to be helped, thanks be to God.*

"Monk!" she calls, and enters the room awash with a bounty of divine mercy and forgiveness, only to find Monk lying in a dead heap against the file cabinet beside the treadmill, which is still moving.

Vera's arm slackens and she spills the coffee all over herself and the rug then drops the mug. "No! Oh my God, oh my God, no!" she says in a whisper. She runs to him and shakes his shoulders, pulls him by the feet until he's laying flat, then pushes his chest in and out, the way he's shown her a million times, but there is no response. She opens his mouth and administers CPR, but she is getting nowhere. He can't possibly be dead, she thinks. He can't be. She dials 911 several times, fumbling, pressing all the wrong buttons, her hands tremble, but finally she connects and a woman answers. She screams at them to get to her house and they want to know why, and she screams at them just to come because Monk needs help fast and she can't get any air into him. The woman on the other end is trying to tell her how to administer CPR, but Vera can't hear anything, she is just screaming and screaming. The scream seems to come not from her, but from the center of the earth. When she hangs up with them, she opens the office window and screams for a neighbor. "Anybody, somebody, Jessica! Lourdez! Monk is sick! Monk is sick!"

Minutes pass like a week, until the ambulance finally arrives. "Up here," she screams, and they enter quickly, run upstairs, and she meets them in the hall, screaming. "Help! Hurry up! Help!"

They flank Monk, take his vital signs, administer CPR, and finally, apply the defibrillator to shock his heart into beating. He does not respond. To Vera, this isn't really happening. Watching her husband's body lying there lifeless, jerked into motion again and again, is like watching a scene from Frankenstein. It isn't happening. It can't be happening. The paramedics go back and forth with these procedures for who knows how long and finally one of them looks up at Vera and says quietly, "I'm so sorry."

"Noooooo!!!!" she screams, her hands on either side of her head. "No, that's impossible. You're not a doctor. You don't know. You don't know anything."

"I'm sorry," he says, rising.

"Take him to the hospital!" she says. "They can help him there."

As his partner talks to someone on his cell phone, the attendant moves toward her sympathetically. "I'm sorry, Ma'am," he says. "We'll wait with you…"

"But he just saw the cardiologist," she says, trembling. "He's fine. The doctor told him he was fine. He told me he was fine. He just saw the cardiologist!"

"Which cardiologist?" says the man.

Vera's brain fogs over. "I don't...I can't remember."

"What about his GP?"

"Dr. Regan," she says. "Dr. Michael Regan."

"Do you have a priest?"

Vera gasps as it occurs to her. Yes, Father Max. Father Max will make everything right again. He'll know just how to talk to the Lord to make it right again. "I'll call him now," she says to the attendant. She runs to the bedroom, dials the number, and waits.

"St. Jude's Church," answers a high-pitched voice.

"Yes, is Father Max there please? This is an emergency."

"May I ask who's calling?"

"This is Vera Wright and this is an emergency."

"Vera?" The voice softens.

"Yes, this is Vera and it's an emergency. Did you hear me? Please get Father Max." Her voice is breaking up. "My husband is..." She gasps for breath. "They think he is..."

"What?"

"Dead."

"Oh my God. I'll be right there with Father Max. Hang on. We'll be right there."

It was Louise. Vera knows it was Louise. Vera has never been so happy in her life to hear Louise's voice.

All at once, people whose names Vera can't remember, neighbors and friends from the ambulance squad who were taught by Monk in this grade and that, are filling her house, trying to help. Monk is laid out on a stretcher with a sheet over his head, and Dr. Regan is signing his death certificate. Vera keeps pulling the sheet off his face, and finally, she says, "Wake up, damn it! Wake up, Monk Wright! I forgive you, do you hear me?! How dare you leave me, oh my God,

Monk, you can't leave me. You can't! You just can't. Uh uh uh....ohhhhhhh."

Dr. Regan takes Vera aside and offers her a sedative. "Just half a pill," he says. "This is such a shock, Mrs. Wright. It will help you to deal..."

She grabs the pill from his hand and throws it across the room. "You listen to me," she says. "He's not dead. That man is not dead. You think he's dead, but he's not. I don't need this pill."

After a while, the funeral parlor is called, and the black-suited men stand onerously in the corner of the room waiting for her to release the body. But she won't do it. There's a pounding up the stairs echoing in Vera's head, and then Father Max appears, so youthful and bursting with energy. Vera feels hope for the first time.

She grabs his sleeve. "They think he's dead," she says. "They think he's dead, Father Max, but if we pray, he'll rise. Remember Lazarus? Pray for him, Father. Pray over him. Make him get up. Make him!!!"

Father Max pulls a bottle of oil from his pocket. He uses it to anoint Monk's forehead in the sign of the cross. Vera grasps Monk's cold hand. Wake up, she thinks. Do you hear me, Monk? Wake up! She concentrates hard, using every ounce of her diminished ether to breathe life into his cold dead body. Father Max chants over Monk—a soothing mantra of ancient prayers, and everything is blocked out of Vera's mind but this—Monk's cold hand and the ancient Gregorian-like chanting from Father Max. Surely this will work, she thinks. This is the real thing in the real language of the Lord. She feels herself regaining her center. She holds onto Monk's hand for dear life, believing...believing with all her heart and mind that he can be brought back to life as surely as faith the size of a mustard seed can move a mountain. Monk is a mountain that she can move. He was alive this morning, and he can be alive again. She and Father Max together—that's more than one seed. That's two.

In the penetrating silence of the room, Father Max finally retreats from Monk, and says, "Vera..." He shakes his head sadly. "I'm so sorry."

She backs up. "No. No!"

He approaches her, and she backs up again, right into the arms of Louise Lambert, her dear friend, where she weeps and weeps while Louise pets the back of Vera's head and says, "I know, dear girl. I know."

"The hearse is here," says someone.

"What hearse?" says one of the men in black. "No one called a hearse."

From where she stands, Vera can see out the window, and suddenly realizes that in all of this, she has completely forgotten about Mia. But right out front is a custom limousine that could easily be confused with a hearse. "Oh, Louise," she says, "it's Mia. And she needs...she can't...she's so sick..."

Louise gives Vera a clean wad of tissue, and gestures to Father Max.

"What is it?" he says.

"She's come to get help." Vera chokes on her own tears. "Mia...she doesn't know. She wanted us to put her in rehab, Monk and I. She doesn't know. Oh my God, this will drive her back..."

Louise is already clomping down the stairs, followed swiftly by Father Max.

"Mia!" she hears Louise say.

"What's going on, Mrs. Lambert?" says Mia, panicked. "No one will tell me what's going on. Is it my mother? I just talked to her."

"It's your father, dear," says Louise.

Vera sees Mia now at the bottom of the stairs.

Mia takes the stairs two at a time. "Daddy!" she screams. "Daddy, no!"

Vera reaches Mia in the hall, and does her best to steady herself. "He's gone," she says quietly. "I'm sorry, Mia. I..."

Mia's hazel eyes are hollow. She walks past Vera like a robot, and when she sees the stretcher, the attendants, the priest, and the sheet over her father's face, she collapses. Dr. Regan orders everyone out of the room but the paramedics, the priest and the mother.

The paramedics call out her vitals, and they are apparently not good. Before Vera knows it, she is crouched in the ambulance next to Mia, with Father Max on the other side of the stretcher. Louise has been left to handle whatever immediate arrangements are needed for Monk. Father Max prays quietly while Vera holds Mia's hand, which is still warm.

Vera has fallen asleep sitting up in a hospital chair, chin to chest, a smattering of drool on her bottom lip. As she awakens, she is disoriented. Huh? What? she thinks. But it all comes back too quickly as she sees Mia lying on the bed in the darkened room, tubes in her arms and up her nose. And then the realization hits her. "Oh my God, Mia is unconscious and Monk is dead." She gasps. Monk is ... no it can't be. Her eyes are wet, her chest heavy, her head spinning. She twists her stiff neck to the side and is startled to see Father Max asleep in the chair beside her. Well bless him, she thinks. He didn't leave me alone. She checks her watch. It's eight o'clock. She's been at the hospital for hours upon hours, maybe ten in all. So why isn't Mia waking up?

Beside her, Father Max stirs, rousing from sleep. "Huh? Huh?" he says in a confused manner. "Oh," he says, spotting Vera and Mia. He rubs his eyes with his fists like a little kid, yawns and stretches. "How's the patient?" he asks.

Vera shrugs. "I fell asleep, too."

Father Max checks his watch. "Oh my goodness."

"Do you have to leave?" she says frantically.

"Uh, no, no, not at all, Vera. I'll just call Deacon Carmine to cover for me. And I'll check with the nurse, how's that?"

Vera grabs a tissue and dabs her eyes. "Because I don't have any family, you know, outside of Monk and Mia. Not to put any pressure on you."

"I know," he says soothingly. "That's why God provides, Vera."

"God provides?" she says as if her brain suddenly sprouted a leak. "God...provides?" Her chin trembles. "You tell your God he can damn well have his provision back if this is how he provides. How...dare...he..." She shakes her fist in the air. "This is hell."

"Go ahead and rant, Vera. God can handle it. Believe me he knows how hard this is for you."

"I don't think so. No, I really don't. Because if he did, he would wake my daughter up, don't you think? Don't you think that if God knew how I was feeling right now, he would wake her up? Don't you?" She shakes her head. "He doesn't know. He doesn't know a damn thing." She hunches over and caves in to the crush of despair she hasn't dared to feel since she found Monk dead in the corner this morning. And then it hits her—the Vision.

She sits up straight. "The Lord gave me a vision of this," she says.

Father Max's eyebrows rise. "Oh?"

"Yes he did. You can ask Louise. Louise knows all about it. Right in the Stop & Shop. I thought I was going crazy."

"How long ago was this?"

"September, I think."

"Did you tell Monk?"

"No, but I made him go to the cardiologist. He went last week." She shakes her fist again. "The bastard let him off scot-free. Just a few tests, nothing else. Wait till I see that bastard." She sniffles and wipes her nose.

"That's something," says Father Max. "A vision. If you have one about me, let me know."

She glares at him.

"Sorry," he says.

Vera swats the air dismissively. "Go ahead and call Carmine. I'll be okay."

"I'll check with Louise, too," he says, "and the doctor. How's that?"

Vera just sits there and whimpers quietly, occasionally rising to a thin wail of a crescendo. Her chest feels like a block of cement, and no amount of crying seems to break it up. In the middle of a long desperate rattle of a cry, the Lord says, "Hold your daughter's hand, Vera."

Vera doesn't feel the least bit like listening to the Lord, but she does crave the warm flesh of Mia's hand, the long, elegant fingers, the dazzling diamond ring, the perfectly French-manicured nails. She plays with Mia's ring finger for a second, sliding the ring up and down. Then she rises from her chair and holds Mia's hand firmly between hers. "Wake up," she whispers. "Wake up my darling daughter." A flash of warmth rushes down her arms, through her hands, and into Mia's.

Mia's lids pop open like the glass eyes of a baby doll.

"Oh," says Vera. "Oh my." She looks at their mingled hands and says, "Mia, can you hear me?"

Mia half-nods. "Oh, thank God," says Vera. "I've been so worried."

"Mom," she whispers, "is Dad...? He isn't...?"

Vera swallows hard. "Yes," she says.

Tears run out of Mia's eyes. "I did it. I shouldn't have..."

"Not at all," says Vera. "I'm sorry you had to bear that burden all these years."

"Who's with him?" Mia asks.

"Louise."

"Go, Mom. Please? Please go to Dad. He needs you."

"You need me," she says.

"I'm so...dizzy."

"I'm just going to get the nurse," says Vera. "Stay awake, Mia. Please."

Mia nods.

Vera retrieves the hall nurse, who says that Father Max has already spoken to her and the doctor is on his way. Along with Father Max they discuss the best way to handle the situation. When the doctor arrives, they decide to stabilize Mia for a few days and hopefully release her for the funeral services, provided she is accompanied by a nurse. Afterwards, she will enter the rehab center. Vera is satisfied with these arrangements, and Father Max drives her home.

Vera doesn't want to go home. She doesn't know what she'll find, or maybe she does: an empty house. A silent, empty house. But as they round the bend onto Destiny Drive, she sees that cars are still parked outside—Louise's and several others. And when Father Max assists her inside, she discovers that her house is filled to the brim with...Martha's.

Margaret Vitella rushes to her side. "Sit down, dear," she coos. "You look exhausted."

Marian Boyle sets up a cup of tea and a piece of buttered toast on a tray table with a lace napkin and a pink carnation in a bud vase. She sits beside Vera and urges her to eat. "Mr. Sweeney from the funeral home will be here in the morning," she says. "But there are plenty of decisions to be made before then. You need your strength, Vera. Eat." She lifts a piece of toast and hands it to Vera. "We've put a sample liturgy together for you, Vera, and you can tell us what you like and what you don't. We just didn't want you to have to compose the whole thing from scratch by yourself."

Vera shudders. "I don't want to do anything," she says.

"We can do it for you if you like," says Marian. "We'd be happy to, but maybe you could tell us his favorite hymns, Bible passages, and whatever else strikes you."

Vera sighs. "I can't," she says. "Mia..."

Louise rushes in. "Oh Vera, how is she?"

"Sick."

"But she woke up," says Father Max cheerfully. "She's on the mend. And ladies, we need to find somebody to take care of Mia at the funeral and burial. A nurse."

"That would be me," says Debbie Murphy.

I—thinks Vera, but she is too tired to correct anyone's grammar.

"I'm a nurse," says Debbie. "I work in the addiction ward at Canaan General."

Father Max smiles, "Now we're getting somewhere."

Vera excuses herself to go sit on the guest bed where Monk had last slept. She buries her face in his pillow and breathes in his musk. She picks a stray hair from the blanket and runs it through her fingers. Choked with tears, she scans the room for other signs of him and it is then that she spots a piece of paper folded on the bureau. With great apprehension, she unfolds it and reads.

Dearest Vera,

I am so ashamed. I never wanted you to find out about that woman. She meant nothing to me. What in the world was I thinking, risking you, risking Mia, and for what? You won't talk to me, so I'm writing. Please talk to me, Vera. Please please forgive me. You mean everything to me. Please talk to me, Vera.

Love, Monk

Vera holds the paper to her heart and weeps until she collapses in the bed, where she sleeps for hours.

For days, Vera's house hums with activity. As upset as she is to be overcome with Martha's, one by one their kindnesses mount up and eventually, overwhelm her. The way they fluff her pillows, warm her tea, rub her feet, fill-in the silent, empty spaces of her home and her psyche. Why, who in the wide world has ever taken care of Vera this way before? No wonder Louise surrendered to them. Who wouldn't?

With the Martha's here, Vera does not have to do a single thing, barely has to function. Though she knows the morning will bring new challenges—for one, she'll have to pick out a coffin. Oh my God, she thinks, a coffin. Monk in a coffin. And a vivid image of Monk dancing the mashed potato in his little cage dance routine flashes before her, setting her off in a crying jag she does not recover from for twenty minutes. The Martha's wrap her in a blanket and surround her with a chorus of 'oo's' and 'there there's'. Louise helps her upstairs and tucks her into bed. It is only then that Vera realizes that Louise's wrist is still set in a soft cast.

"Oh," Vera sighs. "Your hand."

Louise nods. "It's nothing. Forget it."

"But does it hurt?"

"If it doesn't get better by next week, they're going to operate again, maybe use pins. That'll help."

Vera takes the injured hand gently between hers, looks up into Louise's eyes and says, "I'm sorry, Louise. I was full of my own troubles, and I'm sorry."

At that, a searing heat shoots through her, cobalt light surrounds their mingled hands; they are shocked with a powerful jolt then all at once unplugged with a shudder. Vera's eyes lock with Louise's, and they drop their hands to their sides.

After a minute of silence, Louise lifts her hand and stares incredulously at Vera. "Oh my God, it's healed. My hand is healed!" She shakes it vigorously, moves over to the table and lifts anything...a lamp, a dictionary, a basket of laundry. "It's healed," she says in a whisper. She blinks rapidly as she stares at Vera, who is overwhelmed with exhaustion, and falls asleep.

Chapter Thirteen

Father Max stands thoughtfully at the podium. He takes a deep, cleansing breath, and says, "Monk Wright was a good man. A good husband and a good father. He was a good son, and a good friend. He was a good employee. A good teacher and a good coach."

Vera squeezes Mia's hand and turns around to take in the hundreds of mourners—students, wrestlers, army buddies, neighbors and relatives. She dabs her eyes with the never-ending supply of tissues handed to her from the row of Martha's seated behind her. Monk would love this, she thinks, and then wonders if he's here. Are you here? she telegraphs. Oh, Monk, are you here? She turns back around to face the altar before she loses control and starts sobbing again. She can't sob, not with Mia here for only the day. Mia is flanked by Vera on the left and Debbie Murphy, the Martha nurse, on the right. With the help of God, Debbie will take Mia right back to rehab after the services.

Father Max continues, "I've heard a lot of stories about Monk from his students and friends." He pauses. "I heard he likes to win wrestling matches for one thing."

A snigger swells up in the congregation.

"Oh yes, Monk Wright enjoyed winning alright. And he didn't mind working for it, either." Father Max takes the microphone off the podium and walks to the center aisle. "I heard that Monk saved more than one child's life at that school. Am I right?"

A huge wave of applause crests and dissipates.

"Apparently he wasn't afraid to walk into a burning building to pull an unconscious student more than two hundred feet to safety. I don't know if I could do that, do you? That's the sort of thing we can never know, even about ourselves, until the circumstances are presented. And then, in the heat of the moment, we either run in...or run out. We know what Monk did. He ran in, didn't he? Put his own life at risk. Monk Wright had what I call deep character. He was a hero."

Father Max tilts his head and smiles. "He did a few extraordinary things and lots of ordinary things. For instance, he liked to make bacon and eggs for his family on Saturday mornings. He never missed Sunday Mass. He kept his trusty old Suburban truck a stinky mess. I know—I smelled it once."

More laughter.

"He played a mean air guitar to 'Mustang Sally', and he loved to dance the mashed potato, am I right Vera?"

Vera nods. The giggling in the crowd makes her giggle a little, too.

Father Max moves down a step. "He was a family man. He adored his wife, Vera, and his daughter, Mia, more than anything in the world."

Mia buries her head in Vera's shoulder and whimpers. Vera pats her daughter's head.

Father Max gazes out. "More than one of us is probably wondering why a loving God would take the life of a man like this...such a good man with so much to offer the world. With so much vitality. And such a generous heart." He lets this idea settle for a second. "Before we ask why God decided to take the life of this good man, maybe we should ask why God decided to put this good man on the earth in the first place. Faced as we are with his absence, it's a whole lot easier to see how downright holy his life really was. And your own life, for that matter. And mine.

"That's right—every blessed ordinary minute of Monk Wright's life was holy. He was made by God for God, and he lived his life out on this earth under the close watch of his Lord and Creator. He made some mistakes; he wasn't perfect. Perfection is not what makes us holy. Getting back up and trying again—that's what makes us holy." He takes another step down.

"Monk was a humble man. Not that he wasn't given to sportsmanlike bravado now and then."

Another burst of laughter.

"But humility isn't about degrading ourselves, imagining ourselves to be less than we really are. Perhaps we like to think of ourselves as insignificant, because then we can expect less of ourselves. Yet, the truth is—God expects a lot of us. He expected a lot of Monk." Father Max sweeps his arm from right to left. "And judging from this body of witness, I would say that Monk Wright delivered on the Lord's expectations. Wouldn't you?"

Applause and a few cheers.

He strides to the left. "Monk was important; still is important. And so is his family over here. And so are his students and his colleagues. His relatives and his friends. Monk was important not because he died, leaving us bereft. The degree of bereavement is not the only measure of a man's importance. No. Monk was important because he lived.

"Brothers and sisters, let me tell you about a miracle. Are you listening?" He pauses. "The miracle is that one day God decided to focus his omnipotent energy on some specific and unique qualities he wanted expressed in the human family, and that energy, which we call pure love, was channeled so powerfully into a focal point that it crystallized into matter, and eventually became Monk Wright. Monk's parents, in cooperation with His divine grace, became co-creators with God, bringing this holy man into our midst. As your parents did for you, and mine for me. But make no mistake about it; we are all comprised of the super-substance of the Lord. He is with us and in us and around us every living minute of every day. We are his living temples. When God says he will always be with us, he means it not just in an abstract spiritual sense, but in a real and tangible sense." He leans forward. "He is part of our very... cellular ...makeup. Now that, brothers and sisters...is a miracle."

Father Max sighs deeply. "Like Monk, each one of us is not only important, but critical to God's plan. We are far from insignificant, as you can see Monk was far from insignificant. From the grief in this church, it is easy to see that the breadth of his significance is so great that we can hardly bear the loss of it. I shouldn't say the 'loss' of it, because it is actually not lost; rather, it is transformed. Still, his material expression is gone. But his spiritual expression is not, as it can never be, because matter does not arise from nothing, and energy cannot be destroyed. Only changed.

"Rejoice in the knowledge that this father, husband, friend and colleague has returned to the One who created him in the first place. That the One who created him loves him perfectly—far better than you or I could ever have loved him here. That he is surrounded by love and grace and his every need is met instantaneously, because he has been brought beyond time into eternity, where we shall all meet up with him again.

"So be happy for Monk Wright, whose holy mission has been fulfilled, who has been called home for his reward. Be happy for him, because as surely as I am standing here in front of you— with the help of prayer and grace—at some point in time each one of us will be following Monk to that same destination. May his journey be a peaceful and a joyous one. May God bless his immortal soul, and the immortal souls of each and every one of you here."

Father Max returns to the altar, replaces the microphone, bows before the Crucifix, and resumes Mass.

Vera is reminded of a dim vision, a dream perhaps, of her parents, specifically her father, who continues to struggle in the afterlife. Is it true, she wonders, that Monk's every need will be met instantaneously? She must remember to ask Father Max about that, because she would hate to give people the wrong impression. For instance, shouldn't they assume he's in the worst possible situation and pray their hearts out for him? Oh Monk, she whimpers, and all at once her chest convulses with grief. Dear God, she thinks, please let it be as Father Max says—please meet Monk's every need. Oh Monk, she prays, I forgive you. I forgive you.

Mia continues to cleave to Vera, boring into her neck and hanging on her shoulder. Vera's shoulder aches, not that she would say anything. This fragile connection with Mia is all she has left of a family, and she will milk it for all it's worth. Mia's dependency is something Vera will have to think about—dependent first on Vera and Monk, then dependent on Frederick, then on cigarettes, alcohol, heroin, and now dependent on Vera again. Had Mia ever been independent?

All points in the ceremony converge as the casket is flanked by Monk's friends, and the recessional hymn "Joyful, Joyful" resounds. Set to the music, "Ode to Joy", this is a hymn with Monk's name all over it. One of the few he genuinely enjoyed. Vera sniffles. He was so filled with life, so joyful himself, how appropriate to punctuate his life right here, on this hopeful note.

She leans against the back of the pew to stand up, and files out slowly with Mia beside her. Mia hobbles on her fashionably spiked heels, her swollen eyes covered by the black net veil from her exquisite wool broad-brimmed hat. Her slim body is dressed in the most elegant black wool, cut asymmetrically with pearl buttons. Vera barely knows what she herself is wearing, but she knows what Mia has on. Mia has that kind of draw. All eyes are always on Mia. She is such an elegant creature, even now, hanging onto Vera's arm as she is, bawling and bawling as she coughs up a decade of regret.

Vera loses sight of Mia for fifteen minutes as they are both consoled by fellow mourners. Later, she searches the crowd for her daughter to join her in the limousine. She places her hand like a visor over her eyes to cut the noon glare, and spots Mia standing with the nurse, Debbie, all of them arguing with a tall, dignified looking man, whose face is too shadowed to identify. Vera watches as Debbie yanks on Mia's elbow, and Mia resists. The man places his arm around Mia's back proprietarily. Vera steps forward slowly at first, then breaks into a near run as she realizes that the man is Frederick Tophet. What in the world is Frederick Tophet doing here?

"Oh, Monk," she says reflexively before she realizes he is dead. "Oh my God," she says under her breath as she makes her way through the crowd to Mia.

"Mia," she calls sharply as Mia is walking tentatively away, Debbie trailing her anxiously. "Where do you think you're going with that man?"

Frederick turns smoothly around and smiles. "Vera," he says, "don't you think you might have told me where you took my wife?"

Vera glares. "Don't you think you might have called to find out?"

He raises his chin. "Well, we're on our way to the burial," he says. "We'll see you there."

Vera grabs Mia's arm. "She's coming with me in the limousine."

"We have our own limousine," he says.

Vera stomps her foot. "She's not going with you."

He takes Mia's elbow, and starts walking away, but Vera runs in front of her daughter and stares through the black net veil into her eyes. "Don't you dare go with that man," she says.

Mia whimpers, "Mom..."

"Don't worry," Frederick says to Vera, "I'll take care of my wife."

"Is that right?" says Vera, on his heels. "Will you take care of her the way you have been taking care of her? The way she got sick in the first place?" She grabs onto his coat and pulls. "I'm talking to you," she says.

Frederick spins around and points at her. "Let's be perfectly clear about this," he says. "Your precious daughter here got sick all on her own."

"Why didn't you take care of her? Why didn't you put her in rehab?"

"She has a mind of her own, if you haven't noticed."

"She's going directly from here into rehab," says Vera. "Directly."

"She's going back with me to the city," he says, "where she can get the best care."

Vera's shoulders sag. "Mia?" she says. "Are you going to let him do this to you? You do have a choice, you know. It isn't his choice. It's yours."

Mia just stands there and weeps, and Vera sees that Mia has no emotional resources at her disposal. She will align herself with the strongest force.

Frederick pats Mia on the arm, turns slightly and says, "Oh yes, and Vera... so sorry about your loss."

At that, Vera runs in front of him and socks him in the stomach with the one-two boxer's punch Monk used to practice on the punching bag that hangs in the basement. "I'll show you... you..." she says. Right pow. Left pow.

"Ooogh," Frederick says, bending over. He straightens up. "Just kidding," he says and shoves Vera aside. She backs up and falls into a nearby rhododendron.

Louise and the Martha's are instantly at Vera's side, helping her up, brushing her off, and fussing over her hair. A few of the larger members of Monk's wrestling team pick Frederick up by the elbows and carry him to his limousine, ordering the chauffeur to drive the son-of-a-bitch out of there before he needs a casket of his own.

Mia, a sodden mess, is escorted by the same team members into the limousine with Vera, Louise, and Debbie, the nurse. Vera is reeling with rage and grief so huge as to suffocate her. Louise strokes her head with one hand as she holds Mia's hand with the other. "Monk would have loved what you just did," she says to Vera. "He'd have been real proud of you."

This is so true, it makes Vera smile.

At the cemetery, Vera lays the last velvet-red rose on her husband's casket and walks away with her head down and her heart like a rock sinking so hard and so fast as to virtually drag her into the grave with him. Since her parents' deaths, she had forgotten how very physical the death of a loved-one is for the survivors. As if victim and survivors are made of the same substance, no one possessing the skills to separate one from the other, even in death. And so, over time, this great tearing occurs—ripping and tearing and frayed fabric. How will it ever be mended, she thinks. Who will ever be able to repair these ragged seams?

She rides with Louise and Father Max back to the hospital rehab with Mia. Vera is feeling so bad herself, she wishes she could check in with her daughter for a few months' rest. But this is not possible. Vera must stand on her own and face her life without Monk. She must be strong. She hugs her daughter, and then watching Mia walk down the long corridor into a vanishing point, the doors close, and Vera is relieved. No one can contact Mia for three weeks, and that includes Frederick.

For Vera, the weeks after Monk's death are suspended in time. She feels as if she is freefalling through deep space, hemorrhaging fear. Her anchor is gone. How could he have left her like this? And where exactly did he go? And how dare he leave her in a state of unforgiveness. "Where are you, Monk?" she asks every night before she tucks in for a restless sleep. "Where are you, Monk?" she asks, already weeping, every morning as she opens her eyes. Although she, more than most, believes in the afterlife— even has contact with it at times—the disappearance of Monk is another matter. Where is all that energy hiding? And oh, how she misses him! The only relief she has is in the knowledge that Mia has been returned to her. Mia, whom she will finally be able to visit tomorrow. And that leaves her with another question: was Monk's life traded for his daughter's? Was such a thing possible—a bargain made on a spirit level between Monk and God? If so, leave it to Monk to make the sacrifice.

December 18—The Lord tells me to hang on, and I am hanging on, just barely. It is almost Christmas, and I have bought no gifts, and made no money either. I don't care about anyone's hair or makeup. I don't even care about my own. My gray roots are an inch long; Louise's are even longer. Good friend that she is, she says nothing. At some point she will have to go to another stylist, because I am not in the mood to mix chemicals for the sake of anyone's vanity, even hers. If my own hair grows to my feet and trails behind me like a veil, so be it. So what. Who cares? If I had whiskers on my chin I would grow a beard.

All is not lost, however, for in taking Monk, the Lord has returned Mia and Louise to me. He even used me to heal Louise's wrist, although he certainly did not need me to do that. The Lord does not 'need' us, I don't think. Or does he? Maybe certain people can only be reached through other humans. After all, would Louise really be healed if a supernatural entity, (such as those who have seen fit to invade my life), bolted out of the ceiling into her arm. I mean, it's possible that such an event would heal her wrist, but I can almost guarantee you that in the process it would also send her straight to the funny farm. Louise is not the most grounded individual I've ever known.

Anyway, the Lord showed me in the simplest way how forgiveness works—how we can all be healed by acknowledging our faults and sincerely begging pardon. For wasn't it Love itself that ran through my arm into Louise's wrist? Love that healed us both? So why then, I wonder, didn't the Lord give me time to forgive Monk? Couldn't he have waited one more day? One more hour? I would have forgiven him; I'm sure of it. I would have told him I hated him, hated what he did. And not only that, but how dare he disrespect us like that—Mia and me—right in the school, no less! Uh!!! But after the fuss, I would have forgiven him. I would have. I forgive him now. He was not proud of what he did. He suffered, and oh dear God, even died for the shame. Oh, Monk. Oh, Monk!

I'm glad Louise is healed, though, and I'm glad the Lord showed me the way to forgive her. But I myself do not feel healed. I feel injured. I do not sense Monk's presence around me, as I thought I might. I have seen spirits and angels of the Lord, but not my own husband. Father Max says that Monk is unconfined by time and space, and as a spirit, he is everywhere. No offense to Father Max, but I don't want Monk to be part of the 'wind that blows' and the 'sun that shines'. I want him to be Monk, and I want him to be with me. To tell me he is everywhere is to tell me he is nowhere at all.

I am trying to get my bearings in this chaos, but it is not easy. Were it not for Louise and Margaret, Marian and Debbie, and the other Martha's, I would never leave my house. They pick me up every morning for Mass, and bring me back home afterwards. They take me shopping, and bring me casseroles. I was wrong about the Martha's. They are not superficial church ladies. They are real heroes. They knocked on Rhoda Preston's door last week and talked her out of the lawsuit. They laid a magnificent blanket of Christmas greens on Monk's gravesite and drove me to the Stone Yard Company to choose a monument. In the morning they will take me to Mass and then Louise will accompany me when I see Mia for the first time in three weeks. That's friendship you cannot buy. It's the Lord's way of providing me with what I need, though it certainly is not what I want. What I want is Monk.

Yours buried in grief, Vera Wright

It is a gray, overcast morning, snow flurries sprinkling here and there. Brrrrrrr, it's a cold one, Vera thinks. She feels some level of actual excitement today, because today she gets to see Mia unspoiled by alcohol and drugs. The doctors had given Mia a shot of something or other to get through the funeral. They couldn't send her cold turkey into that kind of raw pain. Vera was not discouraged by that, did not see it as a step backwards. She saw it for what it was—compassion.

But Mia is not on any drugs now, including alcohol. When Vera sees her, she will be only Mia, the real daughter Vera hasn't seen for who knows how long. Five years, maybe ten. Since early in high school, Mia had an affinity for tobacco and alcohol, though Vera has no idea when the drug use kicked in. At college, perhaps. Vera thinks it must have been hard for Mia bearing all that obvious beauty, attracting all that attention, for such a genuinely shy girl. In high school all the wrong people wanted to be her friends because her father was a popular teacher, and because she was so beautiful. What reasons are those for friendship, Vera thinks. Reason enough to go it alone.

But then of course, there was the incident with Monk and...that hippy. This realization stabs Vera in the heart. She wonders if Mia had come home and told Vera what she'd seen, what would Vera have done then? Would she have left Monk? She shakes her head. Oh, Monk, she thinks, how could you?

Vera dresses hurriedly in a plain black pantsuit, the same one she has worn a half-dozen times in the last two weeks. She only wears black these days; black suits her. Truth be told, it's amazing she dresses at all, never mind flopping around in a ridiculous bright color such as fuchsia or chartreuse, or even navy blue. How did she ever find those colors appealing? No, Vera's world is colorless for now, and for who knows how long. Maybe always.

Louise picks Vera up in her snappy Lexus, and drives her to the rehab center. Louise is all cheery and optimistic — all talk of Christmas and how the Martha's are going to invite Vera to this and to that. Louise's hopeful attitude, mixed with the snow and the bright colored lights and the decorated trees, lifts Vera's spirits considerably. It occurs to her how much Monk would want her to be happy and strong for Mia — strong for herself! And all at once she wishes she'd worn something slightly brighter — a dove gray, perhaps, instead of black. And she has a change of heart about her hair, as well.

"I should have dyed my hair and yours too," she says to Louise. "Not that I care, you understand. I don't. But Mia...you know how much stake she puts in style. I just...maybe I'll embarrass her even more than usual." She looks down at her lap. "Maybe she won't even want to be seen with me."

Louise finds a space in the rehab parking lot and removes the key from the ignition. "Let me tell you something," she says. "You've never really understood where Mia's looks come from, have you? They come from you. You're gorgeous now, and you always have been gorgeous. I'll tell you a little secret." She looks Vera straight in the eye. "Thirty years ago, your looks intimidated the hell out of me. I didn't think you would even want to be my friend."

"Oh, Louise," Vera whimpers. "How can you say that after all..."

Louise touches Vera's arm. "I had as much to do with that squabble as you did. And anyway, look at all the good the Lord has done with two snippy gossipers who felt superior to everyone in the church." She chuckles. "Why, he's turned us into Martha's!"

As they exit the car, Vera says, "I still hope they don't want me to clean, though."

Louise laughs. "Don't worry; they're far more concerned about how they figure into your psychic dreams. I'll be vacuuming long before you will."

"What in the world do you mean?" says Vera.

Louise beeps the lock with her key fob. "Well, just that they know you dreamed about Monk's death before it happened. Exactly the way it happened. That's amazing, Vera. Don't you think? Not to mention the way you healed my hand."

"I didn't heal your hand," Vera says. "The Lord healed your hand."

"Okay, but he did it through you. I was there, remember? It still freaks me out. You might not think it was a big deal, but it was. Margaret says you've been given the Spirit. Not just in one way, but in lots of ways. She says that's highly unusual and that we need to take care of you and pay attention to the way the Lord works through you."

Vera likes the sound of that—'they need to take care of you.' She needs care all right. But as they approach the lobby, Vera says, "I have to be honest, Louise. As far as I'm concerned, those were unique situations that will not recur."

"I'm just saying...the Martha's are not the least bit concerned about you cleaning the church, that's all. They want your spiritual guidance, not your elbow grease." She whispers in Vera's ear. "Margaret told the others you might be a mystic."

"Uh!" exclaims Vera. "Balderdash."

Louise shakes her head knowingly. "It's a possibility you may have to live with."

As they approach the reception desk, Vera straightens her posture and inhales deeply, praying for confidence. Louise signs them in. "We're here to see Mia Tophet," she says.

A large woman with unruly gray hair and a sunflower shirt-dress flips through the Rolodex. Her nametag reads, MILDRED. "Hmmm," she says. "Would that be T-O-P-H-E-T?"

"Yes, that's right," says Louise.

Vera brushes a piece of lint from her shoulder.

"I don't see her name here," says Mildred.

"Well of course she's here," says Vera. "She's my daughter, and we admitted her three weeks ago. This is our first visit. Maybe that's why you don't have her on the list. Maybe someone forgot to put her on the visiting list."

The woman turns in her swivel chair and consults a directory on the table behind her. "I don't see her name here either," she says. "Hold on." She picks up her telephone and dials.

Louise taps her foot and Vera digs through her purse for the doctor's number. If need be, she'll call the doctor directly. The help at these places is 100% volunteer, don't forget, she reminds herself. You can't expect a volunteer to have the scoop on every single patient and visitor.

"Oh, is that right?" says Mildred into the phone. "Okay then." She hangs up, purses her lips and says, "The ward doctor will be right out. Just have a seat over there."

Vera does not want to sit over there. She wants to beat up Mildred until Mildred produces Mia. But Louise takes Vera's hand and tugs. "Come on," she says. "They probably have to conference with you before she can be seen, that's all."

"Well I just talked to them yesterday," says Vera. "They said I could see her today, no problem. They said she was doing well."

Louise sits down primly, covers her knees with her skirt, and places her huge purse on her lap. She pats the seat next to her. "Come on," she says. "No sense worrying over nothing."

Vera grinds her teeth waiting, while Louise flips through an old copy of PEOPLE Magazine. "I didn't know Jennifer Aniston had a new boyfriend!" she says brightly. "I always thought she and Brad Pitt made such a fine couple back in the day, didn't you? I don't know who this new boy is...this...whatever his name is. But he's no Brad Pitt."

Vera does not give a crap about Jennifer Aniston, and she is not in the mood to listen. Thanks be to God, the doors of the rehab ward finally open and the youthful doctor appears in her smart-looking chestnut brown chignon and white lab coat. Why, she looks like a cover girl for Health Magazine. Vera is thrilled to see her. She stands and eagerly shakes the doctor's hand.

"Mrs. Wright," acknowledges the doctor, who then extends her hand to Louise. "Dr. Jasper," she says.

"Louise Lambert," says Louise with a nervous giggle. "Nice to meet you."

Dr. Jasper consults the chart and motions to them both to have a seat. She settles into the chair across from them, removes her glasses slowly and blinks. "I...um." She takes a deep breath. "I...uh. I don't know quite how to say this. I'm afraid your daughter left this morning."

Vera's jaw slackens.

Louise places her hand on Vera's arm. "What?" she says to the doctor. "Excuse us, what?"

"Yes, her husband came..."

"No," says Vera. "No. Don't tell me you let her go home with Frederick. I'm the one who admitted her here. Not him. Don't tell me this. I can't hear this." She places her hands over her ears.

The doctor crosses her legs and waits for Vera's hands to come down. "I understand, Mrs. Wright. However...Mr. Tophet is her husband and Mia is an adult. If she wants to abandon her recovery to go with her husband, there's absolutely nothing we can do to restrain her. It's her choice."

"But he has some kind of hold over her..."

"Yes, he does," says Louise eagerly. "He's a...a watchamacallit...a swami!"

"A Svengali," snaps Vera.

"That's right," says Louise. "A witch doctor."

Vera shakes her head. "A Svengali is not a witch doctor, Louise."

"Well, then what is it?"

"It's a..."

The doctor interrupts. "I'm sorry, Mrs. Wright. I know your husband just died. I realize how hard this must be."

"No you don't," says Vera quietly, and then feels her head cooking up a good head of steam. "You don't know how hard it must be. You can't possibly know what it's like to lose a husband and a daughter in a three-week period of time. Don't say you know, because you don't know." She stands abruptly and shakes down her right pant leg which has gathered some static.

At that, Dr. Jasper rises, too. "Let me know if there's anything I can do," she says softly. "But remember that recovery from heroin is extremely difficult, and the patient has to want it more than anything else in the world. She has to want it more than she wants her husband. More than she wants her father or her mother. She may be back, Mrs. Wright. Or she may enter treatment elsewhere." She turns to go, then looks back. "For what it's worth, her husband seemed to care. He said he planned to admit her to a facility closer to their home."

"He's manipulative," says Vera. "A dangerous man." She is suddenly deflated, and can't stay there a moment longer. She walks away in a stupor of grief. Louise walks faithfully beside her across the parking lot, neither one speaking. They drive for fifteen minutes saying nothing at all, and all Vera can think of is—if it can't be Monk beside me, thank God it's Louise, and thank God Louise knows enough to honor my silence. Vera wouldn't have banked on that level of sensitivity from Louise. Having known her for so many years, Vera would have bet any amount that Louise would be chatting up a storm about some irrelevant celebrity, or Stanley, just to keep a conversation going. Vera is happy for the silence, as engorged with pain as it is, because she does not want to pick another fight with Louise. And if she is preparing herself for anything right now, it's a colossal three-ring fight.

At home, Vera waves to Louise from the door, then locks the door and drops to her knees, consumed with tears. Tears and tears and tears. And more tears. How can the body produce so many tears? Where does all that liquid come from? She cries until she is limp.

Sometime later, she walks on her knees to the couch and empties her purse in search of the prayer card Margaret Vitella had given her yesterday. Saint Jude, patron of their parish, and even more appropriate, patron saint of hopeless causes. If ever there was a hopeless cause, it was Vera right here, right now. Maybe Saint Jude could help. Vera does not want to be like Judas Iscariot, surrendering to despair; she wants to fight it. She wants to reclaim her life. But she can't do it alone.

Finally, she locates the bent card in her wallet, but she can't read a word of it, so hunts through the pile again for her reading glasses, which she locates. She holds the card between her hands and reads it verbatim, "Dear Lord," she reads, "I am consumed with grief and dread..." This line is too true; it sets her off on another crying jag, though she continues to read through the tears. She cries so hard between big sucks of breath that she barely knows what she's praying. "Please come to the aid of this miserable sinner..."

And then all at once, she stops praying. Stops crying, too. All at once she has had it with tears, and had it with God. "Miserable sinner?" she says in disbelief, staring at the ceiling. "Is that what you really think of me? You think I'm a miserable sinner?" With gritted teeth and shaking hands, she tears the card hysterically into tiny little pieces. "There," she says, "how's that? That's what I think of calling myself a miserable sinner. I'll tell you what I am—I'm a hardworking woman consumed with grief. How dare you! Or anyone!"

She leans against the couch to climb off her knees, ransacks the bookshelves for her forgiveness book, and writes in big black block letters: ST. JUDE. And while she's at it: GOD. She barely knows why she wrote it; she has no real intention of forgiving either of them. Can't even imagine it. Miserable sinner that she is.

She looks to the ceiling. "You're supposed to be a PARENT," she says, spitting out the last word. "Down here where I live, a parent is supposed to care about his child." She raises her fist. "If I, as your child, have an obligation to you, then how much greater is your obligation to me as my parent?" She is onto something here, and her eyes are practically bugging out of her head. "Did you or did you not create us and leave us here to guess why? Why can't you just tell us—why?! Did you really put us here as a punishment? Because of an apple? It certainly feels like a punishment. Though I, myself, can't imagine punishing my children this way—banishing them to a life of loss and abandonment. Think about THAT!"

Now she is screaming and jumping around as nervously as a medicine man on the verge of a cure. "We don't know diddlysquat down here and you run around yanking this person from our lives and that! 'Here's some magic for you, child: stand by and watch as I make your parents disappear. Poof! Now Monk. Poof!' Who next?" she screams. "How DARE you treat your children like this?" And then more quietly, "How dare you."

Her eyes narrow as she stomps her right foot so hard a decorative teacup falls from the nearby shelf and shatters. Vera doesn't care about the damn teacup. She feels like picking up the sharp pieces and scratching herself with them. But she won't. She will try not to harm herself, though she does realize that in the absence of her ability to physically harm God, she is in some danger of harming herself.

"Let me ask you something," she says, jabbing her finger at the air. "Just how much more miserable would you like me to be? You give me freaky visions to warn me, and then in spite of that, you take my husband. You take my daughter." Her strength is returning. She can take on anyone today. She is a fire-breathing dragon. "Do you want me next? Is that it? You're not satisfied with my parents, my husband and my daughter? You want me, too? Well, go ahead and take me, damn it. There's no way to survive this punishment anyway. It's HELL! You can call it earth if you want, but it's hell. And furthermore...everybody down here knows it."

At that, a massive blinding gold light with shimmering flame-blue edges pierces the living room. There is no form to it that Vera can make out, but it is very much alive. It is hot and alive and in her living room. But Vera isn't scared. She is too damn mad to be scared. Still, the light is too hot and too bright, and she shields her eyes with her hands as she backs away to the staircase and collapses on the first stair.

Chapter Fourteen

Vera cannot hear the language of the light; it is no language she knows or could even be taught. And she, herself, cannot say for sure if her own mouth opens or utters an intelligible word. Still, there is an understanding between her and the light. Dialogue is clearly conveyed.

"This is not hell," says the light.

Vera is enraged by this lie. How can the light know whether or not this is hell? The light has no body to burn. In fact, the light itself produces so much heat that it's practically burning Vera! She can feel the deep flush in her cheeks, the sweat on the back of her neck, and the prickly heat on her arms. The light feels none of these things!

"You think it's not hell because you're not human," yells Vera. This last statement feels good to Vera—like a lit match against crisp, dry kindling. She is blazing with anger, and it feels a lot better than simpering fear. She will say anything she wants to this...whatever it is...this thing. No boundaries; no censors. And why not? This is her living room, and if the light sees fit to invade her space, she will damn well say what she wants to say. It's about time, she thinks, that somebody spoke up to the light.

"If you lived here with real flesh..." She pinches her arm to demonstrate. "You would know what pain this is. Not to mention mental anguish."

"This is not hell," repeats the light calmly.

"If this isn't fire then why do I feel like a marshmallow at the end of a stick! You listen to me if you want to learn something, whoever you are..." She points emphatically to the floor. "This is hell, right here, right now." She folds her hands over her chest, which is pulsing with pain. "This...," she says in a whimper, "is living hell." She breaks into tears and pounds her chest with her fist. "My husband is dead. My daughter is lost to heroin. My heart is tortured. How do you expect me to survive?"

The light shimmers more softly. "Loaves and fishes," it says.

She raises her chin.

"Bring him five loaves of bread and two fishes, and he will bring you a miracle."

Vera stares agape as the light surrounds her. There is a period of confusion, and the next thing she knows she is once again sitting at the office desk in her salon, scribbling on memo pads about this and that and who knows what else really, since this too, is a language she does not speak.

When it's over, she is completely spent. Her rage is an ember. She stuffs the papers into the desk drawer, thinking one of these days she will try to make sense of them. File them in a notebook by date, perhaps. Or maybe, (dare she even think about it?), show them to Father Max. She rubs her eyes and peers out the window, amazed to see that it's already dark. She checks her watch—5:00 PM. What has become of the day? What has become of her?

The phone rings a few times, and reluctantly, she lifts the receiver. "Hello?"

"Hello," says a musical female voice. "Is this Mrs. Wright?"

"Yes, this is she."

"Well, actually, I'm calling for Mr. Wright. Is he there?"

Vera freezes. "Um, no. Not at the moment."

"Well, would you mind giving him a message?"

Vera holds her breath.

"Mrs. Wright?"

She exhales. "Yes."

"Would you please remind your husband that he has an appointment with Dr. Guthrow tomorrow at 9 AM?"

"Dr. Guthrow?"

"Yes, that's right. For a stress test. He should wear comfortable clothes, because we're going to have him running on the treadmill."

Vera rubs her temples.

"Mrs. Wright? Are you there?"

"I thought...well, didn't he already..."

"Have the stress test?" prompts the caller. "Well, it was scheduled before Thanksgiving, but as you must know, Dr. Guthrow was called to an emergency that day and we've rescheduled it for tomorrow. At nine." She pauses. "Mrs. Wright?"

Vera cannot make her normal voice work, so she conjures up a formal pre-recorded voice from somewhere deep within and responds, "I'm sorry to report that Mr. Wright will not be able to keep his appointment tomorrow."

There's a pause. "I see, well...will you ask him to reschedule?"

"No, I'm afraid not."

"Um. Okay. Well, can you tell me why? Have his symptoms disappeared?"

Vera stares at the phone for a second or two. "Yes," she finally says. "They've disappeared."

"Because, you know, even if the symptoms improve, it doesn't necessarily mean..."

"He's dead," says Vera. "He died of a heart attack. So he can't come in, ok? He can't come in because he's dead."

The woman gasps. "Oh my...oh dear. Oh, Mrs. Wright, I'm sorry!"

Slowly, Vera replaces the receiver in the cradle.

Vera falls into a nearly drugged sleep on the salon couch without dinner. She is so utterly exhausted she can't even make it upstairs. She has no idea if she even locked the door. She doesn't care. She does not care about anything or anyone. Let the robbers walk right in. Who cares? She hopes they do. She hopes they steal every last thing. They can even steal her, although she feels as if she has already been stolen.

No sooner does she drift off to sleep than she is at the koi pond again with her mother, Regina, who is ever more youthful and angelic in appearance. She is as light and energetic as a hummingbird. Vera's face is immediately buried in her mother's chest, sobbing. Regina strokes Vera's hair over and over again.

"Where is he?" sniffles Vera. "Have you seen him? Where is he? I miss him. I want him. I don't think I can go on without knowing."

"He is in a good place, dear," says her mother.

"How can he be in a good place? Home with me—that's a good place."

Her mother gently pushes Vera's shoulders away so she can look her daughter in the eye. "If you knew what had become of him," she says. "You would never wish him back."

Once again, Vera is reminded of how weak her energy is on this plane, because she has to avert her eyes from the glare. Her mother's voice is thick and low, sound waves rolling through water, and Vera has to use all her diminished ether just to focus on her mother's words.

"Look at it this way, dear," says Regina. "On the earth we are all like separate drops of rain. We know what it feels like to be small and separate with just enough awareness to keep our own boundaries—to protect ourselves from being consumed by the other drops of rain."

"So what are you saying?" asks Vera. "Are you saying that now Monk is what? A puddle, a river? That he has rejoined the other dead drops of rain, never to be distinguished again? I don't want to think of him that way. Thinking of him that way is worse than thinking of him dead."

Her mother smiles and shakes her head slowly. "No, no, dear. Now listen carefully so you will get it right. So you will remember." She points her finger to a spot beyond the pond, where instantly, rain begins to fall in separate drops. All at once Vera and her mother are drops of their own, falling side by side. "This," says her mother, "is the consciousness of a drop of rain."

Vera does not like the feeling. It's scary and unpredictable. She has no idea which direction she is falling. She has no idea if she will collide with any other drops, though there are so many of them, it seems inevitable that she will. She tries to protect herself from the others, but this requires too much energy. She does not know when she will hit the ground, either, or where, or how much it will hurt. Will she end up in the koi pond or the grass? Or maybe, God forbid, the pavement? The uncertainty generates great anxiety. She does not want to be this or any other drop of rain.

Her mother continues. "When you depart the earth in good stead and with sufficient light and awareness about the truth of your Origin," she says, "you no longer possess the limited consciousness of a drop of rain." She points her finger again, and all at once, she and Vera are in a cloud, looking down on the rain, along with lightning and thunder, and magically, it seems as if the rain and the lightning and the thunder are happening right in their heads. As if Vera and her mother are causing the storm. As if they are the storm.

"Instead," says her mother, "when you pass to a higher plane, you bear the consciousness of that plane. In this case—the consciousness of the entire storm. But you are still you, Vera. Do you not sense me beside you? We are not the same, but we are one. Like this."

Vera is so happy sharing the storm with her mother. She has never felt happier. She is no longer afraid of falling, but instead, at this perch, is able to understand the sense of the rain and the need of the thirsty earth. And she is able to fulfill that need. So maybe now Monk is part of something larger, too. Something happier and less fearsome. Perhaps he, too, is no longer separate or alone.

"On this plane," says Regina, "you are still you, but not the false you. Not the earth-bound, limited selfish you. You are the real you. The true self. The true self does not fear unity. The true self knows that the only real joy is in unity. The lower self protects its boundaries. It does not want to share. It wants to control its own destiny and possess the whole storm by itself. It wants to remain separate, and spends all its time and energy doing so."

In the next minute, they are again seated beside each other on the teak bench. A magnificent weeping cherry tree cascades its colorful branches downward like the crinoline skirt of a Victorian ball gown, reflecting its glory in the crystal clear pond water. Vera doesn't remember this tree from her earlier visits. Perhaps now because she is more relaxed, she notices this and other phenomenon, such as the bejeweled scales of the jade koi fluttering beneath the surface of the pond. It's so peaceful she just wants to stay here. Then something occurs to her. "Why aren't you and Dad like the storm?" she says. "Why is Monk able to see that way, and yet, you and Dad are still—separate and alone."

"As I said, Vera, I'm waiting for him. He has a lot of waking up to do, and furthermore, he's waiting for you."

Vera sighs. "Then maybe I'll just stay right here," she says. "I'll stay and talk to him, convince him to move on. I'm done with my life, anyway. There is only sadness for me down there."

Her mother jumps to her feet. "You can't stay!" she says emphatically. "You exit on God's authority only, or there is worse hell to pay. And you, child, have much work to do yet."

Vera does not want to do any work.

"With Mia. And..."

"And what?" says Vera. She doesn't need any more problems than that. Mia is already more than she can handle.

Her mother paces for a minute then gets quite serious, but Vera is fading. She has very little time left here. "Find an interpreter," says her mother anxiously. "Find one fast. The world is about to change and the Lord is trying to warn you."

Vera is fading fading fading. "Where?" she says as she spins back to earth. "Who can possibly interpret those crazy sticks and circles? Why can't he speak to me in plain English!"

"Because..." her mother's voice fades to a whisper, "...then the authorities wouldn't know if the writing came from you or from God, would they? This way, there's no question."

"But, Mom..."

"Hurry!" says her mother, though Vera can no longer see her. The word echoes in Vera's head as she rolls over on the couch to a more comfortable position. "Hurry, Vera, huuuuurrrrrrry!"

In the morning, Vera is awakened in the salon by rustling and intermittent tapping in the main part of the house. She sits up, yawning, disoriented, and leans over to peek through the open door. A flash of royal blue fabric moving briskly from the kitchen to the living room tells her it is no robber. It is most likely Louise. Louise persists in wearing electric colors, even though Vera has told her a million times that as far as color is concerned, she's an "autumn", and winter colors don't really suit her. Oh well, that's Louise for you.

But that was the old Vera thinking, and all at once the new Vera is dragged headlong back into her real and present life as she realizes all over again and for the first time this morning that Monk is really dead. This thought drops from her head to her heart like mercury in an iceberg. How can this be, she thinks, rubbing her eyes. How can he just disappear like that? And like every morning after she's convinced herself that it's true—*Monk really is dead*—she has to force herself to get up. Force herself to do the most mundane tasks, such as brushing her teeth and showering. Force herself to eat and be polite to others. Force herself to breathe. She checks her watch: 9:00 AM. Well at least she slept for a change. How in the world did an entire night disappear like that? She hasn't slept like that since Monk died.

She drags her feet to the door and stands there until Louise notices her.

"Ah, there you are," says Louise. "Margaret!" she calls to the kitchen. "Our girl has risen!"

Vera can hear Margaret shuffling around in the kitchen. The smell and sizzle of smoked bacon and the fragrance of freshly brewed coffee waft toward her, and she is comforted by the familiarity of it. Louise hustles about in the dining room, setting placemats and cutlery on the table. "Would you like to take your shower before breakfast or afterwards?" asks Louise cheerfully. "Up to you."

"Um..."

"Whatever you want," repeats Louise as she organizes the place settings.

Vera notices that Louise's hair is in such disrepair, she has taken to wearing an old-fashioned cloche hat even indoors. Maybe today Vera will have the energy to color, cut and set, though she can't imagine it. Right this minute, the task of repairing Louise's hair is equal in Vera's mind to the task of building a suspension bridge across the Pacific Ocean. Vera points upstairs. "Shower," she mutters.

Louise nods and hands Vera a mug of coffee.

"How many are we for breakfast?" asks Vera.

"Just Margaret and me," says Louise.

'I', thinks Vera vaguely, with no real interest in pointing out Louise's bad grammar or anyone else's. These tiny details of life seem more like senseless ornamentation to her at this point. One less thing to obsess over—the erosion of the English language. As if it were ever her job to begin with. She takes her mug of coffee upstairs.

After her shower, Vera dresses in the only clean black clothes she owns—a pair of sweat pants and a turtleneck sweater. The outfit is ridiculous, she knows, but comfortable. And anyway, who cares what she looks like? Louise and Margaret would never notice, what with their own penchant for bad dressing. Vera fits right in to this motley group of women whose wardrobes have long outlasted their expiration dates.

Breakfast consists of Margaret's specialty—bacon and cheese omelets with a side of wheat pancakes and a glass of freshly squeezed orange juice. Way too much food for Vera, but since nobody badgers her to finish her portion, she doesn't care. "This is delicious," she says, meaning it, though she knows she will leave three-quarters of it on her plate.

"Why, thank you, dear," says Margaret.

Margaret's broad girth, covered in her favorite navy plaid suit, comforts Vera somehow. Reminds her—dare she draw the bizarre comparison—of Monk's substantial presence. Even Margaret's square hands are impressive, large, but in a way—gentle. The sizeable topaz ring is out of place in her otherwise sensible wardrobe—an old anniversary gift from Leonard, perhaps, her long-deceased husband.

"What about Mass today?" says Vera mildly. "Why didn't you pick me up?"

Margaret pats her lips with her napkin. "Well, dear, we tried, didn't we Louise?"

Louise nods with a mouthful of pancakes. "Mmhmm."

"But you were not to be budged," says Margaret in her husky Auntie Mame voice. She wags her index finger. "And I might add that we did not need our spare keys this morning, did we, Louise?"

Louise shakes her head, and after she swallows her food, says, "Vera Wright, your door was completely unlocked! Jack the Ripper could have marched right in! What in the world happened to you, falling asleep on the couch in the salon with your door unlocked?"

Vera ponders — should she tell them about her visitation? Should she just come clean and tell them everything? The light? The stick drawings? The dreams? And oh yes — it's coming back to her now — her mother's warning? She searches for an answer, but none comes. "I just...collapsed," she says. "I was just...I couldn't..."

"But nothing...scary happened, right?" asks Margaret.

"Well, I'm here," says Vera. "No one hurt me. No one stole anything."

"No," replies Margaret, "I mean, last night, before you went to bed like that...just collapsing on the couch...you weren't... you didn't have any...I don't know — visions?" She stares meaningfully at Vera.

"No. Just that I was, well..."

Margaret and Louise are both leaning in across the table. "Yes?" encourages Margaret. "We know you have certain...gifts," she says. "There's no point in denying it, Vera. Because the cat is already out of the bag and down the alley after the mice."

Vera is not sure how much of her experience is meant to be shared right here and now, so she leaves it at this: "I want to host a dinner." She looks from Margaret to Louise. "Serving certain foods," she adds.

Margaret straightens up and shimmies in her chair. "Is this little dinner your idea? Or 'someone else's' suggestion," she says, winking.

"Not exactly mine," says Vera quietly.

"I'll be right back," says Margaret, and she waddles into the kitchen. She returns a minute later with a pencil and a pad of paper. "Go on," she urges, pencil poised.

"Just that I am supposed to serve five loaves of bread..."

Margaret scribbles furiously. "Any particular kind?"

"Not really."

"But I mean...Wonder bread? Rye bread? Branola?" She taps her pencil. "Maybe home-baked? Louise, you have a bread machine, don't you?"

Louise nods eagerly.

"Just bread," says Vera. "That's all I know. Five loaves of bread and two fishes is what I was told."

Margaret drops her pencil, her jaw suspended. "Louise, did you hear that?"

Louise nods.

"Why, that's how the Lord fed the multitudes!"

"Yes, it is," says Louise excitedly.

"And our dear friend here has been asked to feed the multitudes as well." Margaret turns to Vera. "Who exactly is to be invited to this...feast?"

Vera shrugs. "I don't know."

"Well then don't you worry one bit about the guest list," says Louise. "Margaret and I will take care of it. Not to mention the place cards."

Vera's mind wanders for a minute and she is vaguely aware of a voice, which says, "Christmas Eve." Well, isn't that interesting? she thinks. The Lord has seen fit to reveal himself to her friends. Her burden is lifted—if she is a mystic, then so are they!

"Well," she says, plopping her hands face down on the table, "now that's a first!"

Margaret blinks. "What, dear? What's a first?"

"I don't get it," says Louise.

"What?" says Vera. "Don't tell me you've heard him speak before? Because that's the first time he's ever done it in front of any company of mine."

Louise and Margaret look back and forth from Vera to each other. Finally, Margaret says, "Done what, dear? Who?"

"Why, the Lord," says Vera, her voice trailing off in the end as she realizes that the other ladies can't hear him at all.

"The...Lord?" whispers Margaret in disbelief. She pats her hair in place.

"Well, what in the world is he saying?" asks Louise, breathless. "What does he sound like? I've never...I just..."

"Perhaps we should pray the rosary," says Margaret. She leans over for her purse. "I've got beads in here that were blessed at Lourdes."

"Not now," says Vera. "Maybe later. He was just telling me that the dinner should be on Christmas Eve, that's all. So, whoever is free on Christmas Eve is invited."

"Well, that would leave me, Doris, and Fiona," says Margaret. "Possibly Marian and Debbie. The others still have husbands to worry about." She places her big square hand over Louise's. "You still have Stanley to think about, Louise. I'm sorry. But if Vera says Christmas Eve—Christmas Eve it is."

Louise's face twists with conflict, her pursed lips moving unflatteringly to the left and to the right. Her unplucked, undyed eyebrows form a deep V. "Well, I'm not going to miss out on Vera's big miracle dinner on account of Stanley, I can tell you that, Margaret. Stanley can have dinner with his nurse. He can have a bag of squashed peas for all I care."

"Big miracle dinner?" repeats Vera slowly, as if she is hearing it for the first time.

"Well of course!" says Louise. "Why would the Lord ask you to serve five loaves and two fishes unless he wanted to perform a miracle?"

"I don't know," says Vera.

Margaret stands and begins to clear the table. "I'm so excited I can hardly stand it," she says. "Imagine being a character in the story of a modern-day saint."

"Oh no," says Vera. She puts her hands up. "Not me. Believe me. I'm just, I don't know...a convenient channel."

"I've read the stories of all the saints," says Margaret. "And believe you me, this beats most of them."

"Just as long as they don't pluck out your eyes like St. Lucy," giggles Louise. "Or...or stone you to death like St. Steven." She rolls her eyes nervously. "Not to mention what they did to Joan of Arc."

Margaret's eyes light up and she grabs Vera's wrists and turns them over. "No stigmata," she says. "Oh well, not to worry, Vera. They didn't all have the stigmata."

"Please," says Vera, "I'm just telling you what I hear, that's all. Don't expect too much. It might be nothing. Just a nice tribute of a meal that doesn't sound the least bit appetizing to me, I might add." She lowers her eyes. "I don't want anyone to be disappointed."

"Too bad about them if they are!" says Margaret. "You've got an inroad to the Lord. The rest of us will just have to keep our minds open, won't we? I'll remind the others to do the same."

"Maybe just tell them to expect dinner," says Vera. "Not a miracle."

"I'll buy the food," says Louise. "One gift the Lord has given me is a big enough pocket book to fund bread and fish in almost any quantity."

"But only five loaves," says Vera.

"And two fishes," says Margaret, clapping her hands gaily. She cocks her head. "What kind of fish, do you suppose?"

Vera shrugs again. It occurs to her that the Lord is really not great with the details. He leaves a lot of unanswered questions. This is where a female God would come in very handy, or an apprentice, such as Mary.

"Not to worry," says Louise. "We've got a few days to figure that out, now don't we?"

After the ladies leave, Vera has the notion to call Mia. From out of nowhere drifts this little flickering of an idea that perhaps Mia will be receptive to a call. After all, Mia can't just resume her old life, can she? Not after she's already admitted to her addiction. And what if Vera was wrong about Frederick? What if he actually did place her in a New York hospital, as he'd told Dr. Jasper? With a flash of optimism, she dials.

The phone rings three times, and then the answering machine picks up. "Hello, this is the Tophet residence," says Frederick's deep and elegant voice. "Mia and Frederick are not..."

"Hello," interrupts a raspy feminine voice.

Vera's heart jumps. "Mia? Is that you?"

"Just a minute." Mia lays down the receiver, and hacks a phlegmy cough. Then Vera hears her strike a match and inhale deeply on what she assumes is a cigarette, but who really knows? She is taking her sweet time getting back to the phone. After she exhales slowly, she says into the phone, "Who's this?"

"Why, it is I!" says Vera. "Your mother."

"Oh yeah, Captain Grammar." She draws on the cigarette again.

Vera is having second thoughts about this call, but pushes herself harder. "How are you doing, dear?"

"What's that supposed to mean?"

Vera's stomach drops. "It means, how are you feeling? No hidden meaning."

"How do you think I'm feeling, Mother? My father is dead."

"Mia..."

"Oh, sorry, that's right, he was your husband. I probably don't have a right to my own grief."

Vera sighs. "Of course you do."

"Frederick and I don't know what you were thinking...putting me in a...I don't even know what to call it...prison, would be the most accurate word." She inhales again. "What would make a parent do that to a child? What kind of motive, do you think? Jealousy? Frederick thinks you're maniacally jealous of our lifestyle."

"That's ridiculous."

"Call it what you want."

Vera sighs. "Is this how it's going to be, Mia? Utter self-deceit on your part? Are you telling me you have no memory of being chauffeured here of your own will to seek help for your addiction?"

"Uhhh," says Mia. "Frederick and I were in the middle of a huge fight. That's all it was. There's no addiction. I was just feeling...vulnerable, that's all."

"And you're not now?"

"No."

"So? What now? You go back to your old life, and I go back to my new one?"

"Look," says Mia. "Let's face it, you and I have had some difficult years. Dad..." Mia's voice crackles with grief, and Vera is hopeful that the idea of Monk will draw her back to Vera.

"Dad's gone," says Vera, "in one sense. But his presence is all over the place."

Mia grunts. Then after a very long pause says, "I know you must be hurting."

"As are you."

"But that doesn't mean we have to hurt together. We have different lives."

Vera stares out the window as tears stream down her face. "If you need me, call," she says. "Any time of day or night."

"Mom, I...I told you I was doing fine." Mia's voice catches again, and this gives Vera hope that somewhere at the end of a long umbilicus her daughter is still connected.

"I'd like to see you, dear," says Vera. "Hear from you. That's all."

In a whisper Mia says, "Just...right now is not a good time."

"Why?" says Vera, at the exact same time Mia hangs up. Vera sits erect in the brightly flowered chintz wingback chair in front of the picture window and keens for her daughter, and keens for Monk. She has no idea how she will ever live through this pain.

Twenty minutes later, on an impulse, she picks up the phone and dials 411 in search of Stella Wyste in Leesburg, Virginia. "Here's the number," says the attendant, and Vera scribbles it down. She stares at it for a full minute before she picks up the phone and dials.

"Hello?" says a female voice.

"Yes," says Vera in a deep put-on voice, "I'm looking for Stella Wyste?"

"This is Stella."

Vera panics. "I'm looking for the Stella Wyste that used to live in Canaan, New Jersey. Is this that Stella?"

"Why yes, it is," she says. "Who's calling?"

Her breath short and her heart racing, Vera hangs up.

December 20—I have been spending a lot of time feeling sorry for myself, and the Lord has basically told me to knock it off. The Lord, as it turns out, is a real taskmaster. Who knew? He tells me he has to be strict, that I need the spiritual discipline. Apparently he's got plans for me I'm in no shape for yet. Well, I can tell you one thing—I'm in no shape for his shape-up plan, either, or should I say—this spiritual boot camp. And I don't have to tell you that I have not even begun to forgive him for taking Monk, and have no immediate plans to do so. But let's face it, other than Louise and the Martha's, the Lord is all I've got, and I am completely under his thumb. I have to listen when he speaks to me, or he will work on me until I diffuse into vapor. Not to mention the rooms full of hot sparklers he sends to get my attention. What are they, anyway? Messengers of some sort, I realize, but...what? Spirits? Angels? Entities?

Yesterday, he said, "Vera, I want each of your dinner guests to write down her intention on a piece of paper, fold it, and place it in a bowl on the dining room table at Christmas Eve dinner." What confuses me is here the Lord goes to all this trouble, but still won't specify salmon or trout. White, wheat or rye. Not to mention that I'm not the best fish chef in the world, unless you're asking for a tuna salad, and I don't think that's what he intends. Oh, and please don't bring me a fish of any sort with a head on it, which is exactly what kind of fish the apostles served to the multitudes, according to the etchings in Margaret's old family Bible. But I'm leaving those details to Margaret and Louise. I'll be happy to intercede for the Lord, but don't ask me to gut a fish.

Oh yes, and the Lord told me one more thing, and this gave me hope. He said not to give up on my daughter. He said that I was "the only wick upon whom he would be able to light a miracle for Mia." That made sense to me, not to mention the perfect grammar. If I give up on Mia, then she is completely on her own. No wick, no oil. She cannot kick heroin on her own. And maybe in some way my faith in her and in God can keep that possibility alive—the possibility of healing her. Just me, quietly believing—not giving up. I'm thinking that this is the miracle he'll perform for me on Christmas Eve. It's the intention I will drop in the bowl. I'll serve the bread and fishes, and he will heal Mia through me. I am nearly giddy thinking of how much sense this makes. How could I have doubted the Lord? When he performs this miracle, I will cross his name out of the forgiveness book. I am ready to trade Monk for Mia—as if I have a choice. He's already taken Monk, so I may as well help myself to his peace offering.

In faith and hope, Vera Wright

On December 23rd, Vera drives to Mass by herself for the first time since Monk's death. She drives his Suburban, inhaling the cold sweaty funk of the torn leather seats with relish. What she wouldn't give to smell his neck again—his arms, his legs, his Clarabelle ears—all of him. Right after a workout, who cares? Oh, Monk, she thinks, gasping. What I wouldn't give to hold you for five more minutes. For one.

The insurance company sent her a check in the amount of $20,000 to replace her stolen sedan. But she doesn't want a new car yet. She wants to drive Monk's. She wants to pretend that he is right around the corner—purchasing a newspaper or a six-pack of beer, or that she is on her way to pick him up from school—la dee dah, nothing unusual. That at any moment, she will pull over to the side of the road, at a bus stop, perhaps, and there will be Monk, with all his wrestling gear, climbing aboard, ecstatic to see her, and she, him. She blots the corners of her eyes and thinks, is that too much to ask? How can that be too much to ask?

The roads are slick from a film of fresh snow, and Vera is driving cautiously, leaning up toward the steering wheel with her purse wedged behind her for support. She needed to get out of the house on her own—without Louise or Margaret or any number of the other Martha's who have been graciously escorting her to and fro. She cannot hide any longer. Louise and Margaret insisted on purchasing the provisions for tomorrow night's dinner, so Vera has been spared that task. But right after Mass, she has to shop for a few Christmas gifts for the ladies. Some fragrant candles, perhaps, or scented guest soaps. Something simple, but just enough to thank them for all their good will. She feels bad enough that Louise had to finally make an appointment at the Hairport for a color and cut. Vera just couldn't do it, not yet. Such a useless, vain career. She may never do it again. Who knows? Who cares?

As for her own hair, she's letting it grow as long as it wants to grow in whatever color suits it, though the dark pewter color ages her skin. Vera doesn't care. She's had it with caring. It's impossible to keep up with her body anyway, the way it inexorably digs its own ditch deeper and deeper every day. Cellulite here; calluses there. Random whiskers in the most inconvenient and appalling places. Skin tags. Think of the hours and hours she'll save just by letting her body do whatever it damn well pleases. Why, it can slip all the way down the sliding board of dignity and splatter on the pavement for all she cares. And without Mia or Monk in her life, the color of her hair seems a ridiculous matter altogether. Perhaps she will care a great deal more about it once the Mia miracle has been performed at tomorrow night's dinner. She can't say for sure, but it's possible. Anything is possible where the Lord is concerned. At least this is what she tells herself.

In the church, Vera settles into her seat before the others arrive. The altar at St. Jude's is draped in festive fans of holly and evergreen; tiny white lights are strung on the rafters and the choir loft. Poinsettias line the side altars in a riot of holiday red. A towering Christmas tree in the corner is tied with hundreds of tiny red and green velvet bows. Vera herself tied fifty of those bows in between sips of eggnog and the odd gingerbread chocolate drop cookie baked by the Martha's special Christmas committee. What was her problem, Vera thinks now — all those years she mocked the very women who were laboring to transform her church into an inspiring temple of worship? Vera inhales the invigorating fragrance of pine laced with the scent of myrrh and frankincense, and thinks, were it not for Mia, she could die right here right now. Could there be a better death than this?

For reasons she cannot figure, this Christmas season more than any other is stimulating a glorious pageant of nostalgic childhood memories: she and her parents in church on Christmas morning; her mother and she in matching navy coats, velvet collars, broad-brimmed hats and white gloves; Vera's shiny black patent Mary Janes over the dainty white socks with the lacy fringe. Her life has been a good one, but she has possibly had enough of it. And anyway, now Monk is gone. According to her mother, Monk is like a great storm in the afterlife — a hurricane or a tornado perhaps. And here she is — a meaningless drop of passing rain, crashing daily onto the hard ground. She doesn't want to be a meaningless drop of rain fighting for her territory, scared of falling and hitting the pavement. She remembers her mother in that same dream, how peaceful she was. How amazing it was to have shared the storm with her mother.

She's ready to share the storm with her mother and with Monk. With everyone. She's tired of being alone.

Margaret and Doris file in on either side of Vera, and she feels safe now. Moments later, Louise and Fiona arrive, followed by Marian and Debbie. About ten minutes later, Father Max approaches the pulpit, and reads Zechariah's prophecy.

"Praise the Lord, the God of Israel, because he has visited his people and redeemed them. He has sent us a mighty Savior from the royal line of his servant David, just as he promised through this holy prophet long ago. Now we will be saved from our enemies and from all who hate us..."

When he is finished, he stares meaningfully at his congregation and says, "How much humility do you think it would take for an eternal God, an omnipotent and omnipresent God, to abandon his supreme position in order to submit himself to the life of one of his own creatures?" He surveys the room. "Hmmm? Anybody? No? Well, I would say infinite humility, wouldn't you? I would say...this is what is meant by the phrase, 'dying to the self'. One must be willing to die to oneself in order to rise to the greater good.

"Brothers and sisters, our God allows some of us to transform bit by bit. Others are asked to die to the self all at once. Either way, we cannot move beyond this plane without dying, both figuratively and physically. Let us all indulge in humility this Christmas season, so that we may become more like the Lord, who descended willingly into the cradle of humanity, suffering all the grievances of an uncomfortable existence, climaxing in horrific suffering and unspeakable death. All for us." He points around the room. "For Roger and Michael and Fiona. Marian and Debbie. Margaret and Louise. For you and for me. Isn't that something?" He sighs. "Isn't that everything?" He bows, and returns to the altar.

Vera is happy he did not go on and on today, although she loves his homilies. But this is plenty enough for her to digest, right here. Thanks to Monk, death and dying are the only things on her mind. Father Max basically said that some people are asked to die to the self in stages, and some are beaten to a pulp all at once. Vera is the latter. So be it. Today she will focus on the virtues of humility and self-sacrifice, as opposed to the panic she is beginning to feel about the loaves and the fishes and the miracle she is expecting beyond reasonable hope at tomorrow night's supper.

Chapter Fifteen

At six o'clock, Vera sits quietly on the wing chair in her living room, composing herself as the women begin to arrive in small clusters at the front door. To Vera, their energy feels restrained, yet potentially explosive, like a group of four-year-olds at an adult party who were warned ahead of time to behave. Vera smiles when it occurs to her that Margaret probably did warn the ladies to behave—no catty gossip, for instance. Margaret can be so bossy, Vera thinks, and yet, what would Vera have done without her? Why, the evening would have been a total flop at the Lord's expense.

Through her picture window, she has an impressive view of the night sky framed by the gathers of her worn woolen draperies. It is sparkling clear out there, and already stars and planets are decorating the black canvas of sky like tiny marcasites, forming the same patterns they might have formed on the evening the Lord himself was born all those miles away. All that time ago. Vera feels humble tonight. She feels holy and humble and scared. What are these women really looking for? she wonders. She knows what she's looking for—a miracle for Mia.

From her corner, Vera watches in amazement as Margaret and Louise graciously take the women's coats, serve the hot cider and cinnamon punch, make all the small talk— "Well now, isn't it lovely outside tonight, Doris?" "A very hopeful occasion, Gertrude..." It's as if Vera has turned the house over to Margaret and Louise, and why not? She does not even begin to have the stamina required to pull off an evening like this by herself. Look at the décor alone! Cedar branches line the mantle and the hall railing. Vera's elaborate crèche, inherited from her grandparents, has been installed in the fireplace, complete with cotton snow on the roof. When they were positioning it yesterday, Margaret said to Louise, "It doesn't snow in Bethlehem, you know. Just for your information."

Vera could tell Louise was confused by this news. Her face was screwed up like a pug dog while she thought about it. Was there snow in Bethlehem? Vera had to think about it herself. She and Monk always used cotton snow on the roof and on the floor, where all the little lambs were herded into a corner of the drift. Everybody used artificial snow on their crèches. Didn't they?

But Margaret persisted, "I'm just saying, Louise, I'll lay down the snow if you want, but it isn't authentic. It's not even mentioned in the Bible. You just think it snowed because it snows here. Not that it's snowing now. But it doesn't snow in Bethlehem, I can tell you that. You can call up the weather station if you like. If you need proof."

"I've always had cotton snow on my crèche," Louise said, then turned to Vera. "It's your crèche, Vera. Do you think it snows in Bethlehem?"

"Oh well, you know...Monk...loved the cotton snow," said Vera plaintively. The word 'Monk' caught in her throat.

Margaret blinked. "That's reason enough to use it, then."

And that was that — the only near-scuffle between them after days of working together. Vera is beginning to love these two the way she might have loved sisters had she been lucky enough to have any. All that easy companionship, and also, isn't it wonderful the way women take care of each other, she thinks. The way they wash the dishes without even asking. Make the beds. Do the laundry. All of it instinctual, matter-of-fact, and without discussion. Not to mention the decorations. In addition to the crèche and fresh fir bundles, there is a miniature imitation tree on a table in the hall. Louise placed it carefully on a linen doily and decorated it with ribbons of lace, tiny glass balls in every color, and topped it with a miniature porcelain angel. It occurred to Vera at one point that these festive touches might be a bit much — what with her mourning and all. But it makes the ladies happy. And the ladies bring Vera the only glimmer of happiness she is capable of at the moment.

Now Vera looks with affection upon Louise gaily serving punch in the emerald green silk shirtdress that hangs just above her ankle, two inches too long, not counting the fallen hem behind her left calf. Ordinarily Vera would have repaired the hem for her friend on the spot. But not now, because now...who cares? Vera's world has taken a continental shift, a hairpin turn. And anyway, if she were to repair Louise's hem, she would be avoiding the larger issue of the dress color, which is totally unsuitable to Louise's coloring, and also her new hairdo.

Vera doesn't know if the Hairport chopped off all the dyed portion of Louise's hair, (creating an unflattering pixie cut circa 1954), because they thought it would be a good idea, or if it had been done at Louise's suggestion. Whatever the reason, the result is as harsh and shocking as if the beautician had given Louise a buzz cut. Her hair is all straight now, and uniformly steel gray. Except for the substantial emerald clip earrings and the diamond elf pin on her collar, she could easily be mistaken for a nun. Well, Vera guesses that being married to Stanley as Louise is, she might as well be a nun. And for that matter, so might Vera, who has not stopped wearing black since the day Monk dropped dead. And then, of course, Margaret, who has been widowed for so long.

All at once, Margaret claps her hands. "Hear ye! Hear ye!" she calls out in her throaty voice. "We have been called to a great feast by our dear friend and newly installed Martha." She turns to Vera and winks. "Shall we assemble?" she asks.

Vera nods wearily, and pushes herself up against the arms of the chair.

"Everyone, check your place cards before sitting," announces Louise importantly.

The table, which is really a series of smaller rectangular tables at the end of which is a reinforced but wobbly card table, is covered in one of Louise's amazing 120" Irish lace cloths. Minus the fractional drop at the end where the card table sits practically in the living room, the table as a whole is decorated beautifully, elegantly. Vera hates to admit it, (especially given Louise's history of no personal aesthetic sense — that is, aesthetic sense she could apply to her person in the way of hair, makeup or wardrobe), but the dining room has never looked so inviting. Why, it makes Vera consider Louise in a different light entirely.

Not that Margaret didn't contribute; she did. For one thing, she contributed her family's massive silver heirloom candlesticks. Also Margaret's doing — sparkly little votives in tiny red glass containers that illuminate each place setting. As large a woman as Margaret is, she enjoys fussing over the tiniest of details. A real paradox, if you ask Vera. For instance, the white cloth napkins are wrapped in strands of artificial holly — also Margaret's doing. And in the center of the table sits a magnificently carved wooden statue of the archangel Gabriel — a gift to Vera from Louise and Margaret. Vera had been embarrassed by the lavishness of the gift, having given the ladies each a simple crystal rosary blessed by Father Max. But Louise, as usual, would have none of that. That's Louise for you. She gives in proportion to what she has, not in proportion to what she gets from others.

When they are all seated, the Lord tells Vera to stand. She is so relieved to be getting some direction from him finally, that she says, "Amen," right out loud. Then she stands, breathing deeply for a moment with her eyes closed. At the Lord's direction, she says, "Everyone who is here is here because the Lord has called her to be here." She is half-listening to him as she speaks, and so is not in complete control. It is a very confusing feeling, but she continues. "Margaret," she says, pointing to her right. "Welcome."

Margaret smiles giddily and waves hello to the Lord.

"Louise," Vera says, pointing to her left. "Welcome."

"Why thank you," giggles Louise.

"Fiona, Marian, Debbie, Clara, Gertrude, Doris, Lily, Daniella, and Rosemary…" She nods. "Welcome to you all, and thank you kindly for responding so enthusiastically to the invitation."

The women fidget nervously.

"There are twelve of us," says Vera, though she herself had not really noticed the significance of this number until now. "Twelve women to take part in a meal of loaves and fishes—the first of what the Lord hopes will be many such suppers. Suppers that will change the face of the earth."

A chorus of "Ohhhhhh" is heard among them.

"Whatever does she mean?" whispers Fiona, who is seated at the far end of the card table extension. She blesses herself out loud, "In the name of the Father, and of the Son, and of the Holy Spirit. Amen."

"What does *HE* mean, you mean," says Doris. "She is speaking for the Lord, remember. He is speaking to us through Vera."

Vera's eyes are closed, her eyelids fluttering, as she continues unimaginably to listen to the Lord at nearly the same time she conveys his words to the ladies. "The Lord wishes to recognize you, the Martha's, in this significant way," she says, "because you are meek and humble as he was meek and humble. You never complain. You clean up joyfully after his people. No task is too distasteful. You are good and loyal servants of the Lord, and therefore, also of the Father. He wishes to recognize you in this way because it is his will that the first shall be last, and the last shall be first, and the meek shall inherit the earth."

"Well," sighs Gertrude. "Isn't this quite the shocker."

"Like the apostles," whispers Doris reverently.

"His true disciples were women, you know," states Margaret with authority.

"Blessed Mother of God," says Lily reverently, her hand to her bosom. "I'd never thought of us that way."

Vera opens her eyes and glimpses the wide-eyed faces before her as she retreats from the Lord's distant voice into her own mind, and sits down, exhausted.

At this, Fiona takes it upon herself to stand. "In the name of the Father and of the Son and of the Holy Spirit..." she repeats in her squeaky voice.

Margaret hunches forward. "Fiona, dear," she says. "What are you doing?"

"I'm blessing us," she says. "I think we need a blessing, don't you? This is a...large undertaking, and there are no men, no...priests to guide us." She opens her hands palms up as she stares meaningfully at Margaret. "Changing the face of the earth requires all the grace we can get." Her nostrils flare as she exhales, facing down Margaret in a clear challenge. "Wouldn't you agree?"

"A blessing is a good thing," says Vera, and reluctantly, Margaret retreats.

Fiona continues, "We ask the blessing of the Lord upon this evening, cutting off all inroads to the enemy. Amen." She juts her chin out and bug-eyes Margaret.

As various ladies parade to the kitchen and back with platters of food, Vera watches as Margaret nudges Fiona and says, "Fiona, just a reminder that Vera is in charge of this dinner. She was called upon by the Lord to serve it, and though I'm sure you mean no harm, it might be best if you left the blessings to our hostess."

Fiona raises her chin indignantly. "If what she is saying is true, Margaret, then we are all favored. Not just Vera. Blessings from us all are called for, don't you think?"

"Hmmph," says Margaret.

Once the feast is displayed on the table, it is quite impressive, really, especially to Vera whose only preparation was a day or two of meditation and automatic scribbling. Instead of getting five of the same loaves and two of the same fish, Margaret and Louise decided to present a variety. There is a loaf of rye, a loaf of white topped with sesame seed, a Parmesan Italian loaf, a loaf of honey wheat, and a loaf of pumpernickel. The broiled fish are beautifully filleted and decorated with parsley, although Vera notes that the Lord certainly did not mention any garnish. The two fish are one long pink salmon and a smaller, though hefty halibut. Something for everybody! No wonder the Lord hadn't specified, thought Vera. He left it up to the women's creativity. Or possibly he inspired them directly, leaving Vera to her own, more mystical assignments.

Vera leans over and whispers to Louise, and Louise, overjoyed, stands and announces, "Vera would like...well, that is...the Lord himself..." Overcome, she fans herself with her right hand. "Okay, let's start over." She spreads her hand against her chest and breathes in deeply. "Okay. At this time, the Lord would like us each to jot down a prayer intention and place it in the bowl on the buffet table before we eat." Hands to each cheek, she sighs with excitement, then shuffles into the kitchen for paper and pens. "Fa la la la la, la la la la," she sings as she distributes them.

On her paper, Vera scribbles, "Heal Mia," folds it, and drops it confidently in the cranberry glass bowl. When the ladies are finished, Vera passes her Bible to Margaret, and tells her the Lord would like her to read Matthew 14:13-21.

Margaret stands regally, shoulders back, and clears her throat. She lifts the Bible and reads, "As soon as Jesus heard the news, he went off by himself in a boat to a remote area to be alone. But the crowds heard where he was headed and followed by land from many villages. A vast crowd was there as he stepped from the boat and he had compassion on them and healed their sick.

"That evening the disciples came to him and said, 'This is a desolate place, and it is getting late. Send the crowds away so they can go to the villages and buy food for themselves.' But Jesus replied, 'That isn't necessary—you feed them.'

"'Impossible!' they exclaimed."

Margaret pauses for a sip from her water glass, and continues, "'Bring them here,' he said. Then he told the people to sit down on the grass. And he took the five loaves and two fishes, looked up toward heaven, and asked God's blessing on the food."

At this, Fiona clears her throat in an obvious way, while blessing herself silently.

Margaret purses her lips at Fiona, then continues, "Breaking the loaves into pieces, he gave some of the bread and fish to each disciple, and the disciples gave them to the people. They all ate as much as they wanted, and they picked up twelve baskets of leftovers. About five thousand men had eaten from those five loaves, in addition to all the women and children."

Margaret sits and they all look at Vera expectantly.

Vera smiles. "It's a real privilege," she says, "to share this act of faith with all of you."

Louise grins. "Shall we pass the food?" she says.

"Yes," says Vera. And as they tear the bread and pass it along, she hears the Lord's voice again and listens. Her eyes close and her lids flutter, and she says, "The Lord wishes to tell you that one of the intentions placed in the bowl will be healed tonight, and in fact, is already in the process of being healed, but this is not the miracle of the loaves and fishes. This healing is a reward for your faithfulness. There will be a healing at each supper."

As she withdraws from this dialogue, Vera can hardly sit still. She squirms and squirms, as many of them do, and then excuses herself and walks upstairs, as if to the bathroom. "Don't," says the Lord. But she does anyway—as soon as she slips into her bedroom, she dials Mia.

"Hello," says a brusque male voice, clearly Frederick.

Vera hesitates then proceeds boldly. "I'd like to speak to my daughter," she says.

"Oh?" says Frederick.

"Yes, I would, Frederick."

He clears his throat. "I, uh, really don't think you want to talk to her right now."

"Why is that?"

"She's…not in a good way."

"What's wrong with her?"

There's a scuffle with the phone, and then Mia says, "Hiiii Mooom," as high as you please and hangs up.

Vera drops her head, chin to chest.

"Have faith," saith the Lord.

Vera blots her emerging tears.

"Have faith," he repeats.

Vera would have let him have it right then and there were it not for the eleven ladies at the dining room table. "YOU have faith," she wants to say out loud, but does not.

Still, he knows what she's thinking and repeats, "Have faith."

She stares at the phone again, half-reaching for it, and finally, picks up the receiver and dials the number in Virginia.

On the third ring, Stella answers. "Hello?" she says brightly, then more suspiciously. "Hello? Hello?"

Vera just holds the phone, listening.

"Monk? Is that you?" she says. "I saw the caller ID. Why aren't you answering, Monk?" She heaves a long sigh and hangs up.

Vera walks to the bathroom and squirts a few drops of Visine in each eye before walking downstairs. As she enters the living room, the women look at her expectantly, and all at once Vera realizes that she has held up dinner. They have all been served but her.

Margaret points cheerfully to the platters of fish. There are a few pieces of salmon remaining, but only one tiny slice of halibut. "Which would you like?" she says.

"You choose," says Vera evenly.

Margaret smiles and muses to herself, "Well then, which shall it be? Hmm hmm hmm. How about...salmon!"

"Fine," says Vera, taking her seat.

"But if you give her the last piece of halibut," says Fiona, "we might see it multiply."

Vera frowns. She doesn't want to prove or disprove Fiona's suggestion, and since the Lord is not giving her his two-cents worth, she remains silent.

"She selected salmon and salmon it will be," says Margaret. She slices the tender meat with a stainless steel spatula, and lifts it ceremoniously onto Vera's plate.

Fiona clears her throat. "She didn't select the salmon, Margaret, you did."

Margaret smoothes her skirt beneath her and sits down.

"What exactly are you afraid of?" persists Fiona. "Are you afraid it won't multiply? Is that why you chose the salmon instead of the halibut? You're afraid there won't be a miracle after all? That all of this is just, I don't know, in Vera's mind?"

Margaret elbows Fiona and Doris taps her on the thigh.

"No one's afraid of anything," says Lily. "Just let the evening take its course."

Vera bows her head, "Lord, bless this meal. May the miracle of the loaves and fishes bring plenty to the far reaches of the barren earth," she prays, though she is not at all sure where these words originate.

This is followed by a chorus of 'Amens' after which they begin their meals. There is an air of great expectation, although nothing obvious is happening. As they all eat, they are also staring at the last piece of halibut. No one reaches for it. The room hums with platitudes about the presentation, the delicious taste, the brilliance of the idea, etc., but each is distracted in her own way. After they finish their small portions, Daniella takes a second portion of salmon, and passes the dish around. Tension mounts as the platter makes the rounds, the supply diminishing rapidly. The breadbaskets are also passed, but the last piece of halibut remains. And when the salmon dish is returned to the table, it is returned with a single slim slice in the center of the platter.

As everyone slowly finishes her fish and bread in silence, they all end up staring at the fish in the middle of the table. Finally, with a huff, Fiona reaches for the remaining halibut. She puts it on her plate and cuts it. They are all captivated. As Fiona takes a bite, Lily's and Daniella's jaws mimic Fiona's chewing motion. All that can be heard now is the sound of Fiona chewing. Squish squish, swallow. Squish squish, swallow. Almost triumphantly, Fiona stabs the last piece of fish with her fork, and places it in her mouth. Squish squish, swallow. But that's all. She simply chews the fish and swallows it. Nothing else happens. Absolutely nothing. No multiplication of halibut, not even duplication. Clearly intoxicated by the attention, Fiona then leans forward and helps herself to the last slice of salmon, sits back, and eats it in two huge bites. Nothing. No new salmon. No new halibut. Not a crumb of bread, never mind twelve basketsful.

When all the food is gone, Fiona runs her finger through the drippings and licks her finger, as if to emphasize the emptiness of her plate—the absolute disappearance of all signs of food, in spite of the fact that the Lord's name had been invoked. The ladies sink collectively back in their chairs.

A moment later, Fiona says, "I think there should have been a priest here. I think that's what was missing. Priests are ordained representatives of Christ. No offense, Vera...it was a good idea and all. But you're pretty much a novice to the spiritual life, wouldn't you say? I mean, you haven't even been a Martha for that long."

Vera feels something close to terror rising in her. What if Fiona's right? she thinks. What if it wasn't the Lord all along? What if Vera herself has been deceived? If this is really you, Lord, she prays, please don't let them leave without a miracle. Then all at once she says, "The Lord wishes us all to stop questioning him."

Gertrude and Clara turn, wide-eyed. Fiona stands, straightening her shoulders. "I have to use the bathroom," she says. "That is, if it's alright with...*him*." She raises her eyebrows at Vera then turns on her heels and walks away.

"Well!" says Louise with false gaiety. "That was a very nice and filling dinner."

"Indeed it was," says Debbie. But their disappointment is palpable.

"Maybe it's because we're all full," says Doris. "Nobody here is starving. So why would the Lord bother to miraculously produce new food for people who are not even hungry?" She looks around. "I mean...that would be wasteful. The Lord is not wasteful. Think of all the starving children in Africa. That's where fish are needed."

Gertrude turns to Vera. "I wonder what might have happened if we'd been a larger group? Say...a multitude?"

"A truly *hungry* multitude," agrees Rosemary enthusiastically.

Lily catches on. "Oh, you mean, might we have fed them all and still had leftovers?"

"Maybe not leftovers," says Marian, "but all would have been fed satisfactorily."

As Fiona returns, the Lord fills Vera's head and she repeats what she hears. "The Lord wants us to know that every time we reproduce this meal in his name, he will multiply our efforts to heal our loved ones in manifold ways."

They are all pondering this when Louise blurts, "I believe!" in a commanding voice. "I do believe that my friend here is filled with the Lord!" She pounds her fist on the table. "I believe that what the Lord says is truth. If you don't believe, you don't belong here."

"I believe, too!" says Margaret, raising her arms joyfully, and one by one they pound their fists, "We believe! We believe! We believe!" Except for Fiona, who, having returned from the bathroom, remains standing. Margaret walks over to Fiona, wraps her big fleshy arm around her shoulders and says, "Come on now, Fiona, we're one for all and all for one, are we not?"

Fiona picks Margaret's hand from her left shoulder. She looks Margaret in the eye and says, "Do not put false gods before me." Mechanically, she nods to the group then walks to the hall, where she pulls her coat from the closet. From there she says, "I think you all should just think about pride. The Lord warns us about it all the time. There's such a thing as a spiritual show-off, you know. Spiritual show-offs do not receive the favor of the Lord." She fastens the large buttons of her mohair plaid coat. "Merry Christmas," she says, and walks out the door.

Once she's gone, Louise throws her napkin in the direction of the door. "Spiritual show-off my ass," she says then mutters, "You're the damn spiritual show-off." Then her eyes open wide and she places her fingers over her lips. "Oops," she says, but Margaret and Doris are already giggling.

"I think we have to seat her in the actual living room next time," says Doris. "The card table isn't far enough away. Or maybe the basement. Do you have a basement, Vera?"

"She has a crawl space," says Louise.

"All the better," laughs Doris. "We'll seat her in the crawl space."

"Well, maybe that's the problem," suggests Rosemary. "Perhaps she didn't feel included."

Vera is having a very difficult time sitting upright at this point, because she does not know how much of Fiona's message was authentic and how much was corrupt. Spiritual pride is an issue, but then, it wasn't pride at all that brought these women together. It was faith! Not one of them, including Vera, is looking for power as far as she knows. As far as she knows, they are only looking to serve the Lord. Vera yawns deeply, but unsatisfactorily. Every atom in her body searches for oxygen.

The ladies chatter for a while then ask Vera when the next dinner will be, and this amazes her. "New Year's Eve," she says, echoing the Lord's words in her mind. Another supper on New Year's Eve is the last thing she wants to do.

"Wonderful," they all say more or less together. Then they clean up, hug their good-byes and tell Vera they'll see her tomorrow in church. Watching them leave, Vera wants to cry. If she were the Lord, she would remove the burdens of each woman, every burden they could name, and some they could not. "Why don't you do that?" she asks the Lord. "Look how loveable they are. How can you not remove their pain?"

Vera wanders back to the dining room table and stares at the cranberry glass bowl on the sideboard. She thinks that she should possibly respect the privacy of her friends and not read the intentions, but she is overcome with temptation, brings the bowl to the wing chair and sets it on her lap.

She unfolds the first paper. "Heal Emily's lupus," it says. Vera nods. This is a good one. Gertrude's daughter, Emily, has had lupus for ten years, and is now confined to a wheel chair. "Please find Roger a job," says the next one. Roger is Lily's husband. He's been out of work for four years. It occurs to Vera that Lily and Roger may be close to losing their home. "Feed my faith, Lord," says another, though Vera has no idea whose petition that might be. There are several others whose authorships are ambiguous: "Heal my nephew's depression." "Please bring my children back to the church." "Stop the abuse in my family." The last one gives Vera pause, but still, she is not familiar with the handwriting. And then there is Louise's intention, clear as a bell in her silky Palmer scrawl, "Liberate me from my petty life and give me wings."

Vera does a double-take on that one, because, well, that is just not the Louise that Vera knows. She looks through all the intentions again to be sure that no other handwriting can be confused with it, because in her entire life of knowing Louise, she has never so much as imagined Louise capable of expressing that kind of poetic need. "Liberate me from my petty life and give me wings." Well, aren't you something else again, Louise Lambert, thinks Vera, smiling. What a simple and unselfish desire — to be liberated from pettiness. Who would have thought? "Liberate her, Lord," Vera prays.

Next, Vera opens her own intention, "Heal Mia," and closes it again. Opens it. Folds it back. It isn't as if the Lord isn't aware of Mia's plight, she thinks. It isn't as if it's a big fat secret in the Kingdom. She convinces herself that the Lord will not let Mia slip through the cracks. Not as long as Vera believes. Not as long as Vera keeps the faith, exposes the wick that will allow the Lord's miracle to alight. And who says that Mia hasn't been healed anyway? Maybe she and Frederick were just in the process of one final fling.

Chapter Sixteen

"The Savior has come!" booms Father Max from the pulpit. He points to the colorful life-sized crèche on the side altar. "Do you believe it? I mean...do you *really* believe it?"

He removes the microphone from the pulpit and sweeps to the center of the altar in his cascading white and gold embroidered robes and says, "If you do believe it, and you understand why he came, then why do you continue to suffer? If he came to redeem us and to deliver us from suffering, then why do we still get sick? Why do we still die? If he died that we may live..." He shrugs. "Then why aren't we really living? Why are our lives so compromised with disease and corruption? Why are we all half-dead with emotional and spiritual malaise?"

He paces thoughtfully past the poinsettias and back, frowning, knuckles to chin — as if these thoughts are just occurring to him. As if he is concocting this homily on the spot. He is flushed and on fire — the way Vera feels in the center of a great supernatural inspiration. She's glad she made it to midnight Mass, though that was certainly not the plan. At home in her wingback chair she had been drifting to sleep, when all at once she found herself reaching in the front hall closet for her coat, climbing into the Suburban and driving to St. Jude's. She had intended to go to church with the Martha's in the morning. She sighs. Her life is not her own these days.

Father Max continues, "It occurs to me that each of us is like a child learning to ride a two-wheeler without training wheels. As long as we think the Lord has his hand on the back of the bike and is running alongside, we believe we can't be hurt. When we look back, and discover he's not there—that we can't see him with our two physical eyes—we fall sideways to the pavement, crash into a tree, or fly over the handlebars—depending on the degree of our faithlessness. Depending on the extent of the obstacles that we ourselves have placed in the path of our faith. Depending on how fast we are going in the wrong direction.

"And I wonder..." He raises his arm in an arc. "I wonder if we never looked back and believed all the while that he was there...if we kept our eye on the forward view... would we ever crash?" His shoulders shrink forward in defeat. "I think it's possible that all of our suffering is brought about by the compelling temptation to look behind us for proof of his existence. That if we never glanced back, never allowed ourselves to doubt, blocked out all distractions, made a true *commitment* to believe, even in times of confusion...if a certain critical mass of us were able to do that...that act of faith alone would end all suffering. Everywhere. And the earth would be renewed."

His eyes shift left to right and back again. "It's a hunch I've had just recently. A hunch I intend to explore further. But the clues are all there, right in the good book, just waiting for us to 'get it'." He scratches finger quotes with his left hand.

Moving two steps down, closer to the congregation, he says, "After all, the infant...the child...the Son of God has already radiated his perfect light upon this earth and upon each of us. This has already happened. If you have any faith at all, you know this. It's certainly not news to any of us here." He looks around. "If it is, please see me later in the rectory."

A general wave of laughter sweeps through the church.

"Okay then," he says, "that being the case—this perfect light already having enveloped us, you might say—is it not then incumbent upon us to reflect that light back upon each other, rather than hiding it under the Biblical bushel? Rather than asserting boundaries and keeping the light to ourselves? Is it not incumbent upon us to keep our eyes keenly forward on the distant reward, and in so doing, in cooperating with his grace...might we then end the suffering on earth? Isn't it possible that our very understanding and belief that the suffering has already been removed...will remove it? That it is we who forget his gift, and who delude ourselves into believing that it isn't real? Or that it's only real under certain conditions? Or that we have to wait to receive it...to prove ourselves in some impossible way. When in fact, he already did that for us?"

He raises his voice and slows down the delivery. "My dear brothers and sisters, listen carefully: Sometimes faith is not so much the presence of belief as the suspension of disbelief." He pauses, nodding thoughtfully. "The suspension of disbelief." He glances at the vaulted ceiling. "So maybe if on one day...any day...we all drop to our knees and tell the Lord we believe, or want to believe, or at least agree not to disbelieve, the curtain of delusion will be instantly lifted, and we will be able to see that we are already at the threshold of the Kingdom even as we walk this earth. A Kingdom whose laws prohibit suffering and death." He raises his arms. "If we just believe."

Later in the service, Vera receives Communion as the choir sings, "Oh come, let us adore him." Back in her pew, she sits quietly with the Lord, her head in her hands, as he tells her that what Father Max is saying, is the same thing that he has been telling her all along. That true belief is all it takes to renew the earth. She is at once agitated and excited by this realization. It makes her feel that finally she will be able to confide in someone, in Father Max, about her so-called gifts. About the mission of the Loaves and Fishes. And eventually, possibly, even about the chicken scratch that she has shown no one, not even Louise or Margaret.

As she exits the church that evening, she is filled with a sense of destiny, the likes of which she has never felt before. As if the messages the Lord is giving to her and to Father Max are identical, and that she will no longer be forced to work in seclusion. That a great burden has been lifted.

On the way home, she inhales the musty smell of the old Suburban, and realizes that none of her own...transformation...would have happened had Monk continued to live. Not that she wishes him away; she emphatically does not. She misses him so much, in fact, that her entire body calls out to his spirit, *"Where are you?"* on an hourly basis. And she is yet to find him. But now she thinks — *what if he is still here?* What if the world as she knows it is no more than a theater curtain waiting to be drawn? And what if she, herself, through a profound act of true belief, has the power to pull the cord?

As she shuffles into the house, she hears someone in the process of recording a message on the machine. The message is so hysterical that the voice is unrecognizable, and the screaming pitch of it makes Vera's blood run cold. Is it Mia? she wonders, as she yanks off her gloves, casts off her coat, and runs to the living room to listen.

"Vera, you have to get here NOW! Where are you? Where are you? Whereareyou?" And then a lot of wailing and screaming, and finally Vera is able to discern that it isn't Mia at all unless Mia has resorted to calling her "Vera". It takes another minute or so, Vera's hand held hesitantly over the receiver — (does she really want to take this call right now?) — before she figures out that it's Louise, and she lifts the phone.

"I'm here, Louise," she says. "I just got in."

In between the screaming and wailing and mucous-drenched sniffles, Vera hears the words, "It's Stanley. I thought he was sleeping, and I left him there for the longest time. But, oh God, then I felt...his body. He's not sleeping...uuuuuhhhhhh, and I just shook his shoulder, and he's...uh uh uh...he's...he's dead!!!!"

"I'll be right over," says Vera. She drops the phone, dials Margaret's cell phone, and rushes out the door.

A soft snow begins to fall as Vera screeches the six miles of Canaan back streets and pulls into Louise's driveway. Margaret, who lives around the block from Louise, has already arrived, her silver Lincoln Continental parked haphazardly on the street. Louise's house is an imposing white brick colonial, a mansion compared to Vera's. It always surprises Vera that her friend has so much money. Louise's lack of pretension is one of her most endearing qualities.

Vera walks directly through the door, up the stairs and down the long hallway into the master suite where she hears the muffled sounds of Louise crying.

Louise is huddled on the couch with Margaret. "Oh, Vera, you're here," she whimpers.

"Yes, I'm here," Vera says, and the ring of her own words reverberates as some kind of déjà vu. She stands for a moment, stunned, absorbing the scene. There lies Stanley, complete with all his tubes, the thin gray skin on his bald head nearly transparent. His tiny shrunken body situated in the center of a massive antique walnut four-poster bed topped with a white lace canopy. The room is absurdly female, Vera thinks, especially considering it has been used exclusively as Stanley's sick room for the last three years. She can't imagine Monk ever agreeing to reside in such a fussy décor, even in a near coma. But that was Monk—sloppy and macho right to the end—literally thrown into a corner of his messy office in an exercise outfit that barely fit him and certainly didn't match. In sharp contrast, Stanley is dressed in red paisley silk pajamas, buttoned to the neck. He is covered to the waist with white lace linens topped with a plump down comforter edged in matching lace. His jaw is suspended, but thankfully, his eyes are closed. Vera couldn't have stood to see his eyes open, not so soon after losing Monk.

Vera walks quietly forward to join the girls. She is touched by the sight of Margaret, still in her bathrobe, consoling Louise on the adjacent couch, stroking Louise's head tenderly. "Our girl has had quite a shock," Margaret says.

At this, Louise opens her throat and wails, "Aaaaaaaaaaaaa. Aaaaaaaaaaa."

"There there," says Margaret. "There there, dear girl. Such a shock; such an awful shock."

Vera can't help but note how much older Margaret and Louise look in this vulnerable condition, dressed in their nightgowns and robes, bare-faced and without makeup, the sides and back of their gray hair flattened to their heads. How fortunate she is to have friends who consider others even before they comb their hair or tend to basics. She glimpses herself in the huge gilded mirror on the wall behind her friends, and realizes that this is the first time in a very long time, if ever, that she failed to take her own advice never to leave the house without lipstick.

As she slips off her coat and removes her gloves, she says, "Has anybody called the doctor to sign the certificate?"

"The nurse called him," says Margaret. "We're waiting for the funeral attendants."

"Oh, Vera," sniffs Louise. "I've waited for this day for so long, but now that it's here, I just...ohhhhhhhhhhh. I didn't...take care of him, Vera. You know how I was. I was sa-sa-selfish. And, uh uh uh, really, I da-did love him in my own way."

"Of course you did," says Vera. "And you're anything but selfish, Louise."

"And then..." Louise sucks air between sobs. "I think...I don't know, but..."

"But what, dear," says Margaret tenderly.

"My pa-rayer inten-tion!" Louise caws.

This intention issue hits Vera too, though she does not want to let her friends know that she had the audacity to read their personal folded slips of paper. "What do you mean, Louise?" she says guiltily.

Louise raises her head. The whites of her eyes are blood red. "The intentions we wrote for the la-loaves and fa-fa-fishes," she whimpers. "I prayed for fa-reeeee-dom, uh uh…"

As this thought sinks in, Margaret looks aghast at Vera. After she has gathered her wits, she says, "Well, I'm sure the Lord is not in the business of killing our family members just because we've prayed for freedom. Am I right, Vera?"

Vera grips her bottom lip with her top teeth for a second or two then reverses the bite to her bottom lip. "I um…" She is hoping the Lord will fill in the obvious blanks, but at the moment he's not playing that game. "I just think that, well…" She folds her arms and says, more as a question, "Maybe Stanley was ready to die?" She nods affirmatively, because this sounds like a good enough tack. "Maybe Stanley and the Lord were just waiting for you to be…independent enough…before bringing Stanley to his eternal home."

Clearly impressed with this line of thinking, Margaret straightens her spine and turns to face Louise. "Now that makes sense to me, Louise, it really does. What if poor Stanley here…"

They all turn to look at Stanley, which sets Louise off again.

"What if Stanley was just waiting all this time until he knew…"

Louise pats the corners of her eyes with a wad of tissue. "How could he know anything, Margaret?" she says. "He didn't even know where I went or what I did. He didn't even know that I was gone on Ca-ristmas Eve." She chokes back a sob, and frowns. "Hell, for the last year, he didn't even know my name."

As Louise progresses into another chorus of sobs, Margaret draws her into a motherly embrace. "There there," she says, rocking.

Vera says, "Louise, that might be true, but the Lord certainly knew exactly where you went and what you did and with whom." She moves toward them and lowers herself slowly on the mint green carpet at the foot of the couch, curling her legs underneath her. "And quite possibly, he communicated these things to Stanley."

Louise stares ahead blankly through Margaret's big arms, absorbing this information. Then she smiles. "Oh, Vera, do you think the Lord communicated with Stanley?"

"Why, of course," says Vera. "He communicates with all of us."

"I guess, in a way, but still...Stanley? Stanley knew his numbers all right, but he never was much for conversation."

At this, they all turn in some kind of intuitive unison to stare at Stanley's corpse, which for some reason sets Louise off into a reluctant giggle that escalates into near hysteria. Vera, who in her entire life had never possessed the will power to turn down an infectious laugh, swallows the temptation to join in.

But soon enough, as Louise continues, a volcanic giggle rises up from Vera's neck into her mouth. She suppresses it by staring down at the carpet. If she looks at Louise, she'll lose it, and she's not sure whether it would best support Louise to laugh or to resist laughing. Vera then makes the mistake of glancing up at Margaret, though, who is clearly suffering the same predicament, and as their eyes lock, the irrepressible erupts, and Vera and Margaret begin to shake with laughter. Soon Vera collapses forward in a heap on the carpet, a limp rag of belly laughter. This is just so undignified she can't believe she's doing it. But it clearly doesn't bother Louise, who by now is laughing so hard she's practically screaming.

Louise slaps her thighs, and says between hiccups, "Hell, let's be honest, living with Stanley...*hiccup*...half the time I felt like one of those alien satellites in the desert searching for signs of intelligent life."

Vera crawls up off the floor and walks to the bathroom to get Louise a glass of water. Louise drinks it, and this calms her back down.

"Ohhhhh," moans Louise. "That was good. That was real good." She drinks the water. "He wasn't much for church, Stanley," she says. "Oh sure, he liked to donate money, but..."

At this, Margaret's eyes widen. "We should call St. Jude's," she says urgently. "For the blessing. Do you think it's too late?"

"How could it be too late?" says Vera, as she lifts the phone off the end table. "I'll call Father Max right now."

Not fifteen minutes later, Father Max appears groggy-eyed, dressed in an old pair of jeans and a black crew neck sweater turned inside-out and backwards. The white label sticks out like a price tag below his throat. His sneakers are untied. Looking at him, Vera's just happy he managed to zip his fly. He does not look one bit like the gifted priest he is. He looks like a dyslexic schoolboy. On the other hand, Vera knows that at two o'clock in the morning he would certainly have to be forgiven this lapse. Besides, come to think of it, by now they all look pretty accidental. How awkward for him it must be to look at Margaret and Louise in their nightgowns, Margaret's huge spreading bosom clearly unstrapped and practically sitting on her knees.

Suppressing a yawn, Father Max nods solemnly to the women, takes Louise's hands in his and gazes at her sympathetically. "God bless you," he says in earnest.

Thank goodness they are all over their laughing fit, because Vera could just see them bursting out in one inappropriate giggle after another just when Father Max wanted to express his sympathy. What in the world would he have made of that? Father Max proceeds directly to Stanley, murmurs a prayer and administers last rites.

"I thought you had to be alive to get Last Rites," sniffles Louise.

Father Max turns to her. "We really don't know when the spirit lifts, now do we, Louise? I like to leave that determination up to the Lord. It's really the sacrament of healing, and I'm sure Stanley's soul could use the balm."

He gathers them all around the bed and prays that Stanley's soul will be raised to the highest heavens. That his spirit will be clothed in garments of radiant light. That his widow, Louise, will be given the strength to lead the material life God still provides her, in spite of this great sorrow.

At the word 'widow', Louise dissolves into tears.

December 30—Louise has buried Stanley, and now the Lord, if I heard him correctly, wants her to move in with me. Is he crazy? And if anyone has to move in with anybody, why can't I move in with Louise? Hasn't he seen her house—how much bigger it is? Not to mention professionally decorated. Not to mention the six bathrooms complete with whirlpool tubs. Not to mention the swimming pool which, come to think of it, I don't believe Louise has ever even used.

Well, the details of the move aren't too clear, I have to admit. But what is clear, is that he wants us together. I'm yet to figure out what it means exactly. But I'm thinking we may know more tomorrow night at the New Year's Eve Loaves and Fishes dinner, which will be held here again at my house. It certainly wasn't my idea to host another dinner so close to Stanley's burial, never mind that it's another holiday, but Margaret insists that we follow the Lord's instructions exactly. I try to tell her that it's the Lord all right, but it's the Lord trying his best to communicate through my clogged and rusty pipes. The truth is, I constantly doubt myself lately, ever since the debacle of Stanley's death on the heels of Louise's prayer intention. Did the Lord really knock off Stanley just to liberate Louise? Not that Stanley had any quality of life left to begin with, but still.

Since nobody else's intention seems to have been answered, Margaret and I can only conclude that Stanley's death was the so-called miracle the Lord promised. I can tell you this, if anybody else dies as a result of tomorrow's supper, that's the end of my career as a...whatever it is I am. A psychic, maybe, although the Bible forbids psychics, so then why would the Lord make himself known through such a person? Margaret likes to call me a mystic, which naturally has its root in the word 'mystery', so I guess it fits because if my life is anything right now, it's a big game of Clue. I will try to abide by the Lord's confusing command to move Louise in with me. Not that Louise will do it, necessarily. And why should she? What is he trying to do, anyway? Start some sort of convent?

And then it hits her...maybe he is.

Vera and the Martha's attend five o'clock Mass on the evening of December 31st, at the Lord's instruction. "Before your next supper of Loaves and Fishes," he said, "receive Communion with the 'Apostles'." His words exactly, though they certainly did make Vera more than a little uncomfortable. She has not yet used the word 'apostles' with the ladies and is not sure she ever will, especially in front of Fiona. But for now, lined up here in the front pew of St. Jude's, they all seem content, including Louise who, though stunned, is so far sitting up attentively and without tears. She's even wearing a diamond broach in the shape of a champagne bottle for New Year's Eve. And she's dressed in her red and black houndstooth dress, so she is not looking grim, as Vera still is, in widow's black. And then there's Fiona who for some reason looks to Vera like the cat who swallowed the canary. But then, that's Fiona for you—a mystery all her own. Well, at least Fiona appears to be happy tonight and that, Vera hopes, will make the supper more pleasant for all of them. Margaret bet Louise fifty dollars that Fiona wouldn't even show.

The ladies are seated in the left front row, dressed in their best wool suits and silk dresses, just below the pulpit where the lector, George Sanborn, is proclaiming the second reading, a letter from St. Paul to the Corinthians. George raises his solemn, gray bearded face, placing his right index finger on the reading to keep his place.

In his radio announcer's voice he says, "Now all of you together are Christ's body, and each one of you is a separate and necessary part of it. Here is a list of some of the members that God has placed in the body of Christ..." George clears his throat.

"First are apostles. Second are prophets. Third are teachers. Then those who do miracles. Those who have the gift of healing. Those who can help others. Those who can get others to work together. Those who speak in unknown languages."

Unknown languages, thinks Vera, shocked. Well, what do you know?

"Is everyone an apostle?" continues George. "Of course not. Is everyone a prophet? No. Are all teachers? Does everyone have the power to do miracles? Does everyone have the gift of healing? Of course not. Does God give all of us the ability to speak in unknown languages? Can everyone interpret unknown languages? No! And in any event, you should desire the most helpful gifts."

Vera does not even hear the rest of St. Paul's letter, because throughout the entire reading, she has been receiving discreet elbow jabs from Margaret as George mentions each of the gifts. This gets Vera to thinking, not about the many gifts the Lord has saddled her with...dare she count them? No. In fact, there is only one gift identified by Paul that interests her at the moment, and that is not the gift of unknown languages necessarily, but the gift of interpretation. The one gift she doesn't have. She wishes to find someone who can interpret her sticks and circles. After all, the Lord has given her the ability, not to speak, but to write in a mysterious language, and there is St. Paul right in the Bible preaching to the Corinthians about the sure existence of that gift. So who is this interpreter and where does she live? Is she among the Martha's? Could it be Louise or Margaret? Vera is so excited she is practically wiggling in her seat. Somewhere out there is a person who will know what the scribble means! Why would the Lord compel her to write such nonsense if there was no chance at translation? And somehow, possibly with the help of Father Max, she will find that person. Why, maybe it's even Father Max.

Vera wants to find her interpreter so badly, she's tempted to write it down as tonight's intention and throw it in the bowl. But then, she thinks, what would happen to Mia? Mia, who has returned none of Vera's twenty or so phone calls through the holidays. Mia, whose life—perhaps even whose eternal soul—is in mortal jeopardy. No, she can't trade Mia for an interpreter. Mia comes first.

Back at the house, the women are bubbling around like bottles of freshly uncorked champagne. There is a new and exciting tension within the group, a sense of belonging that has developed since the last meeting. A new bond, perhaps, in spite of the fact that neither the bread nor the fish multiplied. And also in spite of Fiona's cranky behavior. If this is not the Lord working amongst them, Vera thinks, nothing is. Of course it could also be the women responding to a renewed sense of meaning in their lives.

Margaret, who is dressed endearingly in a large black and white polka dot dress, gaily claps her hands to announce dinner, and they move into the dining room, which Margaret has freshly decorated in silver and gold to celebrate the New Year. A fresh start. A silvery plastic cloth lies beneath a white lacey over-cloth so that the silver sparkles through. Very effective, Vera thinks. The lace tablecloth no doubt comes from Louise's endless supply of linens, and how Louise had time to think of such a thing after her week of mourning, Vera cannot even guess. Sparkly wires covered in metallic gold are wound around the napkins. Silver and gold confetti is scattered across the table. Vera wonders if the Lord might have had something simpler in mind for his Loaves and Fishes supper. After all, he himself did not serve that miracle meal in a fancy manner. But since he hasn't seen fit to comment on the table setting décor to her, Vera has decided to simply enjoy the efforts of her thoughtful friends.

Vera stands at her seat, looking down on the long table of seated women. How excited they look! She notes that Fiona seems pleased to have been moved up from the card table to a more central position, a noticeable improvement. Perhaps her peevish behavior last week really was based on the seating arrangements, you never know. Well good for Margaret and Louise to have taken care of that. And Lillian and Gertrude do not seem in the least bit miffed at their displacement. Points for Lillian and Gertrude, she thinks, for wasn't it the Lord himself just last week who promised them that the last shall be first?

She bows her head, and the Lord instructs her to say, "'I will speak to my own people through unknown languages and through the lips of foreigners. But even then, they will not listen to me,' saith the Lord.'"

She blinks. "What do you suppose it means? I'm not a foreigner."

Doris laughs. "To some people you are," she says. "Everybody's not an American."

Fiona waves her hand. "1 Corinthians," she says with importance. "I believe it was in the first reading tonight." She shakes her head. "If anybody was listening."

Vera nods: 1 Corinthians. Interesting. Not as if she'd had time to memorize that verse verbatim, though. Or even that she'd been listening to that part of the reading, since she can't remember having heard it before. Whatever. But before she has time to cogitate further, here comes the Lord again...she closes her eyes and lifts her chin. "The Lord says to tell you how happy he is with each of you, that you have the faith to return for what will become our traditional dinner." She repeats the Lord's words slowly and in a slight staccato fashion. "He wishes you to know that as faith builds, so does its momentum and its effect on our lives as well as on the lives of our loved ones."

She touches her temple trying to understand this next line. Her eyes are batting around under the lids as if she's being chased in a dream. "He says..." She shakes her head. Can this be? She's aware of a bang followed by some great commotion among the ladies, but she can't afford to pay attention to it, or she will lose track of the Lord and his message. Though she's concentrating hard, she's having a hard time believing it. "What the?" she wants to say to him, but stops herself. If she opens her eyes, the added distraction will cause her to lose focus completely. She wishes the ladies could understand how difficult this is. If they did, they would not be whispering and shuffling about so much.

Vera sighs deeply. "Okay...the Lord says that we are to challenge his church."

There is great mumbling now. "Vera!" someone says in a warning tone, but Vera holds up a finger to stop the interruptions. She continues very slowly, as if she, too, can't believe what she's hearing. "We are to create a new order. Not a new religion; it is still his religion, under his guidance. He wishes us to start an order that will renew his Spirit and bring miracles to the world, miracles that cannot be performed through any other channel at the moment. He says that the hierarchy of the Catholic Church, as it is now, has become too rigid, too comfortable, too institutional, and too concerned with the per... per-pet- (what is he saying?) per-petu-a-tion of...their own power." She can barely hear him now; a curtain is being drawn between them. "He says...he can no longer perform miracles through that church unless it changes. He says it is our job to change it." She coughs three times. "He says it will not be easy."

Vera leans over as if in pain. She can hear the deep voice nearly screaming at her, but it is screaming from another realm, and because of the great commotion around her, she's losing her signal. She tries again. "He says he wants us to tell the Pope two things: first, that the Pope has not been ordaining all his priests, because most of the faithful...who have been given vocations are not...men. They are women. They are you and I." Her chest heaves as she inhales. "He says...we have to ask the Pope to surrender the great material wealth of the Church—the mansions of its bishops and the instruments of gold. He says that material wealth and comfort for the hierarchy was never his message. He says the church has to be brought back to the people. The wealth has to be dispersed. He wants us to initiate the Society of Loaves and Fishes to feed his people who are starving for his message."

There is a great murmuring now, a terrible commotion. Vera grits her teeth trying to hear his last directive. "He says...we are his new apostles, the priests of the Society of Loaves and Fishes. Not nuns. Priests. He says if the bishops will not comply, we will be ordained by the direct power of the Holy Spirit and that our authority will be obvious to many."

Vera leans her fists against the table for support; she is completely drained. She hyperventilates for a minute then drops into her seat. Head in hands, she slowly opens her eyes and lifts her head to ascertain the reaction of the Martha's. But there is only one person in her view. Standing open-mouthed and aghast at the end of the table right behind Gertrude, is a wide-eyed Father Max, dressed, no less, in his Roman collar and black priestly suit. Since when has Vera ever seen him in that outfit outside of church?

She swallows a lump.

"Well," says Father Max. "Well, well." His head juts in and out like a turtle's as he absorbs her proclamation. "This is quite...the scene."

Vera plays absently with her silverware and says, "How did you...who? Why are you here?"

He purses his lips.

"I invited him," announces Fiona as she puckers defensively and plays with the belt of her dress. "I felt, and rightly so, having heard Vera's, well...blasphemy, that a real priest should be in attendance. That a real, genuine, ordained priest should be...monitoring...us." She says 'us', but her head points clearly to Vera.

"The Lord wishes a new religious order to be born of women," says Vera, repeating the words she now hears within her. "Born of women and run by them—a new element of the church to nurture the feminine voice. He says that voice has been absent too long. That the world can no longer survive without it."

"I see," says Father Max. He leans against the wall and stares down at his feet. "Tell me, Vera. When exactly did the Lord start...inspiring you?"

At this, Margaret stands. "Meaning no disrespect, Father Max, but Vera has just been through a great deal and is in no condition to be answering questions like that. If you'd like to have some dinner with us..." She cocks her head at Vera to see Vera's reaction. Vera nods. "Then we'd love to share our bread and fish with you."

"That's right," says Louise almost joyfully. "We will happily share our meal, but in this case, the Lord's message concerns us."

Father Max's eyes twitch left, right and center. He is pale and rocking back and forth in an odd manner. "I don't...I can't really..."

Fiona pushes back her chair, pulling on the gathers of her ruby silk dress as she stands. "I think Father Max and I have had quite enough for one evening," she says. She squeezes past Gertrude and Lillian, hooks her arm possessively in Father Max's, and escorts him to the door. As she reaches into the closet for her coat and purse, she turns. "You like words, Vera," she says. "Everybody knows you're one for words. Am I right?" She slips her arms into her coat. "Well then, I suggest you look up the word 'apostasy.' How's that? Hmm?" To the others, she says, "I hope to see you all back in your right minds at next week's Martha's meeting. Remember that the Martha's are humble people, not given to... Well, anyway, seven o'clock in the rectory." She waves as she walks out the door.

Chapter Seventeen

After the crescendo of Fiona's departure with Father Max, Vera's house echoes with a coda of deafening silence accompanied only by clanging utensils and the click clack of high heels running from the dining room to the kitchen and back. An occasional, overzealous "Delicious!" and "Can you please pass the tuna?" can be heard, and "What a lovely choice—cinnamon bread with raisins!" This last comment struck Vera as absurd, since she could not bring herself to even think about combining tuna or arctic char with the likes of cinnamon bread. The bread was Louise's way of satisfying her sweet tooth, Vera supposed. As if the Lord had produced a three-course meal to the starving multitudes. But aside from the clatter, nobody offers up a meaningful word until Margaret finally clears her throat and says, "We need to agree to believe."

Lillian leans forward, squinting her hazel eyes behind her new black, crystal-studded glasses. Her silky white hair hangs in a trendy chin length cut, which is becoming to her small and animated face. She is nearly the only one left among them who has not been sideswiped from the fashion mainstream. She considers Margaret's statement and says, "I see what you're saying."

Gertrude says, "Just like Father Max himself said tonight at Mass—if you can't make the commitment to believe, you can at least make the commitment not to disbelieve."

Louise pounds her fist on the table. "To hell with Fiona and Father Max!" She blinks nervously. "Well, not to the real hell..."

"No, of course not, dear," says Rosemary. "But you make a good point...we can't be distressed by the shock of every interloper."

"Not that Fiona was an interloper," says Clara. "Not technically, anyway." She pats her mouth with her napkin. "Sometimes the worst offenses are committed by the chosen ones."

"Like Judas!" blurts Marian, and this draws a general hush as the women absorb the significance of this idea.

The women are so supportive, they nearly make Vera cry. Still, she does not want to take anything for granted. She shakes her index finger and says, "But what if..."

"What if what?" interrupts Doris. "What if you're not right? What if all this really is just in your head?"

Vera starts to nod, but then, listening to the words hanging just beyond her right ear, she snatches them from the ether and delivers them to her friends, "The Lord says he will show us the way. He will not leave us trembling. He will deliver us from the upper room." She leans heavily to the right, closer to the source of her inspiration. "He says how can we doubt that women are needed in his church? We need to allow him to show us the way to integrate women into his fold." She frowns, concentrating hard. "He says...there will be many harsh critics."

Chewing thoughtfully on their chunks of bread, the women listen intently, hungry for inspiration and direction. Vera provides them with the Lord's vision—a renewed church in which women would be provided a womb, a safe place to develop their spiritual skills before sharing them with the world. A place where men would be invited only as congregants until the concept of the priestess had been properly birthed and matured in the Society of Loaves and Fishes. And if the Society is not accepted within the current church, well then, it would simply become a church of its own. For a decade perhaps. Or a century. Whatever it takes.

Listening to her, the women mindlessly consume their meals, picking absently at the flaky fish with their forks while passing salt, although no butter is allowed since Margaret insists that butter was not available in biblical times whereas salt clearly was.

When their meals are finished, they stare for a collective moment at the empty platters of fish and the baskets of unreplenished bread, saying nothing. Their mission, they seem to know, is a mission of faith, and though the Lord certainly seemed to be promising a miracle or two, those miracles, they know, most likely would have nothing whatsoever to do with the replenishment of actual food. Which is too bad, if you ask them—it would be so much easier if only the Lord would supply an upfront miracle or two.

"Before cleaning up, please place your intentions in the bowl," says Vera quietly. And as they anxiously pen their deepest desires, she struggles with the Lord who directs her to pray for an interpreter for her language, though she herself wishes only for Mia's healing. "Are you telling me that you refuse to heal Mia?" she silently telegraphs him. But there is no answer. The void is loud. Painfully conflicted, she fills out two prayer slips, one for Mia and one for the interpreter, going silently back and forth, "eeney meeney miney moe," as she directs her eyes from one fist to the next, eventually forgetting which intention is held in which fist. Finally, she opens her right fist over the bowl and drops the slip of paper inside. Withdrawing her other fist beneath the tablecloth, she strains her eyes and reads the withheld intention, "Heal Mia."

Vera forces herself back from the verge of tears. She should not be so attached to an intention or its outcome. She has been told this over and over again. This is how she gets in her own way—by obstructing the ways of God. And she is not the only one with a painful need, she reminds herself. The other women here are also clearly struggling. So okay, Mia's conversion will have to wait. Fine. But what about the other miracles? Was Stanley's death really the answer to Louise's prayer? Technically speaking, when a man has been walking a tightrope over the chasm between life and death for ten years, and he finally dies — it can hardly be considered a miracle. Can it? And then, the larger question — where is the multiplication of loaves and fishes? She knows that issue is on everyone's mind. Just one piece of bread. One slice of fish. Is that so hard? If the Lord could just see fit to pop one chunk of bread in the hand of one of these women...just once! Why, that would change the world right there.

There is a general tension around the bowl once the papers have been placed inside. A deep sigh from Gertrude. A pout from Clara. A few tears from Rosemary. Vera is not the least bit inspired to encourage their hopes and dreams. She is feeling too discouraged herself. Finally, Lillian breaks the silence by saying, "Well, what do you know — my eye has stopped twitching."

They all turn to Lillian, and Doris says, "I saw it twitching, Lily. Earlier. I did." She leans forward, squinting hard to see Lillian's eye more clearly. "I don't know if anyone else noticed, but her right eye was twitching like crazy when Father Max was here."

"And afterwards," says Lillian. "In fact, it just stopped."

Now they are all studying Lillian's hazel eyes, and she removes her glasses for proof. "See?" she says, and shuts her eyes to demonstrate the stillness.

The only thing Vera notices is that Lillian's black eyeliner is applied unevenly and may even be missing a slight dash in the center of the right lid. It's the only fashion faux pas on Lillian's entire body. She is at least five years older than Vera and in better shape than any of them.

Lillian holds her eyelids steady. "See?" she repeats. "The twitch is completely gone."

Margaret frowns. "So what are you saying, Lily? That it's a miracle that your eye isn't twitching anymore? Was that the intention you put in the bowl? That your eye would stop twitching?" Margaret's voice lilts with contempt.

"Well, no," says Lillian. "But still..."

Margaret rolls her eyes. "I don't think the Lord would ask us to go to all this trouble just to cure a twitching eye that was bound to stop twitching on its own. Just my opinion."

Lillian looks down at her lap. "But it was really bothering me," she says.

The corners of Margaret's mouth curl as she considers this. "Well then I'm glad he cured it," she says. "But I hope that was not the miracle du jour—the miracle we're all waiting for. Because if it is, it seems like a big waste of supernatural power."

"Nothing is wasted," says Vera, suddenly reconnected. "His miracles are big and small. His miracles fit the situation. We'll just have to see if anything else happens."

Louise says, "I don't think we can very well start a church of miracles based on Lillian's twitch, Vera. I don't think we should even tell anyone about it."

"That's all I'm saying, too," agrees Margaret.

All at once Rosemary says, "The pain in my back has subsided!"

"See?" says Lillian. "I'm not the only one."

"I'm serious," says Rosemary. Her deep brown eyes open wide as she rubs her lower back in disbelief. "It's gone. When I got here tonight, I wondered if I could make it through the meal, but all of a sudden, after Lillian spoke, I realized my back felt great. The pain is gone." Rosemary's jet-black hair is pulled back into a severe chignon, so that even without the pain in her back, she looks distressed.

"Well now," says Louise with interest. "A backache is a lot more serious than an eye twitch."

They are all taking inventory of their bodies now, testing this and that odd arthritic part, when Margaret palpates her left elbow with her right hand. "Girls?" she says. "I can't believe this! My tendinitis is gone!" She swings her head back to look directly at Vera. "I could barely lift the dish platter earlier, Vera, but now..." She twists her elbow for show and lifts the heavy platter and holds it. "Now I can lift it with one arm. And hold it!"

Doris says, "Maybe my knees are healed." She stands and parades quickly around the table. "They are!" she says, and breaks into a celebratory tap dance. "Look at me, girls! My knees are healed! My knees are healed!" She dances in a circle.

"Glory be to God, will you look at that," says Marian. "The faith of a mustard seed will heal us all."

This gives Vera an idea, and she walks to the kitchen to search her herb cabinet for mustard seeds, which she locates and distributes to each of the women. When they are all holding their seeds between their thumbs and forefingers, she says, "Let us thank the Lord for these healings, big and small." She breathes deeply. "And may the power of our collective faith heal the pain and suffering that afflicts our sisters and brothers around the world."

"Amen," they say joyfully.

As they disassemble for cleanup, they chatter and hum with contentment. "God is good!" one claims. "God is great!" Drying one of the fish platters, Debbie says to no one in particular, "Fiona will be sorry she walked out on this one. What with her breast cancer and all."

Louise says, "What! Breast cancer? I didn't know Fiona had breast cancer."

"Well, she does," says Debbie as she places the platter on the counter. "I overheard it from one of the oncology nurses at the hospital the other day."

"How bad is it?" says Margaret.

"I'm not sure," says Debbie. "I'm surprised she hasn't told anyone. According to my friend, she's having a mastectomy. She obviously didn't want any of us to know."

Margaret nods thoughtfully. "Well, no wonder then..."

"It was her decision to leave the group," says Louise. "No one kicked her out."

They are still discussing Fiona's breast cancer, not to mention her contentious behavior, as they gather their coats and hats. Listening to them review the alarming scene with Fiona and Father Max earlier, Vera realizes how deeply exhausted she is. The evening has been too much for her. Way too much. She taps Margaret's shoulder gently and confides, "I think I'll skip church on Monday."

Margaret turns and cranes her head forward with concern. "Whatever for, dear?"

Vera shrugs. "I just..."

"Dear, dear, dear," says Margaret. She takes Vera's hands in hers. "You can't let Father Max disturb your peace. After all, he's practically a boy. And until we're able to establish our church...that is, until we receive clearer direction, and even after that—we must persevere in the daily sacrifice of the Mass."

"But what if he...what if I...?

"What if what?"

"What if Father Max refuses to give me Communion? What if he...excommunicates me?"

This statement resounds in the living room and quiets them all down. "Well then," says Margaret to the others. "Vera has a very good question, girls, don't you think? What if Father Max refuses to give us Communion? What if the Pope excommunicates us? What then?"

Gertrude plants her fists firmly on her wide hips. "Well then, that will make it obvious, won't it? The day they do that to us, we're on our own."

"We're either apostles or we're not," says Doris resolutely.

"We either believe Vera or we don't," says Rosemary.

But that line does not give Vera the least bit of peace. She doesn't want all that responsibility. After all, who is she to be speaking for the Lord?

On Monday morning, two days later, Vera can't bring herself to attend Mass. She isn't in the mood to challenge Father Max or to accept his myopic viewpoint. Mostly, she doesn't want to stage her rebellion at the Communion rail. Not that she doesn't harbor doubts of her own—not even doubts really, but worse, painful insecurities regarding the Lord's choice to make his wishes known through her, through the mind and mouth of a beautician. What was he thinking? Would she ever be able to accept her role in this preposterous chain of events? Probably not. But when it comes right down to it, she thinks, how could Father Max—how could anyone—question the fact that women deserve an equal role in the church? After all, these are not ancient times! These are not medieval times! These are not even the '50's! Women are educated and sophisticated and—deeply spiritual beings. Furthermore, with the Lord's help, Vera has come to realize that feminine gifts are in fact integral to the very existence of the church. Not as cleaning ladies, either. As preachers and deacons and priests.

Replaying these thoughts over and over, editing and refining them, she moves distractedly about the house in her white cotton robe and fluffy bedroom slippers, drinking coffee and picking at a bowl of dry Cheerios. She retrieves the paper from the back stoop and settles down to do the crossword puzzle. Five letter word for: *raised platform used for sacred purposes.* She smiles, well, *altar,* of course. That was easy. Hmmm, twelve letter word for *Easter...* She sips her coffee. The phone rings.

"Hello?" she says absently.

The caller hangs up. Another telemarketer, Vera supposes and idly walks to the ID box to check. "Wyste," says the callout, and before she loses her nerve, Vera dials back.

"Hello?" says Stella.

Vera hangs up. She sips more coffee and tries to focus on the crossword. Twelve letter word....

The phone rings, and she buries her head in her hands until the third ring, then answers it. "Hello," she says quickly.

"Vera?"

"This is she."

"Well, hello, Vera. This is Stella Wyste, and I'm sorry to be calling you, but my caller ID reports a half-dozen or so calls from this number."

"Oh?"

"So I'm just wondering if someone in your house has been trying to reach me."

"Such as..."

Pause. "Such as you?"

"Me, Stella? Or more likely, my husband?" Adrenaline reels through Vera's veins.

"Well, I don't know why Monk..."

"Oh well, I can't imagine why, either, Stella. But just a wild guess: to revive an old affair perhaps?"

"Excuse me?"

Vera drums her fingers against the table. "You heard me, Stella Wyste."

"Vera..."

"I'm listening."

"I don't know how much..."

"Everything, Stella. I know everything. Sadly, I learned it from my daughter who witnessed you seducing my husband."

Long pause. "I see. Well, I don't think you should be talking to me about this so-called affair."

"Well, to whom do you suggest I talk?"

"To your husband, Vera. To Monk."

"That's quite impossible."

"I'm sure he'd be happy to corroborate ..."

"You listen to me, Stella Wyste, I can't talk to my husband because he's dead. Did you get that, Stella? D-E-A-D. He died the morning after our daughter accused him of the affair with you. I guess it was just too much shame for him to bear. Not that I'm blaming it all on him, you understand. In fact..."

"Oh my God," says Stella. "Just give me a minute here. Oh my God. Monk is...dead?"

Vera's heart pounds. "Yes." How dare this woman grieve for Monk!

"I'm so sorry, Vera. I am. I'm terribly sorry for your loss and for your daughter's loss."

"That rings a little hollow, don't you think? Coming from you."

"I seduced him," says Stella. "I did that; it's true. He was very reluctant. I caught him at a weak moment. He never loved me. He made that clear. If anyone was responsible for that affair, it was me."

"I," says Vera.

"Excuse me?"

"It was I. You're a teacher, Stella. You should speak proper English."

Silence.

"So now you know," says Vera. "He's dead."

"I cared a lot about your husband," says Stella. "I had no right to, but I did. Some things you just can't help. And I'm sorry for you. I really am."

"Well then," says Vera, and hangs up.

Vera's heart is beating a mile a minute. She can't believe she just did that, but she did. And it's over. She spoke to the devil incarnate, and guess what? Her sin was that she loved Monk. Why, who in the wide world wouldn't love Monk? Wouldn't want him to marry her? Oh Monk, she thinks, I do forgive you; I really do. And as much as I hate to forgive Stella, I must. And I do. I forgive her, too. And Lord, while I'm at it, I also forgive Anthony Kimball for killing my parents. He must have suffered, too, and probably still does. And I forgive you, God, for cavorting around in my tidy life the way you have, messing it up in the worst way.

All this forgiveness lays her heart bare, and she places her head in her hands, whimpering until the doorbell rings. Ding dong. Ding dong. She ignores seven rings, and then hears the key in the tumbler, the swish of the door over the high-pile carpet and a rush of whistling wind.

"Vera?" calls Margaret. "Are you okay?" The door closes. "Vera?" she says anxiously.

The fear in Margaret's voice convinces Vera to respond, though she grabs a handful of tissues and messes up her hair before she shuffles into the living room, blowing her nose.

"Vera!" exclaims Margaret. "Are you okay, dear? Time for church!"

Vera blows her nose even louder into the tissue in her left hand while holding up her right. "You better go on without me," she says with a forced nasal twang. "I don't want to get anyone sick."

Margaret frowns. "I'm not afraid of your cold," she says.

"I was up half the night."

"Mmhmm," says Margaret suspiciously. "Okay then, shall I get someone to bring you Communion?"

Vera rocks her head left to right, deciding. "Well, sure, but don't inconvenience the ministers."

"It's their job," says Margaret firmly.

Vera smiles. "Just not Pauline; she stays too long."

Margaret nods. "Louise and I will bring you some soup later."

Vera blows her nose again, throwing her whole head into it for effect.

"Don't let him intimidate you," says Margaret, as she turns toward the door. "Don't let him keep you from the Eucharist."

Vera nods.

"We're either going to do this full bore or not at all. And while we're doing it, we're going to stand up for our rights."

Vera nods again. Why didn't the Lord channel himself through Margaret? she thinks. Margaret has more oomph, more... conviction. She would have been better at this.

"The Lord doesn't reward half-hearted efforts," continues Margaret.

"No," agrees Vera.

"He chose you for a reason."

Why, it's as if Margaret could read Vera's mind. "He chose you, too," says Vera.

Margaret cocks her head and says, "He chose me because he knows I'll knock down anyone in your path." She wags her finger. "And you know what? I will."

Vera stuffs her hands into her bathrobe pockets. "Thanks," she says, grinning.

Margaret steps onto the front stoop and treats Vera to another blast of arctic air, then stomps down to her car. What a gal, Vera thinks. Having Margaret is like having a bodyguard.

After showering, Vera opens her forgiveness book, first scratching out Stella Wyste and Anthony Kimball then adding Fiona and Father Max. She does not want to be excommunicated.

And just how did this all happen, she wonders. She can't begin to believe the changes that have come over her life since that day in the Stop & Shop when the vision of Monk practically attacked her in the corn display. It occurs to her that if her life could change that quickly, that dramatically, than so could the lives of others. Why, just look at Louise! A prisoner in her own house one day; free as a bird the next.

Vera pours herself another cup of coffee, and moves to the office in her neglected salon, where glistening spider webs have popped up in the corners by the sliding glass doors. She wants to knock them down, but as she opens the closet door for the feather duster, she is all at once inspired to write. She sits down at her desk, pulls out her pencil and pads of paper, and almost watches herself from an out-of-body perspective as her hand speedily marks up the pages with clusters of dashes interspersed with circles and seemingly random but measured amounts of space. Hours later, still in her bathrobe, she emerges from the salon and, on her way into the kitchen, the doorbell rings again. Expecting the Eucharistic minister, not to mention Margaret and Louise with some chicken noodle soup, she opens the door while blowing her nose hard. There stands Father Max, dressed in his puffy black jacket and a ridiculous plaid ski cap.

"Well, hello," he says timidly

"Oh," she says, pulling her robe closer. "Oh, excuse me, I...I'm not dressed."

"I understand you're not feeling well," he says. "I decided to bring you Communion myself."

Reluctantly, she stands aside to let him in.

After an awkward moment, she says, mortified, "I'll be right back. I'll just...change, if you don't mind."

"Not at all," he says, and slips out of his ski jacket.

Upstairs she throws on her black sweat suit and a pair of black socks and loafers, runs a comb through her hair and debates the lipstick issue. Oh the hell with it, she tells herself, and drops the tube of lipstick back in the drawer. After all, I'm supposed to be sick.

As she rounds the bend on the stairs, she sees Father Max sitting erect in her wingback chair, watching her descent.

"Well now," he says, "I'll read you some scripture before Communion. How would that be?"

"That would be fine," she says with reserve, nodding politely. She takes her seat opposite his and folds her hands in her lap.

He begins, "And Jesus replied, 'I have already told you, and you don't believe me. The proof is what I do in the name of my Father. But you don't believe me because you are not part of my flock. My sheep recognize my voice; I know them, and they follow me. I give them eternal life, and they will never perish. No one will snatch them away from me, for my Father has given them to me, and he is more powerful than anyone else. So no one can take them from me. The Father and I are one.'"

As he continues, Vera tries to absorb the significance of this reading. Is it really today's gospel, she wonders. Or has Father Max chosen this verse to frighten her? To put her on notice that if she continues on this collision course, she may be risking her eternal life. That she has become unrecognizable to the Father. What does Father Max know anyway, she thinks. Like Margaret said, he's just a kid. A smart kid, but still... Does he really know when the Lord's voice has been heard by a chosen prophet? Should she trust him? Or should she trust the Lord. Oh Lord, she prays silently, please give me the strength of my convictions.

Father Max unclasps the little brass container called a pyx, that holds the Eucharist, but before he lifts the Host, he says, "Vera, do you have anything you'd like to confess first?"

She makes a tent out of her hands and studies them. "No," she says looking down.

"Are you certain?"

Her eyes dart around the room. Why, look at that—another one of those spider webs behind the phone table.

"Okay then, let's repeat the prayer," he says. "Lord, I am not worthy to receive you. Only say the word and I shall be healed."

Vera swallows hard, chokes a little to buy time, and then blurts, "Why am I not worthy, Father Max?"

He raises his chin and shrugs. "Just in the sense that none of us is worthy, Vera. Nothing in particular about you."

"But why aren't we?" she says. "Think about it. What if I were your mother and I said, 'Max, you are unworthy of my love. In fact, you have always been unworthy of my love, and furthermore you can never become worthy of it. And worse, there is nothing at all you can do to change that situation.'" Her voice elevates as she proceeds, "'But because I love you so much, Max, even though you don't deserve my love, I will say the magic words of forgiveness so that you can enter my home. But remember this: tomorrow you will be just as unworthy, and so we will have to repeat this process over and over again until you die.'"

A little dazed, Father Max leans forward earnestly. "Are you saying that you *are* worthy of his love?"

She fixes her eyes to the left on another spider web between the stair railings. "I have a daughter, Father. She's a heroin addict, and you know what? Even though she behaves badly, even though she's addicted to drugs and leads a self-consuming life, she is still worthy of my love, and do you know why?"

He sighs.

"She is worthy because Monk and I brought her into the world, pure and simple. She didn't ask to be born. We created her and brought her into the world, and she is ours. Well...mine at the moment. And for that reason alone, she is worthy of my love. She is worthy of my love not because of anything she has done or failed to do, but simply because she is mine. Because I had a part in making her. So tell me just how and why the Father, if he is our real father, our Creator, could possibly create offspring whom he finds intrinsically unworthy of his love." She smacks her hands on her thighs. "I don't get it."

Father Max scratches behind his ear. He pulls on his chin, and smacks his lips over and over. Finally he says, "I suppose that's one line of thought."

"It's a woman's line of thought."

"I see."

She sits forward. "A mother's line of thought. This whole...philosophy of yours, of the church...is a man's philosophy invented by men. But what if God is a woman? Or what if God is both man and woman—father and mother? And why not? My catechism said that I was made in the 'image and likeness of God.' So God must have a feminine side, don't you think?"

"I suppose."

"Because men are different, Father Max. Monk felt differently about our daughter. After she disappointed him enough times, he felt that she didn't deserve our love. He felt that, based on her behavior, she wasn't worthy of it." Tears spring to her eyes. "But he was wrong. Because after all, wasn't love the message? Love and forgiveness?"

Father Max's Adam's apple bobs up and down noticeably. "Is this why you want to start a women's church, Vera?"

She crosses her legs. "I don't want to start a woman's church," she says. "I don't have anything against men. I love men. I was told to start a woman's church."

"That's the problem," he says. "I'm concerned about just exactly whose idea it was."

"Well don't be. It's the Lord's idea."

He sighs deeply, peering out the window where Vera can already see a light snow falling. "These...voices..."

"Voice," she corrects.

"I see. And yet, who are we to decide whose voice it really is? Do you think, after all, that the Lord really wants to see dissension in his own church?"

She purses her lips. "As a matter of fact, yes," she says. "As a matter of fact, I think he does. That's why he's allowed the perversion to be revealed. Change...dissension... may be the only hope for his church. It may be the only way to get people to understand that it's time for a new and different order. One that doesn't ignore half of humanity."

He strokes his chin several times. "Why you?" he says pointedly.

She shrugs.

"And why the Martha's? They're not theologians…"

"Because they're humble."

He nods, absorbing the possibility. "We'll have to pray about this," he says sincerely. "This needs prayer."

"Yes it does." She holds back a smile.

He reaches for the Host. "The Body of Christ," he says.

"Amen," she says, and takes it in her hand.

Father Max gives her a few moments alone as he wanders around the room, then says, "Is there anything else you want to tell me, Vera?"

"Like what?"

"You tell me — like what? Like when you started to hear the Lord's voice. Like whatever else he may have told you."

At that, Margaret and Louise cackle laughing on their way up the front walk, and Father Max turns at the noise. "Oh well, now you've got company. Perhaps another time, then. May I come back tomorrow? If you're feeling well enough?"

Vera smiles. "Yes," she says.

"How's ten-thirty?"

"That's fine."

He heads out the door as the ladies make their way inside.

"Well, well…Father Max," says Louise, wide-eyed. She cranes her neck to make oh-my-God-I-can't-believe-he's-here eye contact with Vera.

Father Max nods politely, and waves behind him as he rushes to his car.

The ladies close the door. They are encased in a bubble of cold air, their breath still issuing clouds of vapor as they speak.

"What happened?" says Louise in her high-pitched conspiratorial whisper. "What did he say?"

While Margaret hangs up the coats, Louise hands Vera a big pot of soup and a bag of crackers. "Homemade by Margaret," she says, "who else? God, I'm starved. What did he say? What did he say? Out with it."

In the kitchen as they warm up the soup, Vera says, "He asked some questions and listened to the answers. I actually think he's trying to understand."

Margaret wields the ladle high. "I told you so!" she chirps. "You just never know who your allies will be."

Vera shrugs. "Not that we want him to be excommunicated either," she says.

At the table, slowly slurping the soup, Vera says, "Margaret, this soup is delicious. Louise, the Lord wants you to move in with me."

Louise chokes on her own spit. "Excuse me?" she says.

"You heard me," says Vera. "It wasn't my idea, but I've grown accustomed to it."

Margaret sucks in her cheeks. "Why Louise?" she says.

At this, the Lord prompts her to say, "And you, too, Margaret." After she's said it, she can't believe it. How can this possibly work?

Margaret says, "A sisterhood, then?" Her grin is ear to ear.

Vera smiles. "I suppose it is."

"Our own convent?" squeals Louise. "Can you believe it! I've always wanted to be a nun!"

Margaret squints hard at Louise. "Not a convent at all," she says, shaking her head. After a slurp of soup she holds up her index finger and declares, "A rectory!"

Vera chuckles.

"What about the others?" says Margaret. "What about Lillian, Gertrude and Doris? They're not married either."

"I don't know yet," says Vera. "And there's not really enough room here..."

"There is at my house," says Louise. "There's plenty of room at my house."

"I'll have to consult with the Lord on that," says Vera.

"I can't see why it would make much difference where the convent is," says Louise.

"Rectory," corrects Margaret.

"But if we stay here, where would the church be?" pouts Louise. "Where would we say Mass? At my house there are several rooms that would be perfect for our suppers. Not to mention the swimming pool."

"The swimming pool?" says Margaret. "What in the world does a church need with a swimming pool?"

Louise shrugs. "Baptisms?"

"God preserve us," says Margaret, collecting herself. "Where in the world did that come from? Ha ha ha! That was a good one, dear."

They giggle and giggle, then laugh helplessly, holding their bellies for dear life and finally dropping forward on the table in utter weakness.

"A swimming pool," says Louise, still gasping for breath. "For baptisms! Why not! We don't need a city full of Cardinals to tell us what to do!"

"There's no canon law against swimming," agrees Margaret. "Priests swim all the time." Then she smacks the table resolutely. "Louise, you and I are going to meet with a lawyer and figure out what's what. We've got to draw ourselves a plan."

"A non-profit plan," points out Vera. "The Lord does not want us to hoard riches."

"No fancy vestments, I suppose," says Louise.

"Unless we sew them ourselves!" says Margaret with glee. "Oh my, this is fun indeed! I'm quite good with the sewing machine, you know."

"Stanley had a wonderful lawyer," says Louise. "Not to mention his accountant friends."

"Resurrection!" blurts Vera.

"What's that?" asks Margaret.

"A twelve-letter word for Easter!" Vera exclaims. "It was in the crosswords this morning!"

"Well now, isn't that fortuitous," says Margaret. "Prophetic even!" She turns to Louise in earnest and discusses the practical matters of establishing their rectory.

Vera only half-listens to them as a strange sensation moves through her. A tingling in her lower back, followed by a powerful beam of heat that moves through the same area, seemingly crystallizing and reforming her. Opening a door of some kind, perhaps. It's a sensation she vaguely remembers from a dream...in a mountain. She tries to turn it back, to force it away, to bring herself back to the discussion.

"By the way," says Margaret, "has anyone heard from Fiona? About the breast cancer, I mean."

Louise shrugs. "I haven't heard, no. Have you?"

Margaret shakes her head as she grabs a couple of saltines. "No, I haven't. What about you, Vera?"

Vera barely hears Margaret. She closes her eyes and breathes deeply, because the light has disoriented her. Not just disoriented her, but in an odd way, released her. She is so light she feels as if she could lift right up from her seat and float to the ceiling. In fact, the possibility of that happening feels so real that she grabs the bottom of her seat to hold herself down.

"Vera?" repeats Louise. "Did you hear Margaret? Margaret asked you a question."

Margaret leans forward. "What's wrong with you, Vera?" she asks. "Are you okay?"

"She's sick," says Louise, "that's all. She's not feeling well. Right, Vera? It's the cold?"

At that, Vera's head drops forward and bangs against the table as her spirit lifts and floats above them all. "I'm up here," she says. "Look at me, girls, I'm on the ceiling!"

Chapter Eighteen

Vera does everything she can to stop the escalating chaos. Her spirit literally dives down to grab the phone from Margaret's shaking hand, but as hard as she tries, she cannot seem to make direct contact with either Margaret or the phone. She glides right up to Margaret's ear and says as loud as you please, "Margaret, I'm...fine."

Margaret says, "We've got an emergency at #7 Destiny Drive. It's Vera Wright. Female. Early sixties." She taps her foot and drums her fingers, listening.

"Hang up!" says Vera. "I'm right here. I'm alive and fine!"

"She's passed out cold," says Margaret. She listens for a second, her eyes widening to the size of quarters. "Who the hell knows why?" she shrieks. "For God's sake, send someone over to find out why. Could you just do that? Could you just send the goddamn ambulance out here with somebody who knows something about anything."

Vera tries to tap Margaret on the shoulder, but Margaret ignores her. "Can't you hear me, Margaret?" Vera repeats louder. "I'm Fine. Fine! Fine! Fine!" But her words bounce back and forth around the room like empty echoes. And then there's the larger, more alarming issue of her limp body splayed from the chest up across the dining room table, the soup bowl overturned on the crown of her head like an unpinned yarmulke. Not to mention the carrots and noodles in her hair.

Louise, screaming with her hands over her mouth, is trembling all over and working up such an emotional lather

Vera expects to see brain matter flowing out of her ears like lava. While Margaret continues to shriek on the phone, Louise, hysterical now, drags Vera off the chair by her waist. Louise's ankle twists in the process and Vera, still on the ceiling, flinches as she watches her own chin hit the table and her body collapse like a rag doll onto the floor.

"Oh my God, oh my God!" screams Louise. "I dropped her!" Then Louise falls to her knees, opens Vera's jaw with two hands, and attempts to apply mouth-to-mouth resuscitation in between screams. "Oh my God, oh my God!" she screams, then breathes, breathes, breathes. "Oh my God, help, somebody help!" Breathe, breathe, breathe. Until finally, Margaret literally shoves Louise aside and takes over.

"She...IS...breathing," Margaret tells Louise as if she's talking to a four-year-old. Margaret takes Louise's hand and lays it on Vera's chest. "You see, Louise? Her chest is moving up...and...down. Like this. She's...breathing." Her attempt at calmness is betrayed by the rising pitch of her otherwise husky voice. "She's not dead, for God's sake! She's not dead, Louise! When people are breathing, they do not need CPR! In fact, it can be dangerous!"

Vera continues to call out to the women from the ceiling, "I'm fine! I'm fine!" But it all has the feel of the dreams she's had where the sound travels through ether as thick as water, getting pulled into a riptide along the way. It's pointless. The excitement of her new freedom wanes quickly in the face of the panic it has struck in her friends. She's had quite enough of this new little parlor trick, thank you, and dives down with a degree of force intended to help her re-enter her body.

It doesn't work. She's denied entry. Oh my God, she thinks, I can't get back in! She knows she popped out from the lower back, but with her body laying the way it is now, her escape hatch is against the floor. Unless it's possible to re-enter somewhere else? She tries everything—head, chest, belly—even attempting to turn her body over, to no avail. She bangs herself against her body again and again, and then freaks out, "Oh my God! What if I really am dead? Or about to be dead?"

Margaret's continued insistence to Louise that Vera is still breathing brings a modicum of comfort, as does the long luminescent cord connecting Vera's spirit to her body. She thinks she remembers this cord from a dream, too, but can't remember its purpose exactly. Does this mean she can only float a certain distance from her body without dying? Surely Vera isn't the only person to whom this has ever happened? Why are there no books, manuals or videos explaining it, demonstrating the problem and how to fix it? *"Should you manage to ditch your body, simply insert A into B and fold-over C."*

Damn it, someone must know—for instance, the Pope? It seems to Vera that this situation would be more compelling than nearly any other of the nine million problems upon which the Vatican consumes considerable time. Not to mention the government. Why, it's as if the only thing that matters on earth is matter itself.

Fifteen minutes later, after more chaos than Vera, even from her most vertical perspective, can sort out, she finds herself squeezed inside an ambulance between Louise and Margaret. They're praying crazy incoherent prayers at the top of their lungs, prayers Vera is not even sure the Lord himself can make sense of, not to mention the young paramedics in charge. The ambulance echoes with prayers like, "Oh Jesus, if only...well, we'd give up anything...Vera is so...well, how could we do this without... uh uh uh uhhhh...so important. Please just...merciful Lord." Thoroughly shrill, dismembered requests.

Vera is moved to tears she can't shed. Lord, she thinks, why couldn't you have pulled this little stunt on me when I was alone? Why did you do this to them? She wraps herself against her friends, providing heat and light, which is the best she can do. She knows they feel her because they swat the empty air in just exactly the places Vera has made contact—their cheeks, their arms, and the sweet spots on their necks where Vera has kissed them consolingly. How she loves her friends.

But the ongoing ordeal is confusing to Vera, too, and she is fighting off a panic of her own. After all, she wonders, how long can the spirit detach from the body without the body failing? For all she knows, this is the way life ends. The last time this happened, or at least presumes this happened, she was knocked out cold and brought to the hospital by Monk. But now for some reason, her spirit is conscious even without her body. Alive and well and observing the disparate energy of her friends and neighborly paramedics. She floats above the gurney as they wheel her into ER. She watches as the doctors evaluate her, attach her to this IV and that, call out medical terms, draw blood, and run tests. One thing she is relieved about—she feels no physical pain.

"I'm fine," she keeps calling out. "Doesn't anyone hear me?" Just when she thinks she can take no more, she bends at the waist in grief and frustration, then stretches back up and sighs. It is then that she sees Monk.

"Look at you," he says, grinning, as he watches her from a corner of the room. He is still dressed in his old mismatched sweat suit and dirty sneakers. Leave it to Monk not to change his clothes for eternity. "You're beautiful," he says. His body glows.

She glides over to him and lowers herself to embrace him, but it's like two parallel planes of light trying to intersect. Impossible. They can't feel each other, only look. "You've put on some weight," she says.

"They feed me good up here."

"Well," she corrects him, smiling. "They feed you well."

"I miss you," he says.

"I used to think heaven took care of that part," she says plaintively. "I used to think once we went to heaven, we would feel only joy."

His chest heaves. "I'm working on it. What I found out is if you don't work on it down there, you gotta work on it up here." He looks down. "I took a lot for granted. I took you for granted. I'm sorry..."

She nods eagerly. "I forgive you, Monk. I do. You led a good life, all in all."

"Except for that one thing. How could I...? I just...I'm so ashamed."

"Forgive yourself," says Vera. "You must. You can't ascend until you do." Every lumen of light in her new anatomy aches to touch him. To attach to him, even. She feels herself crying, though she can't feel the tears.

Down below, a nurse says, "Oh my God, look—tears! She's crying!"

"Well, I'll be damned," says a doctor. "Maybe she's coming out of the coma."

"I have to go," says Vera to Monk.

He reaches his arm out and says, "First, come with me. I want to show you something."

She is metal to his magnet and cannot resist the attraction. She floats along, above his right shoulder, the luminescent cord tightening as he takes her out of the ER room and into the corridor where Mia is charging down the hall, weeping, "Mom! Mom! Mom! Where's my mother?"

Vera gasps. "Oh, Monk! Poor Mia! She can't lose both of us."

"Just watch," he says patiently.

Mia is a cosmetic wreck with mascara running down her sallow cheeks, her black hair filled with static and flying in every direction. She's dressed in what Vera can only guess are flannel pajama bottoms and a red silk sweater she must have pulled from the closet on her way out. Her feet are clad in mismatched mules. She's thinner than Vera has ever seen her.

Louise jumps up. "You came!" exclaims Louise. "Oh, I knew you would, dear. I knew you'd come!"

Margaret and Louise embrace Mia and escort her to the waiting room.

"They won't let us back there just now," says Margaret. "They're evaluating your mother. Later, though."

But Mia, throwing her limbs forward like a wild animal, forges ahead and pushes open the swinging doors. "I want to see Vera Wright!" she demands. "I want to see my mother. You can't stop me."

A nurse rushes forward to join Mia before she arrives at the bed and says, "Now dear, the doctors need a little space here to see what's going on. But her vital signs are promising. Her brain activity is a little...confusing."

Mia gulps for air. "Did she have a stroke?"

"We don't know, dear, but we're finding out." She ushers Mia out the doors and into the waiting room. "I promise we'll get back to you as soon as we can.

"Don't let her die," pleads Mia. "Please don't let her die."

Louise sits Mia down beside her and strokes her arms and back gently. "Just pray for your Mom," she says. "The Lord will listen."

At this, Mia breaks into a spasm of chokes and sobs. Tears stream down her cheeks and chin as she says, "I did this."

Vera watches from her position with Monk, and she is moved beyond words. He tries to hold her, but can't get the grip that they both would like. "She's healed," he says. "The Lord healed her. He listened to your request and he healed her."

These words issued from the mouth of Monk Wright stun Vera. "Why, Monk," she says, "you know the Lord?"

He smirks, "Well, you know, I've been watching you and the ladies. And I can see what's going on. Not everything, you understand...even from here it's a mystery."

"But you heard me ask the Lord to heal her?" she says absently as she turns to study Mia more closely. "You heard all of that, did you? And all my tantrums?" She turns back around to see Monk's response, but he has vanished. This leaves Vera with a hollowness so deep she has a hard time keeping her light about her. It sags around her, heavy, drooping, and she fights hard to collect herself, to bring herself back to the center. So this is what it looks like, she thinks. The kinetic ether, the spirit light, when it falls apart. This is what it looks like. She studies the room around her and sees Mia, Margaret and Louise huddled together in earnest, their light drained from their bodies and pooled at their feet.

She thinks that she can't survive long like this—outside of her body with her light so disparate—and just as she has this thought, she is drawn back into the examining room, and from there, through her lower back into her body where she alights with a flash, opens her eyes wide and attempts to sit up. "My daughter," she says. "My daughter is here. I want to see her."

The doctor steps back. "Well, what do you know?" he says, grinning. "If that's not a miracle, I don't know what is. She knew the girl was here." He turns to the nurse at the door. "Greta, go get the daughter."

January 20th—well, finally it's happened. After an MRI and a battery of tests, I was released from the hospital fit as a fiddle, and Mia was admitted for addiction. The Lord is kind and merciful, though his ways are mightily strange! Also, before Mia was admitted, Margaret and Louise helped her find a lawyer who has already served Frederick with divorce papers. Mia is being very brave and apologetic and has told me everything about Frederick's abuse. Apparently he lost so much of his family's money 'investing' that he decided to try his hand at something a little faster and easier—drugs. Huge quantities of imported cocaine and heroin, hidden cleverly in the bowels of his parents' own cruise ships. Not to mention the assortment of designer pills made right in the USA. Mia claimed he was responsible for *getting her hooked on heroin—not that she's abdicated all responsibility, just that one day he substituted heroin for her usual pile of cocaine. And from there, of course...she begged for more. When he refused to supply her, said she was 'completely out of control', well, she found her own sources.*

I know I can't trust everything she says yet, but still...God help my child. Bless her and keep her strong, because I find myself getting lighter and lighter, and worry that my time is short. How will I possibly be able to accomplish all that I must? All I've been asked to do? Not to mention the fact that Margaret has already reported Frederick to the authorities, and we have the prospect of a trial on our hands, not to mention Frederick's immediate threats.

Well anyway, later today Margaret and Louise are coming over to pack my things for the movers, who come in two days. Margaret has placed my house and hers on the market, and we've already gotten bids, which believe me, is no small miracle in this market. I'm excited to move to Louise's house, because after this last fiasco, I realize that I need support from people who understand the nature of my issues. I do not want to be sent off in an ambulance every time my spirit decides to take a hike, which it seems to enjoy doing rather frequently of late. It's as if I have no control! I can't picture myself telling a doctor that I'm perfectly fine—that from time to time I leave my body without notice. Oh, and by the way, while I'm traveling around here and there, I even converse with people, like Fiona, who retains no memory of the encounter. I laid my hands on her and healed her, and she'll never know who did it. Not that I'm looking for credit. From all I've seen, credit on earth amounts to debit in heaven. Best to stay anonymous...

Vera's feverish journal writing is interrupted by the doorbell, and she lays down her pen to answer it. Out of old habit, she checks her face in the mirror and is surprised to see very little of the actual wrinkles which she knows map her face, but instead, a glimmer that she hadn't noticed before. Well, isn't that interesting, she thinks. If she'd ever seen that light before, she would not have cared less about lipstick—hers or anyone else's. Why, I look positively glowing, she thinks. If I could bottle this look—I'd make a million dollars! She is barely concealing an inner joyful smile that is bubbling up like a hot spring when she opens the door to find Father Max standing on the threshold.

"Well now, don't you look well," he says. "I was very worried when you went into the hospital."

She nods for him to enter. "Yes, well, that was something else," she says. "An odd kind of thing. But thanks for your concern."

The phone rings and Vera raises her index finger to Father Max, indicating that she would only be a minute. "Hello?" she says into the phone.

"Mrs. Wright?"

"Yes, this is she."

"This is Sandra Dunlap from Canaan General. About your MRI?"

"Well, yes, what about it?" says Vera. She looks at Father Max and points to the couch, but he remains standing.

"The, um, the film? Well, it has a blotch on it of some kind."

"A blotch?" says Vera. "Oh dear."

"Oh, no. Nothing to concern yourself with, or believe me, the doctor would be calling you himself."

"I see."

"But just a...a blotch. Directly on the film itself."

"Well haven't they already read those films? I mean, didn't they read them at the hospital while I was there? That's what they told me, anyway. After all, they released me."

"Yes, but your internist requested that the films be reviewed by another radiologist. A second opinion. It's pretty routine, but this time, there's a, well..."

"A blotch," says Vera.

"Yes, that's what it says here. And they'd like to repeat the procedure with new film. This film is obviously...faulty. Or possibly, I don't know...something was spilled on it. The...blotch is highly irregular, from an outside source evidently. Or as I said...a corrosion of the film itself. No way to know."

Vera shifts her weight. "Well fine then. When would you like me to come in?" She points to the coffee maker and widens her eyes at Father Max. He shakes his head, no.

"Can you come in on Thursday at eleven?"

"Yes, I'll be there on Thursday at eleven."

"Thank you, Mrs. Wright!"

Vera hangs up and smiles uncertainly at Father Max. "So..."

"Something wrong with your MRI?" he asks.

"No, not really. Something wrong with the film."

"So you'll repeat it on Thursday? Not that I was listening."

Vera smiles. "Thursday," she says. "Not a pleasant exam, but well...I'll offer it up."

He nods. "And, um, you're moving?" He folds his arms awkwardly. "That's what Louise and Margaret tell me."

"Yes."

"The Lord?"

"That's right."

"Mmhmm." He scratches the back of his head. "Vera...I've talked to Louise and Margaret, and I'm trying to understand, truly I am..."

"I've decided to show you something," she says brightly.

He stares at her for a minute. "Alright then. Show me."

She walks with him into the salon office and opens the desk drawer stuffed with her writings. "The Lord has shown me the mercy of every other miracle but this one," she says. "I know if I keep these in a drawer, this miracle will never come to light." She takes the papers out, lines them up in order of date, places the bulk of them in a plastic bag and hands a sampling to Father Max. "What do you think?"

He flips through them. "What is it?"

"It's...I don't know exactly. It's what the Lord told me to write down. I just..."

He screws his face up quizzically. "You just sit here for...what? How long? Hours, days, weeks?" He huffs. "And scribble?"

Her heart drops. "Well...yes."

"Vera..."

"It means something though," she says. "And the Lord himself asked me to pray for an interpreter. A translator."

He flips through the pile. "This is not a language, Vera. It's just lines and circles."

"But maybe...?"

He shakes his head. "I don't think so. This is no language. I'm sorry. I think there's another problem here. A form of deception. Not that you're deceiving anyone, not on purpose anyway." He glimpses the ceiling. "You're under great stress, I realize. What with Monk's death and Mia."

Vera rubs her forehead in little circles.

"I know you believe what you..." he can't seem to finish.

"Hear," she says. "I believe what I hear. The Lord talks to me." She grabs the papers from his hands, stuffs them in the bag with the rest of them and places it on the desk. "I didn't ask for this, you know. And anyway what makes you think that men have a monopoly on spiritual experiences?"

"Well, as a matter of fact, I don't think men have a monopoly. There are many women saints. Lots of them. Seers and mystics, even."

"So you've said before, but why do you think the Lord only made himself known on earth to people in our distant past? People like Abraham and Noah? Why other civilizations and not ours? Are we not worth the trip? "

"Well, of course we're worth it. He died for us."

She opens her arms. "Why can't you understand that he's still trying to tell us things? That we're in dangerous times and there are important things that we need to know. Now."

"These things have to be approached from the viewpoint of suspicion. It's highly unlikely...you have to understand how rare the real thing is. And why you specifically?"

"Because I don't know any better maybe? Because I can't block the experiences, not even one of them." She closes her eyes. "God knows I've tried."

"What other experiences?" he asks. "I mean, other than the dinners. And the new church." He points to the bag of writings. "And...and these."

Vera gets the feeling again, the tingling in the limbs and lower back. Oh no, she thinks, not now! Oh God, not now! "I need you to leave," she says.

"Are you okay?"

She leans against her desk. "I'm fine, but I'm tired, and I need you to leave now." A dizziness comes over her, a feeling she can't remember from the other times. She outright orders him to leave. "Now," she says. "Please."

"But you seem to need help."

"I don't need help. I need to be alone."

"Okay then." He grabs the bag of papers before she can stop him, and walks through the door of her salon. "I'll get back to you on these," he says. "I'll have a closer look. Be well, Vera."

No sooner does he exit, than she lies down on the office couch, and in seconds, she is popped out of her lower back, a place called the 'sacrum,' as Margaret discovered in her research. "Oh looky, Vera," Margaret said while flipping through a book on the history of mystical experience, "the lower back is called the sacrum. And the sacrum is the seat of the soul!" This made sense to both of them, and generated a great deal of relief in Vera. Somebody knew something, which means she wasn't the first to experience it! And the fact that she was not alone in her experience may be the single fact that keeps her from going insane.

Vera checks her cord to be sure it's connected to her body, and follows Father Max into his ridiculous fire-engine red Beatle convertible. Once inside, he drops his head and pounds the steering wheel. "Damn," he says. "Damn. Damn. Damn." He stares at the thick package of notepaper and sighs deeply, then starts the ignition and unknowingly, drives off with her incandescent spirit seated right beside him.

The seat belt alarm goes off and he checks his belt, which is secured. 'Bing bing bing' goes the alarm, and he is utterly perplexed, since there are no heavy packages in the passenger seat. 'Bing bing bing.' He leans over and moves the bag of her writings from the seat to the floor, but the binging does not stop. He pounds the steering wheel, frustrated. Vera wants to laugh, but is not sure exactly how much of her vibration is making its way through. Obviously from the seat alarm, her spirit carries more weight than she thought! Perhaps if she laughs he'll sense that, too, maybe even hear it, and crash his car looking for the source.

Anyway, she sees that it's way too much for him, and she quiets down. She thinks priests should know a lot more about the supernatural. Why don't they? It was like a doctor knowing nothing about diet and nutrition! Is the supernatural not fundamental to our spiritual and religious existence? Are we not primarily comprised of spirit and light, not bones and flesh? Are we not, in fact, spirit first and last? So why do our priests ignore the spirit? What are they afraid of? Right then and there she vows to teach some level of her experience in the seminary of the Society of Loaves and Fishes.

The alarm eventually ceases. Father Max turns the radio to a rock and roll station and taps his left foot as he drives.

"Lay-la!" he wails at the top of his lungs. "You got me on my knees, Lay-la!" Vera can't believe priests do this. From time to time, stopped at a red light or waiting at an intersection, humming whatever tune, he reaches down and selects one of her papers and studies it. This makes her hopeful. At one point he starts nodding, rubbing his chin as if he is actually getting some inspiration, making some progress. As if the sticks and circles are beginning to make sense to him.

Twenty-five minutes later, Vera does not recognize her surroundings — where are they? They've driven way up Route 17 North and into the Ramapo Mountains. Now they are driving up a long, heavily wooded dirt path. She worries that it's just too far to travel outside of her body, and as soon as that worry becomes a palpable fear, she awakens on the couch in her salon.

"Oh, there you are, dear," says Margaret. "Resting?"

Vera rubs her eyes. "That's right," she says.

Margaret sits beside her on the couch. "FYI, Vera," she says, "Father Max interrogated Louise and me at the rectory this morning. I think the young man feels responsible for us, poor soul."

This makes Vera giggle, which makes Margaret giggle back. "Can you imagine feeling responsible for a bunch of old hags like us who simply refuse to listen?" says Margaret. She slaps her knees, chuckling. "Why, it's just hilarious when you think of it."

"Old cleaning hags who tell him they hear the Lord!" says Vera. "And have decided to start a new religious order! Without men!" She caves into a helpless laugh.

"A new church, really," says Margaret. "Because let's face it, dear, do we really think the Pope is going to believe a word of this?!" She holds her belly.

Vera giggles in spite of herself. In spite of the dead seriousness of their plight.

"Why, it's just hilarious," repeats Margaret, roaring in her deep timbre. "And everyone around them gets healed..."

She is desperate for breath. "I've never laughed so hard...since..." She chokes. "Since all this...ha ha ha! And who'd have thought the Lord would be such a comedian!"

Vera sits up. "He is, isn't he?"

Margaret says, "Yes he is, and maybe that's the best sign of his presence after all. Not all this damn seriousness, but the out and out comedy of it all."

Vera is very cheered. "I love you, Margaret," she says.

Margaret's eyes tear. "And you, dear girl—why, you're just the best thing that ever happened to me. And wasn't he the clever one, choosing a dear like you!"

As they hug, Vera feels the sensation again. "Oh no, Margaret," she says, "here it comes again. Please don't take me to the hospital."

"Well of course not," reassures Margaret. "I'll sit right here taking your pulse until you return." And at that, Vera disappears again.

Vera doesn't always remember where she's been, but it's usually on some mission of mercy. Today she finds herself with Fiona and her husband, Gordon, on their trip to the hospital.

"You're healed," Vera whispers in her right ear. "You don't have cancer anymore."

She knows Fiona senses something, because she sticks her right index finger in her ear and twirls it as if to clear a plug. Her head keeps turning this way and that as Vera persists, "You're healed. Don't let them remove your breasts."

Fiona bites the inside of her cheek, absorbing this subtle input.

"Another mammogram," says Vera. "Or sonogram, whatever. Don't let them remove your breasts. Another test. Make them give you another test."

Eventually, Fiona turns to her burly husband and says, "Gordon?"

He nods. "Yeah, hon?"

"I'm healed."

He frowns, pulling hard on his handlebar moustache. "What's that?"

She breaks into a grin. "I said I'm healed!"

"Oh no you don't!" he says. "Don't tell me that, Fiona. That's denial. I know you're scared, and so am I. But you've got to have that surgery."

When they arrive at the hospital, Vera keeps at her, "Get re-tested, Fiona. You're healed. Don't let them take your breasts. Keep your breasts." Fiona becomes so restless that she pitches a fit to be re-tested, and eventually Gordon begs the doctor to indulge her, and with great reluctance, the doctor agrees.

"I don't understand," says the radiologist when he compares the two films.

Fiona's surgeon stares in awe. "Are you sure these are the right films?" he asks. "Are you sure they're all hers?"

The radiologist studies them more closely, refers back to the envelopes for identification and then confirms that they do both indeed belong to Fiona Finnegan. They decide to take another biopsy from the affected area in Fiona's breast, and with that, Vera darts back to her body on Destiny Drive assured that the biopsy will bear out the truth. Fiona is healed. Fiona will not lose her breasts. God's mercy knows no bounds.

Weeks later, Vera thinks that for all the scary trouble the Lord has put her through, at this point nobody could feel better about her life than Vera does right now. In spirit, she is able to flit about anonymously helping people right and left while still living safely in the bosom of the luxurious nest created by Margaret and Louise. Her room at Louise's is a veritable palace—a plump mattress with even plumper linens and pillows. The bedding is as light and fluffy as Vera herself feels lately, and when she lies down in the undulating mounds of white cloud, she feels like just another feather on the bed. She could do without the tassels and fussy equestrian-print wallpaper, but she would never tell that to Louise. Louise and Margaret want only to please Vera—to spoil her rotten in the physical world as she becomes more and more present in the spiritual.

"Eat some more stew," says Louise from time to time. "You're looking very...light."

"An occasional glass of brandy won't hurt you, dear," Margaret has been known to say. "It will stimulate your blood. You're looking peeked."

The truth is, with all her meditation and prayer, Vera has begun to lose interest in food. When she isn't out-and-out fasting, she's eating little more than bread and fish, her daily meal, even though she has not held a formal supper of Loaves and Fishes since they moved to Louise's house. Tonight will be their first, the great initiation of the Society of Loaves and Fishes in their new and hopefully permanent home.

Vera is feeling quite light as she prepares for the evening events. Her "halo" as Margaret and Louise refer to the gradually intensifying light that surrounds her, is on the golden side of amber tonight. She is ready for anything. Why, with the Lord, you just never know what's next! She does not concern herself anymore with his agenda. Whatever he wants, she'll do it. After all, Mia is doing so well in recovery, even her doctor is amazed. According to him, Mia's personal realizations have been profound. She is committed not only to her own recovery, but to those of her fellow patients. As far as Vera is concerned, the miracle of Mia's recovery has sealed her covenant with the Lord. Now, Vera belongs to him and him alone.

She dresses in the simple floor-length burgundy velvet shift with a hood, designed and sewn by Margaret herself. "I know you like your sweat clothes, dear," Margaret had said. "Nothing against them. But I think if we intend to start a church, we need to experiment with some uniforms. Try this!" And voila, she pulled the lovely burgundy velvet cassock from behind her and held it up by the shoulders. "Why, it's perfect!" said Vera. So Margaret and Louise labored night and day to finish them for tonight's dinner, one for each disciple.

And now, as Vera leaves her bedroom and fairly glides down the long, high hall, she feels almost too elegant to be representing God. But then doesn't God enjoy feeling good too, she thinks. Well of course he does! And she descends the stairs in her sweeping cassock to a chorus of applause from the other women, who are similarly dressed.

"Don't applaud me!" she chides the ladies. "Unless of course the applause are for the Lord who works through me."

"Praise the Lord!" they all cheer, jumping like children.

Vera can't believe how beautiful they look, all dressed in burgundy velvet and gathered in Louise's elegant atrium foyer. What an unlikely assemblage! Why, they look like a monastery of holy female druids—the first ever to dare priestly duties. And yet...they're the Martha's! The same women who think nothing of hunkering down to scrub the bottoms of church pews with turpentine and toothbrushes to remove hardened bubble gum and God knows what else.

After a brief greeting, Margaret files them into Louise's elaborate dining room, complete with a raging fire in the massive stone fireplace, candles of different lengths and widths burning everywhere—on the mantle, the table, and against the apron of the diamond-paned windows. The lights of the multi-tiered crystal chandelier are dimmed, the table set luxuriously with all of Louise's and Margaret's best silver and linen. It's a feast for royalty!

Just as Vera settles into her comfortable captain's chair at the head of the table and bows her head for grace, the doorbell rings.

"Oh my," says Louise. "Who could that be?"

"Maybe we shouldn't answer," says Clara.

"It's probably just a solicitor," says Gertrude.

"We certainly don't get many of those around here," says Louise suspiciously. The ringing persists until it merges into one steady buzz. "Oh what the heck," she says, rising. She hustles out of the room. "Such a bother. I'll just send them away."

Out of view now, Louise can be heard click clacking to the door on the granite floor. Click clack. Click clack. The door creaks open. "Well, hello!" says Louise in her liveliest voice, and a minute later she walks into the living room with Fiona on her arm.

Vera nods happily. "Fiona!" she says. "Welcome."

"I just want you to know," Fiona says sniffling, "that my miracle was granted. I don't know if you know..."

Gertrude hands her a tissue.

"That, um, well...I know I behaved badly, but I didn't really believe that cancer could actually be cured. Or that the Lord could work through, um, a woman, you know, beautician. I just...I don't know. And it was—the cancer is gone!" She searches for the words. "Vera?" she says, sniffling.

"I know," says Vera, smiling. "A true miracle."

Fiona blows her nose heartily into the tissue. "I'm not here to eat dinner," she says, "I don't deserve to. I just, well, wanted to apologize for my bad behavior. And...and for not believing..."

"For not suspending your disbelief, you mean," says Lillian gently.

Vera rises and goes to Fiona, whom she hugs. "We want you to stay for supper," she says. "Don't we ladies?"

"We do!" they cry.

So, red-eyed and puffy-cheeked, Fiona takes a seat. Margaret fetches another cassock, and they all say grace after which Vera says stone-faced and with eyelids fluttering, "The Lord wishes you to know that the time has come. The world is about to change."

The clinking of dishes and utensils ends abruptly.

"The world is about to become something new," says Vera, open-eyed now, though deeply entranced. "The Lord wants you to wake up to yourselves, your true and higher selves, so that you will be able to reassure those around you in the midst of confusion and chaos. He wishes the clogged arteries of the world to heal so that his full light might have passage through us. He wishes this awakening to initiate through us...the Society of Loaves and Fishes."

Now the feeling comes over her again, only this time it begins at the crown and bores through her head and down her entire spine like a drill, deep and unforgiving. By the time it reaches her knees she is lifting off, spirit and...good God in heaven...full physical body, levitating in full view of them all, up and up until she hovers six feet above them. Her scuffed black pumps drop from her feet, bump against the chair and land on the floor. Though in her mind's eye she is staring out at all creation—the landscape of infinity laid out in a palette of wild, vivid colors and extraordinary shapes for which there are no words but *ineffable*—still she is vaguely aware of the situation at hand in Louise's dining room. She can see the ladies' jaws unhinge; their eyes glaze; the paralysis creep into their limbs. She watches one by one as they swoon, alternately falling to their knees and passing out.

Only Margaret is left standing.

Chapter Nineteen

"Come down from the ceiling, Vera," croons Margaret. "You can do it, dear. Come on!" She pats Vera's chair. "Right down here. Come to Margaret."

In her trance, Vera is only half aware of Margaret's distress. Oh, if only Margaret could see the Lord's true handiwork, she thinks, the heavenly delights that await us all — she would never call me back down to Louise's dining room. She would reach up here to join me instead.

"Vera," says the Lord in a rich and mellifluous voice, "this is the world that awaits you and all of humanity. I have created this for you."

Vera spreads her arms to embrace this world — this new and transformed earth — to consume and be consumed by it at the same time. To become one with its radiance, serenity, and peace, the likes of which she has never before experienced or even imagined. She is ambushed by love, and yet...more than love. For if this is love, she thinks, she has never really known love. Not even with Monk or Mia.

Back down below, Margaret's signals interfere. "Come on, Vera," she says. "That's a good girl. Come on back down to Margaret." She clucks and coos and tsks as she pats the chair.

At the same time Vera is feasting on the spiritual nectar of the Lord's provision, she is saying to Margaret, "I can't do it. I can't come down. I'm trying, but I can't do it." It's as if she's two different people with two different minds. The Vera who is one with the infinite landscape of the transformed earth is not surrendering the least to the gravity of the old earth in Louise's house. But apparently some part of Vera is still attached to the details of common courtesy and dining etiquette, because Margaret continues to talk to that Vera, and that Vera wiggles her legs and tries every trick she can think of to force herself back down, to no avail.

Margaret scratches her head for a minute then kneels awkwardly on the wide seat of the captain's chair. Leaning against the chair back, she slowly elevates herself to a crouching position. After stabilizing herself, she reaches up to grab Vera's right ankle and instantly retracts. "Ouch!" she screams, tottering. "You burned my hand! Whoa! Whoa! Whoa!" She manages to steady herself while muttering, "Dear God, dear God, don't let me fall," then returns slowly to her knees and climbs off. "That halo is hot!" she says, blowing on her hand. "I don't know how you stand it."

"Sorry," says Vera. "It doesn't feel so hot to me." The persistence of this conversation draws her attention closer to the dining room, and she contemplates her condition for a minute. The women are clearly disturbed over her flotation. She says, "Maybe I just don't weigh enough. Maybe I need some food."

Margaret nods and breaks off a chunk of sourdough bread. "I'll toss it up to you," she says. "How's that? I don't want to get close to that heat again."

Vera cups her hands to catch the bread, but Margaret pitches a fastball off target that hits the mantle and lands on the hearth. She breaks off another chunk of bread, removes her shoes, and reluctantly climbs back onto the seat of Vera's chair. Wobbling a bit, trying to balance herself, she holds onto the chair back with her left hand and extends the bread in her right. "Take it; take it!" she shrieks. "Ouch! Ouch! Hurry up and take it, dear, I'm practically sweating blood. Ouch!"

Vera leans over and snags the bread. "Thank you, Margaret," she says and manages to chew it as she refocuses on the magnitude and magnificence of the vision the Lord has created before her. She is drunk with desire to enter it.

"Can you not share this vision with the other disciples?" she pleads to the Lord.

"No," he says. "Absolutely not. They must act in faith upon your description and the miracle of your levitation."

Vera glances down and hears Gertrude exclaim, "Mary, Mother of God!"

She watches as Clara opens her eyes and cries, "She's still up there!" and THUD, passes out again. Vera is sorry for the distress she's causing them.

In a state of agitation, Margaret stumbles down from the chair and over to Louise who is still out cold, her head lying flat out on her dinner plate like John the Baptist. Margaret shakes Louise's shoulders hard and says, "Louise Lambert, wake up and help me out. You're supposed to be one of the strong ones! Hasn't Vera taught you anything these last few months?"

As Vera finishes her bread and gazes out on her singular view of eternity, another event occurs. Something brand new. At the same time she hovers on the ceiling of Louise's grand dining room, she also walks down the stark corridor of the Canaan General rehab center toward Mia's room. Well, isn't this the oddest thing? she thinks. How can I be in two physical places at one time? And to her it feels as if she is completely present in both locations. Since the ladies are still in various stages of consciousness, Vera is much more interested in Mia than she is in them.

She knocks on Mia's door.

"Who is it?" says Mia in a sleepy voice.

Vera opens the door slightly and peeks in. "It's your mother!" she says gleefully.

Mia squashes a cigarette and slides the ashtray under the bed. "Mom? I can't believe you're here! How did you get in?"

"Just walked down the hall," says Vera shrugging. She advances to embrace her daughter.

"But it's not allowed during the week," says Mia. They hug, and then Mia pushes back slightly to study Vera.

"Mom, you're...filled with..." She places her hand up and down Vera's body. "Light and... Ouch! Heat!" She touches her mother's arm. "But you're also... am I dreaming this?" She knocks on her head with her knuckles.

"Not at all," reassures Vera. She sits wearily down on the side of Mia's bed. "It's hard to explain. Even to myself. I am made of light and yet not of light...I don't know. And I'm able to appear in places..."

Mia steps back, her mouth open in fear.

"Don't be afraid, dear."

But Mia's hand flies to her mouth. "You're not my mother," she says in a shaky voice. "Are you? You're not my Mom."

"Of course I am, Mia!"

"You're a hallucination!" She steps back and bites her thumbnail. "All those drugs...oh my God! I'm hallucinating without the drugs!"

Mia's reaction is so infectious, it scares Vera. Is that what I've become, Vera thinks—a hallucination? "No, Mia, no! There's nothing to be scared of! It's me!" She pinches a piece of skin to prove it.

Mia points her finger at Vera as she takes another step back. "You...you ended a sentence with a preposition. And you used 'me' instead of the reflexive 'I'. My mother would never have done that—either of those things. Whoever you are—leave now."

Vera sighs. "I admit it," she says. "I've been letting my grammar go. My life is harder than that right now." She pulls at the ends of her gray hair. "I don't even color my hair anymore. All those wonderful colors...I can't even remember their names. Not to mention how godawful Louise's hair is looking these days."

These details seem to convince Mia. She exhales with relief and pulls on the ends of her raggedy braids. "My hair is a mess, too," she says.

"Your hair is beautiful," says Vera. She reaches up to stroke it.

After a pause, Mia says, "I can't believe you came just now. I mean...right at this moment."

"No?"

Mia shakes her head. "I was just thinking how nice it would be to have a drink. A nice chilled martini extra dry and straight up with a couple of olives."

"That's the devil talking."

Mia nods sadly. "That's what they tell me."

"The devil wears a slinky black dress," says Vera. "With ropes of pearls. Always enticing. Beware of anything too enticing."

"I feel better now, though," says Mia. "Since you came. You're the answer to a prayer. I wanted to get high and now I'm past it."

There's a knock on the door followed by a gruff voice. "Who are you talking to, Mia?" A pause. "Is that smoke I smell in there?"

"Oh Mom," Mia whispers, wide-eyed. "It's the floor monitor. You have to get out now!" She leans across her bed and opens a window.

"When you're released from here," says Vera, "do what the ladies tell you to do. Louise and Margaret, that is. Do what they say. Promise me, Mia."

Mia nods tearfully. "But Mom..."

And at that, Vera finds herself in full consciousness back on the ceiling of Louise's dining room. The ladies are seated peacefully in their chairs reciting the rosary on their beads, except for Rosemary who is fanning herself in the corner.

As the rosary ends, Vera is brought slowly back down to the chair.

Margaret grins. "Well now...you're back amongst the seated!"

"I'm sorry. I don't know what came over me."

Margaret holds up her hand. "No apologies, dear. For heaven's sake, it's just another in a long line of miracles we've been fortunate enough to witness." She nods to the rest of them. "Isn't that right, ladies?"

"Now that I think of it, I remember reading about it somewhere," says Rosemary. "One of the saints..."

"Padre Pio," says Gertrude, clapping. "From Italy—San Giovanni de Rotunda."

"Yes, that's right," says Fiona. "He levitated...and also bilocated! As did Saint Lidwina from Holland."

"I know about Padre Pio," says Clara. "I have one of his relics!"

Vera's eyes shift left to right as she processes this information. "Fiona," she says. "What do you mean, 'bilocated'?"

"That means that he was able to appear in two places at once," says Fiona. "He did it all the time. Maybe more than two places, who knows?"

"So you mean he could be talking to you right now and visiting someone in the hospital at the same time?"

"Exactly right," says Fiona. "You can borrow my book. He also had the stigmata. When his wounds bled, they smelled like roses."

"All the saints smell like roses," says Gertrude. "That's how you know you're in the presence of a saint."

Vera inspects her hands and wrists. "Well, I'm not bleeding. I don't smell like a rose, either, and I'm not..." she nods emphatically, "... a saint."

The others nod noncommittally.

"I'm not," she repeats more forcefully.

Margaret folds her hands on the table in front of her, circling her thumbs for a minute. "Now Vera, are we not all supposed to become saints?"

"I suppose. But these gifts..."

"Does the Lord not take the weak and make them strong?"

Vera tilts her head at Margaret. "Well, yes. I do remember Father Max saying that a time or two."

"Not to mention St. Paul," says Louise. "St. Paul said it long before Father Max ever did. Father Max got it from St. Paul, not the other way around."

Margaret wags her finger at Vera. "Accepting the Lord's gifts with humility is important. Saint or no saint."

"I try to accept them," says Vera. "But isn't this...a bit extreme?"

"Why don't you let the Lord tell us what's extreme and what's not? Hmmm?" says Margaret. "Who's a saint and who isn't."

Vera smiles reluctantly.

"Well then," says Louise as she lifts the platter of scrod, "shall we begin?"

The disciples pray and chat and eat for hours in warm sorority, the fire burning brightly, the candles flickering, the food abundant and the joy apparent. When Vera retires into bed that night, she is exhausted but satisfied that through all these trials the Lord has provided her with a true spiritual family. She draws the feather comforter to her chin, burrows into the mounds of feathery softness, and dozes off to sleep as she prays contentedly, "Lord, whatever you choose to make of my life, I accept."

What the Lord chooses to give her is a night of tossing and turning underscored with a penetrating unrest. Deep in sleep and yet fully awake, Vera is filled with a high degree of confusion and indeterminate discomfort. What is going on! So much is happening; she can't keep track of it! Why, she is visiting her mother, her father, and Monk at the same time she is consoling Mia in the hospital and healing Father Max's cousin of crippling rheumatoid arthritis. And what is this? My God! Why she's smack in the middle of the Pope's bedroom as he is kneeling on an elaborate, velvet-cushioned *prie dieu* bench, engaged in recitative prayer.

The Pope blinks at her and rubs his eyes. "Where did you come from?" he asks, only slightly alarmed. "Who are you? How did you get in here?"

She bows her head slightly. "Your Excellency, I am Vera Wright from Canaan, New Jersey, USA. The Lord has sent me here to ask you to divest his church of its riches. He says his riches are to be donated to the poor, that he never wished his church to amass material wealth." She speaks with other-worldly certitude, and is only slightly self-conscious of her white terrycloth bathrobe and red fuzzy slippers.

The Pope makes a hurried sign of the cross in front of her and sprinkles holy water in her direction. The holy water only strengthens her light, and she glides closer to him saying, "The Lord wishes you to ordain his priests."

"His priests are being ordained," says the Pope, as he sprinkles more water. He leans against his kneeler to rise, but is clearly having difficulty.

"Many of his new priests are women," she says. "The Lord says you are not ordaining the women. The women are key to the future of his Church."

The Pope presses a button on the ledge of his bench. An alarm resounds through the cavernous suite of rooms, and Vera disappears.

In the next moment, aspects of herself that are scattered here and there around the multi-verse coalesce into one integral and super-conscious spirit who finds herself in an expansive field of waist-high, wind-bent wheat. In all its natural simplicity, this is the singular most beautiful place she has ever seen. The skies are drenched in a rich golden light that originates from no apparent source. And then, all at once, out of a vanishing point on the horizon appears a man soaked in near-blinding sunlight and dressed in an alabaster gown that glows fifty feet from all points of his body. In the center of his body is a radiating sphere of crimson. He looks directly at Vera and beckons to her with his right hand.

Her spirit knows no restraint and takes flight with the unencumbered impulse of a child squealing with extravagant delight. "Hello!" she says. "It's you, isn't it?"

"Yes, it is," he says kindly. "It is I. Hello, Vera."

Vera nearly explodes at his familiarity — the realization that he recognized her in the first place, and then beckoned to her. "Where are you living now?" she asks.

He smiles beatifically. "High Water," he says.

"High Water?" she repeats. This is news to her.

"Yes," he says.

"May I tell anyone?"

"Tell everyone," he says. "Tell everyone you know."

Then he embraces her and she feels as if they are one thing, indivisible, as if she will never be able to return to herself alone. And why should she? Is he not her destiny? And just as she thinks it will never end, *must* never end, he slips into a sliver of supernatural light and disappears. She is awash in a tide of ecstatic joy that ends as abruptly as it began.

Vera awakens in her dark bedroom at Louise's house in an aching state of grievous loss. The void is unbearable. Her cheeks are streaked with tears; her psyche stunned by the glazed remains of his presence. All she can think is this — he knows my name. This is knowledge enough to eradicate the appalling weight of flesh and bone she is feeling now — the years of ordinariness recorded within her. "Where are you?" she cries out desperately from her bed. "Come back! Come back to me! Lord, why have you abandoned me?"

And with those words, hundreds of tiny pulsating arrows dart round and round the room like lasers, and just as Vera rises on her elbows to see what this is all about, they attack her from every conceivable direction. She can't protect herself enough, or at all. She ducks under the covers, but this doesn't protect her, and all at once her temples pound with pain and she becomes violently nauseous. She charges from the bed, barely making it to the bathroom, and kneels at the toilet, retching. Even as she vomits, tiny arrows in electric shades of chartreuse, fuchsia and scarlet aim for her eyes, her head, her heart. "Lord, help me," she pleads. "Lord... please...protect me."

But the Lord's presence is no longer apparent, and Vera crawls to her bed, her stomach clutched in spasm, her heart swollen with inflammation, a constant, shrill screech penetrating her eardrums like daggers. "Stop them!" she screams. "Lord, stop them!" She covers her ears and screams, "Stop! Aaaaaaaaaaaaa! Stop it! Lord...Lord..."

At this, footsteps pound down the hall, the door flies open, and Margaret appears in her big polka dot robe. Hers is a huge and powerful presence, and Vera has never been so happy to see anyone in her life. Margaret rushes to Vera's side and envelopes her in her arms. "There, there," she says.

"I'm going to be sick," says Vera.

Margaret runs to the bathroom for a waste can and lifts Vera up so she can use it. She rubs Vera's back as it spasms, but suddenly stiffens herself. 'Ohhh," she says, placing her hand on her chest. "Oh...oh my goodness." She gasps for breath.

"No!" screams Vera, who, unlike Margaret, is able to see the tiny darts penetrating Margaret's body now—her head, her chest, her stomach.

"Aaaaa! Aaaaa!" screams Margaret, who all at once loses her strength and collapses on the floor. "Louise!" she screams in a hollow, raspy voice. "Louise! Help us!"

Vera knows that Louise's room is too far down the hall. She'll never hear them. Not to mention her earplugs. But seeing Margaret in this condition brings Vera to powerful and forceful indignation. Ignoring the searing pain in her head, abdomen and lower back, she raises herself to her knees against the bedpost and yells, "If you have to attack me, so be it! But how DARE you harm my friend!" She grabs Margaret's hand. "Pray with me," she says.

Margaret nods weakly. "What's happening?" she gasps.

"Be gone, devil!" says Vera, and she blesses the air.

In a moment, a great wind blows through the room and the arrows disappear. Slowly, Vera recovers her equilibrium and Margaret sits up against the bedroom wall.

They are both hyperventilating.

When Margaret fully catches her breath, she says, "Mary, Queen of the Angels, Mother of God, and Spouse of the Most High, what was that?"

Vera hears the Lord's words in her right ear and repeats them aloud. "Spiritual warfare," she says. "We must be strong." She listens again. "Pray unceasingly."

Margaret places her hand against her chest, still winded. "Of course," she says. "We should have expected this."

"Warfare on a grand scale," says Vera, listening to the Lord. "Not to weaken us. But to strengthen us."

Margaret stares ahead. "Isn't there an easier way? I mean, they could have killed us."

Vera shakes her head blankly. "No," she says. "I'm getting a 'no'. No easier way. The way is narrow and scattered with unexpected obstacles and harmful debris."

"Nails," says Margaret, huffing. She raises a finger. "Sharp ones. Pointy side up."

"And rusty," agrees Vera. She leans to her right, into the voice. "He says we have to learn to look where we're going. To be completely awake."

"Even at night?" says Margaret. "Even when we're sleeping? There should be a limit!"

"But there isn't," says Vera. "There's no limit. No limit to anything. We've placed the limits on ourselves, he says. But now we have to be awake, Margaret. Even when we're sleeping."

It's all Vera and Margaret can do to stay awake in church the following morning. Louise sits between them, nudging them gently when Vera's head drops or Margaret inhales a raspy snore.

From the pulpit, Father Max continues the second reading from St. Paul to the Corinthians, "Listen to this secret truth: we shall not all die, but when the last trumpet sounds, we shall all be changed in an instant, as quickly as the blinking of an eye. For when the trumpet sounds, the dead will be raised, never to die again, and we shall all be changed. For what is mortal must be changed into what is immortal; what will die must be changed into what cannot die. So when this takes place, and the mortal has been changed into the immortal, then the scripture will come true: "Death is destroyed; victory is complete!"

Vera ponders these words as she stands for the gospel. *We shall not all die, but be changed in an instant.* Really? Isn't that what the Lord has been trying to tell her? She strains to hear as Father Max reads the gospel text.

"'Don't let anyone mislead you! For many will come in my name, saying, 'I am the Messiah.' They will lead many astray. And wars will break out near and far, but do not panic. Yes, these things must come, but the end won't follow immediately. The nations and kingdoms will proclaim war against each other, and there will be famines and earthquakes in many parts of the world. But all this will be only the beginning of the horrors to come.'"

Vera is suddenly riveted when Father Max reads, "'When the Son of man returns it will be like it was in Noah's day. In those days before the flood, the people were enjoying banquets and parties and weddings right up to the time Noah entered his boat. People didn't realize what was going to happen until the Flood came and swept them all away. That is the way it will be when the Son of Man comes.

"'Two men will be working together in the field; one will be taken, the other left behind. Two women will be grinding flour at the mill; one will be taken, the other left behind. So be prepared because you don't know what day your Lord is coming.' The Gospel of the Lord."

"Glory be to you, oh Lord," repeats the congregation before sitting for the homily.

After closing the Bible, Father Max strokes his chin thoughtfully for a moment and says to his congregation, "Do you know a false prophet?"

Vera is stung by his words.

He points his finger emphatically and raises his voice. "Do you know someone who claims to 'know' what the Lord wants for you and for me?" He brackets the word 'know'. "Someone who is always saying, 'The Lord told me this and the Lord told me that...' "

He shakes his head sadly. "I know people like that. People who claim the Lord tells them what to eat, when to turn on the TV set, when to plant flowers, what to wear, which car to buy. Utterly mundane and inconsequential tasks that as for me, don't add up to the Lord's intervention, because after all, did he not create us with some level of self-sufficiency? I mean, there are decisions the Lord makes for us, yes, and others that we clearly make for ourselves with or without his input." He moves to the center of the altar.

"Over the years, these people—people who claim to know the Lord's every thought, who insinuate the Lord into every minor decision, who justify every action on the basis of his imagined directive—have numbed me to the possibility that there may in fact be true prophets among us." He does not look directly at the disciples in the front row, but crosses the altar to the other side.

"Someone reminded me recently that this gift of prophecy has not been lost—did not belong only to Noah and to Abraham and to David, but to many saints across the ages, past and present. The gift of prophecy, in fact, belongs to humankind. To men in general." He drops his voice a meaningful octave. "And to women."

He heaves a long, heavy sigh. "Beware of those posing as the Messiah," he says. "But also beware of the deep sleep of your own subconscious. The deep sleep that believes prophecy in our own day is no longer possible. That it belonged strictly to the distant past. That we who inhabit the earth today are neither capable of prophecy nor worthy of prophets in our midst. That prophets can only be men, powerful men."

He tilts his head. "Brothers and Sisters, be on the lookout for the prophets among you—not the powerful, but the humble and the knowing, the unexpected beacon in the darkness. For the Lord does not abandon us, but makes himself known in surprising places. Take courage, and remember that his messages are often radical, life-altering, and unwelcome. Still, let us believe in his continued guidance and that all things are possible in his name." He bows to Vera and returns the microphone to the pulpit.

Margaret leans right over Louise to grab Vera's hand. "I'd say someone was converted!"

Louise giggles.

"He's got my writings," says Vera eagerly. "Something's up."

"What writings?" says Margaret.

Vera turns urgently to them both. "Promise me you'll follow up on this, and also on the women's church."

"What are you talking about?" whispers Margaret. "Of course we'll follow up on this with you right beside us!"

"And the Pope..." whispers Vera. "The Lord has asked him to relinquish the riches of the Church."

Margaret gasps.

"I've written a letter..."

"To the Pope?!" says Louise in her whisper-shriek.

"Shhhh!" says Zachary Thomas behind them.

Margaret flips around and glares at Zachary with round bug eyes. "Shhh yourself," she says, which gives Louise the giggles, which infect Vera, followed by Margaret, who has to hold her breath to regain control.

After Mass, as they're walking through the parking lot to the car, the white hot light drills into Vera's crown again, down her neck and through her spine in a slow crawl, and with unprecedented intensity. By the time she gets to Louise's car, she feels as if her right leg is walking in this world and her left in another. The light is so hot it numbs her. She is lightening up too quickly this time and it is all she can do to say, "Margaret...Louise...just promise me you'll do what I asked."

Margaret pitches her pocketbook to the ground and scowls. "Stop talking like that!" she says.

"Please, Margaret" Vera says. The light is crippling, degravitating. "The Lord will work his miracles even in my absence." Her voice is becoming too light to hear.

"What absence!" shrieks Louise. "Don't talk to me about your absence, Vera Wright! You just moved into my house and changed my life. You're staying. Don't you dare even think of going anywhere!"

"And mine," says Margaret, her chin trembling. "My life has never been better. Don't leave us, Vera. Not now." Tears stream down her face. "Please not yet."

Behind them, coming from the church steps, they hear a male voice hollering, "Vera, wait!!! I figured it out!"

Margaret and Louise turn their backs on Vera to see Father Max in his puffy black ski jacket and randomly combed, out-of-control hair, racing across the parking lot waving papers in his right hand.

Halfway across the lot, he exclaims, "Oh my God!" pointing in Vera's direction.

Margaret and Louise turn just in time to see Vera rising off the blacktop in a brilliant nimbus of vaporous golden light. "No, Vera, no!" they scream in unison. "Noooooo!!!!!!! Please don't go." Margaret jumps up and down to grab Vera's foot, but she is too late.

All around the parking lot, parishioners are pointing and gasping and leaning against their cars for strength. "What's happening to Vera?" they pant.

"The Lord will work many miracles through me now," she says as the light overcomes her. "Mia will take my place at the table. In time you will join me! Believe it—the world is about to change! It's not about death. Death is an illusion. His Kingdom is already here."

At that, she becomes so luminescent as to be nearly undefined. They shade their eyes from her light, blinking as she unclasps her right fist, releasing something from her palm, which tumbles onto the pavement and rolls to the edge of Margaret's red quilted boots. When Vera has totally disappeared from view, Margaret leans over and picks up the ball tentatively between her thumb and forefinger.

"Why, look at this," she says. She holds it out as they all study it, confused. "Is this...? What is this?" As far as anyone can tell, it's a black rubbery ball the size of an acorn, still steaming with heat. Margaret sniffs deeply then stares at the others. "Well, what do you know," she says, sobbing. "It smells like a rose."

Chapter Twenty

The Bishops assigned to Margaret this time around are all predictably similar—white men with white hair in black and white outfits. If she didn't know any better she'd think they belonged to a cult. Where are the women, she thinks. *Where are the women?* She cannot get Vera's church started fast enough. Women would never do this. Women would believe what they'd seen. Think of Mary Magdalene. She believed.

She loosens the rose-colored chiffon scarf around her neck and sips water from the glass in front of her. She refuses to be intimidated by these men, who by the way have been giving her the run-around for the past six months, not to mention how they're freaking out Louise, practically treating her like an accomplice to murder. Why, Margaret had to shake poor Louise out of her hysteria the last time they'd interrogated her. And let's not forget how they're treating Father Max, not even allowing him to say Mass until after the inquiries.

But Margaret just can't afford to even think about this anymore. She's got to overcome her grief first. Even now, just the thought of Vera's absence upsets her so much she has to calm herself with deep, cleansing breaths. Why, she never even grieved for her husband the way she grieves for that dear girl. Oh Vera, she keens. How I miss you!

"Mrs. Vitella," says one of the bishops. "I'm Bishop McArthur. How are you today?"

Margaret squirms in her chair. "Fine and dandy," she says.

"That's good...good." He consults his notes. "Now, I want you to remember to tell us the whole truth, Mrs. Vitella." He peers over his reading glasses. "Can you do that for us today?"

"I'm not an idiot," she says.

There's a general restlessness on the bench, and then Bishop McArthur says, "No reason to be hostile, Mrs. Vitella. Just tell us what happened. Remember, we're on your side."

"I've already told you three times," she says. "I stick to my story."

The Bishop leans forward on one elbow. "We're not here to indict you, Mrs. Vitella. This is a very serious matter. We need to confirm through separate interviews that your stories don't change over time and that they match each other's. Do you understand that? Generally these interviews are conducted decades, even centuries after a person's death. To be studying a person's...uh, status...within a year, well. It's highly unusual."

Margaret nods reluctantly, pursing her lips. "To repeat what I've already said...Vera Wright is an out-and-out saint. Not a demon. By now I'd think it would be obvious to you."

"Please allow us to draw the conclusions here," says the Bishop.

Margaret raises her chin indignantly. "She received audible messages from the Lord, which she transmitted orally and through her writing. She rose into the sky and disappeared into the light." She fiddles with her scarf. "And as I've said many times, at her funeral repast, we, that is—the other disciples and I—at Vera's request, prepared five loaves of bread and two fishes, nothing more. The fish were cooked and filleted, of course. Grilled, actually. Salmon and halibut—Vera's favorites." She shakes her head. "We'd had several dinners like these before, as directed by the Lord. But this time..."

She can't help it—the thought of their dinners together causes Margaret to break into a series of sobs, which eventually morph into hiccups. "Hiccup!" She raises her index finger.

"Excuse me," she says, "hiccup!" She roots through her purse for a tissue and blows her nose. When she's finished, she says, "But this time...when we served the food...and there were hundreds of people..." She dabs the tissue against her tear ducts and holds her breath for a minute. "Multitudes! There were multitudes; you can ask the Canaan police. The believers came from everywhere, far and wide. Everyone knew about our dear girl...and the food...uh uh ohhhhh..."

"Go on," says Bishop McArthur.

"The food just kept on...well, multiplying. And multiplying. As soon as one fish was finished, another one appeared, and the same thing with the bread...uh uh uh ohhhhhh." She holds up her index finger. "I'm sorry, I just..."

The bishops consult with one another.

Bishop McArthur drums his fingers on the table. "Mrs. Vitella, are you insinuating that Vera Wright was Christ himself? Is that what you're getting at? That she...multiplied the food, and... ascended into heaven?"

Margaret smacks the tabletop. "Of course she wasn't Christ. Christ spoke to her. She was a saint. Didn't Christ talk to a lot of saints? And yes, he took her into heaven. You have her body."

"You mean the ball."

"That's right."

A bishop at the end of the table introduces himself as Bishop Charles. "Mrs. Vitella, did Vera Wright ever say who she thought she was?"

"She thought she was a beautician," says Margaret. "A hairdresser. She couldn't believe what was happening to her. But the proof is in the loaves and fishes, I say." She wags her finger earnestly. "And may I be so bold as to dare any one of you gentlemen to levitate off the bench right now and disappear into the sky leaving a ball of your DNA for proof.

"And another thing..." she jabs her finger. "You can tell the Pope for her and for me that the Lord gave her a specific message. He said, 'Give your riches to the poor and ordain your female priests.'"

"Yes, the Pope is aware of Vera Wright's mandates," says Bishop McArthur.

"They're not Vera's mandates," says Margaret. "They're the Lord's."

Chapter Twenty-One

The district attorney, Ronald Jackson, folds his arms and narrows his eyes at Father Max. "We're not accusing you of anything," he says. "You're here voluntarily."

"Oh really?" says Father Max. "You could have fooled me."

Father Max's attorney squeezes him supportively on the shoulder.

"This is not an official interrogation," says the DA. He stands up and hitches his pants around his huge belly. "It's just...you have to know how unusual...bizarre...this case is. It's just..." His whole body quivers. "...impossible to believe."

"Of course it's bizarre...it's supernatural!"

"Reverend," he says, "with all due respect, the courts are not satisfied. They want some answers."

Father Max squares his shoulders. "We can't prove everything, can we? We can't prove where we came from, for instance. Or where we're headed when we die. Or where she's gone to, for that matter."

The DA shakes his head. "So you're telling me that the ball...the size of an acorn...was all that remained of her physical body?"

"You got the lab results. It accounts for every major organ."

"What about the films. The MRI?"

He shrugs. "You saw the report, didn't you? Interrogated the doctors? A brain anomaly."

Father Max's attorney flips through some papers and says. "The report is right here, Ronald. It says, 'A crystallization, a faint star-pattern, appears over the pineal gland.'" The attorney sighs. "It appeared on the previous MRI, but they thought it was a flaw in the film. Then it repeated twice—different days, different machines, different films. We've consulted a slew of experts. No one knows what it is. No one has ever seen it before."

Father Max taps his hand against the table. "Look, there were twenty-four people who saw her melt into the sky that morning. If I were you, I'd be more concerned with the messages she left behind." He runs his fingers through his hair. "You might benefit from them."

By now, sweat is pouring down the DA's face and neck. "I saw the so-called writings. The notepads. It was just a bunch of nonsense. Scribble. A bunch of circles and lines."

"That's what I thought," says Father Max, "I'm ashamed to admit. But I brought them to an old schoolmate of mine, a mathematician. An oddball, really, but a good guy all in all. Solitary. He works for the government as a code breaker. He studied them for a while, stayed up a few nights fiddling with computer languages, and bingo—a few messages from our Creator in binary code."

The DA stares at the ceiling. "There must be more to it."

"How can there be more to it? It's only the single most shocking event of our time. A simple beautician—assumed into heaven."

The DA waves his hand dismissively. "That's all for now."

Chapter Twenty-Two

"Please calm down, Mrs. Lambert."

Louise can't say which bishop is telling her to calm down this time. She can't remember their names. They all look the same.

"She was my best friend," she says, bawling. "That's all I can tell you. You just...you can't imagine...I don't know what else..."

"But you say she had visions?" urges one of the men.

Louise nods along with the general rhythm of her shaking shoulders. "She saw her husband dead...husking corn, and then later...in the beginning. But she had the loaves and the two fish...but before that he died on the treadmill, just like she saw."

She sips some water.

The man asking her the questions scratches his head. "Anything else, Mrs. Lambert?"

"Well, yes, then she moved in with me and Margaret and...and floated on the ceiling...and cut my hair. She...she had such a hard time with her daughter, but now... and her husband, Monk. He la-la-loved her sooo m-m-much." She drops her head into her arms and weeps inconsolably for what seems likes hours, until finally, she is escorted from the room.

Chapter Twenty-Three

Mia paces nervously, rubbing her sweaty palms against her red velvet cassock. She listens as Margaret and Louise prepare the hoards of people with a welcoming prayer. They have so much faith in her, but why should they? She has not been strong in the past. She has let everyone down more than once. She shakes her head. But she must let go of her past; she understands this. Her mother...her own mother...is a saint, after all. Not an everyday saint, but a real saint, in the process of being beatified. And if her mother is a saint then is she not herself a candidate for sanctity? Or so Margaret tells her. "Why, look at St. Paul," Margaret said. "Knocked right off his high horse with a bolt of lightning right between the eyes! Or better yet," she said winking, "Magdalene. Yes, that's the one for you, Mia—Magdalene. Everywhere you look, the Lord has a way of turning his worst wrongdoers into his holiest saints."

And Margaret is right; Mia knows Margaret is right. And anyway, having experienced extreme evil, is not extreme good her only salvation? For one who has known one extreme, only the opposite will satisfy. No, there is nowhere in between for Mia.

Margaret raises her arms. "And it is now with great joy that I introduce you to the daughter of our Blessed friend, Vera!!! Mia Wright has already been privy to the insights of her ascended mother who has urged her to take on the holy mantle of our fledgling Society."

Mia emerges from the shadows to vibrant, nearly deafening cheers.

"Mi-a! Mi-a!" they chant.

She forces herself to overcome the unworthiness she feels, unworthiness that she has brought upon herself, the cross of unworthiness upon which she hung for so many years. "I am worthy," she affirms to herself. "I am worthy. I am worthy. I am worthy."

She takes her place at the front of the table, laid out on the stage as a feast before the crowds. "We are worthy," she says. "We are all worthy. Release your unworthiness as I release mine. Acknowledge your light so it may be amplified."

She blesses the food. "The Lord will feed you his light so that you may truly understand that your destiny is with him. He will feed you with light if you let him." She blesses the crowds. "Let him," she says.

The crowds file peacefully to the table, served by the Martha's from the basket of five loaves and the platter of two fishes. Each receives a chunk of bread and a slice of fish until the entire crowd of five thousand is satisfied. Mia will never get over this. As long as she lives, she will never understand.

The Translations

*Y*ou on earth want only what is unattainable. Once you have made your conquest, its value is instantly diminished. Yet this truth applies only to the "seen" world, for there is little concern among you to conquer the unseen world. It is critical that you focus on the truly unattainable frontier as it is not guaranteed to you by simple virtue of your creation. There are heavens and there are more heavens, and still more within. When the new world comes, you will have spent yourselves on outfitting your bodies, which will not be brought forth in this form, for the weight of them cannot be borne on the new Earth which has already been prepared and is made of light.

Feed your body and soul on loaves and fishes. Listen to my new disciples and I will multiply your efforts exponentially in order to assist you into your rightful home whose threshold is before you.

Put stock in the unseen. You are heavy and the world is heavier and sinking from its own weight. Continuing as you are, you will go where the lost generations have gone into deep darkness until the true end, except those who are light enough to pass into the new Earth which I have prepared for you. And for those who possess this light, that passage will be seamless. Some are being prepared now for the journey so that they will be able to function on the other side, to wake those who have kept faith, but whose awareness and consciousness are not sufficiently developed to function on their own. The time is coming; pray unceasingly.

You are at odds with each other, and yet you are the same— made of the same light—matter magnified from my own being. There is an incorruptible part of each of you—the part that I prepared for myself so that in the end, we can be united in complete joy and compatibility. Locate that part of you and treasure it; protect it. It is the light beneath the bushel, dimmed to near darkness and doomed to obscurity by lack of attention and nurture, not by me, but by you and your foolish choices. For though I am ever ready to supply its every need, most attempts of mine are returned unused. One must first acknowledge one's need, and then unlock one's door for the supplier.

Simplify your lives. Simplify your minds. Let go of your attachment to routines and meaningless comforts. Shake up your day. Deny yourself coffee one day, breakfast the next. Learn to live with the unpredictable. Be flexible and ever ready for the unknown to intrude. For it will intrude, and all of you will be tested. Only through flexibility will you survive a true calamity, and the calamity is coming. Not one, but many. Reduce your needs. Exercise your reflexes. Live simply and pray unceasingly.

When the day comes, it will not be expected. The experiences of that day cannot be anticipated. However, fear will not serve you. Your only preparation is flexibility, adaptability, and an abiding knowledge of the spiritual world. Your spirit possesses its own anatomy and that anatomy is formed with light, and the density of that light is known only by me. But in your passage, those with bright light will be instantly recognized in the darkness. And those with dim or dilute light will, like shades and shadows, be unseen or barely seen and unrecognizable. After the passage, you will be judged only by the density of your light, for light is the only element that conveys from one earth to the next. The only currency that matters is the light you bear.

Intensify your light with prayer, devotion, abstinence, meditation, faith practices and good deeds, bright countenance, faithful repetition of pure action and simple living.

Anyone whose light is bright is known now by others whose light is also bright, though you may not know why you are so familiar to each other. This is a time of recognition, as your mutual light communicates between you. Now, those who have *chosen to build kingdoms in the physical world, and whose attachments to this world are great, they also know whose lights are bright, for the consciousness of the great can be equal, but the choices different. One chooses tools of material wealth and the other tools of light. The citizens of the world of matter mock the children of light, for everything the light stands for threatens the foundation of matter. In the end, matter will burn in the heat of the light.*

You will arise into the world of light, not the way a helium balloon rises into the sky, but rather, your lightness of being will eventually prevent you from maintaining a vibration low enough to remain in the physical state. And in that perfect and joyful moment, you will not die, but transform, dropping the weighty scales of matter like a carapace. In such a way did my own mother make passage. And in such a way shall my brothers and sisters.

Do not visit psychics, study ancient peoples, or practice complex rituals to achieve your light. Do not purchase expensive equipment to deep-sea dive when your treasure floats on the surface of the water. There is nothing more to my teaching than this: The Being who brought you here will return for you. In the meantime, love one another and keep a simple faith. Shun distractions and keep your eye on the light. Only light matters. ONLY light. And light derives from the Creator. And light is love. And the light does not judge; it does not say, "This light is better than that light." For all light derives from one source. Focus only on your own light. In this short time left, take every opportunity to enhance your own light, and in so doing you will cast light on all those in your sphere of influence, and without effort you will be casting your net widely and your harvest will be great.

Children, who has told you that you are nothing? Who has made you feel so small? For there is great payment due from the prideful who manipulate you in this manner. Do you know how many angels are commissioned to sponsor your journey on earth? How many Michaels it takes to give you heat and keep your blood pumping? How many legions of Gabriels to balance your fluids, how many Raphaels to balance your electromagnetic energy? How many Uriels to unify these processes? I have issued legions and legions of angelic forces and a personal heavenly guardian to accompany and protect your daughtership and sonship for me. I have spared nothing in your protection, guidance, and the nourishment of all aspects of your being. Would I have provided these things for small and meaningless creatures?

Remember only this when they tell you how small and miserable you are: you belong to me. Male and female, in equal measure, are made in my image. Would you tell your own dear children that they are unworthy of your love? That you love them anyway, but no deed, action, kind thought or pure intention will ever make them truly worthy? No, a good parent would never say these things. A loving parent would say, "You are worthy by virtue of the fact that I created you out of nothingness and through no intention of your own." For can you possess intention even before you are created? No.

You were created with limited self-sufficiencies and conditions designed to return you to me freely. If a child is obligated to love and respect a parent—is a parent not under far greater obligation to love and teach and respect that child of his own substance? Yes. A parent's obligation is greater than a child's.

Children, you are worthy, but many of your deeds are not. Do not examine your worth. Examine your deeds.

It is time to put away your guilt and self-deprecation. Time to honor your rightful inheritance in my kingdom, and in so doing, put away your defenses and your weapons of petty superiority and other evidence of your separateness and aloneness—your illusionary smallness. Acknowledge that you are all equal daughters and sons of the Most High. That each of you has been created with full rights of inheritance. It is time to love, honor and respect those who reflect different aspects of Creation and the Creator. Time to build your light and spread your love, because the kingdom is truly at hand. Light and love are the only elements of your present lives that reflect back on your image in the world of spirit, a world from which you came, to which you first belonged, and to which you will inevitably return. Love and light are one. You cannot have love without light. You cannot have light without love.

Even I, who am unlimited, experience limitations through the limitations of my creatures. These limitations that imprison you are in fact the same limitations that protect your separateness. It is you who grasp onto them, who wall yourselves in with the brick of hatred and the mortar of selfishness, not I who assign them. If you surrender your limitations freely, then I will be able to speak and act fully through you. And the terminal point of matter will be transformed into a point of infinity where all things are rendered possible.

Suffering is not my will for you. Joy is my will for you. Do you know the joy of union? The ecstasy of working in partnership with me? Suffering is a result of closing yourselves off. You ache because you will not open, and I am forced through love to pry you open, to feed you by force as a mother bird must open the mouths of her chicks, to push the worms down their throats that they may live. But what if the chicks opened their mouths and joyously took the worms, knowing their value? Would that not be easier?

It is your own value you do not know. You have built a world that denies your own inherent value. It is not I whom you fear, but yourselves. I will turn your darkness to light where you will allow it, even the slightest. I will apply whatever pressure necessary to the blackest carbon within you in order to create a diamond of your soul. It is the incorruptible in you that will finally know your worthiness, claim its right of inheritance, stand before me strong and unassailable, saying, "Father, may I have the keys to the kingdom that are mine alone?"
And with great and unmitigated joy, I will turn them over.

There is no such thing as life and death. You are neither alive nor dead — you are either awake or asleep. There are people walking amongst you on this earth who are in deep sleep, and others fully awake on other planes whom you have already buried. When you are truly awake on the spiritual plane, there is no death, but a seamless transformation into the new and transformed Earth. What you must do while inhabiting the old earth, the temporary earth, is to outfit yourselves with light, that you will be able to withstand the intensity of your new home. For your new home is made entirely of light. If your interior light is equal to the light of the new Earth, you will thrive. If your interior light is dim, you will burn. Acknowledge your light and feed it. You will gain nothing from ignorance but pain and fear. Pray unceasingly for new reserves of light.

The time has come when a critical mass of my people are developed. They are listening. This opens the portal of consciousness to commune with the divine in new ways. Hear me, those of you who are so equipped. Drop everything and prepare yourselves to move on to your new home. Do you not see people disappearing around you in shocking numbers? In strange ways? By seemingly violent events? Hear their voices and learn from them. Pray unceasingly for discernment.

Ninety-percent of all influence upon your lives is unseen. Be suspicious of the seen not the unseen. Believe what you cannot see.

Your actions cannot be tamed until your thoughts are tamed. All fear resides in thought. Fear is what is crippling you.

Do not worry about the thoughts of those around you. It is enough to pursue your own. Your world will not be healed by the apprehension of your neighbor's thoughts, but by the apprehension of your own.

Do not let the past define you. The past deceives. The past is not who you are now or who you are becoming. You cannot move on until your past is understood or until you are able to release it in faith or both. The past does not bear light, nor does the future. Only the present bears light. To be in the light, you must be in the present.

Transformation does not take place from the top down, but from the bottom up. Not from the exterior inward, but from the *interior outward. The great rumbling of truth and consciousness will be heard first by the most humble and spread amongst you in great numbers until the volume is so great it deafens the ears of your leaders. It will not be heard by your leaders first. Not this time. Your leaders are preoccupied.*

The Earth is in its final season in this—its imperfect state. In its perfect state, it, like you, is eternal. For those who have developed their light and shared it generously, the transition will be seamless. The new Earth will rise up to meet you and regardless of how it appears to others, there will be no suffering for those who are prepared. The beauty of the new Earth is boundless and ineffable and a suitable home for your eternal spirit.

Tell your people: the light is being transmitted in wondrous and myriad methods. Unclench your fists that they may be open when the healing light arrives. Unclench your fists and embrace each other. Do not delay.

Acknowledgements

First, I am grateful to all my church lady friends for their spiritual insights and inspiration over the years. If there are miracles to be had, and I am certain there are, it is through them. Gratitude also to my fabulous friends at the Master of Arts in Writing program at Manhattanville College: Sr. Ruth Dowd, Karen Sirabian, and Dianalee Velie, for their unqualified support and endless naughty laughter. Thanks to my readers: Mary Lou Alter, Marian Schumer, MEP, Susan O'Connor, Chris Conlin, Ro Geisler, Kathy Baughman, and again, Karen Sirabian, for their sharp eyes and encouraging words. Thanks to Dr. Kenneth Davis and his wife, Lisa Davis—mystic extraordinaire and dear friend—for countless healings in words, treatments, and profound companionship on the mystical journey. Last but not least, thanks to Tom for his encouragement and support, and Mom for her DNA. Miss you, Mom!